JAN F
A FLYING

Jan Plesman
A Flying Dutchman

ALBERT PLESMAN

UPFRONT PUBLISHING
LEICESTERSHIRE

Jan Plesman, A Flying Dutchman
Copyright © Albert Plesman 2002

ISBN 1-84426-098-4

First published 2002 by
UPFRONT PUBLISHING LTD
Leicestershire

Typeset in Bembo by
Bookcraft Ltd, Stroud, Gloucestershire
Printed by Lightning Source

ACKNOWLEDGEMENTS

I could not have finished this book without the moral encouragement of my wife Felicita.

I would also like to express my gratitude to my daughter-in-law Samira, who provided financial assistance towards publication.

My thanks also to the management of KLM Royal Dutch Airlines for sponsoring the manuscript.

I

ON 16 AUGUST 1938, military recruit Jan Leendert
Plesman arrived at Soesterberg, the Netherlands' most
important military airfield, located close to Utrecht – a city
almost in the heart of the country. Here he had to perform his
military service, to be drilled for six weeks.

His father had also learned to fly at that same military base
during World War I. After the 1914–18 armed conflict had
come to an end, Plesman Senior founded KLM Royal Dutch
Airlines, on 7 October 1919. Nominated its first director, he
laid the cornerstone to an important career. The airline
embodied the realisation of a long-cherished dream, conceived
while flying as a military pilot over the flat Dutch countryside.

Plesman Senior felt convinced that aircraft were to serve
humanity by bringing people together over long distances
instead of separating them forever in destruction.

KLM grew into the crowning success of his life – the final
result of tenacious, consistent work. In order to reach that
goal, Jan's extremely dynamic father drove all those involved
as hard and relentlessly as he did himself.

He did not suffer fools gladly!

Plesman Senior lived and breathed aviation. He used to
say, 'The air ocean unites all people.' Throughout his life he
strongly and insistently fought for absolute freedom of the air.
He was years ahead of his time, a man of vast vision and

strength, so much so that they called him 'the grand old man of commercial aviation'.

Sitting on hard wood benches, eighteen-year-old Jan and his fellow recruits received an initial six weeks of basic training. He was taught navigation, the elementary functioning of aeroplane engines, aerodynamics and craft construction. Once those forty-three days of basics were over, the practical and active part of training he relished most – flying – lay still ahead of him.

At first, he had to fly the single-engined Fokker S-IV training plane. He was then transferred to a Fokker C-V biplane, powered by a Rolls Royce Kestrel engine. In it, he flew 29 hours solo above the Dutch countryside. He buzzed his parents' house without an instructor one day. Extremely worried, they stared up at the sky, watching his low altitude manoeuvres, silently wishing he'd fly back to his base.

During September 1939, he was assigned to Schouwen and Duiveland Island, in the south-west Netherlands, where he received further flying instructions at Haamstede airfield. Even though the Dutch Air Force employed different kinds of aircraft at the time, the planes were nonetheless quite anti-quated ones.

While training to become a fighter pilot, he accumulated 50 hours with an instructor and 190 hours on solo flights. He felt ready, even eager, to learn to fly the Fokker D-21, the Dutch Air Force's standard fighter plane.

Then, out of the blue, came an unexpected doomsday – on 10 May 1940, the German Army, Navy and Air Force invaded neutral Holland. Five days later, a strangled Holland, overrun by the far superior mechanised German Armed Forces, had to slip into clandestinity while busy burying its heroic dead who had defended their neutral country against the ignoble German onslaught.

Rotterdam, the city with the largest commercial harbor on the European continent, was basely and indiscriminately bombed by the Luftwaffe while surrender terms were being discussed between the Dutch and German high commands. Thousands of fires broke out and scores of innocent victims were counted. Consequently, the Dutch government, despite fierce resistance in several parts of the Netherlands, was forced to capitulate on 15 May 1940.

For the first time in the history of armed conflicts, a fire-storm developed after the bombardment of the city by only 57 twin-engined Heinkel 111 bombers.

During the short five-day war, Jan had been ordered to carry out a number of reconnaissance flights over the Grebbeberg, a hill in the heart of Holland where heavy ground fighting had been reported. Flying the antiquated biplane above the hostilities on the ground, he managed to evade the fast modern Messerschmitt 109 fighter planes every time they attacked him. The slow speed of the old Fokker D-17 biplane offered him an unexpected advantage when chased by the sleek, swift German fighters. They overshot him in no time at all, circling away into the blue sky. His plane buffeted wildly in the turbulence they left in their wake.

On the very last day of the war, he took off from the de Vlijt military airfield on Texel island in the north of Holland, attentively hedge-hopping over the flat Dutch countryside, at the same time anxiously observing the sky above him to watch for any kind of enemy activity. He flew to Buiksloot, the secret small auxiliary airfield situated just north of Amsterdam, close to het Y, a busy commercial shipping waterway, and landed there safely.

Following his arrival, he impatiently awaited further instructions. Later during the day, he took off again, this time to proceed on a short, five minutes airborne hop to Schiphol airfield where he should join the first and second Java fighter squadrons stationed there.

Flying low over the heavily bombed airfield, he took his time before initiating the final approach. He felt rather worried at the sight of so many ugly bomb craters obstructing a safe landing.

3

The whole situation really looked rather bad from the air. He had to solve a complicated enigma – how to set his plane down inbetween the numerous holes on the runway and grass. From his altitude, he had to decide on the best approach to bring the old aircraft down without damage to its structure or to himself. At last he thought he'd found a way.

He carefully started his landing manoeuvre by side-slipping the plane, using rudder, elevators, aileron control and engine power all at the same time to guarantee his safe landing. He moved his head, bending over sideways to the left and right of the small cockpit, to gain a better forward view along the fuselage, straining his eyes to observe what lay ahead of him. But just as he pulled the plane straight for the final touchdown he was taken aback by the sight of an obstructing pole sticking out of the ground. He had not spotted it earlier when circling the field.

Desperately and at the very last second, his right hand shot forward to push the gas throttle to full engine power. The plane began vibrating dangerously, an early warning of a stall. With agonising slowness, it began to respond to his commands, regaining altitude, as if refusing to gain height.

His whole body urged it on hopefully. 'Come on, come on,' he whispered.

His efforts successful, he circled the field again for a new approach. Now his hands and feet were busy while his brain functioned with cool rationality. Rushing over the boundary, he finally managed to put the old plane down in one piece, letting it run over the grass of the airfield.

He had made it! He felt a satisfying surge of contentment flow through him. Enthusiastically, he rapped his right fist against the Fokker's side and spoke to it out loud. 'Thank you, you old war horse. We did it together!'

He smiled with satisfaction. Surviving a number of dogfights with fast Messerschmitts and now his safe return made him consider that he had done his duty. It meant the end of the war for him. He was only twenty years old and had fought against the mighty Luftwaffe. With hostilities over, he had succeeded in returning the antiquated Fokker D-17 undamaged to Schiphol airfield. Quite a feat considering the heavy losses the Dutch military had suffered.

He carefully taxied around the deep bomb craters, silently surveying what was left of the hangars, the station buildings and the tarmac. Schiphol happened to be a basically civilian airport but it also accommodated a number of wood hangars at a corner of the field where Java squadron fighter planes were stationed.

After switching off the engine, he sat stunned, immobile, alone in the small, narrow cockpit, taking his time observing the terrible destruction wreaked on KLM's main commercial base. Here he had passed so many pleasant hours as a child in the company of his father when visiting the airport. A deep anger began to grow inside him and he vowed he'd seek revenge on the infamous, evil-minded Germans responsible for it all, for the motiveless wanton destruction they had caused.

Later, after the dramatic news of the Dutch government's capitulation had been repeatedly broadcast over the radio, his faithful D-17 was destroyed by the Dutch military security forces at the airfield. When he saw it go up in roaring flames, he felt terribly upset. He'd become very fond of the old craft after nine months of close association. As he gloomily watched the flames wildly soar it seemed to him as if his own pride and self-righteousness were being reduced to ashes by the all-consuming fire. As if his own wings were being burned and he consequently earthbound!

After a few weeks of uncertainty, bad feelings and listlessly hanging around the field with a number of other Dutch fighter pilots, he was finally discharged. He returned home to his family in The Hague rather disillusioned by having to admit defeat.

His father had seen his life's work – KLM – crumble in a few minutes of senseless destruction during the May days of

1940. The Luftwaffe's bombing of Schiphol Airport, just a few minutes by car from the city of Amsterdam, had been completely unnecessary. The brutal bombardment had wiped out the KLM fleet's home base and destroyed nearly all the commercial planes peacefully parked on the airport tarmac. The buildings, maintenance hangars and ultra-modern engine repair shops had all been destroyed by the time the bombing was over, along with practically everything else around. What had been laboriously built and expanded by KLM's personnel and Jan's father over the years between 1919 and 1940 now lay in ruins.

Home again, he found his family demoralised by the German invasion of neutral Holland. The Dutch had been caught completely off guard by the sudden, treacherous attack on their peaceful homeland by the German armed forces – even though his father had mentioned the threat of an oncoming war within the family circle on several occasions, he had intensely hoped the Netherlands could remain neutral just as during the Great War.

Naturally the main topic of conversation at home concerned how long the war would last. One day, Jan had a long conversation about the overall global situation with his strong-minded father in his study.

'Well, dad,' he said without much enthusiasm, 'what should I do now that the Dutch forces have been beaten so disastrously?' His blue eyes serious, his father replied, 'I don't have a pat answer right now. The war is still raging in all its fury. The general military situation is rather confused. It seems to me the mechanised German Army and the Luftwaffe are far superior to what the Allied Forces can put in the field and in the air to oppose them. I'm afraid England won't be able to indefinitely hold out against German military might all by itself. Perhaps, my boy, if the United States were to enter the war along with the British, the strategic balance would tip in favour of the Anglo-Saxon forces again. The same as happened during 1914–18.'

Jan nodded. 'If I should return to the Technical High School in Delft to continue my studies in engineering, I'm afraid the Germans will force me one day to work for their war efforts in a factory in Germany. That kind of work doesn't appeal to me at all. As you can well imagine I don't intend to get snared into it,' he stated firmly.

His father stared at him. 'You're right. Why don't you stay at home for a while and rest. It'll do you good. By the end of 1940, when a lot of enigmas have been solved, we'll take another look at the overall strategic European situation.' Plesman Senior seriously studied his son, waiting for a comment while he lit a cigarette. Jan did not smoke.

He smiled thinly at his father. 'That might be the best solution for the time being. But what are you planning to do now that KLM has practically been wiped out here in Holland?' he asked with a tinge of anxiety in his voice. 'It must weigh on your mind a great deal.'

His father replied gloomily. 'At first, I'll have to cut the KLM personnel down to a skeleton staff. It means a very unpleasant choice for me. Then, despite the present negative overall situation, I'll have to start planning for the post-war period. Don't forget, Jan, the Company is still active and will continue to be so in the West Indies. KLM still operates three flights a week from the Middle East to the Dutch Colonies and on to Australia.' Jan's father took a deep breath and continued. 'The war will contribute in an explosive way to new, unheard-of inventions. And also to fantastic technical developments in military aviation first and in commercial aviation later. There will be four-engined commercial transport planes cruising at over 300 miles per hour, flying long distances non-stop over the oceans of the world. Once the war is over, there will be an unlimited, pent-up demand for commercial air traffic. Everything the war destroys will have to be built up again.'

His father sounded confident, even convincing. It slightly encouraged his son.

He eyed his father wanly. 'Well, if we can both stay alive until the end of the war, the future won't seem so black after all,' he said hesitatingly.

Jan's father slowly shook his head. 'No. And even though the outlook seems black, yet we must remain optimistic. We must consider these unfortunate times as a passing, fleeting moment in history – a speck of dust in time and space. Develop a good work plan of some kind for yourself to keep your mind occupied.' His steady blue eyes bored hard into Jan's. Then he spoke paternally, 'Satan finds work for idle hands. Remember that, my boy.'

Good-naturedly, Jan remarked, 'As usual, I think you're right.' Then he got up, walked out of the study into the hall and up the stairs. Once back in his own room, he started putting in order his engineering books and his troubled thoughts, and to consider seriously the new life awaiting him in German-occupied Holland – one he was totally unaccustomed to.

The comfortable house he lived in was situated in the dunes on the outskirts of The Hague, close to the North Sea. It was surrounded by sports fields, tennis courts, a small wood and a park. He intensely loved the pleasant, easy way he had been educated before the war – the luxurious environment in which he had passed his best carefree Hague years. But now that marvellous pattern was completely upset.

He had attended a good high school not far from his home and had been one of the three top seventeen-year-old students in his class. He possessed a fine mind and excelled in mathematics like his father. Those mystical, enigmatic formulas and combined numbers posed no problem at all.

But now that hostilities were over, he felt terribly discouraged. His spirits fell to a new low. He also became concerned. The immediate future in Holland under German occupation looked bleak indeed. He felt convinced that returning to Delft, to the Technical High School where he had studied engineering before entering the military, would put him in danger of being conscripted by the Germans into performing forced labour for their war machine. He wanted to avoid that at all costs and intended to do something about it.

When alone in his room, stretched out on his bed, hands behind a weary head on the pillow, he gave his personal situation a lot of thought. And every evening, along with his family, he anxiously listened to the BBC informing him about the latest disastrous developments on the battlefronts of the world – the latest advances of the German mechanised divisions slicing through the demoralised French defences as if they didn't exist at all.

Seriously weighing the pros and cons, he finally made a fateful decision – not to return to his studies in Delft! He'd stay home for the time being, passively awaiting future events. First of all, he wanted to see how his personal life was going to develop in general in Holland, in occupied Holland.

He was only twenty years old, he could fly a military plane, had been an engineering student for one year, but he assumed there was not a positive future to look forward to in Holland under these dreary, hopeless circumstances, under German occupation.

There was no ray of light at the end of a very dark tunnel. Definitely, there would be no flying for him any more if he remained in his own occupied country. For the time being, his wings had been clipped. As of now, he was earthbound.

In The Hague – the seat of the Dutch government – it was rumoured the German occupation authorities had plans to force all officers of the Netherlands Army, Air Force and Navy to sign a binding declaration giving their word of honour to renounce all further active participation in the war.

He felt utterly convinced he could never seriously sign such an imposed declaration if it ever was presented to him!

Jan and his bosom friend Geert Overgauw – both demobilised Dutch Air Force pilots and Second Lieutenants – planned a meeting at his house to discuss the chances of finding ways to escape from occupied Holland. They wanted to join the Allied Forces somewhere in the world to continue fighting the Nazis.

They saw no real future for themselves in Holland. Both of them were seeking a new and valid purpose in life. They also wanted to feel proud of being Dutch again, to take up the battle anew, to defy the hated oppressor who had so treacherously invaded their neutral country. A small number of Dutch Army and Navy men aboard their warships (especially the latter) had managed to escape to England during the black days of May 1940. A few Dutch pilots had joined the British Expeditionary Forces at Dunkirk and Cherbourg, fleeing to England. But they were only a few – a very few.

Before 1940, during the summer holidays, Jan had taken several bicycle tours through Europe, visiting Northern Italy, France, Germany and Belgium. He knew from experience what he could accomplish and the distances he could cover each day pedalling his racing bike. During the days alone in his room, a rather wild, fantastic idea started to take shape in his fervid brain, of reaching unoccupied France with its temporary seat of government in Vichy.

One beautiful afternoon in September 1940, Geert and Jan, like two conspirators, held a long conversation in his father's home on how to escape Holland.

Jan was the first to speak. 'Geert, I think we should work out a sensible, practical plan to get us away from occupied Holland.' His grey-blue eyes fixed on the other young man. 'For instance, we could try a very risky attempt at riding our bikes to Paris. Once there, we could probably stay with Monsieur Mohr, the KLM director. I know him well: I spent a holiday in his Paris home and still have the address,' he wryly assured Geert. 'Our only problem is getting there, of course,' he added, voice slightly ironic.

With a clearly dubious expression on his face, Geert asked, 'You mean cycling about 300 miles through German occupied territories?' He eyed Jan as if the idea was rather absurd. 'How many days would it take us?' His dark brown eyes questioned Jan seriously. 'You know perfectly well my only experience with bicycles has been pedalling from my house to school and back,' Geert grinned grimly.

Undaunted by his friend's doubts, Jan nodded. 'I figured out we should average some 17 miles per hour. We may be able to reach Paris in less than 20 effective hours of cycling. I sincerely believe we should be able to cover about 100 miles the first day. Then another hundred the next – if your muscles hold out, that is!' he quipped, with a good-natured chuckle. 'We should reach our destination on the third day. We'll have to sleep two nights somewhere along the way. I don't know where,' he added somewhat doubtfully shrugging his shoulders in an impatient gesture.

They carefully studied a map Jan had spread out on a small table in front of him.

'We must get acquainted with all the roads leading south, especially the smaller ones,' he emphasised.

Geert turned his head. 'I know a friend in the south of Holland – close to the Belgian border. I'm sure he and his wife will let us stay over for the night.' Inexperienced as he was, Geert did not have the slightest idea about the kind of dangers awaiting them on the way south. Both young men were groping in the dark about the enormous risks they'd have to face and overcome. 'That means we only have to sleep for one night somewhere along the way.'

Patiently, Jan pointed his right index finger at one spot on the map. 'The second night we'll have to sleep close to this village. It'll be risky, Geert, but let's see how we progress every hour before making any hasty decisions about where to sleep. We can't spend nights in small hotels or boarding houses because guests must be registered. Especially now with the Gestapo everywhere wanting to check on anyone moving. We'll have to find a farm or rest in a barn, or even a wood,' he suggested, his voice indicating the strong doubt he felt himself.

'You must realise,' Geert spoke slowly, 'if we really should reach Paris safely, I'll need a long rest. Four or more days on a bike without the necessary training will be extremely tiring. I never took those long cycling tours you did, criss-crossing through all of Europe.' With his right hand, Geert brushed his dark hair back, sighing deeply while staring doubtfully at his friend.

Jan had expected Geert's comment. 'What would you say to staying over in Paris for three or perhaps even four days? That'll give you enough time to restore your strength. I'm afraid we can't possibly ask for more days of hospitality. Monsieur Mohr will already run considerable risks in hiding us. You must realise the darned Germans have occupied Paris for more than four months. I'm sure there'll be military patrols all over the place, checking the identification papers or other documents of people daring to walk the streets,' Jan remarked warily.

Now, it was Geert's turn to smile. 'Four days will be perfect for me. I'm sure I'll recover my forces during that period of time. Then what?' he queried.

Jan shrugged his shoulders. 'Well,' he answered carefully, 'If we should reach Paris safely and undetected, then we'll still have to cover 220 miles to Vichy. We must try to do that in two days, cycling seven hours a day. I sincerely believe we can make it, because you'll have gained a lot of experience during The Hague–Paris tour.'

He commented dryly, 'Somehow, we must try to gather reliable information on how to be able to safely cross the critical border from occupied to unoccupied France. That particular crossing will be the most crucial moment of our escape to England.' He hesitated an instant to gather his thoughts. 'Perhaps Monsieur Mohr may suggest a safe, useful passage. He should know something about it, I assume.'

Geert took his time to light a cigarette, inhaling deeply while a deep worried frown furrowed his forehead, as if he was mentally weighing the pros and cons of what they were discussing. He felt convinced Jan's wild idea could well turn out to be anything but a party. The risky bicycle tour they were planning happened to be full of dangers and imponderables, being forced to cross vast German-occupied territories, over which they had no control whatsoever.

Jan continued to express his ideas. 'It may well turn out to be a very difficult enterprise. I fully realise that. I also assume it'll definitely be extremely dangerous. Already, the Germans have concentrated many men to guard that all-important border to freedom. People and goods passing through will be closely and attentively checked. You can be sure also the Gestapo will be involved as well. We both know what the penalty is when caught. And it's especially tough for pilot officers like us. Those mean bastards will send us straight to one of their terrible, repressive concentration camps. But, Geert, perhaps Monsieur Mohr might be able to supply us with the necessary addresses of reliable people who may be willing to help us cross that very important border. I'll ask him about it once we are in Paris.'

Jan was only too aware how many obstacles they had to overcome before being able to breathe free air again.

Now it was Geert's turn to ask a question. 'If we should succeed, how far will the Spanish border be?'

With a ruler, Jan went to work on the map in front of him. Once he had finished his calculations, he said, 'The distance from Vichy to Perpignan amounts to about 400 miles. That puts us close to the Spanish border. Once we reach it, we may find someone to help us cross the Pyrenean mountains into Spain. From there, we take a train to Lisbon. I can contact the KLM office there and ask for a free ride on one of the flights KLM still operates from Bristol to Lisbon despite the war. As the son of the founder of KLM-Royal Dutch Airlines, I think I'll stand a good chance.'

Jan had already flown all over Europe to London, Paris, Copenhagen and other cities during his summer holidays. The air was his game, his feast, as he had learned so well from his famous father.

Their conversation was momentarily interrupted by his mother. She entered the room carrying a tray with a teapot, cups and saucers and cakes. When she noticed all the papers, maps and the ruler, she asked, 'Are the two of you planning a trip?' Her beautiful grey-blue eyes were tinged with curiosity but also with suspicion. So many young Dutchmen had disappeared for ever trying to reach England. And now, her own son was obviously planning to escape from occupied Holland.

He laughed slyly at her. 'Maybe,' he said noncommittally. With a worried expression on her face, she left the room.

While Jan poured tea, Geert stared at him. 'How long do you think it'll take us to reach England? It's a rather round-about way, isn't it? Are there any alternatives? I mean other ways to get there?' He asked the questions with a sober expression on his face. He wasn't fully convinced yet by Jan's risky, haphazard ideas, although he didn't offer any of his own.

Jan's forehead creased as he said, 'I estimate it'll take us about 60 days to reach Lisbon, if all goes well. I sincerely believe our risks are reasonably calculated, even acceptable. The major dangers lie in crossing from Holland into Belgium and from there into France. Then, of course, we'll still have to overcome the obstacle of passing the border from occupied to unoccupied France. But we'll just have to accept those risks if we want to escape from Holland,' he commented deter-minedly. He had made up his mind! Being strong-willed like his father, he was prepared to face whatever danger lay ahead, risking his life to gain freedom again.

Doubtfully, Geert shook his head. 'I don't know what to say. Let's hope for the best. What we'll certainly need is a good dose of luck, Jan. That's the only contribution I can give to your plan. Trying to escape to Sweden by boat, which has been done before, is no easier nor will it guarantee a better chance. I've heard the Nazis have already arrested a number of people who've tried to make it across that way. I wonder if we shall ever see any of them return again. So many have already died trying to reach England,' he added thoughtfully. 'Stealing a boat to cross the Channel to reach the Allies is also very dangerous. A few days on the open sea, with German motor-torpedo boats, fast patrol boats and U-boats controlling the North Sea, is also extremely risky. Yes, I must admit, your plan definitely has its fine points. It even seems realistic. It will take a long time, but then we have plenty of that to spare, don't we?' he asked as an ironic, bitter smile creased his lip.

'If you're ready to accept the risks, then we have to set a date,' Jan insisted. 'I think the right time will be towards the end of the year, when the days are short and the nights long. I suggest the 30th of December. We stand the best chance for success during the post-Christmas period when most people, and I assume the Germans as well, will be preparing for the New Year festivities. The German occupation forces should be more relaxed in their vigilance.'

Ever so slowly, Geert got up out of the comfortable chair and moved over to the window where he stared out at the dunes in a pensive mood. Then he turned towards his friend. 'All right. Count me in.' After his significant words, they shook hands as if to confirm their decision. 'We must prepare a list of all the necessary equipment we may need for the trip – food, spare tyres, sleeping bags, woollen clothing to keep us warm, a flashlight with extra batteries and all that. We'll also need binoculars,' he added as an afterthought. Pedalling through occupied territory meant they would have to scan the horizon on a regular basis to check on German troop move-ments all the way, and of course roadblocks manned by German security forces.

That afternoon, once the departure date had been set, they prepared a list of necessary items. Now that their long meeting was over, they finally turned cheerful and even opti-mistic. Life offered a purpose and meaning once again!

They'd have to face danger but also the challenge of a new beginning that would give them the right to be proud officers – and free Dutchmen – to take up the fight against the Nazis anew.

Jan and Geert kept talking while he served his friend cold Dutch jenever. Raising his glass, Jan said, 'You know, Geert – the entire world is focusing its attention on the Battle of Britain raging right now. It overshadows all other war events. But remember, no one must ever forget that if the Dutch Air Force and the ground forces had not put up such fierce resistance at Waalhaven Airport [Rotterdam] and at Ypenburgh and Valkenburg airfields close to The Hague, resisting the well-trained German airborne troops and paratroopers, the British people might well have been forced to start to learn to speak German.'

Geert did not understand him right away, asking, 'Why don't you explain yourself better, Jan?' Thinly, Jan smiled at his friend. 'Well, Churchill – a master of history – should have paid the Dutch more due respect. The Luftwaffe attacked Holland with a total of 929 aircraft, of which 450 were Ju 52s. Dutch Forces managed to destroy 328 of them on the ground and in the air. That represents a loss rate of 35 per cent. The Luftwaffe lost 236 Ju 52 three-engined transport planes, most of them at Waalhaven airfield. And Geert, most important, many of those planes were piloted by instructors from the Luftwaffe's blind-flying schools. Lufthansa pilots accustomed to night flying and instructional staff did not return from their flight and consequently the training of new recruits suffered heavily. It was a bitter pill to swallow for the Luftwaffe. Those experienced instructors should have formed the core to train a new generation of young pilots for their bomber units.'

Following his explanation, Jan continued, 'After the heavy Norway invasion losses, plus those suffered here in Holland, the Luftwaffe was forced to reorganise. They needed a breathing spell which allowed England to build more fighter aircraft to defend the island. The German war factories only produced 150 transport planes during 1939 plus 400 during 1940. Had they not lost all those aircraft in Holland and a good percentage of their experienced pilots and instructors, the Battle of Britain could well have turned out quite differently. I'm not saying or pretending the Dutch saved England but the Dutch certainly contributed in considerably weakening the Luftwaffe's transport capabilities at a most critical moment in history.'

Slowly, Geert nodded his head in agreement, 'My God, Jan – I never thought of it that way!'

He stared hard at his friend. 'And neither did the British!' he exclaimed with irascibility in his voice and downed the rest of his jenever.

II

THE WAR, which had been stagnant since September 1939, suddenly erupted in all its ugly violence and fury during the initial week of April 1940. First Denmark, then Norway, were attacked and occupied by the German armed might. In early May, Holland, Belgium and France were overrun by the far superior mechanised divisions of the Nazi hordes.

The British Isles seemed at the mercy of the German threat, but before the risky seaborne invasion of southern England by the German mechanised divisions could be attempted, the Luftwaffe had to achieve air superiority over the Channel to be able to protect the invasion forces against the Royal Navy.

In Norway, the Luftwaffe had already lost more than 150 Ju 52 triple-engined transport aircraft. During the five-day war in Holland, another 236 transport planes had been destroyed, most of them wrecked on the ground during the tough battle fought for Waalhaven airfield. After these considerable losses, the Luftwaffe needed a breathing spell before the final attack on Great Britain could be launched.

Once the greater part of the British Expeditionary Forces at Dunkirk had been rescued, practically every able-bodied man and woman in England was mobilised to repel the German military forces threatening the very existence of the British Isles.

An Australian girl – Diana Boulton – also joined the WAAF in London. Born in the Sydney suburbs, where she had lived for fifteen years in a pleasant home cosily furnished by her mother, she was now going to fight the invader. Her father, a wealthy, self-made man, had provided well for the family. He had married rather late, just over forty. His wife, Mary, had given birth to two good-looking daughters – Diana and Jane.

At the end of 1936, Diana's father had unexpectedly fallen ill. Following a short period of hospitalisation, he died. It had been the most horrible shock Diana had experienced up to then. She had lost the father she intensely loved. Mrs Boulton, a woman with a strong personality, suddenly found herself faced with the hard task of having to bring up two daughters all by herself.

She had always intended to give her two daughters a European education. A few months after the funeral and the termination of the school year, she decided to move to England. She wanted to be close to Diana and Jane once they began their studies at a London university.

During the forty-day leisure trip on the luxury liner from Sydney to Southampton, Diana and her mother walked the spacious promenade deck together many times, arm in arm, animatedly discussing the past in Australia and what the future held for them in England. Diana would never forget the awful, sinking sensation she felt when seeing the Australian coast fading away in the sea mist.

One evening, while the sun set like a glowing blood-red fireball in the Indian Ocean, Diana, in a melancholy mood, reflected about her father and the aching, agonising void his death had left in her. After her mother joined her, she slipped one arm around her shoulder with a protective motherly affection and softly asked, 'It's really beautiful, isn't it?'

During the long silence following her words, Diana turned her head toward Mrs Boulton and noticed the film of moisture in her mother's dark brown eyes. She could only imagine how much her mother missed her father too.

They remained where they stood for a long time, leaning against the rail, until it got damp and cold. Her mother said, 'Let's go inside and look for Jane so we can eat dinner together.'

Mrs Boulton had so very carefully planned everything, but her good intentions were completely upset by the outbreak of war in September 1939. Diana was eighteen and Jane seventeen at the time. When the war really exploded in all its ugly fury in the spring of 1940, the two Australian girls joined the WAAF – the Women's Auxiliary Air Force.

Once enrolled, Diana threw herself wholeheartedly into her work, learning about fighter planes, bombers, plotting aircraft, the speeds and altitudes planes flew at. After a few months of intensive training, they were assigned to their first operational duty in an operations room on the south-east coast of England. Now they too formed part of the Royal Air Force's daily activities and were exposed to the many bombing raids the Luftwaffe carried out over the south of England.

A tiny cog in the works in the precise machinery of Fighter Command, Diana felt profoundly impressed by the efficiency of the ground control sections so intricately interconnected with one another, participating and even anticipating the moves of the German Luftwaffe, thanks to the use of that very secret weapon radar, a superior aircraft location system.

The Royal Air Force Command seemed like a huge spider crouching at the centre of a widespread web, fine threads interdependent on each other, and with one very decisive purpose in mind – to defeat the aggressor, the Luftwaffe. Those invisible electronic tentacles reaching out over the Channel searched for the enemy in order to warn the waiting fighter pilots, to advise and direct them on the best course to follow to engage the brutal invader.

The operations room in which Diana performed her duty contained a big, flat table in the centre of a hall. It was covered by a horizontal map showing the contours of western France,

Belgium, Holland, the North Sea, the Channel and the southern part of England. Several drawings of different types of aircraft hung on the walls.

Up on the first floor, there were surrounding catwalks and glass-panelled rooms facing out on to the hall. From there the Operations Officers obtained a clear view of everything going on below, making it possible to gain at a glance the necessary overall impressions of the aerial circus, so precisely reproduced by the movements of the small coloured discs representing the squadrons engaged. The WAAF women shifted the small discs on the horizontal map with long wooden rakes which they held like croupiers at a roulette table, receiving their instructions through headphones.

As the coloured discs were pushed back and forth, they dramatically reflected the human conflict taking place at tens of thousands of feet in the airspace above the south of England, the Channel and parts of western Europe. At the most, a few hundred Anglo-Saxon pilots engaged and fought their Teutonic counterparts in man-to-man duels. These were very often resolved in a tenth of a second when a plane and its pilot had to confront or pass through a hail of bullets, illuminated in such a sinister way by yellow-orange tracers streaking through the thin upper air towards their target.

Everyone in England, from Churchill to the man in the street, anxiously waited every passing day for the final results of those intense aerial duels. The very future of Great Britain and perhaps of the world could well be decided by the outcome of the titanic air battles in which hundreds of bombers and fighters were engaged.

At times, the intensive, precise work Diana had to carry out in the operations room was hectic, dramatic and nerve-racking, especially during the sensational, emotional days of the Battle of Britain. At the end of a particularly heavy day, she would finally collapse into a deep, exhausted sleep. Resisting the Luftwaffe was a demanding task, completely draining her.

By the end of 1940, after suffering desperate, irreplaceable losses in pilots and aircraft, the Luftwaffe was forced to change tactics and reduce the massive daylight bomber raids on military airfields located in southern England. From that point on, the greater London areas became the prime target for night bombing. Daylight losses had become too heavy. Luftwaffe moral had sagged badly after meeting with a real enemy – the courageous RAF fighters who stood up against the Messerschmitt 109s and 110s plus the twin-engined Heinkel 111s and Dornier Do 17s. The considerable Luftwaffe losses were partly due to the grotesque tactical errors committed by the vain, fat, drug-addicted Commander Hermann Goering.

During April 1940, Diana met George Wilson – a young English fighter pilot. She had noticed him in a crowded, smoke-filled dance-hall. She had exchanged furtive glances with him and liked his urbane style. He was six feet tall, had dark hair, twinkling blue eyes and a pink, clean-shaven, chubby face. He radiated easy warm charm. She considered him a fine young man with many qualities.

After he'd been introduced to her, Diana found out from him personally that he was also actively participating in the intense air war then raging over England. During the second half of July, when the heat of the air battle began to settle in, George was airborne practically every day to meet and engage the enemy bombers approaching from France. Intense fatigue was reflected in the deep, drawn lines around his young eyes. Already he had shot down seven Luftwaffe planes.

Diana and George managed to meet several times when he obtained a short leave. Then they dined and danced intimately, pretending they couldn't care less about the deadly air war raging in the blue skies above England. They only had eyes for each other. Once they got to know each other better, their emotional feelings grew more profound. One night, George had gently and tenderly made love to her. As of that moment, Diana had changed into a mature woman. Later, when making love, Diana felt as if she'd entered into another world. George was the first man who'd taken her, to whom she had lost her virginity.

On several occasions, George told her that discussing marriage made no sense at all because the war was far too close for realistic plans. He was involved nearly every day in so many dogfights, had to face death practically every time he went up in the air and didn't feel he could possibly offer her any security. Although terribly in love, Diana reluctantly agreed with him.

They sought each other out every off-duty moment, just talking and fondling; that's all necessity could afford them. Sometimes, when the weather looked good, they lay next to each other on their backs in the fresh green, clover-filled grass of the countryside surrounding George's base.

At times, when looking up at the sky, they could clearly observe the many criss-crossing white vapour trails the high-flying bombers and fighters left behind. And they could also hear the angry sharp rattle of machine-gun fire or the slower rat-a-tat of the Messerschmitt fighter planes' cannon, when engaged in aerial combat.

One beautiful balmy summer day, when they were relaxing together in a green field, Diana could not contain her curiosity, shyly asking him, 'George, when you're up there,' – she made a sweeping, all-embracing gesture with her right arm up towards the stark blue sky above them – 'what's it really like?'

'Do you really want to know?' George asked her. He stared deeply into her violet-blue eyes as his reflected a kind of sadness, a tristesse – like a hunter right before pulling the trigger of his rifle to shoot a beautiful, unsuspecting deer. 'It's not very nice really. When you have to face an armada of hundreds of German bombers accompanied by fighters to protect them, it's the kind of sight you'll never forget for the rest of your life. They usually approach England in tight formations. Seeing them come at you so massively grouped together, off in the distance, while you're still climbing, desperately clawing for and gaining altitude, makes you feel awfully small and insignificant. You really feel scared. It's the truth, Diana,' he said softly with a faraway look in his eye

Then, as if warming to the subject, he continued. 'When you're up there,' – he pointed his index finger at the sky – 'it seems as if there's no end to the rows and rows of bombers coming over from France. Sometimes it really seems as if a long, drawn-out, dark threatening cloud extends over the entire Channel. You might compare it to those thick clouds of starlings migrating and suddenly changing course and direction to make such weird formations in the sky. A number of times we meet them head on, trying to disperse them, to destroy the lead planes, but it can be extremely dangerous because you're approaching each other at a closing speed of about 600 miles per hour. At the very last possible moment, you have to dive under or fly over them. You can't imagine how awfully quick it all happens. You have no idea how we slice like lightning through those massed formations. The fighter planes mix in the resulting, developing dogfights and then it's each man for himself. The other day, I came out of a cloud and found a Messerschmitt 109 right in front of me by the purest of chances. I don't think the pilot even realised I flew right behind him. I couldn't possibly miss blasting him out of the sky. All I had to do was push my thumb down on the joystick firing button to let him have it. I opened fire and the plane in front of me disintegrated into hundreds of metal fragments. Poor chap! But, Diana, if I didn't get him, he would have got me or one of my colleagues. Better a Hun than one of us.' George grinned wryly with a hint of disdain.

Diana admired him openly. Playfully, she tickled his cheek with a blade of green grass. 'Please go on, George,' she urged him excitedly, her cheeks glowing red. He was describing a completely unknown, mysterious world to her that she would never penetrate. Diana felt curious and wanted to know more about it.

Noticing her interest, he continued. 'When you get one on your tail,' – he demonstrated with his hands – 'it's quite a different story, mind you. Waves of utter fear run through you. You can feel drops of cold sweat running down your spine as you watch your enemy in the rear-view mirror above the cockpit. It's an awful sight. You quickly say your prayers when you catch sight of the Messerschmitt 109's ugly, dark prop-spinner with a black hole in it. That's how threateningly close the plane is flying and manoeuvring behind you. So you have to try to out-dive or out-turn him and you may still make it and survive. You can also steeply turn down into a tight spiral. If you don't, you're forced to go through that instant of hell exposing your craft to gunfire from his two machine guns and two cannon. I can tell you, dear Diana, that's the critical moment in a dogfight. You could still be lucky and get away with a lot of bullet holes ripping through your aircraft and perhaps even save yourself by parachute. Otherwise, all you can expect is a hail of bullets which could mean the end of course,' he added, lending sinister significance to his words. 'Nowadays, with the ugly firepower those German fighter planes have, it's all over in a fraction of a second.' He stared sadly at her while she leaned over him.

'Oh, that's horrible!' she exclaimed. 'Please stop, George. It's an awful story. You frighten me.' Quickly, Diana bent her head, kissing him softly on his eager lips. Then she caressed the contours of his chubby, sunburned face with her hand, letting her index finger delicately trace the deeply etched fatigue lines around his eyes and mouth.

'Well , young lady, you wanted to know what it's like up there and I plainly told you.' Slyly grinning, he took her into his strong arms at the same time. She purred contentedly, like a happy, satisfied cat. Carefully he took her head in both his hands, at the same time staring deeply into her beautiful blue eyes, kissing her willing lips, drawing her on top of him.

Diana made no objections, she responded readily. 'Hold me tight, George,' she whispered eagerly in his ear, revealing her growing desire for him. Suddenly, quite unexpectedly, they furiously made love in the open countryside beneath the blue sky.

Later, their desires spent, they remained there for a long time without speaking; words had no meaning at that point.

When shadows began to lengthen, they reluctantly left and slowly strolled back to his base, hand in hand, happy and deeply in love.

What did fate hold in store for both of them?

III

DURING the months of October and November 1940, Jan discussed the various aspects, the pros and cons, of his escape plan with his father, too. Although he fully realised what grave risks his son and Geert Overgauw were going to face while cycling through occupied Holland, Belgium and France, he did not make the slightest objection nor could he add much to what Jan had explained to him.

His father told him, 'It's a good idea to go via Paris. Interrupt your trip for a few days. Pick up the necessary strength at Monsieur Mohr's house. Once you're there, please tell him I do appreciate whatever he may do for you. Also wish him the very best. There's very little else I can do these days.' His father smiled ironically. 'You know that Monsieur Mohr lives on the northern outskirts of Paris. You don't have to cross the city. That's an important point, Jan. Avoid the city's centre. Say hello to Mrs Mohr, too. I remember she's a superb cook.' With a hint of mockery to his voice, his father said, 'Perhaps she'll let you taste one of her cooking marvels.'

'I hope so,' Jan said.

'Monsieur Mohr is a very honest, decent and intelligent man. Listen well to what he suggests for the second part of your trip. I'm aware your plan is full of hidden dangers, yet I approve it, Jan.' His father eyed his son seriously. 'You do need lots of luck. You realise that, don't you? Let's hope your attempt will be a success,' he concluded in thoughtful mood.

Letting his father's words of wisdom sink in, Jan told him, 'Under the present circumstances, there are few other practical ways of escaping from Holland. They're all dangerous, loaded with imponderables,' he added crisply.

His father nodded. 'I agree, it's not easy to escape, otherwise half the Dutch population would have left the country already. Now Jan, once you're in Paris, be very careful. Also be patient in all circumstances. Obey Monsieur Mohr and listen carefully to anything he may suggest. He's the best man to give you well balanced advice on how to proceed from Paris to unoccupied France. You can trust him completely. We can't say the same for many people today,' his father added bitterly.

Together they took their time to go over the details of Jan's plan. His father could not find any obvious errors in what his son had worked out. The idea was simple but they ran the serious risk of encountering German patrols checking their documents anywhere along the route south. And what if they should be stopped? They had to cover more than 300 miles!

His father was only too aware of the grave dangers his beloved son would have to face on his way to freedom.

During the following days and weeks, Geert and Jan began overhauling their bikes, cleaning and oiling every moving part carefully. Jan owned a lightweight racer especially built for him by an English firm before the war. Geert's bike was somewhat heavier, yet a good one, solid and fast. They packed all the extra supplies they needed into two personal leather bags. At last, they were ready for the big adventure: a leap into unknown darkness – darkness abounding with far too many imponderables, uncertainties, hidden dangers they had to face.

The penultimate day of the year 1940 was a cold one. After a hearty breakfast with his parents, Jan went to fetch his bike from the garage.

His mother stood waiting in the garden. He walked over to her to say goodbye. Once outside the comfortable warmth of the house, they stood shivering in the early morning cold. Jan noticed how nervous his mother was. She repeatedly asked him, 'Have you got everything you need, Jan?' Her restless, worried eyes fixed on her son with great affection. Now and then, while they were waiting for Geert, she wiped her hands against the sides of her winter coat. 'Will you be careful, Jan?' she asked again. 'Don't do anything rash. Consider everything carefully before you act.' She spoke softly to him as if her kind, motherly advice was going to protect him. Her beautiful grey-blue eyes looked at him with profound maternal love while he impatiently stood next to his gleaming racer. Twice his mother raised her hand as if to say something. But she didn't utter a word, watching him, instinctively knowing everything that could be said had been spoken. There was nothing more to add. It meant a definite goodbye and who knew for how long?

In the meantime, Geert had arrived. Jan bent over to kiss his mother's cool cheeks. She tightly hugged him close to her for just a moment, eyes brimming with tears as she whispered into his ear, 'Please be very careful.' Then she let go of him, not knowing when or if she would ever see him come home again. She quickly placed a hundred guilder note in his cool hand.

Jan's father walked the young men to the gate. He shook hands with Geert, then turned to his son. Their eyes held for an instant – both realised and understood what the departure and the parting of their ways meant. They had fought some titanic battles, both possessed very strong personalities, yet they knew how profoundly they loved each other. Many times, they had behaved like two fighting cocks, each vehemently defending his point of view. His father had only got his way thanks to his iron willpower.

'On your way, the two of you. Make the best of it and may God bless you both,' he said, voice quivering with emotion.

The two young men mounted their bikes. When Jan reached the corner of the road where he'd lived the most pleasant years of his life, he looked back one last time. He saw his parents waving goodbye with their warm shawls. His eyes blurred for just a moment; then he set his mind on the trip ahead, moving on, pedalling furiously, forcing the gloomy emotions to the back of his mind.

The first day went rather well. They were able to make good progress despite a cold, freezing wind. Geert came along nicely, following Jan's lead. On their way south, they passed the cities of Rotterdam and Dordrecht, fortunately not encountering German roadblocks.

As they finally approached the huge Moerdijkbridge towering high over the Rhine river and cutting the Netherlands in two, they despaired. They had to cross it to continue south to Breda but to their consternation they noticed a sentry box in the far distance, at the entrance to the huge metal construction, with a German soldier in front of it.

They halted, stiffly climbing off their bikes, to take time to silently and patiently study the bridge and to contemplate the critical situation in which they found themselves. They noticed there wasn't much traffic passing over the bridge, and wondered what they should do next.

Jan turned his head towards Geert, asking tensely, 'What do we do now? Pretend we're innocent citizens or act like young students on their way south to visit relatives for the New Year festivities?'

Both stared nervously, tightlipped, towards the enormous steel bridge towering high over the flat Dutch countryside. Was it an evil omen of what was to come for both of them?

Geert shrugged his shoulders. 'I suggest we try crossing. If we can't make it past the guard and should he send us back again, then we simply pedal home to The Hague. In that case, we'll have to try and find another way to cross the river. There may be a chance we can find somebody who's willing to row us across during the dark hours of night,' Geert suggested, his features tense.

'Do you know anyone around here who owns a boat?' Jan sounded somewhat irritated when asking the question, making it sound sharper than he intended.

While still staring at the imposing bridge, Geert shook his head. 'No, I don't. But there must have been others who managed to cross over,' he insisted, stubbornly aware other Dutchmen had reached England via the southern route.

Hardly at ease, Jan took his time to observe the level countryside. 'The way I see it, the only solution is to keep going and face whatever may confront us. Let's hope for a bit of good luck. I can't really think of any other way. Shall we give it a try, Geert?' he suggested, his face worried.

Geert nodded his head. 'All right. Let's go, and keep our fingers crossed.'

With their hearts pounding in their chests, they mounted their bikes again. Slowly, they pedalled towards the impressive bridge and their destinies. Would they make it past the German sentry?

The threatening, low-hanging, dark grey clouds raced along the horizon as if they were about to fuse with the landscape below, driven by the cold, harsh westerly winds so frequent in Holland. They could also feel the threat of snow in the gloomy sky above them. It all looked exactly like a scene painted by one of the famous sixteenth-century Dutch artists.

Discussing and working out plans back in Jan's comfortable home had been exciting; but they were now faced with harsh reality. The cold, the unexpected German guard – it all seemed quite frightening to both of them, as if the whole carefully planned escape was bound to go wrong from the start.

The young German sentry stood inside the dark green wooden guardhouse, impatiently shifting from one foot to the other because of the icy gusts blowing outside. The incessant wind howled uncannily through the heavy metal girders of the huge bridge high above the flat land, creating a sinister, threatening noise. The water in the river below was whipped to waves capped by white foam. The whole scene made a grim impression – it didn't bode well for them.

When the German soldier saw the two cyclists coming closer, he briskly stepped out of the sentry box, signalling them to stop. In harsh German he asked, 'Halt! Wo geht Ihr hin?' The young guard sternly glared at both of them from beneath the rim of his olive-green steel helmet. His presence could spell the ruin of all their carefully prepared plans and hopes.

Jan replied calmly, 'We're on our way to visit relatives in the south for the New Year festivities.'

Suspicious, the soldier kept his rifle aimed at them, walking around the two bikes while observing them attentively. He also checked their baggage. Then he finally made up his mind, asking, 'Why didn't you take the train? It's much too cold to be out on a bike.' Jan read the doubt in the guard's cold, untrusting, sceptical eyes.

Jan stared straight at him. 'We do not have enough money for the train,' he lied. He stated it firmly and then resignedly awaited the final and possibly fateful reply. He felt clammy all over his body due to the awful tension he was feeling.

Now it fully depended on what the young German soldier was going to say. Would it be a yes or no, they anxiously wondered.

It was freezing on the bridge high above the river. The wind blew forcefully at the three men shivering in its icy gusts. Again, the German peered doubtfully at them, as if weighing his answer. Then his eyes suddenly relaxed, a smile flickered across his toughened face and he said to Jan, 'That's a nice bike you have there. I own one in Germany. Wish I had it here.' He shrugged indifferently, stepping back into the guardhouse, waving his right arm to indicate they were allowed to continue.

Doubtful at first, Jan and Geert faced each other in disbelief. They heaved deep sighs, weary eyes revealing their utter surprise. Slowly exhaling, shaping twin jets of vapour in the cold air, they hadn't fully grasped the consequences of the soldier's words yet. A sense of utter relief swept through them. They had overcome the first serious obstacle on their risky enterprise south by sheer good luck. How many more would they have to face?

They climbed back on their bikes again and quickly pedalled away, afraid the German guard might change his mind. Looking back over his right shoulder, Jan took in the scene he would never forget. It had been touch and go but fortunately they had made it safely past their first hitch.

In the evening, they finally reached the home of Geert's friend. They felt very tired. It took a long time after Geert rang the bell for the tense face of his acquaintance to appear. He held the front door ajar to see who'd disturbed him at that hour. The moment he recognised Geert his face relaxed.

Opening the door wide, he invited them in. 'Come in! I'm glad to see it's the two of you and not the Gestapo one can expect at this particular late time of the evening!'

After Geert had patiently explained why they were there, his friend immediately offered them two beds for the night. Now they found themselves in a small, well-heated, cosy house. At last, Geert and Jan visibly relaxed in the friendly atmosphere. After all the first day's hectic excitements they could let themselves go, allowing their tight nerves a rest.

When Geert complained about leg muscle pains, his friend's wife handed him a small bottle of sloan oil. Jan gave him a light massage. Afterwards Geert felt somewhat better.

They had been cycling for over seven hours with an ice-cold wind blowing hard over the flat land. Both felt grateful when their host poured them an abundant Dutch jenever, warming their stomachs.

Their host's wife offered them a hearty meal consisting of a good steak, potatoes, cauliflower and chocolate cake for dessert. Staying up late into the night, they excitedly discussed the brutal effects and also the ugly consequences of the German occupation on the local southern Dutch population. The outlook was grim. The near future seemed bleak indeed for the Dutch. Those remaining in Holland were going to face an unknown, abominable existence they had never experienced before in their peaceful country.

The next morning, Jan and Geert were up at eight. They breakfasted with their host and his wife who had prepared fried eggs and bacon for them to give them strength and energy for the second stage of their very risky attempt at reaching southern France.

Attentively, Geert and Jan listened to a variety of ideas suggested by Geert's friend. He patiently explained how they should proceed over the many small country roads leading into Belgium offering them a fair chance to remain unobserved. Finally, they thanked him and his wife and left in semi-darkness. It was 31 December 1940, the last day of an eventful year for the Dutch.

Once outside the warmth of the house and moving forward again, they followed the narrow road Geert's friend had indicated. It led to a thick wood where they finally managed to locate the sandy footpath used for centuries by smugglers to cross over into Belgium. Carrying their bikes on their shoulders, they carefully and stealthily proceeded on foot.

They stopped every now and then, tensely listening for the threatening sound of anyone moving in their vicinity. It was a new, frightening experience to get accustomed to. They felt as if they were common thieves out on a felony.

When they noticed the first road sign, they consulted their maps and found out – to their great relief – they had been following the right path. They had succeeded in crossing the border unseen. Now they were on their way to Paris via Antwerp. They had managed to pass their second important obstacle unobserved!

Nothing else happened that day as they actively pedalled on. At times, in the far distance, they spotted mechanised

German troops on the main roads and avoided them. Yet the sight of the hated enemy made them doubly cautious. As they continued to travel over country lanes, they repeatedly had to stop to check their position on the roadmaps.

Fortunately they didn't run into any military patrols or road checkpoints – not even that second day. It seemed as if a lucky star was guiding their way, much the same as once a celestial body had indicated the way of three Kings.

Late that afternoon, when shadows were lengthening, they approached the French border and decided to spend the night in their sleeping bags in a small wood they found along the road. From that moment on, no one would help them – they were completely on their own. It was not a comforting thought and was a very cold experience. Jan, in fact, had never felt so icy in his whole life, vainly longing all night for his own comfortable, well-heated home in The Hague and his mother's pampering.

The next day, when already well inside France, their incredible luck held. No military patrols or checkpoints interrupted their advance to their goal, Paris. When wanting to swiftly move its troops, the German army only made use of the main highways, leaving the smaller ones to the local populations, reluctant to travel under any other circumstances anyway.

Pedalling south, they also passed Compiègnes, the famous historical spot where the 1919 and 1940 Armistices were signed between the German and French armed forces in two railroad carriages.

While approaching the northern suburb of Paris, they were even more careful. At last, after asking directions of several pedestrians, they found Monsieur Mohr's house. They were both physically exhausted, unshaven, dirty-faced and in need of all the sleep they'd lost the previous night. But not having been captured during their three days on the road made them intensely happy, proud and satisfied they had travelled that far. Their safe arrival was the first goal of a long, long journey south towards Spain and a new future. Yet so many things could still go wrong!

They still had to cross the border between occupied and unoccupied France and had to pedal more than 400 miles before reaching the Spanish border.

IV

EVERYTHING seemed all right one afternoon on the penultimate day of September 1940 when Diana Boulton was summoned to the office of the operations room's Commanding Officer.

Upon entering the small, spartan, soberly decorated space, all she noticed was a plain desk with a chair and two wooden seats in front of it. Photographs of military planes, some dating back to the 1914–18 war, hung on the walls. On the desk stood a lonely, framed photograph of a young RAF pilot in uniform, standing in front of a twin-engined Vickers Wellington bomber.

As soon as she saluted the CO, he welcomed her kindly. 'Please sit down, Miss Boulton. How are things going in the operations room? Do you like the hectic work we've experienced during the past couple of days?' The CO stared inquiringly at her. 'May I call you Diana?' he asked hesitatingly.

'I have no complaints, sir,' she firmly replied. 'The work is interesting. I like it. But sometimes, I have to admit, it's rather dramatic and also tiring.' Diana hesitated a moment, then added, 'Especially when you know the men fighting the Luftwaffe up there.' She smiled wanly at the CO, as if to excuse herself for making the observation.

'I know it's hard work, but remember Operation Command bears the burden of a large part of the air war in this area. It's not as glamorous as being a fighter pilot, of course. You must be well aware of the frightful losses we suffered these past weeks, but the Hun fortunately lost far more.' After these words, the CO stared straight into her eyes, asking, 'Don't you have a friend among the pilots?'

Diana didn't suspect anything yet: she was still under the impression the CO had called her for a friendly chat, even though she felt surprised he had asked her if he could call her 'Diana' instead of 'Corporal'.

'Yes, sir,' she replied evenly. 'I believe his squadron must be in action today.' Now she suddenly became aware how tense the man sitting stiffly in front of her looked.

'That's exactly why I summoned you to my office. It is my unpleasant, most unfortunate duty to inform you he's missing in action. He never made it back from his last flight. He was engaged in quite an aerial battle with a considerable number of enemy planes. The other pilots in his squadron reported seeing his plane go down. They didn't spot a parachute. I'm sorry, Diana, I don't have better news for you,' the Commanding Officer said compassionately.

After hearing the shocking, terrible news, she quickly turned her ashen face away from the CO as her eyes became big and terrified, slowly filling with tears she desperately tried to fight back without fully succeeding. In the room's deep silence, her whole body shook; Diana sat curled up in her chair as if her stomach hurt badly, while spasms of grief racked her. At last she managed to pull a handkerchief out of one uniform pocket, making an effort to dry the tears away. Then she made a courageous attempt at facing the man sitting motionless, as if frozen, behind the desk.

'I …' she started, then hesitated. 'Forgive me … sir … I … can't … help … it.' Her voice broke and she couldn't keep it steady, despite her mental efforts.

Diana tried desperately to control herself. She spoke with extreme effort. 'Although … we all know … it could happen … any day … one always hopes … and always prays … it won't.' She sniffed the words, heartbroken. In despair, she urged herself, 'Please God, give me the strength I need to go on living.'

The CO nodded his head with understanding. 'I know, my dear girl.' His eyes also misted for an instant as he stared at the portrait of the pilot on his desk. 'I lost my only son in this awful war. I can understand a little of what you must be going through. If it can be of any help, I can give a you a few days off.'

Tears slowly rolling down her marble white cheeks, Diana managed to look up at him. 'Could I … have … a few days?' She took a deep breath before going on. 'That way, I can visit my mother. She lives in London,' she added hesitatingly.

'That can be arranged. Report back to me for further duty in a few days. You know you must continue, don't you?' he inquired sympathetically.

'Yes, sir.' This time, she managed to answer firmly.

He spoke to her like a father. 'Life goes on, you know. It's so very sad to lose a loved one but time heals all wounds – you'll see.' He sighed heavily. 'Unfortunately, I have some experience in the matter.'

When Diana entered her mother's flat, Mary Boulton immediately realised something terrible had happened to her daughter. Taking Diana into her arms, she asked worriedly, 'What is it, Diana? What's happened?' Then she let her daughter cry out her grief, despair and deep shock.

'Oh, Mummie! George was shot down!' she cried. 'He's …,' she hesitated a second before pronouncing that dreadful word, 'dead.' Voice quivering, she said softly, 'I'll never see him again!' She wept on her mother's shoulder, desperately sobbing, 'Hold me, Mummie … please … hold me … tightly.'

Her mother comforted her. 'My poor, poor child,' she murmured, deeply anguished, observing her elder daughter. 'There's so little I can do for you right now. I think the best remedy for you is a good night's sleep. Come on, go to your room and undress. I'll prepare a strong sleeping powder for you.' Mrs Boulton put Diana to bed with a heavy dose of sedative.

After her mother had turned off the lights, Diana lay immobile on her back, wide open eyes staring around in the darkness surrounding her, slowly becoming accustomed to it. She fully realised the nightmare world she would have to live in as of now would be a dark, unlit, cold ambience.

Barely audible, she whispered into the dark nothingness, 'My dearest George, I loved you so.' Trembling in the dark, she understood only too well he would never come back to her, to kiss her, touch and caress her, love her.

Her immediate future looked so terribly empty, as if she walked alone on an infinite beach stretching out in front of her without the slightest hope of reaching the end to meet other people, communicate, nurturing a tiny speck of hope to feel alive again, to live a full life again.

Agonisingly slowly, tears slid down out of the corners of her eyes onto the pillow beneath her head; then Diana turned over and desperately cried and cried, only falling asleep due to sheer exhaustion and the effects of the powder her mother had given to her.

The next morning, Mary Boulton silently entered Diana's bedroom with a cup of tea and a freshly baked orange cake she knew from experience her daughter liked. She stood in front of the bed for a moment, tenderly looking down at Diana, now sleeping peacefully as if nothing had happened at all. Her blonde hair spread out over the pillow, her smallish face in absolute composure, her features completely relaxed – she looked so lovely, so rested and so terribly vulnerable.

Heaving a deep sigh, Diana's mother opened the curtains a bit, letting the morning sun filter through. She seated herself on the foot of the bed, gently shaking Diana out of that deep, sedative-induced sleep.

'Diana – wake up my dear.' Patiently, she waited for a reaction. Then she softly spoke again. 'I suggest we take a walk together in Hyde Park today. I remember you needed a few new things to wear. We'll do a bit of shopping as well this morning.' She took her time, observing how her daughter slowly shook the sleep from her lovely blue eyes. 'Come on, Diana,' she urged her kindly. 'I want you to be active. It's the only way to keep your mind busy.'

Languid, catlike, Diana luxuriously stretched her body beneath the blankets, still half asleep, sluggishly staring at her mother while a weak smile of recognition started to play on her lips. Then, she suddenly sat up, as harsh reality reflected in her face. She was now wide awake and the sad, depressing knowledge with her – clearly visible in her eyes. Tears – that she rather unsuccessfully tried hard to blink back – welled up.

Quickly, with one swift movement, her mother moved over to her, protectively taking her daughter into her arms and holding her tightly. 'Don't give into any self-pity, please,' she encouraged Diana. 'This is what life's all about really. Happiness and sadness, good luck and bad luck, seem to alternate. Death's an uninvited guest who turns up any time, anywhere, throughout time … unsought but always threatening to be around. There's no use fighting it. It's like ebb and flow. Remember, when your father died, I had to carry on despite the deep pain I felt just to take care of the two of you by providing you and your sister with a home and a good education as well. At the time, I thought London offered the best solution for the three of us. Come on, drink your tea while it's still hot. Then take a shower. It'll do you good. We'll leave in half an hour. The weather looks fine for a walk.'

Diana wearily nodded. 'Yes, mother.' She faced her, eyes filled with tears. 'I'll miss him so. He was so kind, so charming. Churchill got it so right when he called the fighter pilots our 'finest'. Just think, mother, he was only twenty-two when he died. Can you really imagine that? His life ended at only twenty-two,' she emphasised. 'It's terrible, but you're right. We must go on, mustn't we?' Diana asked, heaving a deep sigh.

'I know. Come on, up you get,' Mrs Boulton insisted. 'We have a busy day ahead of us.' Her mother pulled the blankets away, uncovering Diana.

Diana took a long shower and got ready. Once she had finally finished dressing, she joined her mother. Steadily, at a brisk pace, they walked arm-in-arm for an hour in Hyde Park. Then Mrs Boulton took her daughter to lunch. To keep Diana's mind busy, she accompanied her to several shops in the city centre so she could buy her a few things.

At one stop, Diana chose a blue cashmere sweater and cardigan matching the colour of her eyes. When she tried them on, critically studying herself in the tall mirror, the tears she had gallantly fought back suddenly welled up in big, crystal clear drops slowly descending unchecked down her cheeks. Immediately her mother moved to her side, lovingly placing her arms around her shoulders, encouraging her daughter. 'Just go ahead and cry, my child. Just go ahead and cry,' she repeated softly. 'Let yourself go. Don't fight it. It'll be good for you,' she encouraged her daughter. Discreetly, the saleswoman turned her head away. She knew, like so many others, what dreadful human suffering the war caused.

During the next couple of days, Diana's mother did everything she could in an attempt to try and keep Diana's mind off the hard, cold truth that George would never be around any more to keep her company. After a week at home, Diana informed her mother she felt strong enough to return to her work in the operations room.

Her wounded heart bore its first deep raw scar from then on. The hurt would stay with her for a long time, a very long time.

Once back at the Air Force base, she reported to the Commanding Officer first, then went back to her duties in the operations room, shifting the coloured discs over the table so familiar to her.

After squadrons had returned from the Continent or from the many operational flights over the south of England, and the losses were reported, indifferently chalked up on the blackboard, she quickly looked elsewhere, afraid her emotions would show while observing those harsh, merciless, cold figures.

Again many families had lost a son, had been deprived of a loved one. Diana realised the agony the damnable war caused.

One month passed before the wreckage of George's plane was found and his remains identified. Diana obtained permission to attend the funeral where she also met his parents. There was so little she could say on such a sad and sombre occasion – an embrace, tears, a feeling of hopelessness, a word of encouragement, softly whispered reassurances and that was all. The one she had loved so intensely was gone, leaving a terrible emptiness behind.

The rest of 1940 went by, as did 1941. Diana kept herself busy by dedicating herself completely to her work in the operations room as if it eased her grief. At least, shifting the coloured discs kept her mind active.

During this period, she met several eligible young men. They became good friends and nothing more. Diana had also been in correspondence with a young Tank Corps Captain who had been transferred to North Africa to fight the German Afrika Corps. His letters stopped arriving after a certain date. She was later informed by one of his friends that he'd been killed in action close to Tobruk in Libya, during fierce tank battles with Rommel's mechanised divisions.

Now and then, Diana went to dances where she met friendly, eager officers and non-commissioned men but there wasn't one who could warm her wounded heart. She had no real, steady boyfriend although she happened to be good-looking.

The silence, the emptiness was hers – as well as the deep grief of having to go on without the one she loved. Nobody could intrude upon it. Diana was also afraid of becoming emotionally involved and perhaps being hurt again. At times, she would sit motionless in a chair, wistfully staring into nothingness for hours. And there remained always that raw, cruel, cold question – 'Why, God, why?' But she hardly expected an answer.

She recalled so well the happy and exciting emotional moments she had spent with George. In her reveries, those images took on dimensions impossible to match. They had known each other for such a short period, yet to her it seemed like eternity.

At times, she felt a nauseating, suffocating pain of missing him, like a growing malignancy she bore within, filling her with deep despair, almost destroying her will to go on living.

Diana's wish to remain uninvolved emotionally didn't mean so much an antisocial attitude but rather a very cautious temporary withdrawal within herself. She felt the necessity of protecting herself against the chance of having to suffer again, even though she didn't want to wither away either.

She absolutely wanted to avoid that at all costs. She carefully had to rebuild her life on new, solid foundations. The past would never be a reality again. And she intensely wondered what the future would hold for her.

V

WHEN ENTERING Montmorency, a suburb located northwest of Paris, total disaster nearly struck! On turning a corner, they ran into a German checkpoint in the middle of the street. It looked as if their lucky star was abandoning them.

Quickly, Jan shouted to Geert, 'Turn around immediately and let's enter that side street.' Right that very instant his heart thumped wildly in his chest due to the brutal shock of having noticed just in time the German soldiers busily checking pedestrians' documents.

Jan and Geert pushed their pedals hard gaining speed to avoid the threat of being questioned. A few moments later, a middle-aged Frenchman, typically dressed in a velours jacket with a dark beret on his head, made a sign to them to stop. But both hesitated, not knowing if the man could be trusted. However, having no other solution to their problem, Jan slowed down and, with a serious, searching look, closely observed and weighed up the Frenchman. At last, he decided to stop and talk to the man.

'Hé, jeune homme,' he said to Jan. 'Vite, vite, suivez-moi.'

Hesitantly, Jan nodded his head as if weighing the odds, then answered, in his best school French. 'Vous … me pouvez … aider?' he inquired carefully.

'Oui, oui, moi aussi je déteste les Boches, je les ai combattu pendant la Grande Guerre. Alors,' he urged, noticing their hesitation, 'il n'y a pas de temps à perdre.' And again he insisted, 'Suivez-moi!'

He indicated an old dilapidated building and explained, 'Là vous pouvez rester sans être découverts. Quand les Boches sont partis, je viendrai pour vous avertir.'

Jan sharply observed the Frenchman; then, at last, he stuck out his right hand to shake with him, 'Je … vous … remercie … pour … votre gentillesse.' Jan smiled at the man and they were on their way to the construction the man had indicated.

After they had been hiding for a few hours, the Frenchman came back and carefully explained that he belonged to a resistance group called 'les Maquis'. He informed them that the Germans had left and Geert and Jan again mounted their bikes and were on their way.

After a rather short ride through the periphery of Paris, Jan at last anxiously mounted the steps leading to Monsieur Mohr's front door. Having reached the very first and most important objective in the French capital, Jan and Geert nurtured high hopes for the near future.

After he had rung the bell, a moment later the door was cautiously opened and kept narrowly ajar, as if the ones inside expected unforeseen visitors. Monsieur Mohr's worried face appeared, sharply observing the two unexpected arrivals. The instant he recognised Jan, he quickly opened it wide, letting them enter into a narrow corridor while at the same time nervously looking up and down the street to see if anyone had noticed the two young men. Then he immediately insisted on hiding their two bikes in the cellar, making Jan wonder about all the secrecy. Only much later did he understand why.

Monsieur Mohr studied Jan's face with intense curiosity. 'Jan, what a surprise to see you. For heaven's sake, my boy, what are you and your friend doing here in occupied Paris? It is very dangerous, you know?' His worried eyes searched the two young Dutchmen's unshaven, dirty, tired features.

Jan introduced Geert and then explained, 'We escaped from Holland and we're trying to reach unoccupied France. That's our first goal. But our real objective, Monsieur Mohr, is to reach Perpignan in Free France. I've heard rumours that one can cross the Pyrenean mountains to enter Spain. Once there, we hope to reach Lisbon by train and make contact with the KLM Royal Dutch Airlines office. That briefly happens to be our plan and intention, Monsieur Mohr.'

After a number of sharp questions, Monsieur Mohr shook his head in disbelief. 'You and your friend must have run incredible risks, riding on your bikes through occupied France! Really, Jan, you were never stopped at any German Army checkpoint?' he asked with a strong hint of doubt in his voice, then continued. 'Were you never asked for documents, or something of the kind? It's really against all reasonable expectations and hard to believe that two young men crossed through such a vast, occupied area without ever having been stopped anywhere. You two must have consumed more than your share of good luck,' Monsieur Mohr finally concluded, still shaking his head in disbelief.

Jan smiled shrewdly. ' We do realise that, Monsieur Mohr. Perhaps it all turned out that way because we picked the right time of year. Or perhaps we were truly fortunate. However, I can assure you other ways of escaping from occupied Holland also require plenty of good luck. And they're certainly no easier.' Jan laughed contentedly through the layers of dust and dirt caked on his face. 'We barely met a living soul, pedalling through the cold on our way south. To me, it seemed as if everyone had holed up underground like scared rabbits sensing danger – perhaps German danger.' He laughed thinly.

'I understand,' Monsieur Mohr said. 'I just wanted you to know I'm utterly amazed. I'll help the two of you. You can count on my complete assistance in getting you to the south of France. Tell me, Jan, how long are you planning to stay in Paris?' he asked cautiously. He had many other important matters to deal with but he couldn't possibly reveal to Jan what they were all about.

Jan shrugged, 'It all depends on you, Monsieur. I hope you will let us rest for three days at least. Then, if all goes well, we'll leave during the late evening of the fourth day. Do you think that's feasible?' he asked, a slight frown creasing his smooth forehead. He realised only too well he and Geert were imposing on Monsieur Mohr's valuable time and hospitality.

The KLM director energetically nodded. 'Oui, oui, it can be arranged. I'll have to ask my wife to buy some extra food without causing any kind of a stir. That's not easy these days,' he sighed worriedly. Having settled the matter of their stay, Monsieur Mohr accompanied them to an upstairs room, showing them a bathroom where they could shave and clean up after their tiring trip.

An hour later, they were seated in easy chairs in the ample sitting room, both clean and wearing freshly ironed shirts, while Monsieur Mohr placed cool French beers in front of them. They immediately started to exchange experiences about the bitter, empty life forced upon them by the German occupation. Monsieur Mohr also melancholically mentioned the good old days when KLM employed their commercial planes, Douglas DC-2s and DC-3s, operating them all over Europe and the Far East with incredible regularity.

'Ah, Jean, Royal Dutch Airlines was highly appreciated by everyone and now …' he dejectedly threw his hands up into the air. 'Who knows when it will spread its wings again?' he shrugged with a typical Gallic gesture.

Jan conveyed his father's greetings. 'He told me to wish you well. He said that's all he can do these days.' Just then, Madame Mohr announced dinner was ready. Jan and Geert fully relished the marvellous dishes she had prepared for them and Monsieur Mohr poured a delicious French wine. Following the delightful meal, Monsieur Mohr opened a bottle of port wine and brought both up to date on the difficult period the French were experiencing.

'Yes,' he confirmed, 'the good old days are gone probably forever. The future looks gloomy indeed. The war will completely destroy the old values as we knew them. No one can realistically predict how long the German occupation of France will last.'

They considered it could well take years with England on its knees and America still undecided. Monsieur Mohr also told them that he felt convinced the Nazis were going to lose the war in the long run but it would take many years. Final victory over the German invaders implied a long-range goal, a gigantic battle causing many victims. It was a sombre evaluation yet it would prove to be rather realistic!

During the days while Jan and Geert stayed hidden at Monsieur Mohr's house, Madame Mohr did her very best to spoil the two Dutch guests. She prepared her finest meals and as a result Geert started to feel much better. The annoying pain in his leg muscles gradually disappeared.

Monsieur Mohr strongly advised them both to stay inside. 'Don't ever stand at the windows. I'm not sure whether my house is under observation by the Gestapo or the German Sicherheitsdienst.' Jan was to find out why Monsieur Mohr had to be so careful at a much later date.

On the fourth day, he and Geert got ready to leave after dark. On a detailed map of France, Monsieur Mohr had patiently pointed out the route to follow. In even the most critical circumstance, it would be the safest one to follow in order to reach their next objective – Free France.

'When you get close to the unoccupied French border, you'll find yourselves in rolling countryside covered by woods. Your direction must be Vichy. Jan,' he continued seriously, 'approach that all-important border with the utmost care. Take your time first to observe – maybe even for an entire day and from an adequate distance – all border activity going on at the checkpoints. Look for places where you might cover the ground without having to go through border control. As far as I know, there are no mine fields in that area yet. Take it easy, be patient, observe the procedures and how long they take, exactly what the guards do. Then, when you finally decide which way to go, follow that path. And, Jan …' – he urged firmly – 'stick to it! That's the best advice I can give you for a safe arrival in unoccupied France. I sincerely hope you and Geert will succeed in sneaking through. Once you've made it across, use all your strength to get as far away as possible from the border.' A deep frown creased Monsieur Mohr's forehead as he spoke these words. 'I must emphasise that, Jan, because you could run into one of those mean collaborators operating inside unoccupied France. Yes, Jan, France unfortunately also produces those despicable, characterless traitors who'll report fugitives for Judas money. They've little to learn from the Nazis or the Gestapo for their vile, vicious, intermediary treachery.' Monsieur Mohr sighed heavily, as if he personally felt responsible for those disgusting French double-crossers.

'Also be careful – extremely careful – just beyond the border,' he insisted. 'If nothing happens there, you can relax during the last stretch. Enjoy yourselves a bit when you reach Perpignan and work off all the tensions you endured.'

Monsieur Mohr stopped for a moment, sighing heavily again. 'The south of France is so beautiful at this time of the year. I sincerely wonder if I'll ever see it again?' he commented, eyes reflecting gloom and dejection. Then, at last, he handed Jan the address of a Dutchman who lived in Perpignan and helped others to reach Spain. 'Memorise it and give the piece of paper back to me. Contact him. He knows how to help you cross the Pyrenees into Spain. Just tell him Monsieur Mohr sent you.'

Upon leaving, Jan expressed his gratitude, warmly thanking Madame Mohr for her kind hospitality. 'Thank you, Madame Mohr, for everything you and your husband have done for us. I'll always remember.' Turning to Monsieur Mohr, he said, 'Geert and I will follow your practical advice. I can only hope for the best. You do understand, of course, neither one of us wants to be captured and end up in a concentration camp in Germany or Poland,' he said with a good-natured chuckle.

'All right, Jan. The best to both of you and may God bless you, my boy!' Monsieur Mohr hugged him tightly for a second. He had never had children of his own but intensely liked the son of his Dutch boss. The boy possessed character and was straightforward. 'I hope you'll make it safely to England.' He stared hard at Jan, saying, 'Once you're there, please do everything in your power to free all of us again. Fortunately, the Royal Air Force gave the Luftwaffe a good licking. Perhaps it was the first important step to final victory over those Nazi bastards. Oh, and, Jan, also say hello to my old KLM colleagues in Lisbon and London. Tell them Monsieur Mohr, along with all the rest of France, is most anxiously waiting to be free again.' Silently and meaningfully, they shook hands.

In a serious mood, Jan said, 'I promise you, Monsieur Mohr, I'll do everything in my power to give you back your freedom!'

'Goodbye, Jan – goodbye Geert – it was nice to meet again.'

Monsieur Mohr carefully opened the front door, holding it ajar and peering down the dark street to make sure the two young men could leave without running any risk. Then he walked down the steps into the street. Once he was certain everything looked all right, he signalled them with his right hand. Jan and Geert swiftly slung their bikes over their shoulders, descending the steps as well. Down in the street, they mounted their bikes and, waving a final salute to Monsieur Mohr, were on their way again to face new, unknown dangers.

After a harrowing night, pedalling slowly and attentively through unknown streets and country roads, they finally found a thick wood where they could rest for the entire day. They had reached a point about 130 miles from that all important border to freedom but didn't exactly know what lay ahead. In order to pass the long hours they ate and highly appreciated the delicacies Madame Mohr had prepared for them.

When it became semi-dark, they started to move again, carefully and slowly cycling through the dark night towards their destination. Every time they noticed moving lights, their strained nerves tightened considerably. The following morning they felt absolutely exhausted, not only from physical exertion but also from stress and tension. With only a few miles to go to freedom, every move they made became of the utmost importance and could possibly even be disastrous.

So many young men who had made the attempt to escape from the German occupation had been caught by German security forces. Just when success seemed right around the corner, they had been captured to be deported to a concentration camp in Germany or Poland.

Lady Luck really has strange ways of picking her winners!

After carefully searching for a safe spot to hide, Jan and Geert finally decided on a secure place in a small, dense wood. From their vantage point behind the trees, they tensely observed the German guards in their grey-green uniforms checking the two divided parts of France. They could hear the harsh brutal shouting of the guards. For a long time, Jan studied the scene below him through his binoculars and noticed the sullen, resentful expressions on the faces of those passing over the border. The men and women looked like zombies walking automatically in single file. Everyone slowly shuffling along showed serious, annoyed expressions on their features. Bitterly, Jan became aware no one laughed.

At last, he spotted a narrow gully a few miles to the right of the border checkpoint and quickly pointed it out to Geert.

'I think we could sneak through that hidden passage. Our illegal crossing might pass unobserved over there.' He pointed to the spot with his right index finger, animatedly discussing their chances with Geert.

At one o'clock they ate and then rested for the remaining daylight hours to gather all the strength they needed for the final, most dangerous part of their escape south to freedom at last. Resting in his sleeping bag on the hard, cold ground, Jan longingly reminisced about the good old times in his comfortable home in The Hague.

Finally, after darkness had set in, they lifted the two bikes on their shoulders, slowly and attentively advancing through the windswept countryside towards the gorge. The only noises they heard were the typical moaning, creepy, mysterious sounds of the night, with dogs barking and an owl hooting in a distant tree.

Carefully, they proceeded step by slow step, tensely, nerves stretched to their very limits. Every now and then they halted, taking deep breaths, listening hard for any unexpected noises which might signal the presence of those they did not desire to meet. Above them, clouds drifted by in the sky but they also occasionally noticed a few bright stars twinkling in the dark. It was winter.

Fortunately, the ground beneath their feet felt soft: there were no stones or pebbles on the path they had chosen. As a consequence they made no noise while they steadily progressed.

By now, Jan's heart was racing, thumping in his chest. Even though it was rather cold, small drops of sweat stood out on his forehead and upper lip. He felt terribly tense, perfectly aware one false step could mean absolute disaster for both of them. He looked back over his right shoulder at Geert following close behind, observing his shadow slowly moving ahead. A beam of hope flashed through his mind – perhaps they were going to make it after all.

But right then, suddenly and inadvertently, Jan stepped on a dry twig unseen in the dark. It snapped loudly beneath his weight. In the ghostlike, total silence of the night, the noise sounded like a pistol shot. Both froze on the spot in the hushed darkness surrounding them. They felt absolutely terrified, hearts pounding wildly in their chests as they tensely waited for some kind of reaction from the blackness ahead. Had the German guards heard the noise as well?

Standing completely motionless, barely breathing, they resembled a marble statue of the first two cyclists classified in the Tour de France – two immobile figures with bicycles on their shoulders.

Ever so slowly they sank to the cold ground, waiting, hiding, as if nailed to the spot. For a long time they remained like that, passively awaiting whatever was to come. An eternity seemed to go by.

Both felt the same unnerving sensation, as if a thousand pairs of eyes were watching them, curious and intense, from the pitch-black darkness surrounding them. It felt eerie, nerve-racking. They felt scared to death, not knowing what was going to happen next – and they silently waited. Minutes ever so slowly ticked away.

By now, both realised more dogs were barking in the distance. The sounds of harsh German voices, talking and laughing, seemed to be much closer. These sounds carried far in the total silence of the night as they hugged the soft ground. He and Geert kept on waiting for a long, interminable time, not knowing exactly what to do next. Perhaps a quarter of an hour had passed when Jan finally signalled with his right hand, urging Geert to his feet. Very cautiously, they rose and started to walk forward again like two cats on a night prowl.

After proceeding cross-country for over two hours, they found a narrow, winding country road leading south. They assumed they were in unoccupied France at this point but weren't completely sure. They believed they had made it and could safely mount their bikes again but they couldn't be certain yet. They had not come across any road signs indicating they really were in unoccupied France.

As Monsieur Mohr had suggested in Paris, they had to put as much distance as possible between them and the border they believed they had just passed and left behind them.

The early morning aurora started to show on the distant horizon in a wealth of fantastic, multi-coloured displays of light – pink and purple colours mixing in the sky – while they kept on going, pedalling inexorably towards their goal, even though dead tired. It was now seven in the morning; both were physically as well as mentally exhausted from the nervous tensions of the previous night. Yet they managed to keep on going until eleven, when their last reserves of strength ran out and they could not proceed any further. Breathing had become difficult, laboured and loud. They had reached the absolute limit of human endurance.

Jan and Geert had been on the move for more than eleven hours. For part of the time, they had progressed slowly on foot in the darkness with extreme care over small, unknown country roads leading south. They instinctively felt they should be within unoccupied France – but they weren't sure yet!

Finally, they noticed a road sign: one arm pointed north towards Vichy, the other one south to Clermont Ferrand. At last, they were sure they had made it to freedom! Jan enthusiastically slapped Geert on the shoulder, at the same time performing a kind of joyful Indian dance in the middle of the road. They had finally reached what they had set out for.

A French farmer happening by that moment on a horse-drawn cart eyed them with curiosity. It must have been something of a shock to the farmer seeing two young men dancing on the road early in the morning around two racing bikes lying on the tarmac, both unshaven and rather dirty, but terribly happy, as reflected by the euphoric expressions on their faces.

Jan tossed Geert an amused glance. 'Do you think you can still keep going for a little while? I prefer to go as far as we possibly can today. But first let's buy something to eat and drink. I feel thirsty and famished. What about you? Then we'll decide what to do with the rest of the day.'

Exhausted, Geert nodded wearily. 'Ja, Jan, I agree. Let's move on. I've really reached the end of my physical energy after last night. I've really had it. I don't think I've ever been as frightened in my life when you stepped on that damned twig. My God, I thought it meant the end of the line ... all our efforts for nothing ... but our good luck held and nothing happened. Once we've eaten some food, I promise I'll do my very best to carry on, using what little strength I have left – if there's any left, mind you,' he said, with a very tired smile.

Later on, when they found a roadside café, they sat down at a table, asking for coffee, bread and cheese. Once it was served, they relished the food as never before after the awful tensions of the night. They remained for over two hours; then they wearily got to their feet, stiffly mounting their hard bike saddles. Jan and Geert forced themselves on for another three hours, pedalling calmly, completely at ease, since there was no reason to hurry any more. They added another 50 miles to the distance already separating them from the border. Now they were at least a comfortable 125 miles inside Free France. It felt good and great to be free again – away from those nasty German occupiers.

The first night in unoccupied France, they decided to sleep in a small hotel they found along the road en route south. During early evening, sitting in a small dining room, they enjoyed an exquisite dinner and finished a bottle of red Bordeaux wine while talking animatedly. They didn't have to speak in very low voices any more – they were free! When they finally crawled into the beds in their room, they slept as if in a profound coma. At last, their overstrained muscles relaxed under the cool, clean bedsheets. They no longer had to pedal for their lives. They no longer had to feel scared.

The next morning – 9 January 1941 – they woke up at nine, luxuriating, and later enjoying an excellent breakfast with lots of French cheese, crusty, freshly baked baguettes and coffee in a completely relaxed atmosphere. They had no more German guards or checkpoints to worry about!

At eleven o'clock, they mounted their bikes – their destination was Perpignan. The weather looked beautiful: a cool, crisp, winter morning breeze while the sun warmed their curved backs as they pedalled along the big roads leading south.

The next three days of cycling were much easier. They made good time and a bright, warm sun kept beating down on them. They felt elated when pedalling along the roads leading to the Spanish border, admiring the contrasting colours and the splendid beauty of the rolling French countryside, so well painted by van Gogh, the famous Dutch artist. This time, of course, they followed the main roads, no longer having to fear the unexpected movements of mechanised military German troops or unexpected checkpoints.

Jan and Geert were masters of their fates again – and it showed, even reflected in the happy, carefree expressions on their features. They continued south towards the blue Mediterranean, the scenery becoming more beautiful with every passing day. Both admired the sloping hills, tiresome to climb but so marvellous, once over the top on the other side, to freewheel down into the next valley.

Monsieur Mohr had given Jan the address of a Dutchman in Perpignan who could help them cross into Spain from where they still had to reach Portugal and Lisbon.

When, after some questioning, they finally located the Soler house, Jan and Geert were completely surprised and in a way shocked to find a number of other Dutchmen there, also waiting to cross the Pyrenean mountains. Monsieur Mohr hadn't mentioned their presence at all. They were totally unprepared for the bitter surprise which could well mean a considerable delay in their plan to reach Lisbon.

Jan introduced himself to the house owner. 'My name is Jan Plesman and may I present my friend Geert Overgauw. We have cycled all the way from Paris. Monsieur Mohr, the KLM director, gave me your address. He sends you his very best regards and also informed me you could help us get into Spain safely.'

The man observed them kindly. 'Welcome to my house. A friend of Monsieur Mohr is a friend of mine. What can I do for you, Jan?'

'We'd like to cross the mountains and continue into Spain as soon as possible. We're both pilots and I strongly believe we're urgently needed in England. Perhaps you can tell us what we should do.'

The man nodded. 'Well,' he spoke hesitantly, 'you've noticed the other Dutchmen who arrived before you. We've established a rule that everyone must wait for his turn. I have to warn you, considerable time might pass before yours comes up. It may last as long as two months. It depends on imponderables I cannot reveal at the present moment. I have to get you over the mountains into Spain to good, reliable people who will not send you back to occupied France and a concentration camp. It has unfortunately happened in the past when we didn't have the necessary experience and the right contacts on the other side. We've lost some very dear friends that way.' The man added significantly, 'In Fascist Spain, there happen to be many Nazi informers and Fascist collaborators who may contribute to send fugitives back to the Germans in that part of occupied France which borders Spain.'

'I understand,' Jan answered, unable to conceal the deep disappointment he felt. 'It's a pity and a waste of time we have to wait that long but I'll accept it if you say so. We are already grateful to have come this far and thank you for your hospitality.'

Three long, lonely, boring months passed before their turn finally came up. It was already mid-April. The mountain peaks were still covered with deeply layered snow. When they left Perpignan, Jan and Geert took one last melancholy look at their faithful racing bikes – those two metal wheels, tyres, frame and saddle had become dear to them. After all, the bikes had safely carried them to their destination, the south of France. Jan gave them away to the owner of the house.

Following their French guide, they laboriously started to climb higher and higher up the Pyrenean mountains. At 5,000 feet they already had to wade through very deep, waist-high snow during their 'illegal' crossing into Spain.

They struggled along, step by step, to over 9,000 feet, their breathing becoming more strained by the minute the higher they went. But the French guide urged them on. 'Courage, allez, on y est presque! We can't stop along the way in the open. We must keep going. We are nearly there.' He pointed to a spot up the mountain where they distinguished a log cabin.

Even after shadows started to lengthen and it grew dark, they slowly continued climbing up the mountain paths, resting every hour, then every half-hour. They progressed as carefully as they could, closely and tiredly into the thin air, following the mountain guide's steps.

Inhaling the rarefied, cool, dry air became an increasingly painful process. It burned their throats and lungs. Their shoes seemed to get heavier by the minute. The muscles throughout the lower parts of their bodies began to feel numb. Each additional step became a titanic, mental struggle between willpower and physical exhaustion.

It was well past midnight when at long last the guide stopped at a woodman's small log mountain shed. Jan and Geert had used up all physical reserves hours before; they had by now reached the absolute limit of their endurance.

They gratefully rested, sinking down on a hard wood bench inside the cabin, their weary heads lolling down on their chests while the French guide prepared a log fire to make tea.

Jan and Geert felt the oppressive silence of the surrounding mountains. Nothing stirred, as if they happened to form part of a completely different world. The only sound was caused by the crackling of the wildly leaping flames in the hearth. At last, after downing some food, they rolled out their sleeping bags and crawled stiffly into them, falling asleep instantly as if they'd been doped.

Early the next morning, after only five hours sleep, the guide woke them. Once outside, they were again forced to struggle through a pass 11,000 feet high. At last, after two days of climbing, the longed for descent began. At the end of their tour de force, which had lasted for four days, the guide delivered them to a 'safe' address inside Spain.

When saying goodbye to the two tired Dutchmen, he smiled encouragingly. 'Bonne chance à vous deux. J'espère vous arriverez bien et sains en Angleterre. Au revoir.' Jan and Geert gratefully shook his hand.

By the end of April 1941, they finally arrived in Madrid. When they called at the Dutch Embassy to pay their respects, they were received in a rather cool, indifferent way. It was not what they had expected. They were not exactly welcomed with open arms but rather with neutral unconcern. Both had looked forward to a much warmer reception after all the dangers they had faced. What Jan and Geert did not know, of course, was how a few Dutchmen before them had created considerable problems for the Dutch Consular staff. One strong Dutchman had broken the jaw of a Guardia Civile in a drunken brawl, causing annoying difficulties with the Spanish Government for the Embassy staff.

A few days later, they were able to board a train for Lisbon where they arrived at the beginning of May 1941. Here, at long last, they found a much more gratifying reception at the KLM Office. The Portuguese KLM director, Mr Van Vliet, offered warm hospitality. His wife also did everything possible to make their short stay a pleasant one. Someone was finally taking care of them, spoiling them with good food, wine and charm.

Jan also got a chance to talk to KLM's chief pilot – Koene Dirk Parmentier, an excellent pilot, who had become world-famous during 1934, at the time of the London–Melbourne Air Race. The city of Melbourne was then celebrating its 100th anniversary and Sir Macpherson Robertson had organised the spectacular Air Race to call attention to the memorable event.

The KLM management had entered a twin-engined Douglas DC-2 commercial airplane: it came in first in the handicap race and second in the speed race. It had represented a tremendous success for KLM and Jan's dynamic father. Parmentier, of course, had been the KLM plane's captain. Parmentier's clear blue eyes stared at Jan in surprise when he met him.

'Fancy seeing you here in Portugal! How's your father? When did you see him last?' He fired these questions away at Jan, showing how much he cared about the welfare of the company's General Manager.

Jan smiled. 'Oh, quite well, thank you. You can imagine how much he hates every moment of the German occupation. Who knows how long he'll have to face that hardship before being able to take up his activities in commercial aviation again!'

Parmentier looked knowledgeably at him. 'I understand. You know, Jan, I think I was very lucky to escape from Holland. On May 13, 1940, under cover of night, we found one aircraft still in a condition to fly at Schiphol Airport. I just got the plane off the ground in time to keep it from being destroyed by the Luftwaffe. Now, we use it extensively on the regular hop we make between England and Portugal. I have plenty of work to keep me busy here, regularly flying from Bristol to Lisbon and back.'

With his eyes twinkling, Parmentier continued. 'I want to tell you a funny story. We often have two KLM Douglas DC-3s parked here at Lisbon Airport. Both belong to the company but one flies with camouflage colours to England while the other with German markings and flown by German pilots follows the Frankfurt–Lisbon route. A strange coincidence when you think of it. Sometimes the planes are parked next to each other, like they were at Schiphol Airport … two estranged brothers on the tarmac of Lisbon Airport.' As he spoke, an amused grin crossed the pilot's face.

Jan chuckled. 'That's an interesting story, Mr Parmentier. Too bad my father hasn't heard it.'

Parmentier interrupted him. 'I know your father's heard about it. Via secret channels we keep him pretty well informed. The latest developments in civil aviation in the United States, and the world in general, are also passed on to him. Don't worry, your father is not falling behind on new aircraft being developed by Douglas, Boeing and Lockheed.'

Enthusiastically, Jan said, 'That's marvellous! I'm sure he appreciates that. I didn't know. By the way, may I introduce you to my good friend Geert Overgauw who came all the way from Holland with me. He's a pilot too.' Jan's expression turned serious. 'We would really like to fly to England as soon as possible to join the Royal Air Force. Could you help us by any chance?' He stared questioningly at the KLM Chief Pilot.

'I'll inform KLM's manager. You have my complete cooperation. As soon as two seats are available, you can have them,' Parmentier confirmed.

A happy smile crossed Jan's face. 'Thank you. In fact, Mr Van Vliet told me we could be squeezed in tomorrow if you accept us.'

Parmentier eyed him sharply for a second. 'OK, it's settled. Welcome aboard. By the way, I must inform you, you're not to expect any leniency from British security once you safely reach England just because I happen to know you. You must realise the British are very thorough indeed in their security work. They have to be. They'll question you for a long time before clearing your entrance into England. Security has to make sure it doesn't meet with an invasion of German spies. I sincerely hope you and Geert do understand that.' To emphasise his words, he sternly looked from one young man to the other.

The commercial air service KLM maintained between Bristol and Lisbon was well known to German intelligence. The Luftwaffe could have shot down the unarmed commercial KLM planes any time it so desired, either above the Atlantic Ocean or the Bay of Biscay. But German intelligence found the flights useful for their own purposes and interests.

The KLM DC-3s flew from Bristol Airport to the furthest south-west part of England where KLM captains landed at St Mawgan or St Eval airports to take on the maximum load of fuel guaranteeing a safe crossing over the open sea to Lisbon.

German intelligence made good use of English newspapers like the *Daily Mail*, *The Times*, the *Daily Express* – and many other publications and weekly magazines. Diplomatic mail from Arab countries represented in London but sympathetic to the German cause was useful, too. In turn, English intelligence used German and Swiss newspapers, carried to Lisbon by the other KLM DC-3s on their flights to and from Frankfurt, to find out what was happening in Europe.

One unfortunate day, however, when Leslie Howard – the famous English movie star rumoured to be the chief of English intelligence in Portugal – happened to be on board the KLM plane, it was shot down over the Gulf of Biscay. Everyone inside the plane, commanded by Captain Tepas, died in that horrible incident (1 June 1943).

On several flights, Captain Parmentier was also attacked but always managed to escape by flying very low and zig-zagging over the surface of the sea. With two DC-3s and one DC-2, and despite the raging armed conflict, KLM maintained the Lisbon service during the whole war. About 1,700 commercial flights were carried out on a regular basis, amazing everyone in the aviation world.

On 23 May 1941, Jan and Geert embarked at Lisbon Airport to be flown in luxury to Bristol aboard the KLM DC-3 piloted by Captain Parmentier.

Their continental adventure was over. They had succeeded in escaping from occupied Holland and were now on their way to a new future in England. Little did Jan know that he would never meet Monsieur Mohr again. Later, in Paris, he helped hundreds of young men and women escape to the south of France until the Gestapo henchmen arrested him, abducting the KLM executive to a concentration camp in Germany from which he was never to return.

When the wheels of the DC-3 touched down on the Bristol Airport runway, Jan and Geert had arrived at their destination. In spite of all kinds of obstacles they had made it!

However, despite all Captain Parmentier's recommendations, upon arrival they were immediately taken into a kind of protective custody by the British security services. They were thoroughly interrogated about what they might have seen during their remarkable bicycle trip through occupied Europe. They were queried why they'd come to England, how they'd managed to escape by pedalling their bikes through territories occupied by the German forces. And so it continued, for three interminable days of endless questioning.

After all, it was quite exceptional, pedalling all through occupied Europe and not having been detected once by Germans manning checkpoints.

Jan and Geert felt deeply disappointed: those continuous, insistent demands seemed so unfair after all they'd been through together. They had risked so much to reach England and once there they had become suspects. Reluctantly, in the end, they came to understand the necessity for so much questioning and information-gathering from them. On 27 May 1941, they were finally released from the Patriotic School in London where the questioning had taken place. They also had to present themselves for a thorough physical check-up. Afterwards, they had to confront a Royal Air Force selection board. They had to answer questions about their flying experiences, the total hours flown in Holland, what kinds of planes they had piloted and if by any chance they had any other flying experiences.

At last, they were cleared. Jan had to report at Grantham airfield, east of Nottingham, in the heart of England. Separation time had come: Geert also had to proceed to an airfield to take up training on bombers. He still firmly hoped he could become a Spitfire fighter pilot.

The parting of ways came after more than seven months together. 'Parting is such sweet sorrow' – and it was true for them as well the moment they had to say goodbye. They fought back personal emotions while shaking hands; then each went his separate way towards the RAF adventures awaiting him.

Jan started military training in England on 2 August 1941. At first, he wasn't sure whether he'd be accepted on fighter pilot training. A great deal of it depended on him, how he performed during the first weeks of basic flying instructions. He had not flown for fifteen months.

The great, intense air battles over Great Britain had been fought exactly one year earlier but the air war still raged on: English cities were being regularly bombed at night by the Luftwaffe. During the day, the air war had considerably slackened. The Luftwaffe urgently needed most of its planes to carry out the massive attack Hitler had ordered to conquer Soviet Russia. Operation Barbarossa was in full swing as of 22 June 1941.

After over a year of military inactivity, Jan had to get used to discipline again – had to get up early in the morning and follow link-trainer instructions – an artificial cockpit on the ground simulating the pilot's conditions, exactly as if he were in mid-flight.

During August, Jan accumulated many hours of actual flying, which included operating a twin-engined craft. The Wing Commander in charge of training informed him he was accepted for Sunderlands – four-engined flying boats.

When he heard the bad news, Jan felt terribly and bitterly disappointed. His dream of becoming a Spitfire pilot was completely shattered. He wondered in disgust if he'd risked so much for such meagre results.

A few days later, the Wing Commander summoned him again. This time he informed Jan he'd changed his mind and recommended Jan for fighter pilot training. At these words, Jan's spirits rose sky high.

In the meantime, he'd been told his father had been arrested in The Hague by the Gestapo. He'd been taken from his comfortable home to be transferred to a nearby prison. He was now being held as a hostage by German security in Holland in solitary confinement.

When he asked around, he found out his father's arrest had been principally due to two Dutch pilots – Hidde Leegstra and Piet Vos – who had escaped on 5 May 1941 from Holland to England in a twin-seater Dutch fighter plane: a Fokker G-1 with German markings. And also to Govert Steen, a pilot friend of Jan's, who'd stolen a Fokker T-8W (a twin-engined seaplane on floats) on 6 May and flown it single-handedly to England. Following Jan and Geert's escape from Holland at the end of 1940 and now those of these three other pilots who'd fled in an even more spectacular way, German security suspected Jan's father of being the brains behind it all.

Also unknown to Jan, the German secret service operating in Lisbon had noticed him in Portugal and had reported his presence to the German Sicherheitsdienst in Holland.

Jan felt furious and bitter – his father had to suffer such degradation for something he was in no way responsible for. But what could Jan do?

First, he had to start all over again with flight training, flying a Tiger Moth biplane and a twin-engined Anson. He felt satisfied and proud about becoming a real fighter pilot. He wanted to repay the Germans in kind for what they'd done to his country and his father in particular. But he had barely arrived in England. Still, Jan eagerly looked forward to military action – to downing his first Luftwaffe plane. If he could achieve that, he would feel he'd repaid the Nazis in some way for all the misery they had caused his country.

Two months later, he got his first short leave and decided to spend it in London. Once there, he met a number of his old friends and colleagues from Soesterberg and Holland. Several of them had also escaped in the most incredible ways from Holland. These experiences were completely new to him and he had to get accustomed to an entirely different way of life.

During training, he had only used English and now it was a pleasant, emotional feeling to be in contact with his own countrymen again, to converse and exchange ideas in his own language – making small talk with his Dutch friends about life in general in England and in Holland in particular, of course.

In Jan's considered opinion, training progressed far too slowly. He had expected the flying aspect would be much faster after his own experiences as a pilot in Holland. He had also hoped to be ready for military action and operational flying in far less time. He was impatient for action and had good reason to be. But the RAF was thorough: it trained its pilots well and took its time doing it!

After all, the RAF had gained its vast experience during the Battle of Britain, when so many fine young British pilots – just out of OTU (Operational Training Unit), with only a few hours of practice on Spitfires and Hurricanes – had been tossed into the raging air battles to save Britain from the relentless Luftwaffe onslaught. These young men had been knowingly sacrificed. Once the Battle was over and won, the top brass had decided 'Never again!'

The RAF didn't want pilots only good for clay pigeon shooting by the Luftwaffe. It wanted good all-round pilots, well trained, ready and able to shoot down the opposite side – the bandit – the Luftwaffe.

VI

AFTER GEORGE had been shot down and killed, Diana made it a habit to regularly visit her mother in London during leaves. She needed the moral strength her mother gave her. One evening, towards the end of 1941, she was home again, enjoying a late tea with her mother in the cosy flat's sitting room.

Mrs Boulton watched her daughter attentively, asking, 'How are you getting on?' She was becoming worried about Diana, who seemed incapable of forgetting or of letting go of the sombre reminiscences of her lost first great love – ever since George had died in September 1940, over a year before.

Diana answered evasively. 'Oh, you know, the usual routine. There's not much variety to my life.' She glanced apologetically at her mother. 'The operations room, the work to be performed there and every once in a while a movie or a dance.' She shrugged her shoulders imperceptibly, then continued, 'I don't like going to those dances much any more. I don't know why but feeling a man close to me is terribly irritating, and boring as well.' She smiled thinly at her mother, as if asking to be understood, distancing herself from everything that went on around her.

Mrs Boulton did not want to mention George's name; it would only upset her daughter. 'Well, are there any other parties or events to take your mind off your work?' she asked gently.

Surprised, Diana looked up at her over the rim of the cup she was holding. 'Why the sudden interest, mother?' she asked mockingly.

'To tell the truth, I've been a bit worried about you lately. It seems to me you've completely withdrawn from the world, from everything going on around you. Forgive me for saying it, Diana, but that's wrong. You are so young and so lovely – please don't shut yourself off from all of us,' her mother begged her.

'I know. It may be wrong but it's so terribly difficult to step back into life again as if nothing had ever happened. George and I loved each other intensely; everything else is a mere shadow, a mere void of what we felt for each other.' A film of moisture covered her eyes, expressing the inner emotions she had to fight back.

'That's it, Diana,' her mother affirmed quickly. 'I believe you have to force yourself to open up again. Right now you're like a Dutch tulip in the cool early morning, its petals firmly shut. Yet I know very well there's a warm heart beating inside you,' she insisted.

Diana smiled kindly at her mother, appreciating her personal interest. 'How poetic can you get? But mother, I promise you when spring is on its way, I will mend my ways and shed my hurt feelings like a lizard dropping its tail. Know what?' Diana asked firmly. 'I shall return to the world again. At least,' she said cunningly, 'I'll make a serious effort to do so.'

Content, her mother eyed her. 'You do that, my dear. Now …' Mrs Boulton inhaled deeply before continuing, 'I have taken the liberty of renting a cosy, small apartment here in London for you and Jane. You can use it during your leaves. I've told you and your sister about the birds and the bees and expect both of you to use your brains and be clever girls. Do you understand what I mean?'

A knowing expression appeared on Diana's face. 'Don't worry, mother. I know how to handle myself,' she assured her. And right then and there, images of her and George making love in the wide open meadow flashed through her mind.

'Good!' her mother exclaimed. 'Would you like more tea?' When Diana said yes, Mrs Boulton lifted the tea-cosy to pour her daughter another cup.

Staring at her mother over the rim of the cup she held in her slender right hand, Diana told her, 'You do understand I can't force the situation. I suppose I'll be prepared for the occasion when the right man comes along. Your remarks are true, though, I must make a start and break free of the stale past and start living again. It won't be easy, mother.' Diana sighed deeply.

Gratified by her daughter's improved mood, Mrs Boulton observed Diana with a tender look. 'That's it! Tomorrow morning we'll visit the apartment. I do hope you and your sister will like it. I've kept myself busy these last months arranging the furniture. No easy task, mind you, with everything being rationed these days.'

'Oh, mother you shouldn't have gone to all that trouble, but I am curious. I really do want to see what you managed to get together.' Turning serious again, Diana asked, 'Do you think there exists some kind of equilibrium to everything taking place in life on earth?'

Her mother didn't understand her remark right away, asking, 'What exactly do you mean?'

'Well,' Diana hesitated for a moment. 'Let's put it this way – do you think the positive, enjoyable events will be counterbalanced at a certain moment by unpleasant, perhaps sad ones later on?'

Mrs Boulton shook her head slowly. 'I really don't know. At times we meet people who seem to be blessed only with sheer luck. Then we later find out they've also been through rather dreadful experiences. I don't think there's just a black or white side to life. I believe there are also many grey, over-lapping areas, if you understand what I'm talking about.' Her expression serious, she observed Diana, wondering if she understood those words.

'I think I do, but I must admit I imagined life would be a little more kind to me after Dad died and we left Australia. I really thought luck would have extended a helping hand to me. But George is gone. You know, mother, it never really occurred to me he could be shot down one day. Perhaps I was too caught up in a young girl's dream world without solid foundations. I should have been more realistic.' A rueful smile played on her lips. 'So many other pilots died but I never imagined it could happen to him.'

Surprised, Diana's mother looked at her. 'Do I detect a note of self-pity?' Mrs Boulton asked with a sly twinkle in her eyes. 'You have to take the negative aspects of life along with the positive ones. I don't really know if the former will eventually be balanced out by the latter. I really just don't know,' she repeated softly, more to herself than to Diana. 'Yet I believe we can't possibly be blessed by everything good in life while someone else is burdened with all the bad. It seems so terribly unreasonable and unfair to me.' With those significant words, she smiled encouragingly at Diana. 'You're still so young and lovely. Your future is still an open book. Let's hope you'll be very happy when you come to the right page.'

Imperceptibly, Diana shrugged. 'Perhaps, when I come to it, I will be … Who knows?' She smiled evasively.

VII

DURING AUGUST 1941, Jan continued his training as a pilot. He had to fly on different kinds of aircraft. One of them was the Miles Master, a reasonably fast, single-engined airplane, the forerunner of the Hurricane and the Spitfire.

On 20 August, the military airfield's Commanding Officer informed Jan he was going to be transferred to Ternhill, an airfield situated close to Wolverhampton, where he would continue his training and learn to fly Hurricane fighter planes. It meant a small step forward in his flying career.

The next day, he arrived at Ternhill late in the afternoon. After a rather tiring journey, he was pleasantly surprised to run into a Dutch friend – Govert Steen – the pilot who had made that remarkable escape from occupied Holland with a twin-engined Fokker seaplane stolen right out from under the German guards and single-handedly flown to England. A fantastic and most courageous enterprise!

'Hé, Govert!' he exclaimed in Dutch when they met.

'Dat is een tijd geleden dat wij elkaar zagen! Hoe gaat het met jou?' (It's been a long time since we last met! How's everything with you?')

A bright laugh spread over Govert's features. 'Well, as you can see, I'm still alive and kicking,' he commented happily.

'How are things with you?' he inquired, showing his interest in Jan's well-being.

Jan grinned thinly at him. 'As you can see, I'm being transferred from one RAF base to another.'

Govert nodded, stating, 'That's part of becoming a fighter pilot. I think the RAF definitely wants to give us a Baedeker tour of Great Britain before sending us on operational flights over occupied Europe.'

Eyes revealing how interested he was in Govert's experiences in England, Jan asked, 'What plane are you flying at this base?'

'Hurricanes – I hope to pilot Spitfires in a few months.'

'That's the aircraft I'd like to fly,' Jan commented enthusiastically. 'But I'm afraid it'll take a while.'

Govert nodded his head. 'Better not to be too optimistic. The RAF takes forever to train us. But what else can we expect? We're merely Dutch pilots. Perhaps the British command believes we fly planes with wood clogs on our feet,' Govert exclaimed, smiling at Jan in a slightly bitter way.

At the new RAF base, Govert and Jan often reminisced about the good old days back in Holland and how they had enjoyed the lifestyle they were accustomed to as students in Delft: they hadn't a worry in the world. Now they were being trained by the RAF in England and were totally aware how time sped by without their participating in any real war action. They wanted to become a part of the raging air war – to help bring it to an end. But time passed while they kept on flying trainers – when the weather permitted.

On 8 September, Jan bitterly wrote in his diary:

The weather is awful. The fog shut the airfield down for six days straight. There was absolutely nothing to do. I felt thoroughly irritated by the enforced inaction. What an utter waste of precious time! I feel more imprisoned than ever before. Even though I happened to be a virtual prisoner after the capitulation in Holland, I could at least plan things for the future and try to figure out a way of making them work. But even that seems impossible here and now.

Govert and Jan were eager young men but the dullness, boredom and bitterness made them age far beyond their years. The utter futility of passively hanging around military airstrips and not doing anything important resulted in devastating effects on their nerves and morale. It began to show on their faces, too. Their goal at the outset of their risky escapes to England had been to pick up the fight anew against the German aggressors – to participate actively in the titanic struggle to defeat the Nazis' armed might on the European continent.

On different occasions, they'd risked their very lives to catch up with the Allied Forces, to join them in order to fight against Europe's oppressors. They felt eager to shoot down one of those arrogant Luftwaffe pilots but they were kept earthbound for the time being by the RAF brass.

Due to inactivity and the resulting monotony, the Dutch pilots passed far too much time drowning their sorrows in drink and aimlessly chatting at the bar and far too little time flying at that stage of their training.

With Govert Steen around, Jan at least had a Dutch compatriot to talk to on a regular basis, exchanging opinions in his own language. Since his arrival in England, he had already been transferred several times. Being rather shy and introvert, he found it tough making friends at every new airfield he was sent to. Just when he got to know different people better, he was transferred again. He fully realised there was a war going on, and he had to obey orders, yet it wasn't always easy for him to get accustomed to those constant changes.

The second half of 1941 proved to be rather unsatisfactory for both of them. 'Zij moesten door de zure appel bijten' – as the Dutch saying goes, 'You have to bite into the sour apple' – if they ever wanted to become operational Dutch pilots.

Jan took his instructions seriously when on solo flights above the English countryside practising acrobatics, loops, spins, half rolls, barrel rolls, slow rolls, steep turns, climbing turns and low altitude simulated air attacks. At least those exercises made him feel in a more positive mood. Useful, but they hardly sufficed him. He would have preferred immediate operational flying over Europe. As a pilot, he felt prepared for it. After all, he had already accumulated 199 hours solo in Holland – many more than inexperienced RAF pilots when they had been tossed into the Battle of Britain during the summer of 1940 after only very brief Spitfire practice, of not more than ten hours.

He felt bitter about it all, but kept on going tenaciously, hoping to be a Spitfire pilot one day, and impatiently looking forward to it.

At Ternhill airfield, he had to continue link-training on the ground. During the days and weeks that passed, he became more confident about his flying capacities. His airborne training continued, weather permitting. Yet he felt happy every time he was informed he had deserved an upcoming leave.

When away from Ternhill, he usually went to London, where he was sure to meet some of his Dutch friends. He could always find them at the Dutch Club where most of his fellow countrymen based in England were leave customers.

Whenever he went there he heard many stories and rumours about Holland's condition under its harsh German occupation. Jan wondered how his parents, brother and sister would endure it. At the Dutch Club, interest was of course mainly focused on Holland, but his country meant little to the non-Dutch back at the base.

While on leave, he was informed that four students – very close friends of his back in Holland – had already been killed in action. It made him ponder his personal situation.

He had escaped from Holland on 30 December 1940. It was now the end of October 1941 and he had not fired one shot at the German enemy. He felt very upset about how things were progressing in general. He became disgustedly aware that other Dutchmen who had arrived in England after him were making much faster and speedier promotions. It thoroughly irritated him. It appeared they had an inside track to the upper ranks.

One night during another London leave he went out with the Dutch pilots Piet Vos and Hidde Leegstra. They were the ones who had made the incredibly dramatic escape from Holland in a twin-engined Fokker G-1 fighter plane. Their escape and their daring stunt had, in a way, contributed to the arrest of his father by the German Sicherheitsdienst who now held him hostage in a prison close to his own home.

The three of them enjoyed a wild evening on the town. They downed too many drinks and Jan's head was really flying. Under the influence of the alcohol, his brain spun off in all directions. When he finally made it back to Piet Vos's apartment, he found a bed and more or less passed out. Piet also came home during the early morning hours, drunkenly mumbling, 'Where are my pyjamas?' He tried looking under several chairs, stumbling over them, but to no avail. Jan was peacefully sleeping, wearing the object of his host's frantic search.

The next morning, he was up at eight o'clock but suffered from a rather pounding head as a consequence of the night before. He had to return to Ternhill airfield where the ever so slow training awaited him. He held his head under a cold water tap to clear the alcoholic mist from his mind.

After a tiring train ride Jan arrived back at the base. When evening fell after his first day of flying, he mulled over his own life, over how flying instructions crawled along at a snail's pace, over how he had found himself separated from his family in Holland. He often wondered how his father was being treated in that small, solitary confinement cell measuring six feet by twelve. Those were definitely not happy considerations as he walked along the edges of the airfield in the gloaming. And he tried hard to work out the gloomy reflections whirling in his young brain.

He walked on, hands jammed deep inside his trouser pockets, head down, fronting the winds sweeping over the field. He was forced to face reality and those solitary walks were a necessity; he had to examine his own position in the enigmatic life facing him. The walks partially cleared his melancholic mental processes.

At times, he also felt a pang of guilt: perhaps his own escape from Holland had somehow contributed to his father's problems and hardships in that lonely, tiny prison cell.

For days on end the weather could suddenly turn foul and dreary. As a result, the gloomy hours made him feel quite homesick; his life had been so easygoing and pleasant before the Germans invaded Holland. When flying happened to be impossible, he spent the slowly passing hours writing in his diary. To the blank pages he entrusted his deepest, darkest secrets – at this time, black, sombre reflections describing his dismal inner feelings.

Brooding over his particular situation, he thought back to the friends and acquaintances he had known before 1940, ever since his engineering studies at Delft Technical High School. He would never see some of them again: their young lives had already been snuffed out in the great conflict raging in Europe and throughout the world. Death reaped a rich harvest indeed!

But there were others he never wanted to renew acquaintance with. They had betrayed their country, dishonouring the Netherlands by defecting to the hated enemy – selling their souls to the Devil Hitler. Jan spat on them for their vile collaborative actions. But some of the best were gone forever. Whatever positive, creative contributions they might have made to mankind in the future were lost for all time, while they lay buried or were never found again.

During these gloomy, reflective moods, he also reluctantly wondered how he would react to his own death if ever it should come. He didn't fear it, totally confident, while mentally strong enough to calmly meet the Grim Reaper, his conscience clear.

He was fully aware life on earth happened to be predestined. Some people were allowed more time, others less! He didn't know to which of the categories he belonged. Death was unavoidable, definite in itself. Once it had made its choice, it happened to be irreversible!

The end could come slow or swift, suddenly. He completely understood that. Death was always present – an invisible, uninvited, silent, cruel, patient passenger on every flight he made.

As he jotted his thoughts down in his diary, he also touched upon the bitter plight – the immense, endless suffering – of millions of Europeans bottled up on the other side of the North Sea. All they had to live on was hope. They fervently wished each passing day would be better than the one before.

Perhaps the German leaders would finally see the madness of what they had unleashed and also the futility of continuing the massacres of the war by sending a whole generation of young Germans to their deaths. Perhaps those misguided leaders were still ready to save their own people and the German nation from total destruction. Perhaps they might still ask for a peaceful solution to the raging, utterly destructive conflict. But the Devil Hitler had no intention of doing so!

Sometimes, he felt angry at the whole world: so many days had uselessly gone by – and so agonisingly slowly. He fully realised he still lacked the necessary preparation and experience to complete anything positive or constructive that could contribute to the Allied war efforts.

And the hard knowledge truly obsessed him when he stared out of a window at the impenetrable fog hugging the airfield preventing him from practising his flying techniques.

He was a very honest young man, with a clear, sharp, uncorrupted mind. Healthy, strong, over six feet tall, he had fair hair and grey-blue eyes. His firm jaw revealed how determined a character he possessed. He cherished his personal ideas about life. Hard on others, he did not make friends easily, but was never soft on himself. Forever seeking perfection, especially in his flying techniques, he always demanded the very best of himself and the aircraft he piloted.

At times it strained man and machine!

He took a day lost to bad weather or fog personally. He hated the empty hours wasted away at the airfield while impatiently waiting for the weather to clear. Hanging around the base or the mess, loafing, doing absolutely nothing, leafing through old illustrated magazines, got him wondering, during those interminable minutes and hours, what his dynamic father would have done or suggested to keep his son's mind alert and active in those dreary circumstances. Unfortunately, ground fog, haze, or just plain foul weather unsuitable for flights at Ternhill airfield lasted for many days.

Jan at least had his friend Govert Steen to talk to during the long evening hours. They reminisced about their Dutch Air Force period, about flying the old, antiquated Fokkers.

Govert told Jan he would soon be transferred to another RAF base where he was to pilot the famous Spitfires. As amateur strategists, they both launched endless ideas on how the war should be won. The invasion of Europe and its realisation was, of course, a major topic when they chatted.

On days when the weather was declared unfit for flying, Jan sometimes visited a Dutch military camp at Wolverhampton to change atmosphere, chatting and exchanging opinions with other Dutch officers there: it helped him overcome his feelings of disappointment. The Dutch camp commander was an old colleague of his father. They had been pilot trainees together at Soesterberg during the Great War.

One day, Govert walked up to him with a mysterious smile and asked, 'Would you like to join me and have tea with two elderly ladies?'

Jan shrugged. 'Why not?'

Govert, suppressing a wry grimace, said, 'Well, I must tell you they are no beauties but they're rather kind. I must admit their biscuits and cakes are excellent.'

'Okay, let's go,' Jan replied with a sly grin.

When Jan and Govert arrived at the comfortable house, two friendly, blue-eyed, grey-haired women around sixty welcomed them. The young men were accompanied into a cosy, tastefully furnished sitting room. A couch and three easy chairs were set up in front of an open hearth with a log fire burning in it.

Once seated, Jan at first chatted about trivial matters with the elderly women he'd just met. He felt happy to have kept Govert company, to escape from the rough male atmosphere at Ternhill. He rather appreciated speaking politely in that kind of different, warm atmosphere. It strongly reminded him of his own home in The Hague. And the whole setting brought to mind his mother, who had also always served tea and cakes in the afternoon.

One of the elderly ladies did all the talking, while the other listened silently to what was being said. She poured the tea and at the same time asked him, 'Do you take it with sugar and milk?'

'Yes, thank you,' Jan replied shyly.

As they relaxed in the easy chairs, the ice was soon broken and a warm ambience enveloped all four. The flickering flames of the fire in the hearth also made their contribution.

The loquacious lady asked him, 'Are you adapting to our way of life here in England? It must be quite different from the way you lived in Holland.'

A quick, rueful smile flashed across his face. 'It's not all that different really but I do miss family life and my friends in Holland. A war is being fought and I certainly cannot have everything my way, can I?'

'How true! Do you enjoy flying? Is it very difficult? I quite often see those fast planes fly so dangerously low over my house and I always wonder what the young pilots at the controls must be thinking while they're landing. How do they manage to keep their craft up in the air?' she asked with interest while her kind blue eyes twinkled as if to encourage both young Dutch visitors to speak about their own experiences.

Good-naturedly, Govert and Jan laughed. 'It's not all that complicated, really,' Jan explained. With his hands, he gave a demonstration. 'If you push the joystick forward, the plane descends. If you pull it towards you, the plane climbs. When you shift the joystick to the left, your wing on that side drops. Pressing the rudder pedal with your left foot, you effect a turn in that direction. If you want to swing right, it's the other way around.' He demonstrated patiently, moving both his hands and feet together, explaining the cockpit steering mechanism's workings.

The elderly lady carefully watched his hands as they moved through the air. 'How very interesting,' she commented. 'Well, I'm too old to learn to fly but perhaps my friend could pour you another cup of tea,' she said in a kind voice.

The afternoon flew by pleasantly. The two elderly women succeeded in making the two Dutch pilots feel right at home in their cosy house and in getting them to talk about their personal lives. Having already entertained other pilots over to tea, they knew what to do and say, quite aware how much the young men appreciated relaxing far from the tense atmosphere of military bases.

When the two young men left, Jan commented, 'You've been so kind. I'm truly grateful. You were so patient listening to me.'

The two women stood at the front door saying goodbye. One of them spoke, 'These young Dutchmen are nice.' Then they went back inside the comfortable sitting room, discussing what to do the next time another couple of pilots turned up. It was their small but highly appreciated contribution towards peace.

Once they were back at the base, Jan said to Govert, 'Thanks for taking me along. I enjoyed a very pleasant afternoon.'

Govert grinned at him. 'So I noticed. You were practically teaching that fascinated old lady how to fly.'

Jan nodded. 'True,' he admitted. 'But I really did like the warm atmosphere in that house. It reminded me so much of my own home in The Hague.'

After Govert Steen had been transferred, Jan was alone once more. Little did he know he would never see Govert alive again.

On certain days, his thoughts would suddenly race off to past events – back to the tensions he'd experienced during the cycling trip from The Hague to Paris, furiously pedalling his bike while his morale was sky-high. Following his escape from Holland he had eagerly anticipated somehow seeking final revenge on the Germans occupying his country and keeping his father locked up in prison.

But now, in England, he had to overcome dark periods of gloom alternating with feelings of disillusionment at the way things in general proceeded. He felt so very insignificant while caught up in the midst of an aimless life, a little flying now and then when weather permitted, and those interminable evenings standing at the bar with pointless, inane verbal exchanges in the company of strangers, or almost strangers.

He didn't know how to keep carrying on; everything around went so slowly, as if he were a small fly with one of its six legs stuck in a sweet, sticky substance, blocking its free movements.

There were moments when he felt he watched a movie with frustratingly slow motion, delayed action on the screen.

During the English months, he found it difficult to really discuss his deepest feelings, his worries and ideas about the future with anyone – introverted as he was. He would have given anything in the world to be able to talk to someone he could completely trust about the emotional strain he was being put under at times.

He now lived among strangers and was based in a foreign country. Even though he greatly admired the brave Britons, who were carrying the full burden of the war all by themselves, he felt lonely, so lonely, time and time again – especially after Govert had departed.

Before his escape from his homeland, he could approach his mother and completely confide his personal troubles to her if a serious problem cropped up. Sometimes, he could even disturb his busy father. But in England, the impatient young pilot still hadn't met anyone he could trust with his anxieties.

In the evenings, standing at the bar drinking a cool beer, he chatted with other pilots about superficial matters in general and, of course, the different techniques used in flying one particular aircraft or another. They never brought up one really serious, deep, original thought. It remained in orbit, perhaps even in another dimension, it was never mentioned.

When he suffered these bouts of gloomy depression, shapeless, inconsistent, disconnected and sinister thoughts flashed through his active mind. All his brain could produce were inconsequential vapid ideas instead of really fresh, good, positive, outstanding ones. It irritated him: he felt the surroundings were terribly superficial, lacking any real moral values.

Jan compared himself to a young thoroughbred with a weight handicap, moving too slowly in relation to its true potential. And those dreary, endless English winter days certainly didn't relieve his glum moods.

At times, he felt enveloped in beleaguered emptiness, being propelled forward in ever so slow, lazy progress along a sluggishly flowing river. The magnificent, dynamic momentum that had made him feel like a giant when cycling from Holland to the south of France had faded away. Or so he thought, right then.

Reliving past events, mentally exploring his whole Dutch past, he resented how empty and ineffectual his present frame of mind had become; as if the neurons in his brain operated small tentacles, hanging on to, enveloping what had been. He couldn't tear himself away from those old emotions and kept continuously flashing back to everything that had happened to him in Holland before his departure to England.

He had escaped from Holland to secure a *new* future, that he was ready to give his life for. But this inactivity, this terrible slow ticking away of time as if the two hands on the face of a clock never covered each other, as if they were purposely moving against him, was all so contrary to his very nature – and to what his highly active, energetic father had always taught him to be like.

Now and then, these gloomy moods were interrupted by a little party at the bar; but he regarded these simple occasions as mere superficial interruptions in the maelstrom he happened to be a prisoner of. After the temporary, alcohol-induced stimulation had worn off and artificial excitement dissipated the following morning, he found himself sometimes sinking into an even more cheerless mood. When that happened, it seemed as if he'd plunged into a very deep, dark, exitless tunnel, tumbling down head over heels into an endless black hole.

During the difficult winter weeks, he even tried writing to his mother. The letter was to be given her in case anything happened to him. Though he began it several times, giving it a lot of thought, he never finished what he began. Those wordless white pages kept staring back at him. What he needed to say could not be expressed or written. What he kept hidden deep in the recesses of his mind would never be set down on paper. What could have perhaps been of great human value to others who would read those pages later, remained locked up inside never to reach the pages of his diary. The only result from all those desperate, sad moments – even with all of his considerable efforts – was the awareness that nothing he regretted about past faults or shortcomings could be changed or put right any more.

What had been formed part of the past, and that was that – gone forever! Much as he would have liked to try, he couldn't possibly change or modify what he'd done wrong, make things different, or repair what damage had been dealt. At that point, his parents lived on the other side of the Channel under German occupation while he sat at a wood table along with his melancholy thoughts in a British Nissen hut.

When the weather turned bad, his spirits descended like a deflating balloon miserably falling to the ground. It seemed as if all his efforts, all his enthusiasm had been wasted. It was really disheartening to stare out of a barracks window at the impenetrable grey English fog so frequent during those winter days, grounding him.

Jan was an impatient, young fighter pilot with no time to lose or waste. He wanted to fight the enemy, the Luftwaffe.

The only positive news he heard during 1941, and considered excellent, came over the BBC when it announced, on 22 June 1941, that Hitler had ordered his mechanised army and mighty Luftwaffe to invade Soviet Russia. Now the Allied Forces had a real, favourable chance of invading Europe. The Germans would be needing most of their armoured divisions to cross the flat Ukraine, thus weakening their army and Luftwaffe strength in western Europe considerably. The enormous US production potential and latent armed power had not been tapped at all yet. America still had not joined the conflict although aware Europe was bleeding to death. The British production efforts for their troops were at maximum capacity but even topmost levels barely managed to supply their armed forces. Not only that, their military output was also often inferior in quality to what the German armed forces were already using, or to what was being developed for them – with the exception of the Spitfire.

All these factors, totally beyond Jan's control, contributed greatly to making him feel depressed. Time was a determining factor in his low moods. He felt as if water was steadily flowing through his clenched fists. Hard as he might try to stop it, helplessly squeezed fingers could not keep the water from escaping elsewhere.

When he went to London on leave, he visited the Dutch Club, meeting friends. These short trips made him feel a little bit better. However, there were times he couldn't help feeling homesick: someone singing a familiar Dutch song tore him up inside causing stomach flutters. Or hearing Duke Ellington's jazz music touched a raw emotional chord. At home, in The Hague, he had collected everything the Duke had ever recorded. He still felt profound emotional involvement with Holland. He still couldn't tear himself away from those nostalgic thoughts and reveries. Very often, when alone, he felt terribly lonesome. His solitude was a heavy burden to carry.

Once leave was over, he returned to Ternhill Base, where he was informed he would have to follow a night flying course. All in all, it meant positive practice, even though the new kind of flying routine could be dangerous. Once airborne, flying on instruments only was quite a new experience and sensation.

In the black of night, he totally depended on those small, silent instrument needles informing him about the flight condition of his plane, when speeding through the impenetrable darkness surrounding him with a blacked-out England below him.

The tiny needles represented the only safe way to fly back to his base. In the cockpit, despite the ever present, trusted, regular purr of the Rolls Royce engine, Jan experienced the awesome silence and loneliness of puzzling his way out of a flying enigma back to Ternhill.

On one of those night flights, a colleague made a fatal evaluation error when coming in for a landing and crashed on the runway. He died in the ambulance speeding him to the hospital. Jan attended the funeral. It meant a rather sad, emotional affair, opening his melancholy wounds again.

Aware of what had caused the accident, Jan decided on the spot that he would start retiring early and skipping the bar with its empty, meaningless atmosphere. He wanted to stop drinking and replace it with early morning workouts: he needed a clear mind for his night flying exercises.

During the Ternhill period, he passed several tests and on 4 November was finally admitted to fly Hurricanes. It was a good improvement and quite a change for him. He felt much happier and somewhat better about taking the right steps to become a real fighter pilot at last.

The Spitfire of course was still Jan's dream. So much had been said and written about the plane's excellent flying characteristics, he wondered just how he'd eventually manage. For the time being, however, he was stacking up hours on the Hurricane. It was a good workhorse – but the Spitfire was a real thoroughbred, a plane a man could fall in love with.

When Jan took off for a London leave, he met all kind of people in trains or buses. He sometimes got involved in conversations and found out how others were reacting to the war. With some he made immediate contact, attentively listening to their war stories. Elderly people told him how they'd fought the Germans during the Great War and how their sons and daughters were doing their share to defend the island.

Finally, on 17 December 1941, Jan received the news that he had to transfer to Llanbedr, a military base in North Wales, where he was going to be trained to fly the famous Spitfire. When he arrived at the new airfield, his initial duty was limited to becoming acquainted with its surroundings by making a number of flights in a Tiger Moth.

The weather at Llanbedr was not exactly cooperative either. Fog and low hanging overcasts seemed to be normal here, too. The following day – 18 December – Jan turned twenty-one. Standing alone at the bar, he drank a glass of beer to his own health.

During the next few days, he received instructions on how to operate the plane. Finally, on 23 December, the great day and adventure arrived: he was allowed to fly the Spitfire solo!

That morning, he eagerly stepped on the wing of the camouflage-green-painted plane and entered the narrow, chilly cockpit. The typical smell of a fighter plane – high octane aviation gasoline, glue and leather all mixed together – excited him. He relished it like a panther in the jungle picking up the prey's scent.

Once seated, he carefully took the joystick in his gloved right hand, testing the light movement, the easy and smooth balance of the ailerons and responsive elevators while his feet were busy feeling the rudder's free play.

The parachute he wore fitted perfectly into the metal bucket seat. He accurately fastened the safety belts over his shoulders and lap. Now, at last, he felt ready for the big occasion and a sigh of contentment escaped his throat. Slowly, he moved the Plexiglas hood forward, leaving it half open. He felt a thrill being fully prepared to leave the ground, fully entrusting himself to the elements.

When Jan switched it on, the Rolls Royce engine caught right away. He listened to it attentively, appreciating the beautiful smooth purr of its twelve cylinders.

Once it had reached the right temperature, he inserted the oxygen mask and microphone plug. Then, after the ground crew gave him the all clear signal, he carefully taxied to the end of the runway, swinging the plane's tail left and right for better visibility.

After he had received permission to take off, he went through a final cockpit check. When certain the instrument needles stood in their correct positions, he turned the plane into the wind and pushed the throttle forward, feeling the craft come alive.

The tail lifted off after he had reached the right speed and gained clear visibility of what lay ahead of him. Lightly, he pulled the joystick towards him and the Spitfire nimbly jumped off the runway into the air. To Jan, it seemed like a panther in mid-flight as it leaped towards an unsuspecting animal.

He was airborne! At long last, he commanded his own Spit! He smiled with satisfaction: the feeling he experienced right now was so exhilarating. He pulled the wheels up, closed the hood completely and concentrated on flying and commanding the marvellous plane.

Manoeuvring the controls, he felt a deep surge of elation and complete satisfaction sweep through him. It was a delayed success but well worth all the troubles he had gone through to reach the final result. The risks he had taken together with Geert, travelling all the way from Holland to England – the time lost, suffered so dramatically for the past few months, while training for the big event – he accepted all of it at this very instant of pure happiness, piloting the wonderful plane. He possessed a natural sense of how to fly the fast plane.

He realised everything that had happened to him had been completely beyond his control: the delays, the gloomy moods he had had to struggle against in his morale, his mental attitude. Almost a year had passed since he had left his parents and his comfortable home in The Hague, but at long last he had done it! He now commanded the famous Spitfire, and he thoroughly enjoyed every second of it. This plane – and the reliable Hurricane – had given the Allied pilots a chance to save England during the Battle of Britain in 1940.

So few had fought so bravely and gallantly to earn the admiration of an entire world by beating the mighty Luftwaffe against heavy odds, at great human sacrifice.

He felt good at the controls of the Spit. Concentrating on its smooth handling characteristics, he went into a series of rolls. Then he pulled the plane up sharply and banked it steeply: it responded beautifully. He observed the instruments in front of him, checking if all the needles stood in their correct places.

He felt euphoric, in seventh heaven. It was the same kind of sensation he had experienced kissing his girlfriend for the first time and walking home reminiscing over the emotional moment.

He was extra careful coming in for his first Spitfire landing. With the hood half open, he set it down lightly: a well balanced, very smooth, elegant, nicely handled touchdown. He then slowly taxied to the parking area, switching the engine off, shifting the Plexiglas hood completely back, and deeply and contentedly inhaling the cool Welsh air.

It felt magnificent – superb! He could have sung for joy!

Leaving the cockpit and still standing on the root of the wing, he knocked his clenched fist against the Plexiglas windscreen, saying with a satisfied grin, 'Thank you, Spitfire! I hope we'll become good friends.' Then he lithely jumped to the ground, totally satisfied. He'd done it! His goal had been achieved! A feeling of total well-being swept through him. He'd never felt that good before during his stay in England. The second half of 1941 had finally come to a happy ending!

It had been such a fortunate year at first when travelling south on his bike, but the last six months had been rather difficult and also emotional for him. Yet he had done it: he had overcome all his personal troubles and achieved a positive result.

At that very instant, Jan had become a Spitfire pilot!

He would have liked so much to be able to face his father now and proudly tell him about it personally. Taking pride in saying, 'I did it! I made it! I achieved what I set out to realise. I've succeeded with the plans we discussed in your study.'

But, unfortunately, his father was imprisoned, all alone, in solitary confinement, in cell 545 of Scheveningen prison, close to his own comfortable home. Often he sat brooding in silence and thinking about his son Jan – the boy he loved so intensely.

After the emotional flight, Jan returned to his quarters in an excellent mood, and found a letter from his father on his bed:

22 November 1941

Dear Jan,

I'm writing this letter because 1941 is ending and there are some things I want to say to you. The past year has been a very dramatic one for humanity ... perhaps even the bloodiest in the history of the human race.

Because men have forgotten how to evolve and consult one another, we have seen the terrible slaughter of human beings. Millions have lost their lives and many millions more have been thrown out of their houses and properties, forced to live in fear under terrible stress and abject misery.

I sincerely hope 1942 will bring us a good, solid peace. I deeply pray wisdom, tolerance and love for one's fellow man may reign once more and the enormous threat of total destruction of humanity dissipate never to return again. I hope 1942 will bring tranquillity, order and peace.

I also fervently hope you may find happiness during the coming year and safely return to us and your parental home.

I'm certain you'll meet many people and also take time to have some fun. Be careful when skiing. [Jan's father couldn't possibly use the word 'flying' because of German censorship.] Don't try any exercises you haven't seriously practised beforehand. You'll find speed increases can come so suddenly, and to such a degree, it's impossible to control them any more.

An accident can take place unexpectedly and I do look forward to seeing you again soon, alive and healthy, in your own home.

It would be so nice if we could be reunited again to live in peace, to thank the Lord for his protection. My health is fine but I spend so much time fretting about the developing drama of the world. People could live so well if they just spent a little more time trying to understand one another better. With modern production methods now available, the rich earth could produce enough for all of us. We only fight over how to divide it amongst us while there is enough for everyone.

I hope you'll have a pleasant Christmas and I wish you a glorious end of the year and a prosperous 1942.

May the Lord protect you, my son. Chasten your character and soul so that you may become a good and useful human being and live in a world which should never again be forced to experience the terrible drama we are now part of.

In the small space I'm forced to live in, I so often pray the Lord to help us follow his gospel of love and reciprocal understanding for all. Pray we may all live in God's magnificence and glory.

My dear Jan, may God's mercy also be on you. Don't ever reproach yourself for what happened to me because I'm proud and very grateful you are my son. My love is completely dedicated to you and for you. Be brave, honest and cheerful. Learn and train yourself well. Say hello to my old friends and accept my best wishes and thoughts of love. A strong embrace,

Your father

After he had read the letter, Jan realised it was written under emotional stress in the prison cell. The references to God were typical of a man whose freedom had been forcefully taken away. Yet he felt grateful his father had written to him.

Without Jan really being aware of it, a very dangerous, adventurous and emotional period full of mental ups and downs in his morale had come to an end. And now he was a Spitfire pilot, fully trained by the RAF and ready to finally meet the Luftwaffe!

VIII

THE YEAR 1941 turned out to be a rather uneventful one for Diana Boulton.

She regularly performed her duties in the operations room, spending most of her leaves with her mother in London. Sometimes she would attend a dance or go to a movie.

Now and then, she would awake with a start in the middle of the night, plagued by bad dreams, peering into the blackness surrounding her while images of George whirled in her brain. Alone in the dark, she would softly whimper, 'George, why did you have to leave me?'

Moisture would gather in the corners of her eyes as she stared at the ceiling of her small bedroom. A tear would roll onto the pillow beneath her head, then she would slowly drift off to sleep again, as if nothing had happened. The next morning, she couldn't even recall the incident. Gradually, these fleeting, disturbing sleep interruptions faded away as the images of her first love were forced back deep into her subconscious – encapsulated, to be locked away forever.

Little by little, Diana's subconscious began chiselling away at the images of what would never be again. It was, somehow, a natural process, just like wiping chalk off a blackboard so new words could replace the old on the cleansed surface.

Though she wasn't yet aware of it, Diana ever so slowly emerged from a state of deep depression which had cut her off from the rest of the world. She'd been shut inside a plastic time bubble separating her from reality for far too long.

Whenever Diana visited her mother, Mary Boulton noticed with pleasure her daughter's imperceptible improvements.

Diana's face was no longer waxen like marble, some colour had reappeared on her cheeks, her eyes no longer had that dull, defeated expression; a little sparkle had returned. Diana even managed to break out of her self-imposed cocoon to tell a funny story about some incident at the airfield where she was based. Her mother, well aware it did Diana good, let her talk as much as she wanted to.

Perhaps the year 1942 marked the return of Diana to life again. Her mother felt she deserved it: she was such a nice, charming young woman who had been so deeply hurt when George failed to make it back from his last flight. It had all been so sudden, so completely unexpected. One day her daughter had been in love, the next she looked like a living zombie. Now, at last, there was a ray of hope, indicating that Diana was becoming alive again, active again – at least so it seemed to her mother.

During one leave, Diana told her mother, 'You know, we were hard at work in the operations room the other day when the loudspeaker announced one of those big Flying Fortresses was in serious trouble returning from a bombing raid on Germany. The American pilot informed the control tower he was going to attempt an emergency belly landing at our airfield. Even though it was against all the rules, we all ran out of the ops building to watch the badly wounded bird approach the field. Two engines were out, the propellers feathered and we wondered how the pilot kept that big heavy plane aloft. A lot of smoke poured out of one of the two remaining functioning engines. The pilot advised control he couldn't lower the landing gear due to hydraulic problems. We all tensely observed the outcome, praying for the poor fellows on board the stricken plane. At last, the big plane set down on the wet grass, touching it with its tail first then bouncing wildly and sliding roughly forward at a terrific speed. It only slowed down as it hurtled towards the field's boundary. It was quite a sight, I'd never seen anything like it.'

Mrs Boulton listened to her daughter's story with growing interest. 'Then what happened?' she asked.

'Suddenly, the big monster made an unexpected turn dead centre in the field, coming straight at us. You should have seen us scattering in all directions, like a bunch of scared chickens in a poultry yard. We were screaming like mad, trying to avoid being run down by the blasted thing. It finally came to a complete stop just fifty yards from our ops building.'

'Well, you must have been scared out of your wits!' her mother exclaimed.

'And how! Then the fire engines came tearing over. There were men all over the place in asbestos suits chopping the fuselage with axes to get the crew out. One young sergeant, a rear gunner, was badly wounded, His uniform was soaked quite red with blood. He looked terrible, such a poor white-faced kid, and moaning in pain. The ambulance drove him straight to the hospital. We later found out he was going to live.'

Her mother interrupted Diana, asking, 'What about the others?'

'Oh, they were all right. We do criticise these Americans so much! It's just not fair, mother, to go around saying "They're over here, overpaid and over-sexed!" You should have seen the poor chaps once they were safely out of the wreckage. They trembled and shook like a bunch of frightened boys just out of high school. Fortunately, they recovered a bit when we handed out shots of whisky. One of them wanted to hug me, but I managed to hold him off with a kind word of encouragement. Then a truck drove up and took them off to their airfield. Yes, mother … we all do our share in the damn war, don't we?'

Encouragingly, Mrs Boulton smiled at her daughter. 'We all do, don't we, darling … You mentioned some whisky. What about one? Just the two of us?' she asked kindly.

'That's fine with me. Why not?'

Once Mrs Boulton had prepared the drinks, they sat together and she asked, 'How are things going in general?'

'Not too badly, as a matter of fact,' Diana replied. 'You know, we have a loudspeaker in the ops room. When the squadrons are over France on their sweeps, or escorting bombers and engaging the Luftwaffe, we can overhear most of what they're saying over the radio. Sometimes the expressions are quite funny with a lot of foul language included. On other occasions, it's awful listening to a pilot screaming as he's going down … or even more horrid when a bomber or a fighter plane is on fire and the pilot and crew are still locked inside. That's when we feel so utterly helpless. But, then again, the varied accents you hear are truly amusing. They go from Irish to Scottish, from Australian to Canadian, from foreigners like Frenchmen to Americans lately … and there are also a few Dutch and Belgian pilots.'

'It must be interesting. You seem to be telling me the whole world is up in the air fighting the Huns, even though they still appear to be rather strong.'

Diana nodded. 'Make no mistake about it – the losses I see chalked up every single day speak for themselves. They are considerable. We still have a lot of missing or dead pilots, poor chaps, and planes. The Luftwaffe is far from being beaten yet.'

'When do you have to go back?'

'The day after tomorrow.'

'Good! Let's make the most of your leave then.'

Diana laughed good-naturedly. 'All right, mother, what do you suggest?'

'Let's dine out. I'm in a good mood and I see the whisky put a touch of colour on your cheeks.'

'Right! Let's have some fun. We've only one life to live even if we experience so much in that limited space of time. But, even though one believes in Creation and all the rest, it's so hard to come to terms with death and all the destruction taking place around us. We live in a strange world, mother!' Diana emphasised.

'We do,' Mrs Boulton commented. 'We do indeed!'

IX

WHEN 1941 came to an end, Jan let his mind wander from past to present events, letting them intermingle, removing them from their fixed dimension. He longed so much to embrace his mother for just a moment, to verbally express the deep devotion he felt for her. He wanted so much to say, 'Mother – may I wish you a merry Christmas and all the best for a happy New Year. Thank you for everything you've done for me. Even though I can never find the right words to express it, I'm really grateful.'

In a reflective mood, gazing out of a barracks window at the grey mist hanging over the field, he realised he wouldn't be able to personally speak those words – and the letter he had tried so hard to write remained incomplete, unfinished.

On 21 December, Jan wrote in his diary:

> I still haven't finished my letter to mother. I'm ashamed of myself, but it's terribly difficult for me to express my thoughts clearly. It's also tremendously hard on us because we're not allowed to correspond with our parents – yet we're the ones who run all the risks of never seeing them again. I've forced myself to sit down and write her the letter to be given after the war if I should die. But it's so difficult to write a letter like that. I get into such miserable, gloomy states of mind when I

think of all my shortcomings and all the errors I've committed in my life. It's too late now to do anything about them any more, unfortunately. I do feel rotten having to admit it but all my efforts seem to have reached this dismal, final result.

Jan still suffered greatly from not being able to communicate with his mother and family in Holland.

Vividly, he recalled 30 December 1940 in the garden, when he and Geert were departing, and how she had swiftly slipped a hundred guilder note into his hand as if that was her way of protecting him. He had been impressed not by the small sum but by the kind gesture. Deeply touched!

He also remembered how she had nervously stood in the cold of the morning of his departure, grey-blue eyes expressing the deep, intense love she felt for him. Both of them knew the invisible emotional ties binding them together would be severed inexorably, perhaps forever, the moment he went around the corner at the end of the street – just as they had been when he was born, leaving the safety and protection of his mother's womb to enter the world. Beyond that corner, the separation had become final. He would be alone to face the unknown that lay ahead.

Now he saw in his mind the events taking place again, but in slow motion – his mother waving the warm shawl – himself finally reaching the corner and going around it – doing what had to be done to go forward to a new existence.

The separation had become permanent!

Something else he desired was to be able to face his father, to apologise for all the fights they had had. He sincerely regretted his errors and the many difficulties he had created back in the family circle. He had been so stubborn and obstinate during the years prior to his escape to England. Nor had he been easy on himself and those close to him.

He was all alone, away from his comfortable home in The Hague, during Christmas 1941 – an otherwise rather joyous time. But the Christmas spirit did not cheer him. The whole world engaged in war, his father a hostage of the Gestapo, imprisoned in a small cell – while he felt so cut off in England.

Soldiers, sailors, pilots and, unfortunately, civilians were being killed by the thousands every day in Soviet Russia and North Africa. And the worst was still to come, now that the Japanese, with their treacherous attack on Pearl Harbor on 7 December 1941, had also entered the raging worldwide conflict. They had not only set the Pacific ablaze, but had also caused the United States to enter the war.

As he pondered all this, Jan felt as if life looked like a thin sheet of ice covering a deep, dark lake with a lonely man skating on it. Was the ice going to sustain him or would it crack beneath his weight, plunging him into the cold, black, threatening silence lurking below? Would the elegant, slicing, dancing movements of the man give him the necessary strength to carry him to safety over the threatening, ice-cold water if he continuously shifted his weight from one skate to the other? It was a perilous dance – with Death, perhaps? Did these strange images carry the meaning of his own future?

Life seemed at its lowest ebb to Jan on this gloomy 1941 Christmas Day. His very first Noel among strangers he hardly knew, far away from his beloved family. Yet a sparkle of hope was perhaps present in his subconscious mind.

He found good food and drinks in the mess but still could not shake off the sentimental, emotional ties binding him to Holland, to The Hague, the city where he had spent his most pleasant years, to dear friends, father, mother, family – and all, despite a whole year passed in England. The British had their own habits, ideas, the famous stiff upper lip. He tried hard to adapt to this new way of life but it was terribly hard on him. After all, he was only twenty-one years old. Dejectedly, he stared at the nicely decorated Christmas tree with its colourful glass balls and silver garlands. It had been lovingly adorned but to Jan it was merely a symbol of melancholia at the end of 1941 rather than a sparkling hope for his own future.

Jan strongly believed life itself could not be all. An indefinable 'something' existed somewhere – something to look forward to, hope for and believe in. But he did not know yet what it really meant, nor its form or dimension.

He could neither see into nor penetrate that unknown expanse. The thoughts of the past flashing through his restless, active mind were only geared to his own reality and his emotional ties with Holland. As a pilot, he was accustomed to thinking and acting in three dimensions. His studies at Delft Technical High School, however, had taught him there happened to be four, or even more when the time factor entered the equation.

During the Christmas period, Jan meditated on how the wars on Earth had turned humanity away from Christian teachings – especially those regarding love. On 25 December, sitting alone at his writing table, he put these words down in his diary:

Christmas 1941

Today just doesn't seem like Christmas. To me, it only means the day we remember the birth of child Jesus … even if the whole world is at war. There should be a message of hope but there isn't. The things I now write down in my diary are not logical or reasonably thought out, yet they well up inside me as I proceed.

I sincerely believe life on earth is not everything, but I cannot clearly imagine what the hereafter is like. I'm certain it exists … this cannot be all there is to life … But how far we've all strayed from the Christian teachings of love!

I did not pass this Christmas in reflection … I simply couldn't do it. If father ever reads these words, they'll hurt him. I know that and I'm sorry about it. I apologise. But if I really began meditating on how miserable, how rotten everything is, I would certainly do damage to my brain for I don't really believe in God yet.

Once again, father, I apologise for disappointing you like this, but I find no other way to express what I feel right now. Please don't think I've forgotten everyone in The Hague when I experience these dark moments. Every single day, I think back to how things were when we were a united family and did all those things together ... and I also think back to my obstinacy and how it ruined complete harmony between us. Doing the opposite of what you wanted gave me a kind of inner, burning energy. But I now realise how that energy was misplaced outside our world and eventually brought me to a dead end. That energy, clashing with everyone, got pushed back inside without taking another direction. I know, feel and think it has just gradually faded away by itself. That's exactly what I experience now, sitting here at my writing table, setting my thoughts down in my diary. It explains a great deal, especially about what I feel were my failures, my lost battles over the years. I did a lot of reading before, in my room at home. But I haven't touched a book ever since those long months in the Soler house in Perpignan. I never used to care at all if I started arguing with someone. The past year has wiped away that obstinate streak of mine, sometimes making me regret the change. It could possibly mean a deep change in the dark recesses of me ... the wildness I've known is possibly turning into something better now – into a real desire to work and study ... both things I never really did back at home in The Hague.

When humans fight a war, both sides have crowds of believers, praying in their respective churches for God's help to win the conflict. Jan had instead come to the conclusion that people degraded God to their own level that way, behaving like frightened ants scurrying in all directions, not knowing where to go, without a destination. God's love, he assumed, was above all conflicts. It was given without prejudice but one had to believe in Him to start deserving that love, to start giving it back. These were the meditations Jan confided to his diary on that 1941 Christmas Day.

He was only twenty-one and these thoughts whirling around in his mind, floating free as he let them do, certainly didn't make life easier for him – especially during his frequent walks alone around the airfield in the evenings when he wasn't flying.

He hadn't found God yet, hadn't been able to reach Him, even though he'd been closer than most when airborne in his Spitfire. Perhaps his journey towards God began that very Christmas 1941, during those trying days when the only reflection he could concentrate on was how miserable a state the world happened to be in. There was so little of the love he felt was so vital and necessary.

Jan was keenly aware he had disappointed his father on several occasions: he had rested such hopes and expectations on his capable, intelligent, second-born. That energy – that negative energy he had written about in the diary. But now, at the end of his first year in England, Jan realised that damaging blaze was being reduced to a small, impotent flame. It had seemingly faded away slowly, day by day, making way for other and better aimed energies. He also felt a new awareness of being alive, a new determination to live and love in a broader sense than before.

He had been through such highs and lows, through such intense emotional bouts, during 1941. But now the year was ending, and he was a fighter pilot in one of the famous Spitfires. That was something tangible he could grasp onto. He had obtained a 'result' at last! Yet he had still to meet the Luftwaffe.

On 31 December, he received a letter from his father. The elder Plesman was still imprisoned and therefore wrote in a rather stilted style:

Dear Jan,

December is a month for family festivities. But in our case, separated as we are, it only makes one feel further apart. We also think back to happier days. and times when the family played an important role and people were far kinder to one another.

Millions of people have now been torn apart. This Christmas and New Year will be a sad and lonely one for many, perhaps also for you. Therefore, my wish to you for a happy 1942 is more serious and heartfelt than ever. I hope the year will mark the return of the kind of peace inspiring mankind to take up the banners of love and reason again.

God takes us by the hand, and let us hope for a lasting peace with war banned forever.

I sincerely hope you feel the Christmas spirit and find yourself in friendly surroundings. May the Lord take you into his Almighty protection and bring you safely back to us. I've also gratefully learned you've found God as well and intend to abide by his rules, believing in them.

I am well and able to speak to your mother. Sometimes we talk about happier, more united times. I have been informed by relatives your studies are proceeding well, that you are healthy and full of pep.

It has already turned cold here. I fear this will turn out to be a sombre winter for all of us. Christmas, the feast of light, will unfortunately be passed in profound darkness. And so it will be in the hearts of the 'misguided' who will pray for an end to this horrible conflict and plead for the return of logic and love.

As a young man, you may be of a different opinion, even though I know how generous and sensitive your heart is. I hope you feel strong and that your studies may proceed with good luck, reflecting the kind of results you desire.

Your mother is outstanding under these difficult circumstances. She takes care of me and the children despite all the severe complications involved, never letting anything depress her. She's truly a Rock of Gibraltar for all of us. Even your father must now bow his head and bend to the winds. I eagerly look forward to the day I can resume work in commercial aviation once this mess is finished. You probably know how hard it is for me to be patient!

I wish you a Merry Christmas, a Happy New Year and a prosperous 1942, with the hope and desire we may all be reunited next year.

Your father

Jan felt deeply moved by his father's words. He realised what desperate, inhuman, tough prison conditions his father had to put up with while writing. His father, at 52, had already spent over eight months in solitary confinement.

It was not very easy for Jan to imagine his energetic father all alone, locked up in a small cell, sitting on a hard wooden chair with a piece of paper in front of him on a prison table, trying to write him a letter and keeping German censorship in constant mind. When his father used the word 'study', or 'your studies', he meant Jan's flying since he could not possibly express his real opinions.

Still, he appreciated the way his father had tried to convey his wishes for Christmas and the New Year. Jan too looked forward to a better year which might allow him to accomplish something important, to finally engage the enemy, the Luftwaffe.

Jan's father – a man of great energy, vision and decision – had dedicated his whole life to commercial aviation. KLM Royal Dutch Airlines had, under his aggressive, creative and active management, grown to become a famous international airline prior to 1940. Plesman Senior was one of Holland's most distinguished citizens and had inspired his sons to also go into aviation. Wherever he had accompanied his father around Holland, Jan had heard people whispering 'There goes Plesman!' Sometimes it pleased Jan: feeling proud to be the son of such a well-known man. But there were times when that notoriety irritated him profoundly.

Could that have been the main motive behind his choice of becoming a pilot when he joined the Dutch military in Holland? Was there a subconscious drive within him to try and emulate – or surpass – his famous father? Was that what principally drove him on, that had created those negative energies leading him at times to openly clash with his father? They were both strong-headed.

Or was the desire to become a fighter pilot just part of his nature, desires, personality? Perhaps he still had not found the answer to those questions.

Jan was not the athlete his powerfully built father had been. He played neither football, nor tennis, nor hockey. He had relentlessly and restlessly spent all his physical energies pedalling his racing bike on tours throughout Europe.

Jan possessed a real sense of honour; there was no malice whatsoever in him. Whenever he got involved in fist-fights back in The Hague during his schooldays, it had always concerned a question of principle and at times he went home with a bloody nose. Jan's education made him direct, honest and straightforward: cunning and astuteness were certainly not his trademarks. His stubbornness led him frequently into conflict with others.

But now over a whole year had passed since he'd escaped from Holland and Jan had left most of those headstrong, pig-headed characteristics behind, becoming a strong, tall, well-built, handsome young man and an excellent pilot.

One of Jan's greatest moments in 1941 had been when Parmentier, KLM's chief pilot, had gracefully touched the Douglas DC-3 down at Bristol Airport. At that precise moment, Jan had felt a great surge of joy and absolute satisfaction within him. It meant the final, positive result of a long, adventurous trip. He had accomplished what he had set out to do: to reach Britain and join the Allied Forces to help fight the Germans occupying his country.

On the last day of 1941 there were no flying activities. Jan kept himself busy writing letters to friends, including Geert. He would have given anything to spend the last hours of the year with his friend, to reminisce about the eventful trip they had made throughout France, and their final safe arrival in England.

After half a year of training and flying, Jan felt he was perfectly ready for operational action and combat. A positive result had finally been achieved: he piloted a Spitfire and was anxious to meet the Luftwaffe again – but this time under very different conditions. His plane was now at least equal to the fast, manoeuvrable Messerschmitt 109s. He did not have to engage his Teutonic counterparts in an antiquated Fokker biplane!

Weighing all the factors involved, Jan looked forward to 1942 with confidence and great optimism.

Perhaps by now the reader may have formed the impression that Jan Plesman was a frustrated complainer. That was definitely not the case! He possessed a strong character and very strong will-power; after leaving Holland, however, and his close family, he had had to overcome bouts of low morale, mainly caused by the slow progress of flight training by the Royal Air Force and the bad weather conditions so prevalent during the 1941 winter months in England. Jan had reason to be an impatient young pilot, wanting to fight the infernal Nazi war machine for all it had done to his country and especially to his father.

X

ABOUT THE various early stages of the war, Jan had developed his own personal opinion. He considered the 1940 battles in Europe had been badly lost by the Allies. A small but very significant victory had been won during the Battle of Britain, in which the RAF had thoroughly beaten the mighty Luftwaffe. The year 1941 had enabled the British military forces to consolidate their global positions even though they had suffered heavy losses and disastrous defeats in North Africa and in the Far East after the Japanese had initiated their attacks on the Philippines, Malay, Singapore and Indonesia.

Soviet Russia was now receiving and resisting the heavy blows of the armed, mechanised German might. Fortunately, the Russians courageously held their ground, resisting the vicious invasion of their homeland, sacrificing millions of human lives to halt the onslaught.

The Pacific war would represent a long struggle following the vile Japanese attack at Pearl Harbour. He thought 1942 could perhaps be the intermediate stage before final victory over the Germans and Japanese in 1943, as increased weapons production became available in and from the USA to balance the negative situation on the main battle fronts.

On 1 January 1942, Jan wrote in his diary:

I hope 1942 will be the last year before the big battle. 1940 was defensive, 1941 consolidation while 1942 will be dedicated to building up armoured strength, arms production and still more production. The year 1943 will bring victory and liberation and we'll all go home. We must accept this timetable. It will become increasingly tough for all of you in Holland. We stand here helpless and impotent and I unfortunately realise it more and more with every passing day.

Jan picked up the latest news about developments in Holland at the Dutch Club: things were getting worse and he was certain the Dutch population was going to suffer increasingly during the coming year.

The damp, cold English climate was not much of an ally either: Jan caught a severe cold which kept him grounded for over three weeks. On 6 January he wrote in his diary:

I still suffer from a heavy cold and my ear is blocked. Last year, at the same time, I also had a cold when I was hidden by the French Maquis at Montmorency, northwest of Paris.

After a few days at the local hospital, he was allowed to return to his base again. Once there, he spotted his name on the scoring board and found out, much to his dismay, he was next to the bottom in Spitfire flying hours in his group of pilots. Jan swore he would catch up, weather permitting.

At the end of March, he was ordered to Southend airfield, located on the Thames estuary. At long last, the time had come to participate in operational action, perhaps even air battles against the still mighty Luftwaffe.

On 28 March, Jan flew his first active sortie – an air patrol over a convoy slowly progressing through the English Channel. It consisted of six ships proceeding in Indian file. Circling above them, he clearly distinguished the freighters, but did not encounter any Luftwaffe intruders during his first operational flight.

On 31 March, the squadron was temporarily transferred to Hornchurch airfield for a few days: it had become a famous place during the Battle of Britain.

On 4 April, Jan made his first operational sweep over northern France. The pilots were called at 7 a.m. He washed and dressed carefully, walked over to the mess and ate breakfast: boiled eggs, toast, butter, marmalade and lots of strong coffee.

Later he stood alone, gazing silently out of the window, feeling meditative as he stared through the early morning haze hugging the ground, observing the aircraft parked off the green field. Now they stood immobile, but once in the air and engaged they would spit fire at the enemy.

Jan weighed the personal thoughts whirling actively in his mind, not knowing precisely what to expect that day and wondering out loud, 'Shall I be standing here again tonight?'

He judged himself perfectly capable of facing death with detachment, as if he stood above it, as if it would never physically brush him nor cross his flights over Europe.

Well, he thought to himself, this is my first operational action over Europe and though I feel ready and eager, I still wonder how many I'll make. In silence, he observed the other pilots getting ready, and joined them for the usual pre-flight briefing, wondering what was going on in their minds.

After the briefing, he walked slowly over to his plane, and climbed on to its wing and into the cockpit, settling down in the bucket seat and fastening the seat belts. Everything felt awfully cold to his touch – the joystick, the switches, the canopy – it sent shivers down his spine. A bad omen? Perhaps.

He started blowing on his cupped hands to warm them. With the canopy still open, he calmly waited for the signal to start engines. When it came he was ready, and the Rolls Royce engine caught at the second attempt, growling noisily as if it wanted to demonstrate it too was ready for action.

The squadron consisted of twelve Spitfires which took off in pairs. As the planes left the runway they went into a V-formation, flying close to each other. On his first operational flight over the Continent, Jan was kept rather busy following radio instructions from the flight commander and at the same time watching out from the cramped cockpit for the Luftwaffe. Every so often, he would glance at the instruments in front of him to check the oil temperature, and then monitor the other planes flying close to him. Altogether, it was an exciting and confusing experience, but he liked it!

He flew on the right outer section of the formation – the 'sitting duck' position, so called since the enemy when swooping down out of the sun was bound to attack him first!

On 4 April, he again went on a sweep over north-west France and upon his return wrote in his diary:

A sweep is quite a happening the first time. You don't get a very clear picture of what is really going on around you. I flew Blue 4, behind Conard. After we left France, on the way back to England, after having attacked several ground targets, Blue 2, with Divoy at the controls, was hit by another Spitfire in flight over the French coast. His tail was sheared off and the poor guy went down in a wild, uncontrollable spin. Fortunately, he managed to get out just in time and I observed his parachute open. By now, he's a prisoner of war. I felt terribly upset when I noticed his Spit spinning wildly down, out of control, knowing Divoy was still inside.

On 8 April, Jan flew again over western France and on this flight engaged a Focke Wulf 190 and a Messerschmitt 109-E. He fired at both of them but unfortunately without a result.

On 12 April, he made another sweep over north-western France, and then again on the 14th, 15th, 16th and 18th. On the 26th, he was airborne again over occupied France and again on the 29th. He finished the month of April with three sweeps on that last day. April 1942 had been busy, exhausting and also emotional. But he still had not downed a Luftwaffe plane yet.

Jan had been rather lucky while learning how to behave on those operational flights. In fact, he had accumulated more than 22 hours of operational flying during April, by flying fourteen operational flights over France. Many more flights followed, giving him more experience with every flight he made.

From Southend airfield, he flew to the most northern parts of Holland, flying along its coast, and once, on an exceptionally clear day, he was able to distinguish the house he had lived in on the outskirts of The Hague. He also made several sorties over Belgium, while the town of Lille in northern France was the farthest he penetrated into enemy air-space above occupied Europe.

Flying over this particular part of France and Belgium, Jan vividly recalled his school history lessons about the summer infantry offensive from July through to November 1916 at the Somme river and the one at Passchendaele in 1917. These attacks were commanded by General Douglas Haig. Senseless battles which caused enormous losses in human lives: 400,000 at the Somme, 240,000 at Passchendaele. The young British infantrymen had died, had been sacrificed, for practically nothing. A whole generation was wiped out by the heavy machine-gun fire that had been brought to bear on the human onslaught by the unfortunate British soldiers.

By now regularly in action, at last Jan was achieving what he had intended all along when leaving Holland. He felt fine being active. The bleak, negative thoughts which had plagued him during the second half of 1941 were gone, along with the depressions he had to fight against. To him, it seemed as if a strong wind had cleared the airfield of a thick fog that had been clinging to the ground.

After a few weeks of intense operational flying from Southend, the squadron got a new squadron-leader – Duncan Smith, popularly known as 'Smitty'.

Jan thought the world of him and they got along marvellously. Smitty possessed a pleasant personality, and was a good and enthusiastic leader. Jan learned a great deal from him during the flights over Europe that Smitty personally led and commanded.

During the time he flew in this squadron, Jan felt really happy. Smitty's inspiring, lively leadership also made him feel more confident during the many operational flights they carried out together.

Very often, once they had safely returned to base again, Smitty, gesturing vividly with both hands, would describe to the pilots the different phases of the mission they had concluded that day. Listening attentively, Jan learned the finer points of flying technique. The experience he gained from it considerably improved his chances of survival.

At that time, there were about forty Dutch fighter pilots flying in England, spread across various English squadrons, all under British command. The idea was launched of putting together a Dutch fighter squadron just like those of Polish, Czech, Canadian, French and other nationalities. The task would not be an easy one, but Dutch authorities in London accepted and even promoted the concept. New trainees would be needed to make up the numbers required for an eventual all-Dutch squadron – the RAF insisted on at least sixty active pilots as a minimum. Also, the Dutch Navy would have to loan out a number of their pilots to meet the necessary numbers. The plan was good but its organisation would be a problem.

During one of his leaves in London, Jan visited the Dutch Ministry of Defence to find out more detailed information about the launching of a Dutch fighter squadron. At the time, he felt it was a good idea, but he could not foresee what personal trouble and pain it would later cause him.

During one leave, Jan learned that his friend Govert Steen, flying with the British 129 Squadron, had been shot down on 5 June 1942, on a sweep over northern France. Jan was shocked and upset: he would never see his young companion and likable friend again. Yet again the Reaper had struck!

Back at the base – and completely out of the blue – there was more bitter news: experienced Dutch fighter pilots from the various English squadrons were to be transferred to Castletown – the northernmost airfield in Scotland.

After flying operationally for over a hundred days – fifty flights over Europe – Jan was forced, on 23 July, to leave the base with which he had become so familiar. All the Dutch pilots in England were removed from active duties for a rest period. They would eventually form the rank and file of a Dutch fighter squadron now they had gained operational experience.

With great reluctance, Jan had to gather up his personal belongings, leave Southend and proceed to Castletown, a tiny village located at the northern tip of Scotland. On arriving at his new destination, Jan thought it was the loneliest, most god-forsaken place he had ever visited in his whole life, a dismal contrast with the pleasant atmosphere he had enjoyed in Southend.

Jan truly regretted having to say goodbye to Smitty and the other pilots whom he had begun to like and appreciate, and the feelings had been mutual.

One day at the bleak Castletown airfield, Jan saw a Spitfire diving towards the field. As usual, he watched the pilot's manoeuvres with great interest. To his utter horror, however, Jan realised the pilot was pulling the plane out of a piqué much too late. Something was awfully wrong!

'Pull up, man!' he shouted at the top of his voice. In despair, he looked at the terrifying event unfolding before him – there was absolutely nothing he could do.

'Pull up!' he shouted again, horrified. Nothing happened. The plane continued to hurtle straight down – the pilot's final flight! The crash was terrible. The awful sound of metal being shattered into thousands of fragments as the plane hit the ground was bloodcurdling and macabre. Jan would not easily forget it. The young pilot was killed instantly.

Jan ran to the crater caused by the plane's impact. On being told the pilot's name, Jan realised he only slightly knew him. He was amazed by his indifference to death: studying the remaining ragged pieces of the beautiful, elegant Spitfire, he thought he was probably more sad about the loss of the plane than the man who had flown it. The thought thoroughly shocked and disturbed him.

Had a crash like the one he had just witnessed taken place before the war, at Soesterberg in Holland, the remaining pilots would have been profoundly shaken and shocked. But here in England – especially in Castletown, this lonely place – Jan was not emotionally touched by it. It was merely another occurrence; that was that, and life went on as usual.

That evening, while Jan was at the bar drinking a beer, another pilot spoke to him. 'Did you see the crash this afternoon?'

Jan nodded. 'I did. Too bad the sergeant didn't pull out in time.'

'Yeah,' the other pilot commented. 'Another beer?' he asked evenly.

Jan shook his head. 'No thanks, I'll just finish this one, that's all. I don't feel like more tonight after what happened this afternoon.'

'When does your next leave come up?' the other man asked indifferently.

'Next week, I think,' Jan replied unenthusiastically.

'Well, lucky you! I don't get mine until the end of September.'

From the way their conversation was going, Jan realised only too well the unfortunate sergeant had already been forgotten. Looking around at the others in the bar, he noticed everyone was having a drink and a laugh before turning in.

115

The dead man had been erased from the young pilots' minds. Maybe they all drank too much in order to ward off the ominous premonitions of their own fate present every day and on each flight they made.

Death was not sitting out one single dance. It was always there. The day's dramatic events had confirmed this for Jan once again.

On 14 September, he went to London on leave. By sheer chance, he ran into Smitty while walking in the centre of town.

Jan shook his hand enthusiastically. 'Smitty!' he exclaimed happily. 'How are you? I'm so happy to see you!' He stared with pleasure at his former commander: they had made so many flights over Europe together.

'Not too badly, as you can see for yourself. I'm still alive and kicking!' Smitty smiled warmly. 'But tell me, how are you and your Dutch countrymen getting along?' he asked, clearly interested.

'It's a rather dreary story and I'd rather not tell you about it, Smitty. We've been sent to a god-forsaken base in the north of Scotland – Castletown. I've never seen a more desolate airfield in all of Britain,' he commented unhappily.

Smitty noticed Jan's veiled eyes and the sadness of his expression. Good-naturedly, he laughed at the young Dutch pilot, tossing him a mysterious glance, and kindly inquired, 'Would you like to join me at the Shepherds?' The Shepherds was a small pub where RAF pilots regularly met when in London.

Jan hesitated for an instant after the unexpected invitation, then readily accepted. 'Thanks, Smitty, I'll join you with great pleasure.'

When they entered the pub, there was a burst of noise as Smitty was welcomed with a loud cheer by all present. It was quite a surprise to Jan to discover a great number of young airmen gathered together. He found he and Smitty were surrounded by the Battle of Britain's most famous group of pilots. They were celebrating the top score of a 1940 September day during which they had shot down 102 Luftwaffe planes.

Jan, of course, did not belong to this small and exclusive group of brave and lively men but, as Smitty's guest, was accepted just the same. He stood among Great Britain's 'finest', as Churchill had called them, and felt thoroughly impressed.

Jan deeply appreciated being in the presence of those great, courageous pilots, even if only for a moment. In such small numbers, and at incredible personal sacrifice, they had saved their island from the Luftwaffe onslaught.

He listened to their exciting stories with deep interest. Like all pilots, they gestured with their hands to describe their different flight manoeuvres. After part of the evening had passed pleasantly and intimately, having shared a few hours in the presence of these exceptional young men, Jan felt he could no longer impose. He went over to Smitty and said, 'Thanks for your kind invitation. I had a wonderful time.' Then he bade them all goodbye.

Once outside, Jan's head overflowed with dramatic thoughts and imaginary fantasies. Alone and forlorn, he walked through the dark, blacked-out streets of London. He proceeded dejectedly to the Aero Club, where he had booked a room for the night.

Perhaps the utter loneliness, the dreariness, of Castletown was a heavy burden; all Jan knew was that during his lonely walk he boiled with inner fury. Those famous, brave pilots could look back at something real and tangible. Their achievements, their victories had been scored. They had won a memorable victory over the Luftwaffe. Meanwhile, Jan felt like a tiny ant – still at the very beginning, without having shot down a single Luftwaffe plane, despite having fired at a few.

Now he was being kept at Castletown for a rest period. He felt like a race horse confined in a narrow starting-gate, eager to tear off but reined in by the jockey.

Every now and then Jan did a bit of flying – far too little as far as he was concerned. The whole blame could be put on that damned, ill-fated attempt to try and put together an all-Dutch fighter squadron. He deeply hated Castletown.

The day after seeing Smitty, Jan had to return to the north, to the Dutch squadron. In the meantime, he had discovered that his friend Geert Overgauw had been on a course, trying to master the fast twin-engined Mosquito – a tricky plane.

An ominous threat of bad luck seemed to hang over the airfield on 13 October. And it would indeed come true – one of the Dutch pilots was going to die that day. Someone had to fly a shipping recce over the North Sea – the man chosen for the mission would not return.

Flight operations had first asked Jan if he wanted to fly the recce that afternoon. Since the flight didn't provide him with many credit points in the flying hours system, Jan had declined. He felt terrible about the other man's fate. His conscience troubled him deeply when he heard the tragic news, but what the hell, he thought, this was the destiny of war – one moment you're alive, the next you've had it, your candle has been snuffed out and the Reaper has booked another one.

That same evening, while on standby, Jan passed his time reading *The Last Enemy* by Richard Hillary, a famous Battle of Britain pilot, who had suffered atrociously from burn wounds and whom Jan had met on that memorable evening at the Shepherds when Smitty had invited him there for a drink.

Jan enjoyed the book: it gave him something to think about – exactly what he needed that dreary evening.

Squadron Leader Johnny Johnson's impressions of Castletown, contained in his book, *Wing Leader* are in total contrast with the dismal description of time spent by the Dutch pilots at Castletown presented in Jan's diary:

We soon fell under the spell of its wild beauty and the warm hospitality of its inhabitants. Lord Tichfield had no official connection with 610 Squadron; he wrote to say we were welcome to hind-shooting on his nearby deer forest at Berriedale. We shot quite a few beasts and sometimes the whole squadron dined on venison at the Dunnet Hotel. We shot mallard and widgeon when they flighted to Loch Heilen, and flushed the grouse from great stretches of heather covered moorlands.

Jan never mentioned any of these activities in his diary – neither being invited by anyone with an estate or vast property in the Castletown area, nor dining on venison or mallard or grouse. But perhaps the local citizens thought those alien Dutch pilots still went around with a black cap on their heads, a long-stemmed white pipe in their right hand, wearing a striped vest, baggy trousers and heavy wooden clogs on their feet.

The extreme boredom at lonely Castletown cost Jan and his Dutch colleagues a great deal mentally. Each minute of the long hours, days, weeks and months spent at lonely Castletown faced them with the challenge of having absolutely nothing to do!

At last, on 15 October 1942, Jan was transferred south. Once again, the Dutch fighter pilots had to proceed to several operational British squadrons. The original plan of the exiled Dutch government in London to set up an all-Dutch fighter squadron had been temporarily and dismally abandoned.

It was Jan's opinion that the clumsy, ill-considered attempt had been a total failure because of bad planning by the Dutch authorities in London. How he despised those lazy, inefficient bureaucrats wasting his valuable time! He had lost three complete months!

He was sent to Ludham airfield, a satellite of the big Coltishall military base in Norfolk, on the east coast. While flying south, Jan's spirits soared: he was eagerly looking forward to more action against the Luftwaffe.

At this airfield, Jan flew Mk Vc Spitfires, models which had been provided with extra fuel tanks under the wings to allow more extensive sweeps over Europe. These Spits were armed with two 20 mm cannon and four .303 machine guns.

On 24 October, Jan's first operational flight from Ludham took him to the Dutch coast. During the flight, he clearly distinguished the white beaches and dunes of Holland below him in the bright, sharp, crisp autumn air. At last, Jan was in action again and felt fine, eager to even the score with the Luftwaffe.

He could finally look forward to shooting down his first enemy plane, to blasting it out of the sky. When he returned from that first sweep over Holland, he felt completely at ease, calm, in full control. He had taken it all in as a perfectly normal performance.

A few days later, the base commander informed Jan he was to report to the Dutch Embassy on 30 October. The Dutch Queen intended to decorate a number of Dutchmen with the Merit Cross.

In Jan's citation it stated that Jan had earned his decoration 'For the careful preparation of his escape from Holland to England. For the courageous and tactful way in which he prepared his getaway to join the Allied Forces.'

As Jan entered the Embassy, he noticed quite a number of his fellow countrymen. After a short speech, the Queen personally handed out the decorations.

The small, grey-haired lady possessed an aura of authority. She looked straight in the eyes of each man she decorated and had a firm handshake for everyone. She was Wilhelmina, Queen of the Netherlands.

When she stood in front of Jan, he had to bend forward to enable the Queen to put the ribbon over his neck and shoulders. Then he saluted smartly.

Jan was impressed by the atmosphere and happy to see his friend Geert, who received the same decoration.

Following the ceremony, the two young men went to the Hong Kong, a well-known Chinese restaurant. Once seated, they launched into a lively discussion: they had so much to talk about, so many opinions and experiences to discuss. In celebrating their meeting, they downed a lot of drink.

'Do you still remember how we didn't know what would happen when we left Holland?' Jan asked. 'We were in such a fighting mood, we risked everything we had – our very lives – to get here. I must admit I've achieved what I set out for – I have become a Spitfire pilot. But I haven't shot one Hun down yet. You know, Geert, sometimes it obsesses me, because I feel I could even the score for what the Germans have done to my father, my family, me and my country if only I could shoot one down.'

'Ja, Jan,' Geert agreed. 'I do understand your feelings. I can't say I have done anything of much importance either up to now. I haven't even seen the enemy yet. I've been training all the time, that's all,' Geert exclaimed bitterly.

A half-smile began to appear on Jan's face. 'You know, Geert, every now and then, I feel like a hairy, beautifully cocooned caterpillar, completely excluded from everything taking place around it, waking up and going to sleep with its own myriad glum thoughts, isolated from the whole world.'

Geert sighed loudly. 'Let's have another drink. What the hell – why not? Let's pretend we only escaped to England because our Scotch whisky supply ran out when the Germans invaded Holland!'

Jan observed Geert seriously. 'Aren't we bitter, the two of us? And right after receiving a decoration from the Queen! We were so optimistic, ready to show the world what we could do and we've done almost nothing. Still, Geert,' Jan said proudly, raising an index finger for emphasis, 'I do fly Spitfire. That's a tangible result at least. I'm also regularly over Europe these days. And notice how the anti-aircraft fire from the ground is increasing in intensity every day. I can tell by those awful, grey-black explosions and puffs of smoke in the air. It shakes you up, Geert, it really does!'

They became drunk with their steady boozing and created a great deal of noise. Finally, having criticised everything possible, they unsteadily left the restaurant.

Following his return to Ludham, Jan's military life began to settle down. Early morning reveille, and then waiting at readiness for the regular sweeps over Holland, Belgium, and northern France. He gained more experience with every sortie he made, becoming more and more confident during the many flights over enemy-held territory.

Jan assumed he would now be active again, able to contribute to the Allied war effort. His training experience was now to be applied to the real thing – fighting the Luftwaffe in man-to-man duels in the air, inflicting damage on the hated enemy.

Yes, 1942 had been a far better year, with the exception of the three dreary, wasted months at Castletown. If he could only find a real friend with whom to share his innermost thoughts, he might even start to feel at home in England, leaving behind those stale, distant, ineffective reminiscences of Holland, which had bothered him so much.

XI

'A REASONABLE average is perhaps the worst of all things,' Jan wrote in his diary. 'It's neither bad nor good but something right in between.' It symbolised a position he disliked thoroughly, and this was typical of Jan – he only aimed for the best result.

By now, he was accumulating regular flying hours during the many sweeps he flew low over western Europe. He had looked forward eagerly to this kind of military activity. Well prepared by the RAF, an excellent pilot, Jan was still uncontrollably restless to shoot down his first enemy plane, to see it go crashing down in flames, to get even with the hated German enemy.

During one low level sweep over north-western France, the flight commander spotted a number of Focke Wulf 190 fighters at 11 o'clock up ahead of the formation, proceeding at a lower altitude. He immediately ordered his planes to attack the enemy and swooped down.

The Fw 190 was a formidable, awe-inspiring new fighter, equipped with a 14-cylinder air-cooled radial engine with fuel injection, providing it with 1,600 hp and a maximum speed slightly over 400 mph at an altitude of 18,000 feet. It flew faster than the Mk V Spitfires equipped with a 1,400 hp engine which were then being used by the RAF. These Fw 190s had made their first appearance in the skies over France during August 1941. By the end of September the initial skirmishes were fought, and the RAF was badly mauled by the new German fighters. The unexpected introduction of the Fw 190 caused widespread consternation among the RAF pilots, just as the Fokker triplane had done during the Great War.

As the months passed and the casualties sharply increased, it became quite clear the new Luftwaffe fighter plane was one hell of a craft and not to be underestimated. It possessed a high climbing and diving speed, was extremely manoeuvrable, and its introduction took the RAF completely by surprise. Unfortunately the RAF lost a considerable number of both pilots and aircraft. The only real advantage that the Mk V Spitfire offered in aerial combat was its ability to make tighter turns than the Fw 190. Jan had been instructed to be well aware of the small advantage he had against such formidable opposition. At the beginning of 1942, the Luftwaffe introduced the Fw 190A-3, equipped with four 20 mm cannon, which made it even more feared and respected as an opponent.

Only after the RAF introduced the vastly superior Mk IX Spitfire – with a 1,600 hp engine and a four-bladed variable-pitch propeller instead of the three-bladed one of the Mk V – was there again a semblance of equality between the adversaries.

Jan, eagle-eyed, had also spotted the enemy aircraft below him, flying a steady course above the green and brown French countryside, among the white cumulus clouds slowly and majestically floating over the landscape. He could clearly distinguish the black, white-framed crosses on the Luftwaffe aircrafts' wings. His heart began to pump much faster, and adrenalin began to flow into his veins. Jan was tense, ready for action. At the same time, however, he had great respect for the Fw 190's first-class fighting qualities – never to be underestimated.

After the first skirmishes, the Luftwaffe formation dispersed, breaking their tightly-held flight pattern, and circling towards central France as if to invite a chase. From previous experience, Jan knew perfectly well these tactics were to set up a few planes as bait, with the intention of enticing the attacking Spitfires into an ambush by numerous Luftwaffe fighters waiting high in the sky in the French interior, ready to swoop down out of the sun on their unsuspecting victims.

He shouted a warning over the radio to advise the commander to change plans when he spotted him right on the tail of an escaping Fw 190. Jan curved up to one of the other Spitfires engaged in battle with a 190. As soon as he appeared on the scene, the German fighter circled away towards central France. Jan let him go: he was not about to follow him. Looking around, eyeing the sky for further action, all Jan could see was free, clear, deep-blue space and decided to return to base in England.

Jan was not expecting any further action on the flight back after breaking off from the intense engagements over France. In a happy mood, he sang a sentimental Dutch song in the Spit's cockpit, completely oblivious to any danger or impending threat to his life. A tiny black speck gradually grew bigger in the sky behind him: a Messerschmitt 109E was gaining on him. It came closer by the second, while Jan flew totally unaware of the silent killer stalking him. Death threatened him from behind, reaching out for him – seeking his life.

Suddenly, completely unexpectedly, a coloured hail of tracer bullets streaked out of nowhere over his wings and canopy as he flew over the middle of the Channel. It looked as if fierce, intense lightning was striking his plane. Bright flashes of light whooshed past the sides of his cockpit; the orange-red tracers were not only whipping over his wings but also enveloping his Spit. The plane buffeted roughly, and for a second, Jan sat frozen in his bucket seat with utter fear.

In that second, his heart pounded wildly in his chest, pumping at least eight times faster than normal, all at once, in that terrible moment of utter suspense. As a pure reflex and a survival instinct, he sharply pushed the joystick forward and simultaneously shoved the rudder hard with his feet, managing to throw his Spit into a violent downward spin, almost blacking out from the strong centrifugal forces acting on his body and brain.

After the Luftwaffe pilot saw the Spitfire in front of him go down so steeply in such a wild spin, he probably imagined he had hit the pilot and killed him.

But Jan, furious at having been so nonchalant, and despite his bitter surprise and severe setback, managed to pull out of the dive, barely streaking over the sea's surface, levelling out and then angrily climbing back up to altitude through thin layers of clouds. Now, teeth clenched, he set his mind to meeting that sneaky Messerschmitt again – its pilot had so ingloriously attacked him from behind. It was his turn to fly towards that enemy bandit and attack!

He was now the hunter, not the hunted! He was going to show that bastard what he could do in a man-to-man air duel.

Once the Luftwaffe pilot realised he had not downed his prey and it was coming back at him like an angry hornet, he banked sharply away to escape in the direction of France. Jan regarded it as a small moral victory!

Watching the enemy disappear, he gave up the chase and headed back to England, a more experienced flying Dutchman.

There is a hunter instinct in every man – the parrying between the instruments of death had brought it out in him. The better man had won. Even if he had not succeeded in shooting down the Messerschmitt and killing its pilot, Jan judged himself to be the victor!

He had never in all his life been so frightened when – out of the blue – the brightly coloured tracer bullets had sped over his wings and cockpit. Once Jan had regained full control of his Spit, he recalled the famous words, 'Attack is the best defence.'

Jan had decided to fight it out despite having gone through the most frightening emergency he had ever experienced just minutes before. And now, even though Jan hadn't even come within shooting range, the German opponent had preferred to turn tail like a scared rabbit towards the sanctuary of France.

Jan continued to strain his neck, searching the sky around him for intruders. When he saw no enemy aircraft to threaten him, Jan flew back to base, a much wiser young man. Again, he had learned how careful a pilot had to be when airborne – always alert, no instant of relaxation, on the qui-vive, tense and ready for action. A fighter pilot had to give everything over to one elementary rule: the instinct for survival!

That same evening, Jan wrote in his diary: 'I realise by now the Huns really shoot at you. I've never been so frightened in my whole life.'

Death always lurked around the corner. Death stayed on permanent duty, stalking its next victim. It stood patiently, silently, threateningly in the wings, attentively watching his performance. Singing that sentimental Dutch song had almost cost Jan his life.

After landing safely at his base, Jan relished the moment of relief and lightly slid his hand over the Spit's hard fabric, observing a number of bullet holes. How lucky he had been to survive the sneaky, unexpected attack! Then he proceeded to debriefing, where he asked if the flight commander had already returned. The reply was negative.

Only later during the day did Jan find out that his commander had not returned from the flight and was considered missing in action. He was probably another unfortunate victim of the formidable, deadly Fw 190.

A few days after the incursion over France, the squadron's pilots were called to a conference presided over by RAF intelligence officers.

A detailed map had been attached to the wall in the briefing room and one of the intelligence officers was holding a wooden pointer to indicate railway tracks in north-western France. He briefly summarised what was expected from the pilots.

'We've gathered information that Goering and his infamous train are somewhere on the tracks in north-west France, right within striking distance of this base's Spitfires.' He indicated the area. Following a railway track with the stick, the officer explained the next day's mission. There were questions and answers. At the end of briefing, the time and hour of attack were set up.

During the evening, the young pilots excitedly discussed what they were expected to do the next day. They were all thoroughly convinced only a few of them would be standing at the bar the following evening. The operation promised to be very dangerous, and demanded great human sacrifice. Some had too much to drink.

The squadron had to accompany a group of light twin-engined bombers towards the heavily armoured train. The bombers were to drop their deadly loads while the fighters would first protect them from Luftwaffe interference and then attack the train with their cannon if they had enough ammunition.

The next morning Jan prepared himself meticulously. He went about his business with a calm mind, reasoning with himself that there was no cause for unnecessary excitement. It was a perfectly normal operation, just like so many others he'd been through before, except that this particular train was equipped with many anti-aircraft cannon and heavy machine guns.

Once Jan was given the signal, he started his engine and taxied to the head of the runway. He took off behind the plane leading blue group. After the take-off, they rendezvoused at 6,000 feet with the light bombers they were escorting to France, flying in close formation. The big adventure had begun.

To their great surprise, when they reached the neighbourhood of the target there was no train matching the description of Goering's – which would have been defended by six special carriages mounting numerous anti-aircraft weapons. During briefing the day before, the pilots had been shown pictures of the extraordinary train. It had impressed all the pilots. But now, flying low over its supposed location, they couldn't find it.

Reluctantly, the bomber pilots had to fly home with their unexploded bomb loads still locked in the bomb bays. Not a very pleasant prospect!

The fighters shot up several targets they found on the way back to base. The only practical result was a small locomotive they found on a track.

After returning safely, the pilots in Jan's squadron openly demonstrated their disappointment about the day's poor results with an animated bar discussion. That evening, Jan wrote in his diary: 'That's how war is … one moment you are nearly killed without expecting it at all … the next you're mentally prepared for the worst and nothing happens!'

During his first flights over Europe, Jan had decided his number would probably come up after ten – or at the most, twenty – missions. After all, he had read that the average life of a heavy four-engined bomber amounted to only fourteen missions. Why then should he average any more? Why indeed?

By now, Jan was perfectly aware the Luftwaffe really was shooting at them: he had experienced it over the Channel returning from an air battle over France. It was no game that was being played up there in the air! Jan argued with himself that if his number did ever come up, it would be very sad for his parents but the matter would not concern him – he would be dead in an instant. All his earthly problems would be wiped out in a flash. Perhaps it could be compared to an old piece of clothing – worn for far too long, and discarded without a feeling or a thought.

Death as a phenomenon did not really impress Jan. He was completely convinced that birth – the beginning of life – and death – its conclusion – could not possibly represent the two main events in one's life on earth. There had to be more, much more.

Jan had jotted down a number of reflections like this in his diary. Sitting at his writing table, he gave his fertile brain total freedom to touch upon the deepest thoughts it could conjure up.

In October 1942, in a memorandum , Sir Charles Portal – Commander-in-Chief of RAF Bomber Command Europe – stated:

> The object of the bombing offensive in Europe consists in the progressive destruction and also bankruptcy of the enemy's industrial and economic systems plus the unhinging of his moral to such a point that the capacity of armed resistance must be fatally weakened.

During 1942, the bombing of targets in German-occupied Europe progressively increased. So, unfortunately, did the consequent losses of men and aircraft. In a way, it was a Battle of Britain in reverse: the Battle of Europe.

Despite military aggression against Soviet Russia by the German Wehrmacht and Luftwaffe on the eastern front, the Luftwaffe operating in the west had managed to reinforce its depleted stocks of pilots and planes. The German manufacturing plants were capable of turning out some 600 fighters a month, despite the continuous Allied bombardment of their factories.

Improved versions of the Me 109s and Fw 190s came off the production lines to battle against Allied war efforts. The menacing, ever-growing arsenal of anti-aircraft guns on the ground increased in firepower and accuracy day by day. Not a very bright prospect for all those frequently flying over Europe.

On 6 December 1942, Jan had to participate with 167 squadron in a withdrawal cover escort for 93 medium bombers – Bostons, Venturas and Mosquitoes. Their objective was to destroy the big Philips electronic factories located in Eindhoven, in the south-eastern region of the Netherlands. A daylight attack on a Sunday was planned, since the

Philips manufacturing facilities were spread throughout the city and it was assumed the workers would be out of the plants on lunch-breaks when the bombs would fall.

Flying high above the bombers, looking down at them streaking low in close formation over the Dutch countryside, Jan had qualms: the Allied pilots would be dropping those ugly, black-painted eggs on Dutch targets – homes and, unfortunately, people.

Inevitably, some bombs would miss their targets, causing civilian casualties. Perhaps even mothers and children would be among them. Jan's countrymen would suffer, and he knew it, but there was nothing he could do. At any rate, he had only the best of wishes for the bomber pilots, who still had to fly into the very heavy flak thrown up by the German defences around the target area. The bombers had to continue on their way without further fighter escorts. Those were the instructions.

As a Dutchman, Jan was fully aware the destruction of the German-occupied manufacturing plants was a necessity; he had scruples, however, about bombing his own country, especially when some bombs were bound to miss the indicated targets, killing innocents.

On a number of flights over Holland accompanying the big bombers, Jan had observed the bomb bays opening slowly and menacingly – at first, the black bombs would float majestically, following the same direction as the plane, and then sink into their own trajectory, drifting down to the designated target. The sight of those ugly, destructive devices made his stomach contract at times.

Circling high over the Moerdijkbridge, which spanned the Hollandse Diep in the Rhine estuary and linked northern Holland to the south, Jan anxiously scanned the horizon, straining his eyes to locate the returning bombers. He finally noticed them, individual specks in the distant sky above the white clouds, scurrying like a bunch of disturbed ants on a well-trodden path returning to the safety of the anthill.

Jan could see they were still being attacked by the Focke Wulfs and Messerschmitts, swarming and diving around them like a cloud of angry wasps around honey pots. Finally, when they spotted the waiting Spitfires high above, the Luftwaffe pilots desisted, leaving the battered bombers alone while they turned away inland.

Following the raid, the hard facts of the results became known. Jan was dispirited. Fifteen bombers – a great many – had been shot down: an extremely high loss rate, over 16 per cent. Between 60 and 80 airmen, at least, had been wounded, captured or killed, and the actual damage inflicted on the Philips factories had been far below expectations. His squadron suffered no losses during the withdrawal escort as they had not engaged the Luftwaffe over the south of Holland.

The next morning, 8 December, Jan sat at readiness again. The weather was cold and it was actually freezing outside. The wind blowing in from the north-west made it seem even chillier. Upon entering the cramped cockpit that morning, everything he touched felt icy. He shivered in his flying suit. A portent of bad luck for someone still having to fly operationally.

A bright blue sky permitted excellent ground visibility. The wind seemed to have cleared the air, as if a huge vacuum cleaner had swallowed up all the clouds. Jan and one other pilot took off for a sweep of gun positions on the French coast.

Crossing the Atlantic Wall on his way in, Jan made a wide turn to gain a better view of the targets below him. Then he dived towards one of the heavy gun emplacements he had noticed before. Jan aimed his Spit towards it. When he had it well fixed in his gunsight, he pushed the firing button on the joystick and let his four cannon sing their familiar destructive song, performing their lethal work. The other pilot was right behind him, protecting his tail.

After the first dive, Jan made a sharp, climbing turn to prepare for the next attack. Passing low over the gun carriages, he made a tight turn and finished it off with an Immelmann, rolling over to a normal flight position again at the top of the loop. To Jan's utter surprise, the plane, having lost too much speed, started to vibrate violently, beginning to stall. The flying speed was too low to keep the plane up. Jan had to call on all his flying technique to stop it from stalling badly and going into a spin. He was losing altitude at a terrifying rate, the nose of his Spit pointing to the sky above him. Terrified, Jan saw the ground approaching at frightening speed. Just when he thought he was a goner, that the crash was inevitable, he miraculously managed to pull the plane out of the spin, and could level out to get the critical situation under control again. Jan had avoided hitting French soil by a feather!

He was perspiring profusely in the small cockpit. Cold sweat ran down his spine, making him shiver. It had been a very close call indeed. Luckily, he had control of the Spitfire again, and he headed back to the English coast, the other pilot flying wing tip to wing tip next to him. The pilot was looking at Jan. Jan's earphones crackled.

'Are you still there, Jan?' his fellow pilot asked with concern.

'Yes,' Jan replied, his throat tight. 'The dive turned into a very close call. How did it look from your cockpit?'

'I gained the impression you wanted to glue yourself to one of those cannon like a manufacturer's trademark on a barrel. You just got out of that stall in time, my friend,' the other pilot chuckled.

'True, very true!' Jan laughed happily into the mike in front of his mouth. 'It was a good lesson. Still, I think we did some damage to a number of cannon and maybe even to the range-finding equipment.'

'Perhaps, but it very nearly cost you your life. Better be more careful next time,' the other pilot emphasised.

After a careful landing back at base, Jan patiently parked his Spit and switched off the engine. He opened the hood completely and remained seated, inhaling deeply, gratefully filling his lungs with the cold, invigorating English winter air. It felt good to be alive and Jan relished the moment. Then he climbed out of the cockpit and, standing on the root of the wing, knocked his fist against the Plexiglas hood, saying, 'Spittie, the two of us just made it today. You wouldn't like to lose your friend now, would you?' As he spoke, a mocking gleam shone in his kind, grey-blue eyes.

It felt so good to feel solid British ground beneath his flying boots again when he jumped down on to the grass. Jan rushed across the field to the mess and thirstily downed two cups of hot strong tea. He certainly needed that! Some of the other pilots shot him curious glances: they'd never seen him drink his tea so eagerly.

That same afternoon, Jan was airborne again in his Spit. This time, he had to escort a flying boat over the Channel to protect it on an air-sea rescue mission. Jan could clearly distinguish a tiny yellow life-raft bobbing on the water and someone aboard waving.

He kept circling, scrutinising every part of the sky, alert for any enemy intervention. He was a protective umbrella for what was happening a thousand feet below. Once the downed pilot had been rescued and safely pulled aboard the Albatross, the plane took off again, returning to England. Only then did Jan feel free to return to base.

By now Jan was flying a great deal operationally. There were times, however, when he would feel quite tired, even dull and listless. Jan did not realise it but he was beginning to feel the mental and nervous strains of being up in the air practically every day – of flying regularly over western Europe whenever the weather allowed.

Jan felt a weariness, a kind of physical exhaustion he had never experienced before. It was clear in his face, haggard and deeply etched with fatigue lines.

He looked forward eagerly to some days of rest in London: perhaps he would run into a number of his Dutch acquaintances who would temporarily take his mind off flying.

Jan felt as if he were made of lead. He acted like a robot at the controls: a very dangerous mental state for a fighter pilot aloft who had to be wary and alert every single minute of his flight. There were times he wondered if he needed one of those benzedrine pep pills to keep him flying.

Perhaps it was the tension involved in all those hours flying over enemy territory, knowing they were always ready to shoot him down. Or perhaps he was physically and mentally close to a breakdown. Maybe his fine physique could not indefinitely absorb the nervous tensions of flying day after day in the dangerous European air war, heedless of the risks.

And yet the flying continued without a let-up, without a pause for relief. Jan was driving himself too hard, as if his mind was continuously in second gear and never in overdrive.

One day, returning from a sweep over Holland, one of the British pilots Jan knew well didn't make it back. Jan had seen him go down, engine smoking, belly-landing in the North Sea. He had carefully memorised the spot where the plane had finally sunk into the water. As soon as Jan was safely back at base, he immediately asked the commander for permission to take off again to search for his friend.

Permission granted, Jan took off alone, on his third flight of the day, following the route the pilots always followed on operational flights to Holland.

He searched for an hour, trying to pick out a yellow life-raft bobbing in the brownish sea. The Spitfire's range was limited to one hour's flying time. When Jan noticed the red fuel warning light on the instrument panel flashing intermittently, he was forced to return to his base having accomplished nothing.

Jan had not been able to locate the spot where the missing pilot had ditched. Forlorn, he sat alone in the narrow cockpit of his Spit on the flight home. He felt a surge of compassion for the fine young pilot, who had probably been killed. Yet again Jan sensed the ever-present dark shadow of death reaching out for him.

At the end of 1942, Jan was airborne over western Europe on several occasions. On 13 December, he was over southern Holland. During the afternoon, Jan had carried out a 'rhubarb' – flying at low level and attacking whatever targets he encountered – and he had also attacked two Fw 190s. The squadron was now commanded by a new leader, just back from a long rest period.

Once in flight, the squadron headed for the Zeeland Province Islands in south-west Holland. After crossing the Dutch coastline, the squadron leader ordered the pilots to drop their external fuel tanks so they could make a low, fast approach over the Moerdijkbridge, over the Haringvliet – a branch of the Rhine that flowed into the North Sea in that area. As Jan streaked at high speed over the bridge, vivid memories returned to him of that freezing afternoon, nearly two years before, when he and Geert had stood shivering in front of the young German guard who finally let them pass on their way south.

The squadron was now flying at three thousand feet, and meeting intense anti-aircraft fire from the batteries protecting this crucially important bridge.

The flight commander ordered a right turn, leaving the area and heading back to England. Until then, not a shot had been fired, but at that very instant a number of Fw 190s swooped out of the sun, engaging the squadron in a rather confused air battle, circling and diving.

Manoeuvring well, Jan found a 190 straight ahead of him. The plane was sharply outlined in his gun sight for an instant: Jan immediately thumbed the joystick's firing button, firing a short cannon burst at the enemy. Jan's adversary dived out of sight, but he decided not to follow suit, anxiously keeping an eye on his tail via the mirror while searching for the rest of his squadron. Finding himself all alone in an empty sky, Jan went into a steep turn and returned to base.

After landing, Jan was told at debriefing that the squadron leader had not returned. This was both a great loss and a great shock to Jan. How could such an experienced pilot with so many flight hours get shot down? Once again, he was reminded the life of a fighter pilot was very risky indeed. Perhaps the squadron leader should have made a number of training flights before embarking on such an important mission so soon after a long leave. But that was hardly up to Jan to judge. The outcome was merely the same: another good man had been lost. Even though he felt a sense of gloom about the loss of such a fine man's life, Jan just had to carry on.

That evening at the bar, Jan drank far too much and got rather drunk. For two days in a row, fine and skilled pilots had not made it back from missions: they were greatly missed. You could replace lost planes, but not highly qualified pilots, nor fine human beings!

When the personal belongings of both pilots were being gathered the next morning – to be sent home to their next of kin – Jan silently observed how indifferently those possessions were packed and being carried away. It struck him as macabre, and he felt a terrible void, as if his stomach had been scooped out of his body.

At times, the flights over Europe turned out to be a picnic. There were morning take-offs, the squadron flying into formation while over the English countryside. Then the planes headed for the Dutch, Belgian or French coasts. Once they dropped the extra fuel tanks on the other side of the Channel, they swooped low to attack ground objectives like locomotives, trains, barges, bridges and military convoys moving on the roads.

At other times, there were dogfights with Focke Wulfs and Messerschmitts. The Luftwaffe still managed to operate many of them. In fact, their numbers were still superior to those of the RAF opposing the Luftwaffe during the Battle of Britain.

Sometimes, flying over the infamous north-western French triangle, anti-aircraft fire from the ground became more and more concentrated, precise and heavy. Those grey-black puffs of smoke were permanent signs, constant threatening reminders of the continual dangers and risks to which they were exposed and during those flights over Europe. The German armed presence was felt each time they crossed the Channel and saw stricken planes going down trailing black smoke. One Dutch pilot described it in his diary as 'a seething, churning sea whipped by hard winds'.

In the heat of battle, a pilot was often tempted to chase a single Luftwaffe plane inland. But he was likely to be drawn into a group of waiting Luftwaffe planes, to ambush the unsuspecting victim following the bait. Jan assumed this had probably happened to the squadron leader a few days before.

Returning from one flight, Jan found a letter from Holland. He learned his father had finally been released by the German Sicherheitsdienst, having been held hostage for over eleven months in solitary confinement. Many a man would have succumbed under this kind of duress, but not Plesman Senior!

Jan's spirits lifted considerably with this good news – it was just what he needed at that point of his stay in England. Fortunately, his dynamic father had been able to overcome the awful, destructive mental dreariness of solitary confinement by reading and exercising, and had kept his mind active by just plain thinking.

He had managed to keep his vigorous spirits alive, and the letters he wrote to his son showed this. There were no longer all those references to God and religion. Jan felt utterly convinced his father would overcome the unhappy experience and – once the war came to an end – would be able again to dedicate his whole life and energies to commercial aviation.

Even though the Dutch part of KLM's operations had been practically destroyed during the days of May 1940, Jan was certain his father would be able to reconstruct the airline again after the war, making it bigger and more powerful than ever before. The Dutch airline still operated in the West

Indies – Curaçao was its main base for the regional Caribbean network – and made regular flights from Bristol to Lisbon.

Parmentier, KLM's chief pilot, had told Jan that his father had regular supplies of up-to-date American literature on commercial and technical developments in aviation. Most of the material was sent via KLM's offices in Lisbon or Switzerland. And Jan was sure his father had been reading every single word to stay on top of events.

Jan would have liked so much to say, 'Dad, I respect you, admire you and love you.' But he had never managed to say it when back in Holland and now he thoroughly regretted it. He deeply wanted to reach out to his father and break down those invisible barriers which had separated them so many times in The Hague.

Jan had been an obstinate, stubborn, opinionated young man in near perpetual conflict with his strong-minded father: on several occasions, after another fierce verbal exchange, Jan had sped furiously away from his paternal home on his racing bike.

On 17 December, Jan was granted leave and took off for London, where he had booked a room at the Dutch Club. When he checked in, the desk clerk told him Geert had also booked a room. With pleasure, Jan anticipated spending the next day, his birthday, in the company of his friend. That night he turned in early to make sure he would be in good shape the next day. He intended to make the best of his short leave.

Early the next morning, the door to his room was carefully opened: Geert entered, singing 'Happy birthday to you ...'

When Jan was fully awake, Geert presented him with a handsome silver pencil, a sign of great friendship. Jan gratefully appreciated the gesture. Jan later invited Geert to Oranjehaven – a big house near Marble Arch that Queen Wilhelmina had made available to those Dutchmen who had escaped from the German occupation of their homeland.

They stood at the bar with cold Dutch jenevers in their hands.'Geert, here's to you,' said Jan. 'Nice seeing you again.

It's been two years since we left Holland. Time certainly flies by! I'm on operational flights a lot these days but I still haven't shot down my first Luftwaffe plane. I might have got one the other day – I'm sure I hit him at any rate!'

Geert downed the contents of his glass and a sad expression appeared in his dark eyes. 'I'm not doing so well, Jan,' he confided. 'Last week I cracked up a Mosquito unfortunately – while coming in for a touchdown.' Geert sighed deeply. 'I still don't know exactly why, but once the tail wheel hit the ground, the darned plane changed direction and suddenly shot off the runway. I simply couldn't keep it on the right course. The whole tail section was damaged – badly! The wing commander called me to say I'll be transferred to heavy bombers. That's the penalty for damaging a Mosquito – as you know. Too bad, too damned bad, Jan. It was such a wonderful plane to fly.'

Geert took a deep breath, then added, 'I guess that's life.' For an instant, tears of frustration welled up in his eyes. Then he impatiently shrugged. 'What a lousy war it has turned out to be for me. I was so eager to perform something of real importance and now, of all things – after two full years wasted here – I'm back where I started from!' Geert spoke bitterly.

Jan smiled compassionately at him. 'I'm sorry my friend, but "Hou je kop op, man!" – keep your spirits up! Don't let this unlucky accident wear you down,' he encouraged Geert. 'I'm doing a bit better. Before the year runs out, I'll have made fifty sweeps over occupied Europe. At last there's something to be proud of – it's a real accomplishment for me. Now, let's forget our personal problems and the damn war. Let's enjoy ourselves and have some fun on my birthday.' As an afterthought, Jan added, 'By the way, American pilots are sent back to the USA after fifty successful missions.'

Again, they raised their small glasses of cold jenever and tossed the contents down in one.

Late in the afternoon, Jan phoned Joyce – a girlfriend he had met on an earlier visit to London. He invited her to the theatre but she said she already had an invitation to a cocktail party and couldn't possibly break the date at the very last moment.

'If you want to, Jan, I can try and meet you later – maybe at the Shepherds. I promise I'll do my best to meet you there later in the evening. I'm sorry.'

To kill time, both men kept on drinking, talking and reminiscing in the Dutch Club. They also downed a number of those strong jenevers. Then they walked unsteadily to the Shepherds to try and find Joyce.

When she finally showed up, Jan and Geert had drunk far more jenevers than Joyce had sipped cocktails at her party. The difference in alcoholic intake between them certainly showed – and attracted notice!

Once she sat down, Joyce told them how annoyed she was to find herself in the company of two half-drunk Dutchmen. Geert was especially rough on her, heavily criticising women in WAAF uniform fighting the war.

With an alcoholic mist befuddling Geert's brain, he blurted out all kinds of wild remarks. At one point, he drunkenly looked at Joyce, derisively saying, 'Women should stay at home and work in the kitchen – they shouldn't try to fight wars along with men. Fighting is for men, not for women!'

Joyce had been patient and was a good sport but she finally decided she had had enough – she stood up and left in a huff.

Jan quickly stood as well, wobbling, leaving Geert at the table in his alcoholic stupor, and tried to catch up with Joyce to apologise.

Joyce had looked forward to seeing Jan again, and liked him for his good manners and sincerity. But he had disappointed her this time. When Jan finally and unsteadily caught up with her, in the blacked-out streets, he realised, though befuddled and full of alcohol, that meeting Joyce in those conditions had been a bad mistake.

He looked at her and apologised. 'I'm sorry, Joyce – but I should tell you my friend Geert is extremely sad and discouraged today. He cracked up a Mosquito so they've transferred him to heavy bombers. Really, Joyce – he's been a very unlucky pilot here in England. Please forgive him for his behaviour tonight.' Jan looked at her sheepishly, begging for her forgiveness.

Joyce laughed at him good-naturedly. 'All right, both drunken Dutchmen are forgiven. Come, give me your arm. I'll steer you, you drunkard.' Chuckling to herself, she took his arm firmly under hers, trying to keep him on a straight line through the dark streets to her apartment. Every now and then, he suddenly lost his balance, weaving to the right or left of the street, dragging her along. 'You know, Joyce,' Jan slurred, 'it's not easy for my friend Geert. He's been away from his family for over two years. His flying activities have not produced the desired results. After having crash-landed a Mosquito last week, he has to start all over again, but now on heavy bombers. I hope you'll understand.' Jan was mumbling more to himself than to Joyce.

'Of course I understand. But tell me how *you* feel!' Joyce eyed Jan with concern. 'I think you downed a few too many too.' As she spoke, she smiled warmly, her lovely mouth showing her even white teeth.

With a naughty twinkle in his eyes, Jan glanced at her. 'Well, I suppose I did,' he admitted. 'I shouldn't have after phoning you.' He wiggled his index finger at Joyce. 'I shouldn't have, but I just wanted to keep Geert company in a moment of grief. You know, Joyce, the two of us had such a terrible, harrowing time escaping from Europe. And since today's my birthday, we both kept on drinking to my good health. I probably got too sentimental about it,' he added apologetically.

'Oh, Jan – congratulations!' she exclaimed, turning towards him and lightly kissing him on both cheeks. 'Happy birthday! Why don't you come up and I'll make you a nice strong cup of coffee. It'll help you find your way back home.'

Jan nodded. 'Thanks, that's awfully nice of you. I'm not being a bother, am I?' he asked, staring at her. He was still rather unsteady on his feet.

'No, no! Here we are. I'll lead the way.'

Joyce guided him to her front door. He stood there, fragile and slightly swaying against the wall while she searched for her keys in her bag. Once inside the apartment, she eased the drunken Jan into a comfortable chair, and then got busy in the kitchenette. After a short while she returned with a cup of hot and strong black coffee.

'I hope it's all right,' she said hesitantly. 'Here you are, Jan. I only made one cup. I can't sleep if I drink any before going to bed. It might just be a false idea but I'd rather play it safe. I have a lot to do tomorrow.'

Slowly sipping his coffee, Jan stared at her over the rim of the cup. 'Thanks, Joyce, this is a nice birthday present. I appreciate it. How are you doing these days?' he asked, curious.

'Oh, don't worry – I'm getting along. You know, we WAAFs are not supposed to complain. All in all, I must admit my life's not too bad. What does frighten me, though, are the night bombardments. They scare me stiff! I lie there in my bed, not knowing if the next bomb dropped on London will have my name on it. When I've survived the night and arrive at HQ the next morning half-dead from lack of sleep, I'm so mad at those damn Germans I just want to work harder than ever – to give those lousy Huns a taste of their own medicine!'

Jan nodded, feeling better already. 'Good for you, Joyce! What a war! I wasted nearly half a year training at one military base, then another and another. After that, they sent me to the most god-forsaken part of the country in the far north of Scotland. Now I'm finally operational – and weather permitting, I fly nearly every day.'

He looked seriously at Joyce. 'It's tiring, you know, being up there every day.' He lazily moved his right hand towards the ceiling as if to indicate the sky above them. 'It all happens

143

so fast if anything goes wrong. One moment you're all flying together in tight formation and the next you're separated from each other, flying all over the sky, hunting, trying to shoot down a Focke Wulf or a Messerschmitt. It's everyone for himself. At times it's quite confusing with all those planes flashing through the air.'

Joyce watched him tenderly, following the movements of his hands. 'It's really awful up there, isn't it, Jan,' she said, a kind softness in her voice.

''You know,' Jan went on, 'the other day – during a sweep over France – I was attacking a moving train. At first, I flew very low past the engine cabin, waving my wings to warn the driver and fireman first – in order not to kill innocent passengers. I could have easily fired at the train by coming up from behind over the carriages. To thank me, the damn engineer hid the train between a dense row of trees along the track, making our attack nearly impossible. In fact, my wingman damaged his wings in the tree tops and almost crashed. Joyce, there's just no recognition any more for a pilot's gentlemanly gesture.' Jan smiled ironically.

Joyce acknowledged his words, smiling warmly back at him. 'Jan, you're such a nice fellow and such a drunken darling – I can understand how you must have felt when your gesture was not appreciated. Please be more careful the next time and stay alive. You're not invulnerable, you know. When you have to attack a train again, do think of yourself first. Will you do that – just for me?' She looked at him tenderly, tilting her head so her blonde hair cascaded down her shoulders.

'Okay, Joyce – I'll do that. Thanks for the nice cup of coffee. I really needed it right now. I'll be seeing you – and I'll behave better the next time, I promise!' Jan slowly rose to his feet, still swaying slightly, but ready to leave.

At the door, Joyce stood on her toes and gave him a friendly kiss. Then Jan was off along the dark blacked-out streets, trying to find his way through London to start searching for Geert.

First, Jan returned to the Shepherds and asked the people at the bar if they had seen Geert leave. Getting no satisfactory answer there, he carried on to the Oranjehaven, and then to the Dutch Club, where he finally found Geert – collapsed!

With some difficulty, Jan managed to load a complaining Geert on his shoulders and carry him back to Geert's room. He lay Geert on the bed, removed his jacket and left him as he was, carefully covering him with two blankets. Finally, dead tired, he headed back to his own room – to sleep off an eventful birthday.

Jan's twenty-second anniversary had started off so nicely with a little birthday song and a present, but had nearly ended in a drunken brawl with his best friend when he tried to put Geert to bed.

The next morning, Jan was up at eight. After breakfast, he went shopping. He also arranged for Red Cross parcels to be sent to his family and his aunts in Holland, and made a donation to the Red Cross for prisoners of war.

Having done his duty, Jan went back to the Dutch Club, where he found Geert sitting at a table enjoying an abundant breakfast, a big cup of strong black coffee in front of him. He had partially recovered from the rough experiences of the previous night. Geert apologised for his bad manners and behaviour. 'You know how it is, Jan. This lousy war is really wearing me down. If only I hadn't suffered that damn accident with the Mosquito, I might be operational by now. But I guess it wasn't meant to be,' he said with a deep sigh.

'Don't let it get you down,' Jan encouraged Geert. 'Pick yourself up. I'm inviting you to lunch and then I have to get back to the base. My leave is over. Let's enjoy ourselves. You're my guest.' They went off to Maxim's where they enjoyed the food.

Their conversation often returned to those anxious days cycling through Belgium and France on their way to freedom.

After the meal, they said farewell and went their separate ways – Geert to learn to fly Lancasters, heavy four-engined bombers, Jan to return to his dangerous missions over Europe.

The armed hostilities continued – unabated.

What would be the fate of Jan and Geert – what did the future hold for them?

XII

ONE EVENING just before Christmas 1942, Diana was sitting with a few friends in the WAAF mess at Ludham airfield. Much banter was flying back and forth, in a room filled with blueish smoke. Toulouse-Lautrec could not have painted the scene better in its matt, lustreless colours.

People were continually entering and leaving, but at one point Diana's attention was drawn to a tall, handsome RAF officer striding alone to the bar. He stood there by himself for a while, sipping a beer and observing those present, now and then exchanging a few words with others standing nearby.

Diana noticed with interest his regular, oval face, his finely sculptured, straight nose, wavy blond hair and a firm jaw, expressing strong character. She thought his eyes were blue. From his brief glances at others, Diana thought he might be rather a shy young man. His eyes met hers for a moment, only to look elsewhere immediately.

At that very moment her heart began to beat faster – much faster. For the first time since she had lost interest in so many things, something started to stir deep within her. All at once she had met unexpected turbulence after a long, lonely flight in the dark.

After finishing his beer, the young officer left, but just before disappearing through the door, his hand already on the handle, he glanced once more in her direction. Their eyes locked for a second and Diana felt the blood rush to her cheeks – she thought she must be blushing. All at once, she felt warm all over, as if an electric current had been plugged into her and the resulting heat was flowing freely through her, leaving such a nice, comfortable feeling. Then the officer had gone.

Would she ever see him again?

Trying to hide her personal interest, Diana innocently asked her companions if they knew the man who had been standing alone at the bar drinking a beer.

One of the men spoke up. 'That chap? Yes, I know him. He's from Holland. I think his name is Jan, or something like that. He's rather shy, doesn't speak to the girls much, but can he ever fly a plane! That flying Dutchman really has it at his fingertips. He manages to get the very last ounce of performance out of a Spitfire. I've seen him stunting over the field at an awfully low altitude – really frightening! I believe he flies a lot of missions over Europe. He must be a very tired pilot – he's in action every day he can get off the ground.'

That was all Diana could find out about this interesting Dutch pilot. She was excited to hear he handled a Spitfire so well.

A few days later, she saw an announcement about a Christmas dance. Normally, she would have thought twice about going, but this time she immediately decided to go. Perhaps I'll meet him again at the dance, she thought to herself.

That Christmas Eve, feeling really good, Diana entered the WAAF mess and happily admired the gaily decorated tree and the brightly coloured garlands hanging from the ceiling. Her eyes slowly and hopefully swept over the room and then the bar, expecting him to be there – but he wasn't!

A pang of disappointment shot through her. Had something happened to him, perhaps? Diana was seized by a feeling of deep anxiety she had never before experienced. Had anything gone wrong during his last mission, she wondered?

She knew there had been casualties that day, having seen the list of missing pilots chalked up on the blackboard in the operations room. But she didn't know the tall Dutch officer's squadron. Was he missing?

Diana felt at a loss. What should she do now? She felt lost and worried – her happy frame of mind disappeared and a deep black mood gripped her. There seemed to be no reason to stay in the festively decorated, smoke-filled room.

She had just decided to leave when an officer she had danced with a few times approached her.

'Hello, Diana. Why that serious face? May I buy you a drink?'

She looked at him indecisively and then accepted, just to pass the time of day. Once she had sat down, she kept eagerly watching the door each time it opened – but the man she was hoping and longing to meet didn't appear. Diana was terribly disappointed – despite the officer's company, she felt completely alone, adrift at sea, directionless and disoriented.

A deep, cold chill ran through her. She wanted to be near her mother, in need of her mother's warmth and strength, which always comforted Diana in moments of distress.

'Are you feeling all right, Diana?' the officer inquired with a concerned edge to his voice. 'You look so distressed.'

She paused a moment before replying. 'No, I feel fine. How about that drink?' she asked, and smiled at him.

'Coming up!' he exclaimed as he turned to the barman.

Once the drinks had been placed in front of them, he raised his glass to toast her. 'Merry Christmas, Diana!'

'Merry Christmas,' she replied meekly and absent-mindedly, her eyes still fixed on the mess door.

XIII

TWO DAYS before Christmas, Jan had to escort a group of bombers to northern Holland. The weather, despite the time of the year, looked fine and the squadron levelled out at 23,000 feet. Looking up through the cockpit hood Jan could see deep dark-blue sky. Far beneath his right wing was the Dutch coastline, and Jan could clearly distinguish its white dunes, the dikes that protected the lowlands from the furies of the North Sea, the polders and narrow canals that divided the flat country into so many precise plots of cultivated land.

From thousands of feet above, it all looked so perfectly peaceful. Jan found it so hard to imagine how millions of his own countrymen, down below, were suffering horribly, silently, every day, their hearts filled with hatred of the harsh German occupation. It all looked so neat, so frail and so quiet from this altitude.

Jan could see the Rhine, flowing through the countryside until it ended its course in the North Sea, while the Meuse flowed in between the Zeeland Province islands in the south-western Netherlands. Jan knew his geography, and it was easy to recognise the clear-cut layout of his own country spread out below him.

Jan remembered vividly how his father, before the war, would say on their Sunday trips in the car, 'Look over there to

your left. What church is that?' Or he would ask, 'What canal
is that over to your right?' Then he'd say, 'Remember it well
because if you were a fighter pilot and popped out of a cloud
or found yourself on an overcast day, then you'd be able to
recognise the landmarks immediately – and get an advantage
on your enemy!'

Jan smiled ruefully in the cramped cockpit. How much he
missed his father's good advice! He had paid so little attention
to it in the past. If only he could step out of the cockpit for a
moment, ring his father's front doorbell and say, 'Hello, here
I am!' and then return to England. But unfortunately there
was a war raging and Jan was on his way to protect the
bombers about to release their deadly cargo on his own
country.

From this altitude, Jan could also clearly see the island of
Schouwen and Duiveland where – at Haamstede airfield – he
had been partly trained by the Dutch Air Force, flying antiquated Fokkers.

Jan was vividly reminded of his elder brother Hans, who
had been flying a Fokker D-21 fighter for the Dutch Air Force
at the time of the German invasion. Hans had shot down
three Luftwaffe planes during the four-day war. In fact, Hans
had logged the highest time in action of any of the Dutch
fighter pilots during those days in May 1940.

Now Jan's mind returned to present reality. How tiny
everything looked from this altitude. In a few minutes, he
would see the bombs float down from the planes he was
accompanying, and explode on Den Helder, once a Dutch
naval base but now used extensively by the German Navy.

Circling high over the target, grey-black puffs of smoke
from anti-aircraft fire filling the sky, Jan saw the terrible blasts
where the bombs struck. Suddenly there was a big bright
flash, followed by a huge fire with mushroom clouds of black
smoke obscuring ground visibility. Probably a number of oil
tanks had been hit. Jan smiled grimly: those Germans
deserved this destruction.

After the bombers made their final runs, they headed back to England. Jan's squadron, a protective umbrella flying high above, also prepared to return home: the Luftwaffe had not offered much resistance. When they entered British airspace, the fighters swung away to land at Ludham. On the flight back, Jan had plenty of time to consider the growing strength of the Allied Forces. He had heard President Roosevelt on the radio, announcing American aircraft factories would produce 50,000 planes during 1942 and 200,000 the following year. These were unheard-of figures but they were being met and even now Jan could see that the bomber offensive was growing stronger each passing day.

Bombers flew over Europe night and day dropping their lethal loads – thousands of tons a day on targets in Germany, France, Belgium, Holland and Northern Italy.

By 1943, the Luftwaffe's indiscriminate bombing of targets in England and the subsequent destruction would be repaid a hundred times over. The air battle for Europe had really begun. The books were truly going to be balanced!

After his last flight over Holland, Jan was ordered to report to another airfield for night flight training. There were few pilots who actually enjoyed night flying. The impenetrable darkness surrounding the pilot had to be conquered by precise calculation, demanding the utmost attention and concentration. It was a strenuous mental effort, and it could be dangerous if one was unwary, but Jan did master the technique in the process of making a number of cross-country flights to sharpen his navigation skills.

The days before Christmas 1942 went by quickly. Jan thought a great deal about his parents and his family in Holland. He reminded himself to write home by 27 December. His parents would be celebrating their 25th wedding anniversary. A letter was the only affectionate gesture he could make, sending it through the KLM Office in Lisbon. He would tell them that everything was fine, that he felt good, that his 'studies' were progressing satisfactorily and he was anxiously looking forward to meeting them again by the end of next year. He could say no more than that, having to take both British and German censors into consideration. They were so diligent with their scissors and deletions while scrutinising a letter.

Jan was well aware from his own frequent flights of the ever-increasing Allied air activities over Europe. He was convinced the war would be over by the end of 1943. He didn't think the German civilian population could withstand the increasing night bombardments the RAF inflicted on their factories and cities – and the devastating daylight bombing by the American Air Force on the German Fatherland grew in strength every passing day.

Walking through the blitzed streets of London during his leaves, Jan had been considerably affected by the sight of the bomb damage. And in 1940 he had visited the fire-razed centre of Rotterdam and witnessed the utter destruction caused by only 57 twin-engined German Heinkel 111 bombers. Now the Germans were on the receiving end of firepower that was at least a thousand times greater. Jan thought it very fitting: the Nazis had brought only death, misery and murder – all the worst possible kinds of cruel and barbarian slaughter upon humanity. He believed this was why the worldwide conflict now raging in all its horror should be over by the end of 1943. The American Air Force daylight offensives were growing stronger and more intense with each passing day due to the enormous production facilities at their disposal in the USA. Jan thought the Germans would eventually have no choice but to surrender. It was just a matter of time. But time and the Grim Reaper happened to be two of the main players in Jan's life.

With nothing better to do on Christmas Eve, a bored Flying Dutchman wandered over to the WAAF mess. As an officer, Jan was allowed to visit it. While standing at the bar sipping a beer alone, he noticed a particularly good-looking WAAF sergeant. Every now and then she briefly and elusively glanced back at him.

From the short distance he stood away from her, Jan admired her soft, thick blonde hair, cut rather short as was the style. She possessed wonderful, vivacious, expressive, deep-blue eyes, a cute and finely-sculptured nose, a creamy-white skin and even white teeth which showed every time she laughed. Jan wondered why he had never noticed her before.

Yet Jan thought he could see a kind of deep-seated sadness hidden behind the cheerful attitude. It made her seem vulnerable, and it intrigued him. She seemed to be burdened by some mysterious inner grief which attracted him even more.

Jan could not get a good look at the girl's figure or legs while she sat at a table with a group of WAAFs and flying-officers, but when she got up to dance with one of them, Jan admired her long, tapered, shapely legs and slim build. Even when dancing, she sometimes glanced over her partner's shoulder in his direction, and their eyes held for a second. It seemed as if two electric currents had come into contact causing a spark.

Jan would have liked to meet her but he didn't know anyone at her table who could introduce him. He talked with a few other people standing at the bar. Having finished his beer, he left early to return to his quarters. Just as he was shutting the mess door behind him, he glanced at her again, and their eyes held for a split second. How much he desired to meet her – but he would have to postpone that to another occasion.

When Jan read the announcement of a dance at the WAAF mess on 27 December, he immediately decided to attend. *She* might be there!

Jan had better luck this time. When he entered the noisy smoke-filled hall, he saw her at the bar chatting with a pilot he knew from his own squadron. Jan decisively strode straight up to them.

'Hello, Harry. Would you kindly introduce me to this charming young lady?' he asked eagerly.

Harry laughed good-naturedly, and introduced them to each other. 'Diana, meet Jan – Jan, meet Diana,' he grinned at both of them.

With kindly interest, Diana looked at the Dutch officer. 'Hello, nice to meet you. Do you both fly in the same squadron?' she asked, turning her head from one to the other.

Jan nodded. 'Yes, we do.' He ordered a beer.

She tilted her head to study him better. 'But you're not British, are you?' she asked, curious, glancing at the sleeve of Jan's RAF uniform: it displayed an orange lion and the words 'Je maintiendrai' beneath it.

Jan shook his head. 'No, I come from a small country – Holland. It's about thirty minutes by air from here.' He gestured with his right thumb and index finger as if he were measuring a small object.

Diana laughed. 'Well it can't be that small, can it?' Her eyes teased him.

'Not exactly,' Jan agreed, smiling. 'And where are you from?' he asked.

'Australia – originally.' Diana hesitated an instant before adding, 'I'm familiar with your country.' Her vivacious blue eyes expressed amusement when she said that. 'At least, from the operations room where I can follow all the squadrons and their movements every day,' she added, a challenge in her voice.

'That's interesting,' he commented. 'Too bad you don't recognise my plane, or Harry's, by identification or you could follow us all the way during our sweeps over Europe. It would be quite a combination – us up in the air and you in the operations room,' he stated. 'Perhaps you could even guide us by telepathy.'

Unperturbed by the remark, Diana asked, 'What's your squadron number? We follow everything that happens in this area from the operations room: the bombers, the fighters – in short, the whole show.' Diana's words contained a touch of pride.

'I'm with 167 Squadron,' Jan answered. 'You must be performing quite a task. May I ask you how many hours a day you're involved in your work?' This time he spoke seriously.

Diana smiled at him. 'Nearly ten hours a day. Women do contribute their share in helping to win the war, you know,' she said challengingly. Diana was proud of her small valuable contribution to the war's outcome.

Jan shook his head. 'I didn't realise you were busy that many hours a day. Tell me, what part of Australia are you from?' he asked, changing the subject.

'I was born in Sydney, but my mother wanted to move to London right before the war to give my sister and me an English education.'

Jan turned his attention to Harry and said 'Look, it's rather crowded and smoky in here – how about moving over to our bar just to change atmosphere? Maybe Diana would like to join us?' Jan gazed at her questioningly.

She nodded approval. 'All right, let's go,' she said firmly.

Together they walked over to the officers' mess. Once there, they were told Diana could not enter as she was merely a sergeant. Her two escorts had completely overlooked military rules. They regarded her as a woman, not as a military entity.

Harry saved the embarrassing situation by suggesting they sit in his car. Fortunately, it was parked close to the officers' mess, and it was the only accommodation available just then. They continued their interrupted conversation in the small car but the formation of frost like a silver lining on the windows as soon as they were seated seemed to make the confined space even smaller, oppressive and eerie.

Jan went and got some drinks from the bar, which they drank in the tight car space. When the young Dutchman handed her a drink, Diana noticed his slim, elegant hands, so much like those of a designer or an artist.

It was rather cold outside but Harry refused to start the motor in order to save gas. The vehicle was not the best of places to be; a short while later Jan offered to see Diana home.

She consented. 'If you'd like to, it's all right with me.'

Jan turned to Harry. 'Would you like to come along too?'

Harry shook his head. 'No, thanks. I'm going back to the bar. It's much too cold for me outdoors.'

It was, in fact, a cool night. The air was clean and crisp. They had to walk some twenty minutes to Diana's billet.

'Well, here we are,' Diana said, once they reached her destination. She pointed out a red brick building. 'This is where the WAAFs sleep. I must go right in. I'm afraid I'm already very late,' she hurriedly said, consulting her watch.

'When can I see you again?' Jan asked eagerly.

'I'm free tomorrow evening if you want. See you then, at the bar. Bye for now and thanks for the drinks.' Diana pivoted around, hurrying into the dark building.

After saying goodnight, Jan walked slowly back to his own quarters. Talking to Diana made him feel fine. He liked her. Deeply inhaling the cool, invigorating night air, he had a feeling of happiness, of light-heartedness, for the first time since his arrival in England – as if a thick haze had lifted to reveal a beautiful, sun-drenched countryside ahead of him. Back at his own quarters, Jan undressed, whistling a Dutch tune, and went to sleep with a contented, Mona Lisa-like smile on his lips.

The following evening, Jan went to the bar in a wonderful mood. After he had waited for over an hour, however, he decided it was time to leave. Diana hadn't shown up. It was a bad let-down. He didn't expect it of her: she seemed like such a nice, well-mannered young woman.

Just as Jan was moving away from the bar, a sergeant approached him cautiously. 'Are you the Dutch pilot who had an appointment with Diana?' he asked.

'Yes. Why, what's happened to her?' Jan sharply inquired.

A fleeting smile crossed the other man's face. 'Diana's been penalised for re-entering her billet too late last night. She's been confined to quarters for ten days and asked me to tell you she's very sorry not to make it tonight.'

Jan was grateful for the explanation. 'Thanks for letting me know. When you see Diana again, please tell her I'll be looking for her in about two weeks.' Jan stared at the sergeant seriously, and asked circumspectly, 'By the way – do you know her well?'

The man nodded. 'We work together in operations control. She's a pleasant, efficient colleague. Perhaps a bit dejected at times. She lost a very dear friend during the Battle of Britain. The poor fellow was shot down in September of 1940. Diana's been sort of keeping to herself and withdrawing ever since then. Her visiting mess the other evening was really out of character.'

'I'm sorry to hear that. The air war certainly claims its victims, doesn't it?'

The sergeant shrugged, not knowing what to say. 'Well, you know how it is,' he commented stoically.

After this short conversation, Jan went back to his quarters. In the meantime, the weather had taken a turn for the worse. He was forced to walk through an icy downpour before making it back to his lodgings, getting his uniform totally soaked. That evening, Jan wrote in his diary: 'Have been in- formed by a sergeant Diana's confined to camp for ten days because she was late. What a mess! I can't say the evening was a great success. Had imagined something quite different!'

All in all, such a promising evening had turned into a gloomy, dreary event. Jan felt blue and discouraged. He had been looking forward with great anticipation to a pleasant evening with Diana, but it had been a complete flop. Well, Jan thought philosophically to himself, we may meet again another time.

But the war was not waiting for them: Jan had to fly over Europe again the next day. Once in bed, hands folded behind his head to prop it up, he tried to visualise Diana. With those images whirling around in his mind, he slowly dropped off to sleep.

Jan went on leave during the next few days. Since Diana was still confined to camp, he decided to go to London. As was his habit, he stayed at the Dutch Club for two days. There he met another Dutchman, Chris Krediet, who had performed fantastic exploits during his time in England since 1940. He had already been twice escorted by English motor torpedo boats to the Dutch coast. There, he had landed in a tiny rubber life-raft on the beach of Scheveningen – a seaside resort. By crossing the beach and the wide boulevard on its other side, Krediet had made it into The Hague unobserved by the German Wehrmacht guards. After a few days in Holland, gathering necessary information, he had succeeded in escaping in the same ingenious way he had arrived. The motor torpedo boat picked him up at the scheduled time, and took him back safely to England – with the valuable knowledge he had obtained.

For these and other courageous actions, Krediet had been personally awarded the Order of William (the Dutch equivalent of the British Victoria Cross) for exceptional bravery, by Queen Wilhelmina.

Jan knew Chris Krediet well from his schooldays in The Hague. He was a friendly, well-mannered young man, and Jan enjoyed talking with him that evening. Chris was able to inform him that Plesman Senior was mentally and physically all right. The prison ordeal apparently had not done any major damage to his mental skills.

During their conversation, Chris told Jan how the situation had developed on the other side of the North Sea. The local scene was worsening rapidly, day by day, and the German occupation was becoming harsher. Many young Dutchmen forced to work in factories in Germany had simply disappeared when they were picked up during the military roundups that regularly took place in the big cities. Consequently, many young men had gone underground.

159

Jan also met another Dutch pilot during this leave, who had made several night flights to Holland to drop off or pick up members of the Dutch Underground. Curious, Jan asked how such an operation was carried out. He had always wanted to volunteer for these missions, and quizzed his new companion about the methods used. At last the pilot agreed to give Jan a rundown on how such dangerous missions were carried out.

'How do you do it?' Jan bluntly inquired.

'Well, I fly a single-engine Westland Lysander. From England over the Channel to the Dutch coast is rather uneventful but you must navigate very precisely. You can't afford to make mistakes and start flying circles over Holland. Once over the Netherlands, all the Underground can give you is one – or two, at the maximum – quick light signals from the area where you have to land. In a flat country like Holland, these signals can be observed over wide distances. I can assure you the Nazis – and the Gestapo especially – do not sleep at night.' He laughed significantly.

'I can just imagine,' Jan commented. 'Please continue – it's really exciting.'

'Underground members use a kind of covered lamp with blue lights to indicate the landing spot where I'm to touch down. Of course, it has to be changed every flight I make to the other side, understand? I can land that marvellous plane and take off again along a short, straight country road. I only need about two hundred yards of unobstructed flat ground for those purposes. That's all. After I disembark people from England and pick up those returning, I am ready for the next flight. You should see the faces of some of my passengers. I think they're more afraid of flying than of the Germans!' He laughed good-naturedly.

Jan listened attentively to every word. How he would like to carry out similar missions!

'Sometime it really gets quite exciting. The last time I took off, the Germans came racing over the road crossing my take-off direction with their headlights blazing. I just barely made it, skimming over the roofs of their vehicles.' The pilot smiled wryly at Jan.

Jan was impressed by the stories he heard from this courageous pilot, but his time was fully occupied by the regular missions he was making over Europe once or even twice a day. Every time out was risky enough for him.

After this interesting visit to London, Jan wanted to visit Geert at his base in South Cerney, Gloucestershire, to see how he was doing and celebrate the second anniversary of their remarkable escape from Holland.

By January 1943, Jan had already flown more than sixty missions. After 1941, 1942 had been much a better year for him. At least he had damaged the German occupiers of his country, and so he began 1943 on a more optimistic note. He looked forward to seeing a lot of Diana. He liked her a great deal, from the little he had seen of her.

In January, Jan wrote in his diary:

> I'm still convinced the Germans are going to lose the war by the end of 1943. They will be forced to ask for peaceful negotiations. At first, the American Air Force activities were slow; but with the passing of the months, they'll develop rapidly and massively. Daylight bombardments over Germany must be terrifying for the local population. I do wonder how long they're able to resist.

Recently, Jan had noticed the first Flying Fortresses and Liberators. Flying parallel to them, he had been impressed by the sheer size of these four-engined bombers compared with his small Spitfire.

Geert was also training regularly – on Lancasters, the bomber that was spreading such devastation over the German Ruhr. This time, Geert was more successful, and was approaching promotion to bomber captain.

England, and its empire in general, had certainly carried the weight of the war for the duration of 1941 and the greater part of 1942. But now, at last, American production facilities were becoming available, and would definitely turn the balance of the war in favour of the Allies. Jan remembered his father telling him, 'I'm afraid England by itself will not be able to hold out indefinitely. Perhaps, my boy, if the United States joins the British, the strategic balance will tip in favour of the Anglo-Saxon forces again.'

Eagerly, Jan looked forward to that victory, to being united with his family in Holland again.

XIV

OVER CHRISTMAS, Jan compared the two letters his father had written in the closing weeks of 1941 and 1942 respectively.

He could clearly see his father's greater optimism in the second letter. The elder Plesman wrote about how much there would be to rebuild once the war was over. One particular sentence struck Jan because it was so typical of his father: 'I hope that, wherever it can be done, a considerable effort will be made to render things and buildings beautiful.'

Jan was also grateful his father had finally told him he should not feel guilty about his escape from Holland and the consequences for his father – eleven months of total isolation in a small prison cell close to home.

Jan was pleased by his father's reassurance that he was proud and thankful for such a son and that he loved Jan deeply.

The second letter was already more optimistic simply because his father had finally been released from his solitary confinement and had been able to return to his home. Jan could tell that his father's words held new faith in a future he would be part of, and Jan was absolutely certain his father's energy would be abundant as soon as the war was over.

Albert Plesman

Enschede, 9 November 1942

Dear Jan,

Many happy returns for your birthday. May the next year bring us peace and you health and prosperity. I sincerely hope your hard work will be crowned with success. I also hope you will make a good career for yourself and will soon be able to shake hands with your parents once again.

Time goes by rather quickly. The year is already almost over. I'm sure 1943 will also pass swiftly. If only people began reasoning again, building a better world. I express the wish you'll work at something which satisfies you.

How are you getting along with the girls over there? Or would you rather wait to meet a solid, steady Dutch girl? Do you visit many good families? Always be sure to keep up good homey contacts: it's important.

I also hope you'll find the time to study, to promote your spiritual life. You can now lay the foundations for a good existence. Strengthen yourself and your character, but also take time off to relax.

I wish you a Merry Christmas and hope you are in a good mood, surrounded by a pleasant atmosphere. We shall think of you when your sister, brother and wife, and your aunt visit here. We shall toast your good health and your brother's in Switzerland. And we'll hope and pray you'll soon be among us, well and healthy.

It must be rather cold in those Swiss mountains, especially because there's so little coal [this is a reference to Jan's flying]. We can live here despite the coal shortage, and I do expect we'll survive reasonably during the coming winter.

As you can well imagine, I have plenty of time for study. When I relax, your mother and I take walks in the

164

beautiful surroundings of our forced temporary accommodation. Your mother is wonderful and a strong moral support. She enjoys the nature here. Our life only becomes rather gloomy here when it rains.

We appreciate and enjoy the living room. which is so big it actually consists of a double sitting room where we also eat and snugly sit around the hearth.

I lost quite a bit of weight last year because of my forced residence but being thinner will be useful later when I go back to my old work.

There's a small pond close to the house where we live. Your mother and I skate on it when it's frozen over. It was a bad summer, still I was able to swim and even play tennis a few times.

Mother and I visit church every Sunday; together we pray for peace and for all those who have to suffer and worry about their children's destiny. How much suffering there is in the world! I only hope a better one will emerge from all this. When it does, we will have to pay a tribute to those who died to make it all possible. May love return to make brothers of men again.

There will be so much to do so that brutalised people can live a decent life again. Many years will have to pass before the world settles down: many social changes will have to take place because of the long war. I hope commercial aviation will play an important role in regenerating what has been destroyed.

There'll be so much to build up again. Youth will have its hands full. I sincerely hope that, wherever it can be done, a considerable effort will be made to render things and buildings more beautiful. Being an architect after the war is over will certainly not be a bad job at all.

I hope you've made a lot of friends and have had enough time for self-thought and study. Jan, I hope your birthday will be a pleasant one. Unfortunately, we cannot spoil you, but we'll drink to your good health and express a wish to the Lord that he might protect and guide you to a better life.

Keep your contacts up with the Almighty, with Nature and the Universe in general. Be cheerful and try to make the best of things. We miss you. Your mother embraces you and I constantly think of you.

Your father

Having read the letters, Jan felt better. His father was now living with his mother in the east of Holland, close to the city of Enschede. From the last letter, he judged his father was regularly working again, preparing plans for the rebuilding of KLM Royal Dutch Airlines once the Netherlands had been liberated. Knowing this pleased Jan immensely.

Jan's mind was put more at ease: it now seemed merely a matter of time before he would be reunited with his family in Holland.

Jan looked forward to it eagerly – but would time be granted to him?

XV

DIANA WAS GOING over the events of the previous two weeks, thinking back to that first night in the WAAF mess when she had been having a drink with Harry and the hall door had swung open to reveal the young Dutchman she had noticed a few evenings before.

This time he had confidently marched straight up to her and Harry. Diana's eyes had widened when she saw him approach. At the same time, her heart had started to beat much faster; in fact, it was pounding in her chest. Once Harry had made the introductions, Diana became aware of a strange sensation flowing through her: a curious empathy for the tall, handsome, strong young Dutch pilot.

When Jan's grey-blue eyes stared at Diana, she felt as if an ocean of kindness embraced her. She also noticed his profound shyness and could sense that he was a highly sensitive lad. His English was perfect, yet she could detect some traces of his accent in the few words he spoke – it sounded charming to her.

A while later, when the atmosphere inside the mess had become rather oppressive Jan had invited her to the officers' mess – just a short walk away.

She had accepted just to please Jan, but the three of them had completely overlooked the rules that prevented Diana – a mere sergeant – from entering the officers' mess.

Jan had immediately apologised. 'If you're patient enough, Diana, I'll get you and Harry a drink from our bar and then we can sip it in Harry's car. What about it?'

Though annoyed, Diana had agreed to his suggestion and they enjoyed their drinks and continued their conversation sitting inside the small car parked outside the mess. The windows had frosted over immediately, making the limited space even more confined and oppressive.

It had been a rather cold and eerie experience, but as a result Diana had met the Dutchman for whom a strange attraction was beginning to warm her heart.

Later, when Harry had excused himself, she had walked back to her billet with the Dutchman, and made a date for the following evening when she would have some hours off.

Jan had stirred Diana's emotions, and was about the same age as George. He did not exactly remind her of George, but there was a certain affinity – both radiated an immense inner kindness. Perhaps George had acted rather more forcefully, but then Diana had only known the flying Dutchman for a few hours.

The following morning, Diana was told to report to her commanding officer. As she stood to attention, she was informed in no uncertain terms that she was confined to barracks after hours for the next ten days – because she had returned one hour late the previous night.

The bad news shocked Diana and made her desperate. How could she get a message to the Dutchman when she couldn't even meet him after duty? She didn't want him to think she had stood him up.

During her entire duty day in operations, Diana was at a loss about what to do. Jan would be standing at the bar that same evening, vainly waiting for her. He would be very disappointed if she didn't show up.

Returning to her billet in a bad, dark mood that afternoon, Diana met a sergeant she knew from the ops room and begged him to contact a tall Dutch pilot at the bar and let him know she had been confined to quarters for ten days.

The next day, very concerned, Diana asked the sergeant if he had been able to pass on her message. He assured her he had spoken to Jan, who had said he understood and was sorry he hadn't paid more attention to the time the previous night.

On hearing this news, an appreciative smile came over Diana's lovely face. At least, the Dutchman wasn't mad at her.

When the ten days had passed, Diana immediately tried to see Jan again in the WAAF mess. To her disappointment, she was told he had gone on leave to London. The information made her feel blue.

Nearly two interminable weeks passed. Finally, Diana saw Jan again, standing at the bar drinking a beer as usual.

'Jan, how are you?' she asked cheerfully. 'Long time no see!' She spoke with a friendly smile, tossing him a fond glance.

'Hello, Diana. I'm sorry you got back late the night I walked you home. It may have been my fault. How have you been?'

Diana shrugged. 'Oh, all right, I guess. I've been working a lot these days and meeting you again I should enjoy this evening. That's the least I can expect after being bottled up for ten days. Don't you agree?' Now her blue eyes twinkled playfully.

'Of course! That's the right spirit. What can I do for you? Would you like to start the evening out right with a drink?' Jan asked kindly.

Diana nodded. 'Yes, please I'll have a small whisky if that's not shocking. It'll be a bit of a pick-me-up after a hard day's work. We Australians love to drink whisky – it gives a little pep, you know,' Diana affirmed with a hint of bravado.

'Now, before we get the time mixed up again, when do you have to be back at your quarters. That way, I'll keep an eye on my watch and make a flight plan – if you understand what I mean.' Jan grinned at her.

'Fine! I'll completely depend on you then tonight. You'll be my cavalier – or should I say my air knight perhaps? How

169

does that sound to you, huh, Flying Dutchman?' Diana asked, a little mockingly.

He half-smiled. 'Sounds romantic to me. But, if you want, I'll be your timekeeper. Tell me how you're doing in the operations room? I'm really interested in your activities.'

Diana stared questioningly at him. 'You know what the ops room layout looks like, don't you?'

'Yes, I've visited several, but please continue.'

'For example, I can follow your squadron when you're out over the North Sea and a part of the European coastline – but I've no idea who's piloting the planes, of course.' Diana threw him a mocking glance. 'We only move discs with squadron numbers. We push them around, via radio instructions we receive in our headphones, over the big flat map with long wooden sticks. A bit like croupiers at a roulette table, you know. I must admit at times it can be quite exciting. Sometimes, it's nerve-racking, especially when we know there have been losses.' As she spoke these words, a shadow passed fleetingly over her features.

Jan stared at her. 'It's a shame you only see the numbers, otherwise you could follow me over Holland, Belgium and north-west France.' Out of curiosity, Jan asked, 'Why is an Australian like you performing military duty here in England?'

'Well, that's a long story. After my father's death in Sydney, my mother moved to London with me and my younger sister Jane. At the time of leaving Australia, my mother thought it would be better for us to study in England. But the war upset all her carefully laid plans. My sister and I joined the WAAF – and here I am! What about you?' Diana shot Jan a questioning look. She wanted to know more about him.

'Well, at the end of 1940, I left Holland with a friend of mine called Geert Overgauw. We cycled all the way from Holland via Belgium and France to the Spanish border. From there, we took a train to Portugal. Then, KLM Royal Dutch Airlines helped by flying us from Lisbon to England. Once I arrived in Britain, I was forced to waste half a year training on several types of aircraft before I was allowed to climb aboard Spitfires. So here I am – flying operationally at last.'

'Have you any specific plans now that you're based at Ludham?' Diana asked, staring into his eyes for a second.

'First of all, I have to shoot down a Luftwaffe plane. That, Diana, represents an absolute sine qua non for me,' Jan stated firmly. 'Then I'll see if I can make it to the end of the war alive. With the numbers of flights we have to carry out these days, it's a big question mark,' he said seriously.

'Don't let it influence you. You'll surely make it home in one piece,' she smiled encouragingly.

'You know, there's a chance a completely Dutch fighter squadron will be formed one day with only Dutch pilots making up the ranks. They're dispersed nowadays among several British squadrons all over England. If the Continent should ever be invaded, I assume we'll probably have to move overseas until the end of the war. Then, when it's over, we'll all go home. Perhaps I'll go to the trouble of picking up my engineering studies in Delft again where I left off. Who knows.'

'Well,' Diana smiled sweetly. 'That was quite a speech! Now I know all about your ideas but tell me, Jan, what exactly did you study and where is Delft – I don't know.'

'I was a student in Delft. It's a small historic city about fifteen kilometres from The Hague where I lived. At Technical High School, I studied engineering but, if I must be truthful,' he laughed at her, 'I didn't get much done the first year. I had to join the Dutch Air Force for regular military duty and then I was mobilised just before the outbreak of the war. I flew operations in a marvellous old antiquated Fokker biplane during the four days the war lasted in Holland.'

'Do you always want to be a pilot?' Diana asked. 'Even after the war?'

Jan shook his head. 'No I don't think so. Maybe I'll return to Technical High School to finish what I started. I really think I'm still young enough.' Jan glanced at Diana again. She felt she was being engulfed by a wave of kindness and warmth when she stared into those deep-set grey-blue eyes. It was like sitting in front of an open hearth while the heat of the flames warmed her, making her feel so comfortable. She had never experienced such an emotional phenomenon before in the presence of a man. Diana even felt a bit intimidated by the new sensation; it had never happened to her before, not even with George – with whom she had been so deeply in love. The odd, indefinable feeling disturbed and disoriented her.

Generally, men stared at her, turning their heads to throw admiring glances. Diana knew she was attractive, with a fine, well-developed body and elegant, shapely legs that she was proud of. But no one she had ever met gave her the kind of sensation the Flying Dutchman did when she met him. She sensed she was being drawn into a new, mysterious world of warmth, tenderness and kindness. Diana felt as if a wave of strong sympathy was sweeping through her – a benign, friendly feeling of being absorbed by some kind of strong magnetic force. Could it be that, ever so slowly, Diana was being introduced into a new world of love?

She studied Jan's face closely. 'Who else in your family has the same colour eyes? They're really nice, you know,' she commented.

Under Diana's intense gaze, Jan blushed. 'My mother, I think. She's a kind – a very kind – woman. I miss her a great deal and, unfortunately, I haven't seen her for over two years.' His eyes misted over.

'She lives on the other side of the Channel, under the harsh German occupation. My father was imprisoned by the Gestapo and was a hostage for over eleven months. He had to pass all that time in a small cell, in solitary confinement, but now I know he's free again …'

'Oh, that's awful!' Diana interrupted. 'Can you send your parents a few Red Cross parcels from time to time?'

Jan nodded. 'Yes, I can. My parents were ordered to move out of their house near The Hague. They had to settle down in east Holland, close to the German border, near the city of Enschede. They weren't allowed to go on living in our Hague house,' he blurted out angrily. The hard expression on his face revealed how much rage was stored within him. The knowledge impressed Diana.

'Are you allowed to write to them?' she asked.

'Now and then – I write via the Lisbon KLM Office but I'm sure the censors cut out half the contents of my letters. I'd like to do so much more for them but I'm afraid it's impossible.' Jan checked his watch. 'Hey, Diana – I think it's time to take you home. Shall we walk like the last time or would you like to ride my bike side-saddle? It's not very comfortable, though,' he apologised with a smile.

Diana also glanced at her watch. 'I still have thirty minutes. Let's walk. The fresh air will do us good,' she suggested. 'I think we'll make it in twenty minutes.'

They left the mess together. It was cold outside.

Jan reached his right hand out. She took it. They silently walked through the dark. The stars above twinkled brightly. The temperature had to be below zero.

When they reached Diana's billet, she turned to him to say goodnight. Jan spread his strong arms around her, enclosing her tightly in them, tenderly kissing her forehead, nose and lips. 'Goodnight, dear Diana – sleep well. Hope to see you soon. I have to be on standby again tomorrow. Perhaps you'll spot my squadron moving over the big map.'

Resting her head a second on his chest, Diana looked up at him, whispering into his ear, 'Dear Jan – take good care of yourself please.' Then she quickly broke free of his embrace, kissed him, and disappeared inside her lodgings, waving at him.

Diana felt good – exhilarated. It had been such a long time since she'd kissed a man and she felt a surge of happiness flowing through her. At last, she had met a friend who interested her. A kind-hearted, good, decent friend.

On meeting Jan, she had immediately sensed his obvious shyness. But she liked him at first sight and, now that she had chatted with him, felt even more attracted to the Dutch pilot.

Smiling dreamily at her own image in the mirror, she noticed how her eyes sparkled just like diamonds in the floodlights of a jeweller's shop window. Her cheeks felt cool and were rosy from the cold night air.

Diana felt happiness flowing through her whole body. It felt as if she was lazily floating down a river, lying on her back on the bottom of a flat boat with the sun glowing overhead, warming her. Just lying there, not thinking about anything in particular – gliding along ethereally.

She sighed happily. It would have been wonderful to hold on to this fleeting moment of happiness forever, but Diana was only too aware harsh reality could tear the feelings away; she had to go on with her daily routine, problems and all, moving those circular objects over the map to track aircraft movements.

This idea shocked Diana – her thoughts and emotions in an uproar, she saw the disturbing vision of Jan in his tiny Spitfire cockpit, on a mission the next day over Europe, perhaps about to engage an enemy pilot in battle – each equally ready to kill the other.

It was like the Middle Ages, she thought. Then, there were knights in shining armour on horses, armed with shields, swords or lances. Now these pilots – knights of the air – sat behind twelve-hundred horsepower engines, an armoured shield protecting their backs, armed with eight machine guns or four cannon on the wings for terrific firepower, approaching and stalking each other at speeds of nearly 400 miles per hour in a three-dimensional fight taking place tens of thousands of feet above the earth's crust.

Diana's stomach contracted into knots. She suddenly felt miserable and confused. She thought she might die merely thinking about what might happen the next day to all those young men up there in the sky – especially her precious Flying Dutchman.

Diana hated war. When the sly, unreliable, hypocritical politicians could not reach a suitable agreement, it was the young men who had to be sacrificed in an insane armed conflict, maiming the future promising generations of every country involved.

And it was almost always the men who crossed swords while anxious women sat waiting for the combat's outcome, wondering if they would ever see their beloved ones come back alive.

So it would be the next day – while Diana followed the progress of 167 Squadron in the ops room, Jan would be one of the active pilots. Sliding the discs from one part of the map to another, Diana would know only the squadron number, not which plane was his. Not until after the planes had landed with their crews would Diana be informed if any of the young men or craft were missing – POWs perhaps – or dead!

Dreamily reminiscing over her meeting with Jan, Diana became aware she had once again developed a strong attraction, a feeling of sympathy, for a fighter pilot – this time, a Dutch one.

Diana remembered vividly how George had told her he could die any day of the week. At that time, during the summer of 1940, the Luftwaffe had a three-to-one advantage in numbers of planes. But despite the Luftwaffe's numerical strength, the British pilots were far superior to the Teutonic ones in spirit, and perhaps also in the overall techniques of aerial warfare, even though German pilots had gained considerable experience in the Condor legion during the Spanish Civil War.

George had also told her about the slight advantage British fighters had over the Luftwaffe pilots approaching from France despite their superior numbers. The British were advised and forewarned by a new invention – radar – which helped keep them informed of the directions from where the compact Luftwaffe squadrons set out on their way to the south of England. It had given the Allied fighter pilots a slight edge over the German ones – just what they needed to over-come the inferiority in numbers and balance the score.

Wistfully, she hoped she would never have to pass through another day of being informed the one she loved would never come back to her. Anything but to be forced to fill that terrible black void again. She had already suffered enough, Diana judged.

She slept badly that night, turning and twisting and tossing on her narrow metal cot. In her nightmares, she imagined dozens of Fw 190s circling around one lonely Spitfire – her Flying Dutchman at its controls, desperately trying to outwit and out-turn the threatening pack of aggressive Teutonic hawks hunting him. Then, at last, the Spitfire banked sharply, showing its light blue belly to be hit by hundreds of bullets, and spiralled slowly down like a wounded bird, leaving a trail of thick black smoke behind it.

With a loud cry of anguish, Diana started awake in panic. Staring into the dark, eyes wide open, terrified, she desper-ately whispered 'No!' into the darkness – 'No, no, no!'

The next morning Diana rose early, and splashed cold water on her face to clear her mind from sleep deprivation and be ready for the day's duties. At breakfast, she drank two cups of strong black coffee to help her confront the day.

Entering the operations room, Diana was immediately aware of the tension always present and tangible when fighters and bombers mounted a massive raid against conti-nental targets. Many of the WAAFs in the ops room had friends among the pilots participating in the hazardous flights over Europe. Their thoughts and prayers always silently, anxiously and hopefully accompanied the flyers putting their lives at stake for the common effort of defeating the Nazis.

Unobtrusively, Diana took her place on one side of the big table, ready to shift the small coloured discs indicating the numbers of the squadrons taking part in the raid.

Suddenly, she noticed the disc numbered 167 – Jan's squadron – being pushed over the map in the direction of the

North Sea. Diana felt a pang of anguish and tension in the pit of her stomach. She suffered in silence and forced herself to concentrate on the work, now and then stealing a quick, apprehensive glance at that particular small disc and its movement towards Holland. Before, Diana had been rather indifferent to the dynamics of the discs being pushed across the map; now that damned small object represented a person very dear to her.

After two hours of intense activity, she saw the disc bearing number 167 being pushed back towards England until one of the girls bent forward to pick it up indifferently and put it back in its container. Many discs, each with a different number, were silently waiting to be used again and again. Here, merely impersonal figures were involved. Up in the air, it was a matter of human lives, dear to the girls in operations, fighting to stay alive, being saved or lost on these numerous, interminable flights.

Diana didn't dare ask anyone if 167 Squadron had suffered any losses and continued her duties normally. By the end of the afternoon, the losses were chalked up on a big blackboard. Reading the figures, she noticed to her despair that 167 Squadron had lost two planes! Diana felt crushed. She could have burst into tears in a corner of the big room not knowing who the two missing pilots were.

Could one of them be her Flying Dutchman?

Again, Diana bitterly reflected that women were always the ones to anxiously and passively await the outcome of the raging battle.

When the clock in the ops room read seven, someone took Diana's place on duty. She immediately hurried, even running occasionally, over the big airfield to the WAAF mess where she hoped to find him.

Would he still be alive?

Diana felt she badly needed a drink. Her nerves were so tense, so exhausted from the day's emotions.

Would Jan be standing at the bar, waiting for her?

Diana asked herself this while catching her breath before entering, hesitantly reaching with her right hand for the door handle, not knowing what to expect. She dreaded this moment of uncertainty.

On entering the room and being enveloped by the stale, bluish smoke that hung thick in the air, she shot a glance at the bar. Yes, he stood there, innocently smiling at her in an almost apologetic way. A half-empty glass of beer stood on the counter in front of him.

Diana could have laughed and cried at the same time knowing he was there. Her first impulse was to run over to him, throw her arms around his broad shoulders, embrace him, plant passionate kisses all over his face as if it might protect him from any threat of danger, and tell him how happy she was he had safely returned. Again, she felt warm all over.

But she checked herself and walked normally over to where he stood at the bar. He stared at her tenderly. 'Hello, Diana. Did you have a tough day? The squadron got into quite a show over Holland this time. We accompanied twenty-four bombers to Ymuiden, close to Amsterdam where the huge iron works are – or rather were, I should say. From what I could see, I believe the raid caused a lot of damage. I saw many fires burning out of control. Would you like a drink?'

Diana noticed the twinkle in his tired eyes and the deep wrinkles etched in his face. His drawn features reflected what he must have been through during the past three hours. She did not like the sound of his tired voice, knowing he deliberately withheld his dangerous flight experiences from her,

Diana placed her right hand on his sleeve. 'Jan, I do need a whisky, if you don't mind, after all of today's excitement. Did you lose anyone?' she inquired, with hesitation.

A shadow passed over Jan's face. 'Yes, unfortunately – we lost two fighter pilots. One was shot down over Amsterdam; the other had engine trouble over the Channel on his way back but managed to bail out close to the English coast. I assume air-sea rescue must have found him by now. But enough talk about the damn war! Let's enjoy ourselves now that we're together.'

Warmly, Diana smiled at him. 'I do agree with you.' She raised her glass to him, tinkling the ice cubes. 'Here's to you, brave Flying Dutchman.'

He thoughtfully looked at her. 'Say, Diana, I've got leave coming up soon. Any chance of seeing each other in London? Maybe we could go to a show or a movie. Something like that. How about it?'

She shrugged. 'I can't give you an answer right now. The idea is very appealing. I've got to check the next roster in the ops room. Maybe I can ask next week. Is that close enough to your plans?'

Jan nodded. 'Yes, that's fine – provided the Luftwaffe doesn't prepare any surprises for me! May I say you look very charming tonight? Your blue eyes have a special bright sparkle to them. Is it the whisky, perhaps?' He grinned at her.

Diana looked at him with amusement and satisfaction. 'Or maybe something quite different, Dutchie. May I call you that sometimes?' She tilted her head, a delicate smile on her mouth. She wasn't at all sure if he was going to like that nickname.

Jan showed his surprise. 'Dutchie?' he repeated. 'No, please Diana ...' He shook his head, hesitating a moment. 'I don't particularly like that name. Please call me by my own. If it's good enough for me, it's also good enough for you I hope,' he insisted.

Diana didn't say a word, mysteriously smiling at him, as if it was her secret, as if something stored in her mind would eventually be revealed.

Diana not only noticed the tension lines in Jan's face but she also became aware of a kind of physical exhaustion showing beneath his hollow eyes. She detected the dark circles of fatigue. She fully realised that, despite his cheerful mood, Jan was covering up the nervous strains of that day. She knew from her ops room activity that afternoon that he had flown twice to the other side of the Channel – over four hours of strenuous flying.

Staring at his grey face, she warmly asked, 'Are you very tired, Jan?'

'A little, to tell the truth,' Jan admitted. 'It turned out to be quite a circus today. There were Focke Wulfs all over the place this time. They're formidable antagonists you can't underestimate or you're in for a surprise,' he said in a serious voice.

'Why don't we move over to my private place. My sister Jane and I own a crazy little houseboat close to my billet. She'll be there too. I'm sure you'd like a cup of tea and some sandwiches. Okay?' Diana gave Jan an inviting look.

'A splendid idea! Let's go. How long will it take us to get there?'

'Like the last time – about twenty minutes.'

They left the bar. As soon as they were outside, Diana impulsively threw her arms around his neck. Standing on tiptoe, she kissed him affectionately. 'Jan, I'm so happy. I don't know why.' A radiant smile showed on her face when she stared at him.

He was completely taken by surprise but returned the kiss and softly said to her, 'I'm glad to be with you again.' Then he chuckled and said, somewhat in retaliation, 'Aussie …'

Now it was her turn to look surprised. Hand in hand, they walked to the houseboat where Jan was introduced to Jane – as good-looking as her older sister. Jan thought Jane looked more sexy. Diana entered the kitchenette to make tea for the three of them while he talked to Jane.

'Are you also working in operations, like Diana?' Jan asked.

'Yes, we do the same kind of work. I also have to type reports. Very dull, really. You fellows up in the air, you've got all the fun while we poor WAAFs have to perform the boring work.'

At that moment, Diana entered carrying a tray with a teapot and cups. She carefully set it down on the table, at the same time scolding her younger sister. 'How dare you say "fun"! Can't you see how tired the poor Dutchman is?'

Diana consulted him before pouring. 'Do you want your tea with milk and sugar?'

Jan nodded. 'Yes, thanks, but Diana …' He raised his right hand to stop her. 'Please don't pour like the British do. If I may say what I prefer, I'd like to have the tea poured first into the cup and then add a little milk, please. Here in England, practically everyone puts a lot of milk in the cup and tea on top. In my opinion it makes the tea taste different and, allow me to say, worse.'

Once he had made known his preferences, he smiled apologetically at Diana for being so difficult.

'My! How fancy can one get?' she exclaimed mockingly. 'All right, have it your way, Dutchie. Is that the way they drink tea in Holland?' she queried.

'That's the way my mother always prepared it at home,' Jan replied.

Carefully, Diana filled his cup as he had asked her to. Then she tried it herself, feeling curious. After having tasted it with small sips, she affirmed, 'Well, I must admit, you've got a point in your favour. Indeed, it tastes better – more like real tea.'

Silently, Jan smiled knowingly.

Diana sat down next to him on the small sofa, slipping her arm through his. The three of them valued and enjoyed this peaceful and homey moment together in the small houseboat. Diana with her presence created a warm, cosy atmosphere wherever she happened to be – just what Jan so badly needed.

Jan highly appreciated Diana's gesture of inviting him for a late tea after his mission. They listened to classical and light jazz music. Of all things, she insisted on reading him a number of stories written by Hans Anderson. Jan liked that very much. They passed a pleasant evening and the time flew by. The better Jan knew Diana, the more he realised she was quite an exceptional young woman. She was not only good-looking but also possessed a great, warm, human heart.

At midnight, he had to leave. 'Diana, I have to get back to my quarters. Tomorrow I have to fly to the Continent again. I must get some rest before take-off.'

At the door of the small cabin, Jan turned to Diana. 'You've been a darling, inviting me here to your cosy little place. I feel really rested. Thanks for the lovely evening.'

He also said goodbye to Jane. After Diana had given him a quick kiss, Jan walked out into the dark night towards his quarters. A warm feeling of happiness burned inside him: he was no longer alone. At last he had found a friend and a very true and loving one at that. The balance of his personal interests, as of that evening, had most probably shifted from stale, ineffectual thoughts of Holland and his family, to England. There, a sweet, understanding, exceptional, lovely Australian girl with a quixotic sense of humour – Diana – had now become foremost in his mind. It was just what he needed at that time.

When Diana returned to the cabin, Jane asked, 'Now where did you find that handsome, simpatico Dutchman? He's a darling!'

Diana fixed her younger sister darkly. 'He's mine and you stay away from him! Is that clear?'

Mockingly, Jane stared at her sister. 'You like him that much?' she asked, a trifle surprised.

Diana didn't say a word and ignored the question, but her eyes expressed the same threatening look as a lioness protecting her cubs from danger.

Yes, she realised, she liked Jan very much!

XVI

WEATHER permitting, 167 Squadron engaged the Luftwaffe frequently during the first six months of 1943. Jan flew many escort missions over Holland and Belgium. He also made a number of sweeps and low level attacks on moving targets and as escort to bombers on their runs over industrial targets. Jan noticed bitterly that the hostile flak increased with every flight he made.

In his log book, Jan mentioned:

Close escort to twin-engined Ventura bombers. And also close escort to 12 Boston bombers to Flushing, a small city on Walcheren island. Close escort to 12 twin-engined Lockheed Ventura bombers. Target the iron-works at Velsen, west of Amsterdam.

In his diary, Jan wrote, on Monday 29 March:

Nine o'clock take-off. Rendezvous with 24 twin-engined Ventura bombers over Coltishall. The bombers entered Holland close to the city of Rotterdam to bomb the assigned targets. Return to Ludham at eleven o'clock. Afternoon – second take-off and a sweep over western Holland. It was a beautiful day, not a cloud in the blue sky. Again, I was able to observe the house where I lived with my parents before my escape to

England. Flying high over it made me think a lot. How much time has already gone by since I said goodbye to my father and mother.

Tuesday 30 March:

Quarter to eight in the morning. Carried out several stunt flights over the airfield. I was in the air for over one hour. Later, I had to carry out two exercises in squadron formation flying over England.

Wednesday 31 March:

Squadron flying again over England during the morning. Afternoon free, I could pay a visit to Diana's little houseboat. She's a marvellous girl.

Sunday 4 April:

A show over Holland again. It was a beautiful day. Flew escort to 24 twin-engined Lockheed Ventura bombers which were going to bomb targets around Rotterdam. On the way back we were attacked by a pack of Focke Wulfs. Got one on my tail who shot repeatedly at me but I outmanoeuvred him. After I had landed, I was informed that Cassidy was missing.

That same evening, Jan wrote again in his diary:

It is always the good fellows who don't return from their operational flights. What a dreadful pity he's lost. Shall miss him, he was such a nice chap.

And so it continued. A small city close to Rotterdam – Maassluis – had to be bombed. Dordrecht, the city he cycled past while going south to Spain. Den Helder, a naval base, the airfield on Texel Island, were all hit as were so many other locations in Holland. Zeebrugge and Ghent in Belgium were also hit by the bombers he had to accompany. And on every flight he risked meeting Focke Wulfs.

Frequently, due to the intense anti-aircraft fire from the ground, the bombers were shaken and tossed about as if an earthquake had wracked the air they were flying in. At other times, the squadron was engaged in air battles with Focke Wulfs and Messerschmitts. Several were shot down, but the squadron every now and then lost a number of pilots.

Occasionally 167 Squadron escorted B-24 Liberators and B-17 Flying Fortresses. Flying escort to heavy bomber-groups was no joyride – it required concentrated, precise piloting for more than three hours at least. Spitfires were not equipped with automatic pilots – and then there was the ever-threatening flak thrown up by the German anti-aircraft batteries.

Jan also flew a number of covers for air-sea rescue operations over the Channel and the North Sea.

On 19 April, Jan wrote in his diary:

> Accompanied Beaufighter torpedo aircraft over the Channel. They sank two German ships. It was quite exciting seeing the devastating results of their attack.

By now, Jan had flown more than eighty missions over Europe and had become one of the squadron's veterans. He had seen many come and go, but he and Kees – another Dutch pilot – were still there and active.

For a long time, Jan had looked forward to and expected to be promoted to the rank of Flight Lieutenant. Oddly enough, even though several other Dutch pilots in other British squadrons had received quick upgrades, Jan and his Dutch colleague Kees – dark-haired, with intense dark brown eyes and an RAF moustache – had kept their ranks as Pilot Officer. Both men were sorely disappointed and irritated. They felt they were being treated as second-rate officers. It was just neither right nor fair. Jan was determined to do something about it.

Jan could not understand why the two of them had been excluded from any kind of promotion so far. He decided to contact the Dutch Air Force office in London during one of his next leaves and complain about the unreasonable treatment.

Jan loathed those god-awful accommodating officers in their well-heated offices. They sat so primly and so straight behind their desks – in clean uniforms, with their trouser creases so freshly ironed – while the only minute risk they ran was being bombed during the night when the Luftwaffe sporadically sent one of their bombers on a run over London. Asleep in their warm beds, their liabilities were minimal, practically zero!

When on leave, Jan turned up at the Air Force Office where he spoke to one of the commanding Dutch officers.

'Sir, I have carried out close to one hundred operational missions over the Continent but I'm still a Pilot Officer instead of a Flight Lieutenant. I believe I'm entitled to an advance in rank. Others who took the same training courses I did, and who have flown considerably fewer operational flights, have already been promoted in other English squadrons – a few even to the rank of Squadron Leader. I don't understand why. Since I'm part of the same group, I really can't fathom why I haven't been promoted yet.'

The officer opposite him stared at him rather stiffly, nervously shifting about in his chair. 'You may be aware we are still trying to put together an all-Dutch fighter squadron. We want you to gain as much experience as possible while you fly with the Royal Air Force.' The man took a deep breath before continuing. 'Then, when you become part of the Dutch squadron, you can expect much quicker promotions.'

Smiling bitterly at the officer, Jan said, 'That may be right, sir. But I'm over Europe practically once, if not twice, a day while waiting for that to happen. I can assure you those operational flights are no picnics! The Luftwaffe are not exactly shooting peas at us from the ground or in the air. I may not even be alive any longer when the all-Dutch squadron is formed. I insist I be promoted Flight Lieutenant at least, having carried out so many missions. May I remind you, sir, American pilots go home after completing fifty flights over Europe. I've effected close to one hundred and have received no promotion so far. That's unfair, sir!' Jan spoke heatedly, becoming angrier by the minute as he spoke to the motionless bureaucrat in front of him.

The officer blinked nervously. 'I promise you I'll look into the matter of your delayed promotion. You must realise I have to contact the Royal Air Force. However, you may rest assured I'll give your request the utmost consideration.' A stereotype answer from an archetypal bumbledom apparatchik. Spoken in a voice as dull and empty as the bureaucratic mind in which it was conceived.

Jan glared contemptuously at the insignificant little official in front of him. If looks could kill, the inconspicuous uniformed invertebrate would have been dead right on the spot.

Jan got to his feet, saluted smartly and sardonically stated, 'Thank you for your interest, sir.'

Disgusted with it all, Jan left the building in a huff. The conversation had turned into a total failure – as he had anticipated. Unhappily, he realised he hadn't obtained what was rightfully his. His brain pounded with a deep anger at those indifferent government servants sitting motionless behind their desks on their fat buttocks, indolently waiting until the war was over, without getting involved too much, without running any real risk of being killed.

If these dwarves ever ventured to make a real decision, they could make a mistake which might delay the automatic promotions built into the systems of their military careers. A well-placed stamp on a document meant more to them than the just claims of a fighter pilot regularly meeting the enemy head-on in air combat. Some of the most dangerous fighting of the war was being carried out by those who had risked their lives to come to England and fight, who were airborne nearly every day, meeting the mauling German war machine as it still ground away, with many victims as its grim result. The Nazis had not been defeated by any means: the losses of pilots and planes chalked up on the blackboards at many British airfields were stark reminders that the Luftwaffe was fighting back.

Having nothing else to do and in a sombre, morose mood, Jan proceeded to the Dutch Club to forget all about the irritating experience. By sheer coincidence, and to his pleasant surprise, he ran into Geert – also on leave in London.

'Hallo, Jan – how are things with you?' Geert looked Jan over. 'You are angry. I can see it from the expression in your eyes. Tell me, what happened to you? Can I be of any help?' he inquired sympathetically.

Having no one else to reveal his grudges to while Diana was still at Ludham, Jan told Geert about what had made him so angry. 'I've just returned from the Dutch Air Force headquarters. Those characters told me I still have to wait for my rightful promotion to Flight Lieutenant. Be patient, they said, even though I've flown more than a hundred missions over Europe.'

Geert shook his head compassionately. 'For Heaven's sake, Jan, let's not ruin our afternoon talking about the Dutch staff at the Air Force Office here in London! I've never seen such a bunch of lazy incompetent bureaucrats. But what can you do? We seem to be the tiniest teeth in the gears of a big clock relentlessly ticking away without getting any recognition for our efforts.'

Jan sighed heavily. 'You're so right. Let's not spoil our afternoon griping away. It creates such a negative atmosphere and we're in London to enjoy ourselves. Right?'

Geert nodded. 'Right! Let's have tea and cakes first, and then a touch of the stronger stuff later.'

'Ja!' Jan commented. 'But you take it easy with the liquor – I still remember the last time. We do have plenty of time ahead of us, don't we?' he asked with an ironic smile.

'We certainly have. It's no use fighting windmills. Hey, that sounds funny coming from a Dutchman!' Geert remarked and they both laughed, breaking Jan's tense, angry mood.

Over tea, they reminisced about their former years in Holland. Life had been kind to them. Their fathers – as managers in big commercial firms – had provided them with the necessary financial means to study and fully enjoy their free time. But then they had had to join the Dutch Air Force for normal military service and had flown plenty of hours in Holland on those antiquated Fokker planes.

Once in England, Jan and Geert had been utterly disappointed by having to repeat most of the flying practices and procedures they were already familiar with, causing them to lose valuable time. Both had expected a very intense short training course in flying after their arrival in England, to be followed by missions in Hurricanes or Spitfires, or even bombers.

Anyway, here they were, sipping English tea in the Dutch Club. Two and a half years had passed and Geert still had yet to drop his first bomb on a European target. He was still busy training on four-engined Lancaster bombers but approaching the critical moment when he too would regularly fly operationally over the Continent.

Cup in hand, Geert said, 'Jan, you've at least something positive to your credit. You're approaching the crucial point. You've been over Europe over a hundred times and have never been shot down. But, my friend, your survival percentage is becoming rather unfavourable to you,' Geert commented speculatively.

'Don't scare me, Geert,' Jan smiled thinly. 'I know that's true but I still have to shoot down my first Luftwaffe plane. You know, during an aerial combat with a Focke Wulf the other day, I think I got one. It went down, spinning out of control, but I wasn't sure of the outcome: I had to return to the bombers to protect them. Maybe I did get my first one,' Jan said with a hint of pride.

'Did you report it as a probable?' Geert asked anxiously.

Jan shook his head. 'No. And I haven't claimed all the flights I made to the Continent, or air-sea rescue, not passing over the European coast line as completed missions. Others have. But perhaps the film shots will confirm my claim to have hit a Focke Wulf,' Jan spoke with a hint of pride.

For a moment, Geert stared seriously at his compatriot. 'Jan …' he spoke hesitantly, as if he were doubtful about what he wanted to explain, 'if anything should ever happen to me, will you visit my parents in Holland after the war and tell them about our lives here in England? What we did and didn't do? In short, tell them all about it.' Again, Geert hesitated. 'You know, I think they would really appreciate it,' he added as an afterthought.

A fleeting, melancholy smile appeared on Jan's mouth. 'Will you do the same for me?' he asked soberly.

Geert nodded. 'You know, it's not that I'm afraid to die. But there are moments I'm scared stiff – when a part of the plane doesn't work right, engine failures and all that. Mind you, I'm still training. I haven't got the operational experience you've accumulated,' he laughed dryly.

'I die a thousand times every flight over to the other side,' said Jan. 'When you see the sky around you covered by all those black mushroom-like puffs of greyish smoke indicating heavy hostile flak, you do realise the intensity of anti-aircraft fire. It seems to me it's growing in strength every day. I can assure you, Geert, it makes you wish you were somewhere else when you're flying through it. Still, I set my mind on the kind of fighting I do and accept the consequences. You can't simply step out of your cockpit and say "Excuse me, fellows – I think I've had enough!" Don't you agree?' Jan stared at his friend.

Geert shrugged. 'Hell, I'm sorry I brought the subject up in the first place. Let's forget it.'

But Jan insisted. 'I want you to know I've officially written down that Koen Parmentier, KLM's chief pilot, is my next of kin here in England. If something happens to me, I hope he'll inform my father about what I tried to do. He's a fine man and extremely capable. When I talk with him, he sometimes reminds me of my father, even though he's much younger.'

'Okay, I think we've said all we can on that subject. I hope we'll both return to Holland alive and laugh about our war adventures and experiences,' Geert grinned slyly at Jan.

Once they'd finished their tea, they went to the Aero Club for a drink. There they met colleagues of different nationalities from other squadrons. Later on, they visited the Shepherds, where they joined a group of Belgian and Norwegian pilots. Having downed quite a number of drinks, they all needed to eat. The whole group marched off to the Hong Kong to enjoy a Chinese dinner.

Afterwards, Jan and Geert said goodbye to the group and went back to the Dutch Club where they met a number of Dutch pilots. Jan discussed the pros and cons of forming an all-Dutch fighter squadron with them. There were moments when the discussion became heated – quite a few pilots argued that a completely Dutch fighter squadron only served as a political move on the part of the Dutch government in exile – a ceremonial horse to be displayed during a parade once the war was over, nothing else.

When they seriously calculated how many Dutch pilots were available right then in England, by listing the ones they knew on a sheet of paper, they came to the conclusion that a Dutch squadron was actually feasible. An operational squadron could indeed be made up exclusively of Dutch pilots.

The next morning, when their leaves were up, Jan and Geert went their respective ways, Jan to his fighter planes, and Geert to mastering Lancasters, coming closer and closer to flying actual missions.

Back at the base, Jan was informed there had been several flights over Europe during his absence. On one of the bigger raids, ten bombers had been shot down, a considerable loss. Jan judged that this must have been a rather bad show.

Perhaps the fighters had been escorting the bombers from too great a distance, enabling the Luftwaffe fighters to streak through the formation's empty airspace. Jan could not evaluate the operation – he had not been there. At any rate, it demonstrated the Luftwaffe were alive, not sleeping. Since 167 Squadron had returned from the fateful mission without any missing planes, Jan thought it was a rather strange, unfortunate operation.

Diana and Jan were now meeting regularly. They spent many hours together on the small, cosy houseboat. Kees, who had been introduced to Jane by Jan, had also taken a liking to Diana's younger sister.

Their meetings were easy and pleasant since the two Australian girls and the two Dutch pilots got along very well. One evening, the two men had been invited to a little party of Jane's on the houseboat. She had also asked a number of other pilots and their girlfriends to come along. Jan and Kees went to the houseboat and found three other couples already there. Jan wondered how so many people could squeeze into such a small place but it worked out all right.

Once the introductions were over and a number of drinks downed to relax everyone, a friend of Jane's suggested they play strip poker. Jan had heard of that particular card game but never played it before. They first had to explain it to him. He agreed to participate under one condition: Diana should be his partner.

Jan was wearing a flight jacket, a blue turtleneck pullover, RAF trousers, shoes, socks and underwear. Diana was dressed in a grey sweater and matching cardigan, a flannel skirt, stockings, shoes and underwear. When the card game started, there were four men seated around the table while their girlfriends stood behind them to root for their partners. In the first hand, once the cards had been shuffled and cut, Jan had two pairs – two tens and two jacks. Attentively studying his cards, Jan threw one on the table and was given a seven of hearts.

One of the players opened the score, offering his jacket. Diana immediately countered, 'I offer Jan's jacket. I'll see you.' She studied the faces of the other players to see their reactions; two of them withdrew but Kees, who had Jane behind him, kept playing. Jane's face betrayed no emotion.

After Jan placed his cards face-up on the table, he noticed Kees had three queens and the other player had three nines. Diana had to help Jan take off his jacket, and handed it to Jane with a defiant look in her eyes.

New cards were dealt. This time Jan had two aces and three other cards. He asked for three new ones and noticed another ace among them. Diana squeezed his shoulder with one hand, bent over him and whispered into his ear, 'Come on, Jan. You're doing fine this time.'

Diana studied the others closely, how they shifted the cards they held, how they exchanged some for new ones from the stack. She tried to fathom their emotions from how they stared at the cards and the expressions on their faces, she noticed if small and victorious smiles were playing at the corners of their mouths, and how many cards they discarded. Having seen Jan's cards, Diana was utterly convinced she and Jan would win his jacket back. Diana offered Jan's pullover, eyes challenging as she made her play.

One of Jane's friends offered his jacket to see Jan's cards while the other two players withdrew. Triumphantly, Jan started to display his three aces, one after the other, smiling, certain he held the best cards. To Jan's complete surprise, the other player had a straight flush. Jan had lost again!

Helping him to take off his pullover, Diana stared apologetically at him. Jan now sat in his undershirt, trousers, shoes, socks and underwear.

It became rather warm in the houseboat cabin, with ten people crowding its small space. The loss of a jacket and a pullover did not make him feel cold at all.

The poker game continued. Because of his inexperience, Jan finally found himself seated in his underpants and nothing else. Diana, standing behind him, silently admired his strong build and well-developed chest.

When the time came to change partners, the girls seated themselves on the laps of the men; most of the latter were already missing one or more pieces of clothing. Diana sat on Jan's lap; he was only wearing underpants. She fondly kissed him on the cheek, whispering into his ear, 'Don't worry, Dutchie. Just wait and see. Your Diana will win back everything you've lost so far.' Jan noticed the excitement sparkling brightly in her lovely blue eyes.

After the first deal, Diana held three kings, and it looked as if her promise might be kept. She requested two new cards but they didn't offer anything to improve her chances.

Bravely, she opened the score. 'I start with my shoes. Anybody offer more?' She openly glanced at the other girls, attentively observing them.

'I'll see you,' Jane said. When Diana demonstratively put one king after another down on the table, Jane smiled slyly and placed three aces next to Diana's kings. Diana had lost – again.

Impatiently, she shrugged, handing over her shoes. She turned to look at Jan. 'Unlucky in cards, lucky in love,' she quipped with a warm smile, playfully ruffling his fair hair.

The game went on. All of them became more excited as girl after girl progressively shed some of her clothing. At a certain moment, Jan – still wearing only his underpants, with Diana on his lap – found she was wearing only a bra and panties. She looked simply lovely, cheeks glowing red from the drinks and the fascination of the game. She didn't want to give up at all but there remained little for her to offer to stay in the game.

One of Jane's friends announced, 'Last hand coming up!' He began dealing the cards carefully. While she was shuffling them, Diana noticed she held three kings and two tens. Now, at long last, she was absolutely certain she had the best chance and didn't ask for other cards. She looked carefully at the others, then courageously and brazenly opened the bidding. 'I offer my bra to whoever dares to call me.'

Diana's challenging words were met with a second of shocked silence. Unperturbed, she turned her head to look at Jan, hugging him, and said throatily, 'I'm certain to win this one. Don't be shocked now, Dutchie.'

'What if you lose?' he asked nervously.

'Then, I'll have to give up my bra,' Diana laughed mischievously. 'Will it embarrass you terribly, Dutchman?' As she stared intensely into his eyes, hers expressed the naughty mood she felt. She moved her head forward until it came to rest against Jan's forehead. 'Don't be afraid,' she whispered.

Kees checked Jane's cards carefully, finally announcing, 'We withdraw.'

Another girl also quit the game. Now it was Diana against one of Jane's WAAF girlfriends. She challenged, 'I bet all the clothes I won so far against your bra.' Her partner took advantage of the occasion to quip, 'Then we'll get a look at the goodies!'

Diana sharply raised her right eyebrow, shooting him an angry, displeased look. He turned beetroot red and shut up.

Very slowly, and in dead silence, nine pairs of eyes anxiously followed her every move. Diana put down one card after the other, then watched her opponent do the same. The latter had three aces and two jacks. Diana had lost!

Diana looked coyly at Jan. 'I'm sorry. Can you please unhook my bra?'

Jan, hands shaking and clumsy, fingers unpractised, managed to unhook it at last. Diana swiftly grabbed it, placing it on the table; simultaneously, she covered her breasts with both hands in a lightning move. Jan couldn't help but notice how elegant the shape of her firmly moulded breasts looked. At the same time, he could smell her smooth white skin and her perfume by Chanel – Cuir de Russie. He also caught sight of her neck arteries pulsating rapidly. Never before in his life had Jan experienced such an unexpected yet exciting encounter.

Following Diana's bold display, all the players rose to their feet, shouting, 'Hurray for Diana!' With one lithe move, she retrieved her bra from the table, instructing Jan, 'Hook me up again.'

The game had turned out quite exciting; time had flown by swiftly. Everyone was in an exuberant mood. The war had been forgotten for just a few hours of unlimited fun. Not one lascivious thought had passed Jan's mind when Diana was sitting in his lap, practically dressed like Eve for a part of the evening. His admiration for her bubbling sense of fun had increased considerably. Now the game was over, everyone reached for their clothes and began to dress fully again. One of Jane's friends had a good voice and started to sing a popular song; they all joined in. After a last round of drinks, Jan and Diana excused themselves, desiring a bit of fresh air. They left for a walk in the dark, cool night. They put on their warm overcoats and strolled along the river, holding hands.

There was an amused expression in Diana's eyes. 'What an exciting game that was!' she exclaimed. 'You lost your clothes as quickly as I did. If we ever should play it again, we'll have to be more careful to hold out a bit longer. Were you terribly embarrassed, my Flying Dutchman?' she asked, tossing back her head and laughing roguishly at him.

Jan shook his head. 'No, I wasn't embarrassed. It was quite a new experience for me, learning how that particular poker game is played. I really didn't know anyone could lose their clothes in only a few rounds,' he said, grinning.

Diana rested her head in the hollow of his neck. 'We all had a rather tiring day. That was the main reason, I didn't object to the suggestion of playing strip poker. It came at the right moment. It did in fact loosen us all up a bit. Did you like it?' she asked, teasing him with a naughty look in her eyes and shaking her head, tossing back her blonde hair.

Jan inclined his head slightly. 'Yes, I did. I don't have such a lovely girl sitting on my lap without her clothes on every day!' He laughed, revealing the deep fatigue wrinkles around his eyes.

They felt light-hearted, carefree and happy. During these momentary seconds of joy, of pure felicity, only one shadow loomed over their serenity – the intuitive knowledge, temporarily forced to the back of their minds, that these moments together could well be the last. The ugly war, always present in their subconscious, clouded their lives. Death waited so patiently along the young pilots' flight paths over Europe, reaping without respite its human harvest. Day after day, the pilots went up, and each day some did not return. That was the score. It was always present – inexorable, ominous, sinister. The scythe ready to cut off another young man's life – it could rarely be escaped.

Diana and Jan were totally involved with each other every time they met. There had not been one argument to cause any tension between them. They gave entirely of themselves.

Diana knew only too well that the young pilots, so cheerful now at the houseboat, had to climb up again into those cold cockpits, into their fighters and bombers, and carry out those dangerous missions she followed in the operations room.

The day that Jan had been in London on leave, Diana had been shocked to see written up on the blackboard the loss of ten bombers in one mission. Losing ten planes on one flight was terrible: it meant at least fifty crewmen had been killed or taken prisoner.

As the bombers had flown over Europe, Diana had noticed how a number of the WAAFs in the operations room had become very nervous and tense. Later, when the cold statistics of the unfortunate mission were chalked up, there had been gasps all over the room. Some of their friends were surely among the victims or POWs.

How intensely Diana hated those god-awful moments of despairing uncertainty. First came those abstract figures being written on the board. Then followed the human aspect – the bitter suffering, the deep grief of knowing, and the utter sadness of losing a dear one.

With detachment, the generals watched and calculated the results of their carefully prepared plans as the inanimate objects were moved across the map. Only afterwards were they informed about the emotional results. Knowingly, consciously, they were obliged to continue sending the 'finest' to their deaths – to win the war, and medals.

Diana saw everything happening from too close a distance; she was now too directly involved when the discs were shifted over the map. And she began to wonder if she should continue her job in the operations room?

One of the objects regularly moving on the map was the disc with Jan's 167 Squadron number on it. It was right beneath her watchful eyes, causing her stomach to tense up nervously every time the disc was impartially moved by one of those long rakes over the Channel, the North Sea or the Continent.

Diana found the strain was becoming too much for her. She needed, she desired a change. She had done her part for three years now. In Diana's opinion, that was enough!

Steadily walking alongside Jan, she asked hesitantly, 'What would you say if I were to apply for a transfer and join the Air Transport Auxiliary? I heard they teach you to fly. There seem to be quite a number of female pilots delivering fighters and even medium or heavy bombers from the factories to the military bases. It might even be interesting for a girl like me. What's your opinion on that, Jan?'

'Well, watching you shed your clothes tonight during the poker game, I dare say your body is all right!' he quipped, jumping away from her before she could pinch him. 'But, seriously,' he continued, 'if you can pass the medical and the eye test, then I agree it might be interesting work for a girl. And I do think you'd make a good pilot. Seeing you take off your bra and all leads me to believe you have good reflexes!' Jan grinned boyishly at her.

Diana moved her head as if to say, 'Do you think only men can fly planes ?' But then she explained, 'In Australia, there's a famous woman pilot called Jean Batten. She was originally born in New Zealand. Before the war, she demonstrated women can pilot planes too. She flew a small, single-engined Gipsy Moth biplane from London to Australia,' Diana said defensively and softly. Then she continued, 'In America there were Amelia Earhart and Jacqueline Cochran who also showed women can command aeroplanes.'

Jan smiled at her mysteriously. 'I know. Jean Batten was a guest in our home in The Hague. She came over for dinner one evening. A number of KLM pilots had given her useful advice when she progressed along the route from Europe to the Far East. It was the same commercial air route KLM planes took three times a week from Amsterdam to Batavia before the war,' Jan explained.

Surprised, she turned her face towards him. 'Jan, you're not pulling my leg, are you? Did you really meet her?' she asked incredulously. 'Please tell me all about her; how she looked, how she behaved and all that,' Diana insisted, moving closer to him, pressing her breasts against his arm. He nodded in agreement, 'Yes, I did meet her. She had dark hair, dark violet-blue eyes, was small – rather petite I'd say, very charming and interesting.' As an afterthought, he added, 'As a pilot, of course,' and laughed heartily at Diana, a twinkle in his eyes.

'Yes!' she exclaimed enthusiastically, 'That's her all right. I remember the pictures I saw in the papers. She made headlines several times. She must be a very gutsy woman.'

'We were home in The Hague when she came over for dinner,' Jan said. 'My father had first spoken to her in the main KLM Office. Then they walked to our house which was nearby. It was an educational evening for us. We listened attentively to her at the dinner table while she described her adventures and experiences flying the small biplane. She spoke slowly and rather precisely, explaining how she had prepared for the flight and carried it out.'

Firmly, Diana said, 'See? I'll apply this very week. If I really do pass my medical, I will also become a woman pilot.' Defiantly, she added, 'A pilot like you.'

She turned her head, staring up at him while her eyes caressed his features. Diana felt so completely at ease with her Flying Dutchman. She couldn't exactly understand why. Was she in love with him? When she was close to him, walking and talking with their bodies touching from time to time, she felt a kind of elation sweep through her. Her problems seemed distant and she relished the intense moments of happiness just orbiting around a source of genuine kindness and love.

When they finally returned to the houseboat, the others had left already. They cleaned the mess up together. When the time came to say goodnight, Diana clung to Jan for a second, kissing him softly on his lips.

'All right, Dutchie. Off you go and thanks for helping me clean up. And Jan,' she hesitated an instant, 'Don't you ever forget that poker game. But be more careful the next time or you'll lose your underpants too!' With an infectious, rippling laugh, she good-naturedly shoved him out the door.

'Goodnight, Diana. Have a good night's sleep.' As if in a dream, Jan walked back to his base. It was six in the morning. He had never felt so good since his arrival in England. Diana had changed a lot for him. The feelings of homesickness he had suffered so intensely faded away as if a fresh wind had cleared the airfield from a sticky, stubborn fog.

The first rays of sun tried to break through the pale grey ground haze hugging the earth, colouring it a light pink. Without any rest or sleep, Jan went straight on to standby. There in the dispersal hut, sitting in a big leather easy chair, he fell asleep in front of an open fire, long legs stretched out in front of him.

The early morning light, mingling with the soft yellow-red colours of the hearth's flames, performed an unreal and weirdly fantastic dance on his calm, now completely relaxed face as he slept soundly. A Mona Lisa smile playing on his lips,

Jan was totally oblivious to the cheerful chirping of early morning birds awakening to greet a new day. He didn't even hear the deep growl of the Rolls Royce engines being tested and warmed up by the busy maintenance staff at the airfield.

Undisturbed, unaware of anything taking place around him, Jan slept, and dreamed of a lovely girl called Diana. Fortunately for him, the weather turned bad and he didn't have to fly. Later, during the remainder of the day, he managed to get to bed and catch up on his sleep.

There would be a big, important mission the next day, however. Twenty-four Spitfires had to accompany twenty-four twin-engined Lockheed Ventura bombers to Rotterdam harbour. Not much happened during the flight over the North Sea. The fighters flew in tight, disciplined formation, a thousand feet above the bombers, spying out for the threat of Luftwaffe interceptors. Once over Rotterdam, they suddenly met heavy German fighter opposition, consisting of a considerable number of Fw 190s.

In the midst of the developing air duels with quite a number of planes circling and diving in the limited airspace, Jan got one on his tail. Anxiously, he kept his eyes glued to the mirror above the windshield to watch what was happening behind him, outmanoeuvring the pursuing Teutonic hunter. The other pilot wasted a lot of ammunition trying to hit his Spit without really being able to gain an effective shot at him. During the intense air combat, Jan remained utterly cool, constantly out-circling his insistent opponent.

The vast experience Jan had gained during his many missions proved to be of great value to him at that point. After some moments of concentrated manoeuvring, he skilfully managed finally to get behind the tail of the Fw 190 that had shot at him. He saw the enemy plane clearly outlined against a white cumulus cloud majestically drifting over the Dutch countryside. Jan reckoned he was less than 500 yards behind his antagonist.

Jan kept his thumb on the joystick firing button, ready to fire his first cannon burst. Once he had the Fw 190 looming for a second in the reflector sight, he immediately depressed the button, counting aloud, 'One, two …' Then, when he saw the aircraft ahead bank sharply to starboard, he released the button to save ammo. The Spit's four cannon had fired regularly; Jan had joltingly felt their vibrations and had seen how his own tracer had passed a little too high over the Fw 190 weaving in front of him.

The Luftwaffe pilot must have spotted the brightly coloured tracer streak above his cockpit and instantly wrenched his plane into a sharp right downward turn.

Jan smiled grimly and this time followed him down immediately in a tight swoop, feeling the blood drain from his head when he returned into a grey-out. The distance between them had reduced to about 400 yards. Jan bent forward eagerly – the enemy plane was once again lined up in his gun sight. Excitedly, he exclaimed aloud in Dutch, 'Nou heb ik je mannetje!' ('Now I've got you, little man!')

Jan blasted the Luftwaffe plane with all he had. He could plainly see how his tracer swept closer and closer to the plane manoeuvring desperately in front of him. Jan adjusted his flight path accordingly and was convinced a number of bullets were hitting the enemy target. But he didn't see any metal parts tearing off the Focke Wulf. Perhaps his bullets had hit the pilot, wounding or even killing him. Right then and there, Jan wondered how old his adversary might be. Yet it was a Fw 190 he had wanted for a long time, a very long time.

During this frantic action, Jan repeatedly threw anxious glances at the mirror above his windscreen to see what was going on behind him, to make sure no other enemy aircraft had been following him through the air chase. Watching the Focke Wulf go spiralling steeply down over Holland and disappear into a low hanging cloud, still spinning wildly and completely out of control, Jan couldn't be sure he had indeed finally shot down a Luftwaffe plane to even the score. He had to pull up, join the bombers again. This time, on return to base, he was going to report it at debriefing as a probable. The film camera would contain shots confirming his claim.

Closely eyeing the sky around and above him, Jan did not see any other Luftwaffe planes. He climbed back up to a high altitude in order to protect the bombers, now homeward bound after the attack. They had done their destructive duty well. The fierce combat had been quite exciting. Drops of perspiration stood out on Jan's upper lip. His heart was still pounding, while his body felt clammy all over from the extreme physical effort, the moment of greying-out on a tight curve, the tension and strain of the fight.

On the return flight over the North Sea, white contrails formed in the cool upper air, criss-crossing all over the sky in wild designs, resembling long white snakes floating on air, entwining and encircling one another at twenty thousand feet like a spectacular serpent's love ritual.

Kees had also participated in the show. After landing, they quickly cleaned up together and went to the houseboat to meet Diana and Jane.

Both girls had apprehensively followed the entire operation on the horizontal map in the operations room. Instinctively, Diana realised how tired the two Flying Dutchmen would be feeling after the day's fierce engagements. She and Jane had prepared a high tea with lots of biscuits, pastries and cakes, looking forward to their visit to the houseboat.

When Jan and Kees arrived, Diana immediately noticed the sharp lines of physical fatigue on their faces, but both were in a cheerful mood and ready to enjoy the latter part of the afternoon and early evening. After spending a few pleasant hours with the two Australian girls, Jan checked his watch. 'I'm afraid we must go. There are two sweeps over Holland scheduled for tomorrow – one in the early morning and one late in the afternoon. You understand, don't you, Diana?'

She nodded her head in consent without saying anything.

The two Dutch pilots were strongly built young men but hardly made of steel. Nor were they robots who could perform their dangerous tasks ad infinitum, automatically handling their craft – a very risky state of mind even for two experienced pilots.

Once they'd kissed the girls goodnight, Jan and Kees hurried back to their accommodation and went straight to bed; they needed rest badly, to confront next day's risky events.

In his diary, Jan wrote: 'We really enjoyed ourselves very much. We talked and ate a lot. The two Australian girls spoiled us in a grand manner!'

XVII

A S SOON AS Diana entered the apartment in London, her
mother immediately noticed a change for the better in her
daughter's attitude. Diana's step looked more dynamic with an
energetic bounce to it. Her eyes sparkled anew with life, and
she had a ready smile again. Once seated at the dinner table, she
was in high spirits, telling her mother all kinds of funny stories
about comic incidents that had happened at Ludham.

Mrs Boulton felt pleased, even favourably impressed, by
her daughter's metamorphosis. At last, it seemed to her,
Diana had broken out from that oppressive cocoon that had
separated her for so long from the world as she had withdrawn into gloomy, bitter thoughts about the loss of her first
great love.

While sipping tea with Diana, she innocently inquired,
'How are you and Jane getting along?'

With a happy intonation in her voice, Diana answered,
'We're doing fine, absolutely super! The other night, Jane
threw a party at the little houseboat and mother, hold tight,
we played strip poker.' Noticing the surprised look on her
mother's face, Diana informed her in detail how she had
passed the evening shedding one garment after the other until
all she was wearing happened to be her panties and bra. She
didn't tell her how she had taken off her bra in full view of
those participating at Jane's party.

'Well!' her mother said, raising one eyebrow. 'I do notice quite a few changes in you! What's happening out there at Ludham airfield? Is there someone you've met I should know about?' She glanced at her daughter inquisitively.

Diana smiled at her mysteriously. 'Maybe I have,' she answered evasively. 'When I'm on leave next time, I'll try and ask him over. Then you can take a good look at him.' She continued excitedly, 'He's quite handsome – from Holland. His father is the director of KLM, the Dutch airline. And do you know, mother, he had dinner at his house in The Hague with Jean Batten, the famous Australian aviatrice,' Diana said breathlessly.

'But what has Jean Batten got to do with meeting this Dutch acquaintance?' Mrs Boulton asked, rather astonished.

'Oh, that's a long story.' A smile curled across Diana's lips. 'I'll tell you about it one day. Now, mother, brace yourself. I've great news for you. I'm going to put in a request to join the Air Transport Auxiliary. I want to become a pilot too,' Diana stated, and looked at her mother challengingly.

'What's that you're going to do?!' her mother inquired incredulously.

'I'm going to be a pilot. I've made up my mind. I can't stand it any more – looking at those darned discs being shifted around over the large map in front of me in the operations room every single day and knowing Jan – that's his name – is up there flying over the Continent with all those nasty Germans shooting at him.'

'Is that his name?' her mother asked, glancing curiously at Diana. 'Might he by any chance be the one who tempted, or talked you, into this flying idea?'

Diana nodded, and smiled. 'That's his name. I also call him "Dutchie" sometimes, but I don't think he particularly likes that nickname. He always raises his eyebrows when he hears it and – yes, mother – he's partly responsible for my decision to learn to fly. I also call him my Flying Dutchman at times.'

Mrs Boulton poured Diana another cup of tea. 'What exactly does he do? Is he perhaps a bomber pilot?' she cautiously asked.

Her mother immediately noticed how a brief shadow darkened her daughter's radiant face. 'No, he's a fighter pilot with 167 Squadron. Judging from the number of times the disc with that number moves over the big map, I must say he's rather active. Nowadays, the pilots are operating over Europe often – even twice a day!'

'Twice a day?' her mother interrupted.

'Uh-huh,' Diana confirmed, nodding. 'You should see them after a safe return. They look so awfully tired, mother. One can only imagine what kind of hell they must pass through during those two-hour sweeps over Europe and the Germans shooting at them – it's not exactly kid's stuff, you know!' Diana exclaimed.

'Does he ever talk about it to you?' her mother asked.

Diana shook her head negatively. 'Not him, he's not the talkative kind. He keeps it shut tight within his brain. Nor does he boast. When I first met him, I immediately sensed his shyness; but now that I know him better, I must say he's a very kind, decent, warm-hearted person.' She hesitated a moment before adding, 'And with such fine manners.'

Diana smiled knowingly at her mother when she said those last words.

'Are you going to leave Ludham then? If you should really become a pilot, I mean?' Her mother's words sounded a touch worried.

'I think so. I'll probably be sent to a flying school in the Midlands.'

Diana and her mother kept on talking until late in the evening. When Mrs Boulton brought a breakfast tray to Diana's room the next morning, Diana was still in a profound early morning sleep. Her mother watched her silently. Diana's face was so smooth, so totally relaxed, yet she looked so frail. Mrs Boulton knew from experience how much, how deeply, her daughter had been hurt when George had not returned from that last flight. And now she had met another fighter pilot – a Dutchman – a Flying Dutchman.

Mrs Boulton knew Diana was a bright, sensible girl with a strong character. She had, over the years, grown into a beautiful, mature young woman. But would she survive a second shock? Or was she like Meissen porcelain – so beautiful, yet so fragile?

She opened the heavy curtains slightly, letting the morning light filter into the bedroom. Diana started to stir lazily beneath the sheets, blinking against the light. Sleepily, she said, 'Hello, mother – good morning. I slept marvellously in my own bed again, without a single bad dream disturbing me. The other day, right after I met Dutchie for the first time, I had a horrible nightmare about a Spitfire with him at the controls being shot down by several of those nasty Luftwaffe planes. It was awful, mother – really horrid!'

'Now, my dear, let's start the day by forgetting all about planes, shall we?' Mrs Boulton insisted. 'Let's work out a nice programme. There's fine weather today, so I suggest we take a walk and then get some shopping done. Is that all right with you?' she asked kindly.

'Yes, mother.' Diana smiled warmly at her, and sipped her tea. She was thankful for her mother's attentions. While Diana had breakfast, Mrs Boulton settled at the foot of the bed, patiently listening to everything Diana had to tell her.

Diana's two days' leave went by quickly and she was forced to return again to her duties in the operations room.

As she bade her mother goodbye, Diana said, 'You've been so kind and understanding. Wait till you see Dutchie. I think you will also like him very much.'

'I'm certain of it, Diana. Now take good care of yourself. See you soon, the two of you.' Mrs Boulton smiled confidently at her daughter.

Once the taxi had disappeared around the street corner, she pensively went back into the sitting room. With intense pleasure, she had taken note of how much better her daughter looked; but that Diana had fallen for a fighter pilot worried Mrs Boulton far more than she had revealed to Diana. If the Dutch boy really was airborne nearly every day, she felt his chances for survival were not too good.

She didn't want to face another day when her daughter would be terribly hurt by the consequences of that damned war. Diana was so utterly happy now – but later?

As Mrs Boulton walked through the streets of London, she kept noticing all those young men in uniform. Lately, more and more Americans, in their smart uniforms, formed part of the total picture. How many of them would survive the onslaught still to be carried out on fortress Europe to liberate the Continent from the Nazis? How many would pay the ultimate price to get the Germans out of France and the rest of Europe?

Pouring herself a stiff whisky, Mrs Boulton wondered what the future held for her and her two daughters? Holding the glass in her right hand, she said aloud, 'This damned war has surely ruined all my plans.'

XVIII

AFTER LANDING at Ludham from his last flight over Europe, Jan phoned Diana, informing her, 'I just got back. The squadron met with a lot of enemy action. I feel very tired. Do you mind if I skip tea today? Tomorrow, weather permitting, there'll be other flights to the opposite side.' He spoke wearily.

Diana felt a pang of disappointment, but she understood so well: those 167 Squadron pilots had been up in the air far too often these last days. Much too often for her taste!

'All right, Jan. Take it easy, and pleasant dreams. Will you dream of me?'

Jan heard her chuckle at the other end of the line. 'I'll do that. I'm sorry, Diana – bye for now.' He hung up, took a quick shower and went straight to bed without eating. The moment his tired head touched the pillow, he fell into a deep, exhausted sleep.

Time passed by – days and weeks. The girls kept on working in the operations room while the squadrons and pilots were active flying their sorties, escorting bombers or going out on sweeps, shooting up ground targets in low level attacks in Western Europe.

Every now and then, another pilot did not return and another new, eager, young face joined the squadron. Jan and Kees had become two veterans of the British 167 Squadron.

Somehow, it all strongly resembled a famous war movie Jan had once seen in The Hague, starring David Niven and Errol Flynn. It was called *Dawn Patrol*, and concerned a fighter squadron during the Great War. Some of the experienced pilots never returned from their flights over the Front. These were replaced by eager young pilots, barely trained to take the places of veterans, who after only a few flights were shot down in their turn or were reported missing in action.

After returning from another mission, Jan wrote in his diary on 10 June:

> A show over the Continent today again. Weather during the afternoon cleared. Take-off at 17.55 hours. Escort for 6 twin-engined Mitchell bombers. Target: Ghent in Belgium. Halfway between the Belgian coast and Ghent, the squadron was attacked by 24 Focke Wulf 190s. I didn't break away from the formation, making short weaving turns from left to right and vice versa to keep them in sight. At a certain point, three Focke Wulfs attacked us from the eight o'clock position and I turned left, giving hard rudder. They sharply climbed. I then tried a head-on attack which unfortunately failed. They out-climbed me. Afterwards, they began a right turn and started to dive towards the bombers. I tried to follow them down for a second but broke off the action since they were already too far away to get a good shot at them. The range became excessive, so I banked sharply and climbed, returning to a position close to the bombers.
>
> Three of the Dutch pilots who should have been close to me had disappeared. The main Luftwaffe attack was over, but I saw one lonely Focke Wulf trying to attack a Mitchell bomber. I was too far away when I gave him a long burst of my cannon. No effect. Returned to base. At debriefing, was informed two of our finest had not returned. Pointless to add they were both capable, fine young men. Damned nice fellows. Shall miss them.

On 12 June 1943, out of the blue, Jan and Kees were informed they had to prepare for a transfer to Liverpool. A Dutch fighter squadron was finally being set up. They were to become members of a new, all-Dutch team.

At last, they were both taken off operational flying. In a way, they had been abused enough: this would be a big change for them. After hearing the news, they decided to go to the houseboat that same evening to inform the two Australian girls about the latest developments.

After he told her, Jan said to Diana, 'You know, on the one hand, I'm glad I'll be able to take it easier for a while. It was really getting to be too much lately. On the other, I'll be sad to leave. You and Jane have created such a pleasant atmosphere for me. I can never thank you enough for it. Both of you helped us keep our heads above water, if you understand what I mean.' There was a serious expression on Jan's face.

Diana gave him a melancholy smile. 'Yes, I do understand. But you and your colleagues wanted that Dutch fighter squadron and now you'll have it! Both of you can take a rest from operational flying. It will be good for you, Jan. Besides, you'll be training with your own countrymen. Later on, if Europe ever gets invaded, you'll return to this base, or one close by – maybe even Hornchurch, you'll see.'

Jan shrugged. 'Who knows, Diana? I'll keep in regular touch with you. I'll send you my new address once I'm there. Let's coordinate our leaves as much as possible, so we can meet frequently in London.' He looked at Diana hopefully, breaking the tension between them.

'Ah!' Diana exclaimed, putting her right hand to her forehead. 'In all the excitement of you both leaving, I completely forgot to give you some very important news. I passed my medical. I think I'll also be transferred in a few weeks.' She smiled uncertainly at him. 'I wanted you to tell me your news first, Dutchie. How do you like it? Diana Boulton becoming a pilot?' Her eyes showed her pride, and her words touched Jan's emotions.

'Congratulations,' he said. 'I think you'll make a good one. You do have good reflexes, I remember – especially when you're playing strip poker.' Playfully, Jan jumped beyond her reach.

Both laughed. At the same time, she gave him a meaningful look. Jan felt the blood rushing to his head – he was visibly blushing. But now the moment of separation had come. He bent towards Diana.

'Take good care of yourself, and pay close attention to what the flight instructor tells you when you start flying. We'll be seeing each other again soon. I won't be flying operationally for a few months. Does that make you feel better?'

But Diana did not speak, she did not answer his questions – she only looked at Jan and loved him.

Diana felt a surge of sadness flowing through her. She had to make a strong effort to fight back her emotions. Yet she also felt relieved that Jan would not be flying into danger again for quite some time – perhaps as much as six months. The disc would continue to be pushed over the big operations room map. It would still bear number 167, but Jan would no longer be part of it. Now the round wooden disc would have no special meaning for her any more.

Eyes moist, she looked up at him. 'Goodbye, Jan – my dearest Flying Dutchman. I wish you the best of luck. Take care, will you? Just for me, little Diana?' She searched his face lovingly, while her arms encircled his neck, hugging him strongly.

They were both tense. He kissed her once and she pressed her body hard against him for a second, as if she wanted to assure him of herself. Then he sighed deeply, calling out to Kees, and they were off, walking back to their base. The two girls stood on the houseboat roof, waving at them until they'd disappeared into the dark of night.

Early the next morning, two Spits flew low over the houseboat. Jan led the way with Kees close on his tail. The two planes climbed sharply. The two pilots waved their wings at the girls standing on the roof, then dived at the houseboat, pulling up at the very last moment. The noise of the Rolls

Royce engines was ear-shattering. After their first fly-by they flew back over the boat again, this time slowly and majestically, waving their wings again as a last farewell gesture.

Diana and Jane had returned to the deck, flourishing white tablecloths in response to their fly-over. The two Spits climbed sharply then, circling away, becoming smaller and smaller, dwindling first into dots and then into tiny specks, disappearing over the horizon into the deep blue sky.

Diana's eyes brimmed with tears. She continued to stare at the vast, empty sky long after they'd gone, wondering how strange it was Jan and Kees were still in their planes, flying towards Liverpool and she couldn't see them any more. They had vanished but they were still there, making progress, nearing their destination. Time and dimension were two enigmatic measures.

Standing alone, Diana asked herself if George could also still be flying somewhere in that vast expanse, the universe. But she, as a human being, could no longer see him any more after he had disappeared from being bound by earthly measures as she knew them.

Could he perhaps have transferred into another dimension but still be present somehow in this one? The thought sent a shiver down her spine. She didn't know the answer. She just kept on wondering sadly, feeling very lonely, staring gloomily at the empty sky above her, until it became cold and she too descended into the cabin. 'Godspeed, Jan,' she whispered hoarsely.

As of now, she eagerly looked forward to meeting him during one of his coming leaves. She felt sure he would be safe for a few months at least, resting, taking it easier and performing only a little flying. The Royal Air Force had grabbed enough of the two Dutch pilots' generosity.

When Jan and Kees landed at the new base – Woodvale, close to Liverpool – they automatically became 322 Squadron at the moment when the Spits' wheels touched the runway.

The new airfield offered reasonable pilot accommodation; the mess and small bar were pleasant enough and well-stocked.

During the first few days, Jan took care of his personal belongings and also brought his diary up to date. He walked around the new surroundings, meeting the other Dutch pilots – only eight in number – some of whom he'd known from earlier meetings at the Dutch Club in London. During the next months, the 'foreigners' – the non-Dutch – were to be replaced by younger Dutch pilots, some of them trained in the United States.

In the course of the following weeks, Jan had to do a lot of organising, while the squadron had to follow a training and exercise program even though it was now all-Dutch. The pilots flew considerably fewer hours than at Ludham. Formation flying had to be practised, along with simulated air combat and shooting practice. The Dutch pilots had to get accustomed to each other and to how they flew Spitfires, learning to think and fly harmoniously as one squadron and not as individual pilots. They were kept busy, and the time flew by quickly. Sometimes they even had to scramble to intercept enemy aircraft reported over the Irish Sea.

One day, an American pilot landed a P-51 Mustang fighter at Woodvale. Jan walked to the new aircraft to meet the pilot and discuss the plane's flying characteristics. The Mustang had a much longer range than a Spitfire. It was equipped with a 1,400 hp engine and flew considerably faster than Jan's Mk V Spitfire.

'Why don't we try a fake aerial combat? Then you'll get an idea how it performs,' the American suggested confidently to Jan, convinced of his Mustang's technical advantages.

'All right, I'll get my Spit ready,' Jan grinned with self-assurance, thanks to his wide experience over Europe.

A few minutes after take-off, they were flying at ten thousand feet and the simulated combat began. After a number of sharp turns and rolls, Jan managed to fly right behind the

Mustang and stayed on its tail. No matter what acrobatics the American pilot tried, Jan clung to his tail like a leech to the skin of a fat pig. He could have easily blasted the American out of the sky any time he had wanted.

The two planes climbed high sharply, circled each other, banked, and sped low over the field with Jan expertly glued to the tail of the Mustang. It was clear the hapless American pilot had no real combat experience. It showed in the crude amateurish way he handled the Mustang.

Once they had landed and parked their planes, the American invited Jan for a beer at the bar. 'I feel as dead as I should be,' he told the young Dutchman. 'Thank you for an interesting afternoon. It won't be easy to forget!' He raised his glass, and added, in open admiration of Jan's flying technique, 'Am I ever glad we're fighting on the same side!'

Jan laughed good-naturedly at him. 'It's all just a matter of practice. You'll be getting a great deal of it once you're operating regularly over Europe. And you'll also get a look at the intense anti-aircraft fire from the ground. It's increasing day by day and I can guarantee those black puffs of smoke will impress you – even scare the hell out of you when your plane is buffeted around by the explosions at those high altitudes.'

The American pilot inquired, 'How many times have you been over Europe?'

'Over a hundred,' Jan replied.

The US pilot observed him speculatively. 'You should be receiving your pension after that many flights. The brass should order you out of operational flying.'

Jan nodded his head, acknowledging the truth of the American's remark. 'I know,' he agreed. 'But that's unfortunately not exactly our situation. The Dutch Air Force in London doesn't count the same way the American Air Force does.'

Before returning to his Mustang, the American said to Jan, 'Good luck, my Dutch friend. Be seeing you one day, perhaps in London.'

At Woodvale, the Dutch pilots had a small British car at their disposal for transportation at the field. One day, the driver took a curve much too fast and lost control of the vehicle. It overturned several times. Kees, who was sitting in the back seat, was thrown clear, breaking a number of ribs in the process. Lying on the wet grass, he moaned in terrible pain and was rushed to a nearby hospital.

It turned out the air knights, so supreme up in the sky, proved vulnerable when involved in stupid earthly accidents.

Several days passed before Jan was allowed to visit Kees. When he entered the hospital room, he saw his friend propped up against a lot of pillows to keep him in a sitting position in bed. He realised the recovery would be a long affair.

After his visit to the hospital, Jan phoned Diana to tell her what had happened. 'Kees will be all right with a few weeks of complete rest. But bad luck and good luck go hand in hand – he won't be flying for quite some time. I have a question now. Do you think you could get a leave during the next couple of weeks? If you'd like me to, I can reserve a room for you here. Perhaps Jane could also come along to keep Kees company – to cheer him up a bit!'

'I think I might be able to get a leave in ten days,' said Diana. 'I'll write and let you know the definite day. If I can make it, I'll visit you and your Dutch colleagues. But I can't make any definite promises regarding Jane right now. I'll see what I can do to encourage her to come. How are you getting along at Woodvale?' Diana's interest showed her concern about Jan's well-being.

'Not too badly. The accommodation is reasonable and the mess quite pleasant. I do miss you though, Diana. Do you know that?' Jan asked quietly.

'Well, I should hope so, Dutchie. Are you Dutchmen all made of stone or something?' Diana chuckled at the other end of the line. 'Just joking, Jan. Hope to see you soon,' she added as an afterthought.

The sound of Diana's voice raised strong emotions in Jan. He was really impressed by her good mood and humour. She was such a sweet girl with great character who had done so much to keep him mentally alert during a difficult part of his life in England. After speaking to her, Jan considered her remark about the Dutch possibly all being made of stone. He had a vague idea of what Diana meant but he wasn't completely sure at all. He wanted to ask her about it later when she came to visit Kees at the hospital.

The days flew by swiftly – navigation flights, low level attacks, formation flying and so on. Before he knew it, Jan was standing impatiently at the station waiting for Diana's train. He finally spotted her among the milling crowd heading for the exit. With intense pleasure, Jan noticed her elegant civilian clothes, making her even more attractive and lovely than the last time he'd seen her in her WAAF uniform.

When Diana neared him, her features relaxed completely and a bright smile crossed her whole face. With a red glow of excitement, she said, 'Don't stare at me as if you'd never seen me wearing a dress before, Dutchie.' She looked up at him and smiled temptingly, giving him a quick kiss on the cheek while he held her at arm's length, admiring her.

'We girls sometimes like to show off and demonstrate we're really girls after all despite the lousy war.'

Jan smiled at her. 'I'm staring at you because you look simply wonderful, smashing! Come on, let's take a taxi to the hospital. Kees is already allowed to leave the hospital two hours a day and he's saved the time to have lunch with us. Where's Jane?' Jan had only just noticed her absence.

'I'm sorry, but Jane couldn't make it this time. I'll try and keep Kees good company for her sake.' She darted a glance at Jan to see if he understood what her words really meant.

Sitting next to him in the taxi, she studied Jan out of the corner of her eyes. His face was rested; the deep fatigue lines had practically disappeared. He no longer had those dark Ludham circles beneath his eyes. In a way, he looked much younger and more attractive than he ever had before. Knowing this pleased her no end.

'You know, I think you look much better here in Liverpool. Your face isn't as tense any more. I believe you look more like yourself. You've become a very handsome Dutchman,' Diana complimented him, and with a provocative twinkle in her eyes she moved closer to him.

Jan turned his head to look at her. 'Well, it's true. I do feel more rested. I've been looking forward to meeting you again. It's been a long time for me. You were always so good to me at your houseboat. I really miss that cosy, crazy little place. It was great fun spending time there.'

Diana looked back at him. 'Maybe one day you'll return. The way the war is going, I think they'll need all the men they can get for the final assault on Europe.'

'Who knows? Here at Woodvale, we don't fly much but we train on all kinds of exercises – like survival courses after bailing out of a plane. But I look forward to seeing some action again. I'm slowly falling asleep at this airfield.'

Diana shook her head vigorously. 'Oh, Jan! Forget all about action.' Her voice was firm. 'Let others carry the brunt of the battle for a while. When I worked in the operations room, I saw 167 Squadron doing more than its normal share. Take it easy for a while. Enjoy it, Jan, appreciate your off-duty time before the brass call you back to active operational flying. Relax – as much as you can. Judging from my experiences in the ops room you've done your duty. You'll see how many pilots they'll need when the invasion starts at last.'

They had arrived at the hospital, where they found Kees in the garden sitting in a deckchair enjoying the sun's warm rays. Diana noticed many patients – some sitting motionless in chairs, others sadly and slowly shuffling along – with a lustreless look in their eyes probably due to shell-shock. Others again were recovering from normal accidents or illnesses, but she also spotted many others recovering from war wounds. A number of them were a pitiful sight, missing arms or legs. The brutal horrors wrought by the interminable war were an awful reminder to her.

When she was close to Kees, Diana encouraged him. 'Hello, old chap, you look fine, just super. I also notice you still possess your classical RAF moustache with the outer tips upturned. Jan told me your chest folded like an accordion. But looking at you I must say he exaggerated.' She smiled warmly at him. 'The hospital nurses must be treating you well. Jan also informed me we can eat lunch together, the three of us. Is that all right with you? I apologise for Jane, she couldn't get a leave. She told me I may give you a little kiss on the cheek on her behalf.' Spontaneously, Diana bent down to place her lips affectionately on Kees' cheek.

Kees smiled happily. 'Let's go have lunch. I'm fed up and bored stiff of sitting like an old invalid in the sun without doing anything.' Kees rose from the deckchair slowly with some effort, grimacing in pain. Diana could clearly see how much time he still needed to fully recover. He would be earthbound for several more weeks.

After lunch, Diana and Jan accompanied Kees back to the hospital. Then they went their way to the centre of Liverpool to get some shopping done. They were on their own – no others to keep them company or interfere with their happy mood. Now they could dedicate themselves completely to one another.

It felt good to Diana, walking arm-in-arm with her Dutchman. They laughed happily at the stories and jokes they exchanged. They were content to be together again and only had eyes for each other. She bought him a few handkerchiefs and a tie; he insisted on presenting her with a bottle of Chanel perfume, Cuir de Russie. He remembered its fragrance so well from that fantastic, memorable evening when they'd played strip poker at Diana's houseboat. Towards late afternoon, Jan accompanied her to the hotel.

He had booked a comfortable double room for Diana and her sister Jane. The view from the room was pleasant enough.

They drank tea together in the hotel lounge, recalling all their experiences at Ludham. Then they enjoyed a leisurely dinner during which they happily finished a bottle of claret. Both felt fine, elated to be together once again, and also a bit light-hearted following the red wine. Diana's cheeks glowed; she felt warm all over while her blue eyes shone like those of a young girl in love.

At the end of the dinner, Diana asked, 'Jan, what time do you have to be back at Woodvale? I'd like you to stay with me as long as you possibly can tonight.' Diana knew instinctively that from now on she had to lead her shy Dutchman very delicately. What was going to happen next represented the critical moment in her marvellous relationship with her Flying Dutchman.

'I'm completely free. There's no flying tomorrow. I've all the time in the world – just for you, dearest Diana.' Jan smiled contentedly at her, completely unaware of what she was leading up to.

'Fine,' she said. 'Would you like a nightcap in my room? I brought a small bottle of whisky along. Not very ladylike I know, but we Australians simply love to sup a whisky before turning in. I want to celebrate our reunion. How about it, Jan?'

'Let's go,' he replied. Together they went up to her room where they talked until late. They swapped experiences they'd been through during the past weeks of separation.

Diana let Jan do the talking and, when she felt the moment was right, kissed him lightly on his lips, pulling him ever so carefully down on top of her.

He responded to her kiss and she became aware of his physical reaction. She smiled victoriously; she knew by now she had won the battle. There existed no more barriers to hold them back. To Diana it seemed as if a green Very light had slowly descended from the sky on its small parachute, as a sign they could take off. They could fly off together into the universe speeding into its endless space, where time takes on other dimensions. They finally loved each other, as if both had known for a very, very long time it was the logical conclusion to a deep feeling of mutual affection that had gradually matured since their first meeting.

Diana felt perfectly happy. She had looked forward to this romantic reunion with Jan, had desired to be together with her Flying Dutchman, but this time she had concluded she wanted everything, and completely.

She was absolutely certain of her deep love for her tall, shy Dutchman. That night, she gave herself entirely to him; there were no barriers between them or anything to restrain their passion.

At last they were together, the most important thing for Diana. They had come to know one another during their walks and talks; but now they met on a completely different level and to her it felt good and wonderful. In fact, it was a unique sensation and experience. She still felt the warm glow of complete satisfaction. Diana lay in the crook of Jan's strong arm, feeling protected as if nothing in the world could ever separate them. She experienced intense happiness and total contentment. She had decided to take the final step and, looking at Jan lying so close to her, knew he felt completely happy too.

She turned her face to him, asking, 'How do you feel?' while her hand softly caressed his cheek.

Tenderly, Jan smiled. 'I feel a beautiful girl in my arms right now,' he said softly. 'But, apart from that, I feel like climbing out of an overcast into the deep blue sky, higher and higher up to the sun. And then racing my Spit just above the white clouds until it gives me a superior, inexpressible sensation of speed. Right above those sun-drenched clouds, I feel completely free in the sky, just rushing into an endless void. That's how I feel. And you, Diana?' he gently inquired.

Diana's expression was mysterious. 'Oh, I feel good too. I just made a big discovery.'

'What kind?' Jan asked curiously.

'That Dutch stone can be melted if the right temperature is applied and if one sets one's mind to it. Do you understand what I mean, Jan?' Once she had asked the question, she stared deep into his grey-blue eyes.

'I think I do.'

That night they were insatiable, discovering one another completely. Even the disturbing thoughts of war were fully banished. They felt happy together, existing only for each other – whispering sweet endearing words.

They experienced moments of exquisite, absolute felicity. Time seemed to have left them alone in that room in Liverpool, not ticking away at its usual speed. Perhaps it even came to a standstill during particular instants of extraordinary happiness. Maybe it lasted one second or an eternity. It was of no importance, really. Their being together represented an unending moment in time – to be remembered for ever.

The excitement of being in love, of discovering one another, gave them a feeling of complete fulfilment. Nothing could be added to it.

Finally, Diana and Jan had surrendered, to find each other entirely.

Could their happiness last?

XIX

SHORTLY AFTER the enchanting, romantic visit to Liverpool, Diana had to report to flying school in the Midlands, to start initial training with the ATA.

At first, before she could be allowed to make her first flight, she had to follow elementary courses in theory, engine performance, revolutions per minute, engine power, fuel consumption, the operation and functions of ailerons, rudders and elevators, navigation and many other important subjects.

Several months went by, but at last the big moment in Diana's life arrived. She was going to take off in a Tiger Moth – with the instructor at the controls, of course. The Tiger Moth, a single-engined biplane practically flew by itself. It had a low stalling speed and was generally recognised as an excellent aircraft for beginners.

Walking with the instructor towards the plane parked on the tarmac, Diana felt a bit nervous. This was going to be it! The instructor indicated the forward seat to her and she placed her foot on the lower wing to climb aboard while he sat down behind her.

In a steady voice, the instructor told her, 'Diana, you can start the engine.'

She held the joystick all the way back as she had been taught, and pushed the starter button; the engine fired and ran smoothly right away. A thin smile played on her lips – she had taken the first step. She watched the needle indicating the oil temperature rise steadily to the right position. Then the instructor said, 'Now taxi slowly to the head of the runway where you'll have to park for a moment. Take it easy – we're not in a hurry. After you receive the all-clear signal, take off.'

Diana nodded to show she understood, and took a deep breath. She taxied the plane to the head of the runway where she waited for the green Very light before being permitted to take off. To Diana, it seemed like an eternity. Meanwhile, she regularly checked the few instruments in front of her to make sure each needle stood in the correct position. At last, the pistol fired and a green light started to descend slowly to earth. Now she was authorised to take off into the same sky where her Flying Dutchman regularly flew. She moved the controls, checking that they could move freely.

Calmly, the instructor told her, 'Go ahead. You're cleared for take off. You know what to do.'

Quickly, Diana pulled her goggles over her eyes, pushed the throttle forward to full power, felt the free rudder movement with her feet and then moved the joystick forward to a slightly more central position. When the speed indicator registered 50 mph, Diana pulled the stick a little towards herself, causing the plane to respond. She was airborne; she was flying, she had left the ground. The small plane carried her up into the sky just like a bird spreading its wings. A little later, when still climbing, she pulled the gas throttle slightly back to cruising power and adjusted the angle of climb to initiate her first, mild turn to the right. She saw clearly the ground below. The houses and farms looked somewhat smaller, and the animals in the meadows, the cornfields, the trees and the hedges dividing the fields passed by beneath her. It seemed as if they were shrinking in size, becoming miniaturised. Diana was elated, and experienced an overwhelming desire to shout out to the whole world how happy she felt at that very moment.

She straightened the plane out to initiate a course parallel to the runway as the instructor had told her to do. Then she passed over the airfield boundary and kept going for a while. Following this manoeuvre, she again made a right turn to align the plane with the runway ahead of her.

The instructor's calm, reassuring voice reached her. 'You are doing well. Take it easy for the landing. Remember I'm right behind you to watch how you move. Go ahead.'

In flying a Tiger Moth, Diana didn't have to think about lowering the landing gear or the flaps because they were all fixed into place on this type of craft. She pushed the stick slightly forward, increased engine power, and pulled the joystick gently towards her as she passed the boundary again – reducing engine power and making a perfect landing.

The instructor behind her had not had to intervene at all. He shouted, 'Good show, Diana! You did it all by yourself! Now take off again and fly a circuit plus a landing!' She continued doing the exercises for about thirty minutes; some went smoothly while a few others were bumpy, but overall she thought she'd done quite well for a novice. She judged her performance as being quite reasonable. The instructor then said, 'Take her back to the apron. This will be enough for a first time.'

After Diana had parked the aircraft and switched off the engine, the instructor spoke encouragingly to her. 'Nice going. You performed well for a first flight. For the next few days, we will be doing these take-offs and landings regularly until you get the hang of it. Later on, we'll make a number of overland flights with you at the controls. And when you've handled it all well, I'll let you make it up there alone. I think you'll be able to handle it in about two weeks' time.'

Diana could feel her adrenaline flowing, and glanced at the instructor. 'Thank you,' she said excitedly. 'I hope I won't disappoint you. I don't know how you felt sitting behind me, but I felt so impressed. I'm so happy I've taken my first step towards becoming a pilot.' As she spoke, Diana's eyes sparkled and she jumped lithely down from the wing to the tarmac, fighting the impulse to plant a kiss on her instructor's cheek.

Instead, Diana strode purposefully beside him to a small control room where her first flight was chalked up on a blackboard – just the same way things were done in the operations room at Ludham. It reminded Diana so strongly of the work she had performed before, of the tension when losses were written on the board and the general satisfaction of the WAAFs when all the squadrons had returned safely without any losses.

The instructor addressed her. 'Well, Diana – take it easy for the rest of the day. I'll see you tomorrow morning at ten.'

She smiled at him confidently. 'I'll be there. You can count on it,' she stated, as she passed a new pupil on her way out to the plane.

Dressed in her grey-blue coveralls, Diana walked to her assigned quarters. Once back in her room, she threw herself on the bed, completely exhausted. Lying back with her head resting on her hands on the pillow, weird images flashed through her brain. She couldn't possibly figure out how fighter pilots manoeuvred those very fast planes, the Spitfires and Typhoons. How could they keep their minds clear and alert, watching the instruments in front of them in the narrow, cramped cockpits, and at the same time still having to keep their eyes wide open, examining the sky for enemy Luftwaffe planes? How could they possibly perform all those activities simultaneously and yet fly so close to each other in victory or four-abreast formations? How could they do it, she marvelled? And yet they did – every day – and she was only too aware of it.

Now Diana fully realised why the faces of those young fighter pilots were so deeply marked by fatigue after they returned from a mission over the Continent. Her admiration for Jan, her Flying Dutchman, only increased.

Lying on her back, idly staring at the ceiling of her small room, she allowed her mind to wander, imagining herself a female pilot at the controls of a Spitfire, streaking through the air at close to 400 mph, the plane responding marvellously to her commands. Already she figured herself in a simulated air combat against her Flying Dutchman. An enigmatic, Mona Lisa-like smile played on her lips as she reflected on it, fantasising what kind of aerobatics she'd have to perform.

Diana sighed loudly, feeling utterly contented. It was so wonderful, she reflected, to be able to command a plane, to be able to fly it to whatever destination she chose. There was something about it that made one feel superior to earthbound people, as if flying made one a real giant, a prima donna of the air. Again, Diana's eyes sparkled brightly – she had definitely found a second love, flying.

Each day during the following weeks, when weather conditions permitted, Diana made more progress, and at last the all important moment arrived. She was going to fly solo. She was going to take off without the faithful instructor and his serene, mellifluous voice calling out behind her. She felt thrilled, this was going to be her great day.

That morning, when she had fully awakened, Diana immediately walked to the window and looked out at the weather, curious. It was a bright morning, with only a few small scattered clouds in the sky; it seemed an ideal day to go up. But Diana also felt a kind of tension. She knew the nerve centre of her body was located close to her stomach, but she forced herself to calm down since she had set her mind to this moment of truth a long time ago. If her own emotions got so worked up before her first solo flight, she could well imagine what tension – even anxiety – those pilots must feel before entering the cockpits of their fighters and bombers ready for missions to the Continent, not knowing if they would ever return.

Diana's flight instructor was waiting patiently next to the plane. 'Today's the big day, Diana,' he said evenly. 'You know exactly what I taught you; that's all there is to it, really. You take the plane up, fly a number of circuits, make a few more take-offs and landings. Then you proceed to the church tower about thirty miles from here, circle around it once and return for the final landing here. Is that clear? Any questions?' His blue eyes in his tanned weather-beaten face steadily quizzed her to be sure she had properly understood.

Diana shook her head. 'No questions. I have a perfectly clear idea of what I'm supposed to do,' she replied firmly.

Dressed in her coveralls, she climbed into the cockpit. This time she took the instructor's seat. The small space had already become familiar to her from the last flights, when her instructor had told her to occupy his seat. She adjusted the seat belts and strapped them on, inhaling deeply a few times to steady herself.

Diana gazed attentively around the plane to make sure everything was clear on the tarmac. Then she started the engine and let it run until it reached the right temperature. She waited quietly until the instructor had removed the blocks in front of the wheels. After he pulled them away, she was ready to taxi to the runway, waving a last time to him as he stood alone on the platform, thumb turned up as a sign of encouragement.

When she reached the head of the runway, Diana waited impatiently for the green Very light. When it appeared in the air, she lowered her goggles over her eyes, checked the instruments in front of her once again, and then took off. At an altitude of around one thousand feet, she levelled off to initiate the first required circuit. Her heart pounded in her chest – she was alone at the controls now. No one else was there to help her. A few drops of perspiration stood out on her upper lip; now and then she bit her lower one, concentrating on what she had to perform.

Effecting her first turn, she forced herself to keep her nerves steady and under control. Subsequently, Diana aligned the plane with the runway ahead, and prepared to carry out her first solo landing. Softly encouraging herself, she said aloud, 'Steady, Diana! Keep it well aligned!' She saw the boundary of the airfield flash beneath the wings of the Tiger Moth, then lightly pulled back on the joystick, executing a perfect landing. It was smooth, soft, elegant, well handled. She felt satisfied and elated. She had done it – and so well! Pure joy flowed through her mind.

Rolling out, Diana shoved the throttle forward again and, hearing the growl of the engine increase, gained speed to take off for a second time. The other circuits she had to make went well too. Diana already began to feel much better, more secure. She felt confident she could do it all by herself. A proud smile crossed her tight lips. Thoughts whirled around in her brain. If Jan could only see me now, she mused.

She relaxed a bit, luxuriating in the sensation of flying completely alone. Diana felt the wind rush against her cheeks, and appreciated the regular purr of the engine and the air whistling through the wires connecting the two wings of the Tiger Moth, as if it were a kind of music. Now Diana was on her way to locate the church tower she was so familiar with, having flown over it so many times before during lessons with her reliable instructor.

The English countryside beneath her looked lovely from this altitude. The rolling hills, the green fields, the small valleys sloping gently, the charming farms, the animals and meadows all looked so tiny, so precisely defined. She enjoyed the moment immensely, taking in the magnificent, colourful spectacle unfolding below her, feeling like a giantess.

Diana kept her eyes on the horizon, every now and then checking the few instruments in front of her, the altitude indicator, the number of propeller revolutions, the oil temperature; once she found all the gauges in their correct positions, she felt confident, exuberant, glad simply to be alive.

Diana found her feelings for Jan growing more intense even though she was so thoroughly enjoying commanding her own flight. She laughed in delight, musing that her love for her Flying Dutchman was also carried on wings.

A few minutes later, she located the church tower, gracefully circled around it and then headed back towards the airfield again.

Diana was elated, fully caught up in the life of a real pilot; that's how she felt as a feeling of utter pride surged through her. She sang out loud in the cockpit, letting her voice be absorbed and carried away by the wind blowing around her head.

Following a well-executed landing, she felt so happy and jaunty that her cheeks consequently glowed with real excitement. She could have embraced the plane she had been flying, the instructor, in short, everything and anyone within her reach. Diana was in seventh heaven – she had done it! And all by herself. Jan would be proud of her!

Diana had completed a very important step in her life. She was now much closer to her Flying Dutchman, could understand more of those hidden aspects of his active operational life that she had hardly ever penetrated before. Jan rarely talked about the frightful tensions, the horrors he experienced in the tiny cockpit of his Spitfire while in action over Europe.

George had also spoken little of what could and did happen up in the deep blue sky when forced to combat the hundreds of Luftwaffe bombers and fighters clouding the skies over the Channel on their way to bomb England during 1940.

Contemplating it all, Diana was happy. Jan – now based at Woodvale – was remote from enemy action.

When she returned to her quarters, Diana glanced at herself in the mirror. Her cheeks still glowed and her eyes shone brightly, yet she now detected tiny crow's feet around her eyes. Little lines of tension after the great excitement of her successfully completed first solo flight. Physically she was exhausted, even though elated with the result. She had made it! She could now face Jan and exclaim, 'I'm a pilot, too!'

Sometimes when Diana had completed her duties in the operations room at Ludham, upon entering the smoke-filled mess, with all its noise and banter, she had remained struck by the tired, even haunted, eyes of some of the fighter pilots on their return from missions over enemy territory.

Oh, they made one hell of a noise at the bar all right, letting off steam, drinking, and loudly describing their flights with typical hand gestures. But Diana had silently noticed the dark lines etched in their faces, as if a sculptor had chiselled them to express the extreme limits of endurance.

During those moments, the pilots looked years older than they actually were. In the hundred and twenty minutes of flight since setting out, they had become 'old' young men – precociously aged in that short period of time. And for some, those minutes of tension had turned into eternity: they would never be tense or take off again. They had found their destination forever – Death!

Once Diana had obtained her flying license, she found she had a leave coming up. She phoned Jan in Liverpool, telling him all about it. They decided to meet in London; fortunately, he had also been able to arrange a short holiday.

Waiting for the train at Liverpool Street Station, Jan paced the platform impatiently. At last, it arrived. He spotted Diana's blonde hair in a sea of bobbing faces and waved to her.

She rushed towards him, spreading her arms wide, a radiant smile lighting up her lovely face. He seized her under her armpits, lifting her off her feet like a feather and swinging her around in the air while the people moving towards the exit looked on with amusement.

'Hello, my dearest pilot,' Jan said eagerly. 'How are you making out these days?' he asked, impatiently staring at her with those grey-blue eyes she loved so much.

Diana smiled at him happily. 'Jan, please put me down. You have no idea how excited I am. I have so much to tell you about my flying,' she said in a husky voice.

'What shall we do? Do we first pay a visit to your mother?' He stared questioningly at her, waiting for her decision.

'Yes, that's fine. That way, I can change into something more comfortable. Shall we also arrange a programme? How many days off have you got?'

'About a week. The planes have been sent to another base to be fitted with new engines and, on top of that, I have three days' leave coming to me. That makes six days altogether. Is that enough for us?' Jan asked, grinning slyly at her.

Diana shot him a provocative look and laughed. 'That will do, Dutchie. I think that will give me plenty of time to tell you all about my flying experiences!'

Outside the railway station, he hailed a taxi and they were on their way to her mother's apartment. She stole quick glances at him. He needed a haircut badly; his locks were far too long for her taste. She also noticed that his face was somewhat drawn and there were two new harsh, bitter lines around his mouth she'd never seen before. Innocently, she asked him, 'How are things in Woodvale.'

With a weary smile, Jan turned to her. 'Well, you know, we're training but don't have enough planes. It's all so disorganised. I honestly have to confess the whole atmosphere of the place is getting on my nerves. I'm more rested it's true, but the whole situation doesn't satisfy me in any way. I had expected so much more being together with my countrymen. Frankly speaking, it's quite a disappointment.' Diana became aware of how resentful Jan sounded when he made that last comment.

Diana put her hand on his arm as a goodwill gesture. 'Don't worry, Jan, I'll take good care of you during these few days in London. I'll make you forget the nasty experiences. We'll enjoy the good things of life. How about it, huh?' She pushed up against him and gave him an encouraging squeeze of the arm.

After she had spoken those consolatory words, Jan smiled at her. His finger tips caressed her cheek. 'Hello, darling Diana. I should not have bothered you with my problems. I should listen to you instead and hear how you're doing as a pilot.'

They sat close together in silence until they reached her mother's apartment. Once inside, Diana went to her room to change while Jan, having greeted Mrs Boulton, chatted with her in the sitting room.

'Any news from your family in Holland?' she asked him. The inquiry was kind. She had dark hair, partly streaked with grey, strong and elegant features; her dark eyes reflected a vigorous personality. She was dressed in a casual beige dress. Staring at her, Jan thought to himself he would not want her as an enemy. He also understood why Diana mentioned her mother so often.

'I've received a number of letters from them,' he politely answered. 'Naturally, they can't write what they'd like to because of German censorship. But other Dutchmen at the Dutch Club in London tell me the situation over there is rapidly deteriorating. I feel compassion for those who have to live under the harsh, ghastly German occupation. It must be terrible. So many young men are carted off to Germany to work in the war factories. No one is safe from the horrors committed by the SS and the Gestapo.' Jan spoke unhappily.

They could hear the sound of a shower and Diana's voice softly singing a popular tune, 'Dancing in the dark'. Mrs Boulton inconspicuously observed Jan and inwardly evaluated Diana s choice.

'In a way, you must be thankful you got out of Holland just in time,' she commented. 'You could also have been one of those unlucky young men being taken away from home and family and forced to work in Germany. Still, I believe it will all be over by next year. Then you can go home again and be reunited with your family and your Dutch friends. Your mother and father must be anxiously looking forward to seeing you again.'

Jan nodded politely. 'Yes, I think so too. The war will last for at least another year. Those Germans are tougher than any of us thought possible. You know, Mrs Boulton, during the very first months I spent in England, I mostly concentrated my thoughts exclusively on my family in Holland, especially my mother. But now, my reflections are increasingly drawn to what happens here in England. Diana is a great moral help to me. In the very beginning, I really felt rather homesick.' He smiled apologetically at Diana's mother. 'I've heard rumours we shall be transferred to the south again in a few months' time. I do believe the 'Big Operation' should be on by then.'

'You mean the invasion, don't you? That tremendous operation will be quite something. I notice so many Americans here in London. They seem to increase in numbers by the day!'

The door swung open right then and Diana entered the room. It seemed as if a bright warm sun had dispersed a few dark clouds in the sky. She had changed into a light blue cashmere turtleneck pullover and a dark blue flannel skirt, with a cardigan over her shoulders. She looked simply lovely and very desirable, Jan thought to himself.

He openly admired her. Diana looked very much a woman and the pullover enhanced her well-proportioned figure and soft curves to their best advantage. Staring at her, Jan realised she had changed his whole life.

Diana cheerfully consulted her mother. 'I'm ready for tea. How about the two of you?'

Mrs Boulton stood and went into the kitchen, returning with a big tray. On it stood a silver teapot surrounded by several small dishes covered with cakes and pastries, cups and saucers.

They sat together in the sitting room just like a normal, peacetime family. That was what Jan appreciated so much in Diana. She created a pleasant, peaceful atmosphere wherever she went; no tensions, no grim ideas about a war needing to be ended. Jan felt as if he were at his own home in The Hague, being spoilt by his mother.

Drinking his first cup of tea, which Diana had barely saved from the British milk-first habit by explaining to her mother how Jan liked it, he said, 'Now, Diana – tell us about your flying adventures. That way, your mother and I can also get some sort of idea about what you've been doing in the Midlands, streaking through the air.' An encouraging smile appeared on his face as he spoke.

Diana stared at them uncertainly. 'Well, if the two of you insist, here I go. First of all, I must be frank and say I like flying very much and appreciate it more and more with each passing day. I'm not afraid. After my first solo flights, I've become more confident. Observing the countryside from the cockpit is really a marvellous, unique experience. Those toy houses, and everything else around, look so peaceful from the air. You get a complete sense of relativity – you are up there worrying about flying, and there's a seemingly quiet world beneath you, at peace and not at war. There might be a husband quarrelling with his wife or scolding a son in one of those small houses – or a boss shouting at one of his employees – but you don't hear any of it, aren't directly involved. You're busy flying and I would like to use the term "soaring majestically" above it all. It doesn't concern you in any way. Is that clear?'

Diana looked questioningly, eagerly, at Jan and her mother to see if they understood her explanation. Then she continued.

'The relativity of it all is really what I like so much about flying. You're alone up there, commanding your plane. You can fly wherever you want to go.' Now she smiled hesitantly at Jan. 'I'm certainly no Jean Batten yet, but given time, I will learn and perhaps become a reasonably efficient transport pilot,' she assured them with pride.

'Good for you, Diana!' Jan exclaimed enthusiastically. 'The most important thing is for you to like it. Just follow the basic rules and nothing will happen to you. If you ever develop engine trouble, then that's a completely different story. What was your highest altitude?'

Diana smiled modestly. 'Oh, I can't possibly compare my flying feats with you fellows, of course. But I've already flown at five thousand feet.'

Now she turned to her mother. 'Your horizon – what I mean is, what can be seen from your cockpit – increases tremendously with altitude. You know, when the day's clear and I'm flying at a great height, I can even see the Channel coastline.'

Diana got carried away telling her story and, like all pilots, used her hands to emphasise how she flew the plane, visually describing the manoeuvres she performed when airborne. She looked simply lovely in her light blue pullover, talking excitedly about her flying skills, hands actively slicing the air around her, her cheeks glowing red.

Jan and Diana's mother watched her in fascination. It was the first time since George's death Mrs Boulton had seen her daughter so full of pep and enthusiasm. It made her happy – and also grateful to the tall, good-natured Dutchman who had inspired Diana to start flying. She liked her daughter's choice. He was a fine young man with excellent manners, with style and class – and it showed.

Had Diana's mother been twenty years younger, she might have taken up flying herself after listening to Diana's lively description of being in the air.

'I'm glad you like it,' Jan encouraged her. 'As I told you, I haven't finished my studies at Technical High School in Delft. However, as a future engineer,' he laughed slyly, 'let's say I'm always amazed, when initiating take-off at the beginning of the runway, at how you still belong to a two-dimensional world. But then, when you gain speed and your tail leaves the ground, you're still in the same dimensional sphere until you're airborne and suddenly become three-dimensional. You become an integral part of a completely different environment. A marvellous, unknown new world, I dare say. You speed through the air, carried by your plane's wings, with the sun high in the sky, the blue, wide open spaces above you and the earth below. You're in full command and can point the plane in any direction you desire.'

Jan looked at Mrs Boulton, explaining, 'That's the beautiful part of flying – you're really as free as a bird.' He spoke enthusiastically. 'When I'm in my Spit at a high altitude the sky looks dark blue. I am aware of a sensation there's something beyond us, an undefinable, mysterious force directing all of us. I've felt that emotion on several occasions. Perhaps it sounds weird to you, but that's what I experienced.' Imperceptibly, Jan shrugged his shoulders after these significant words, as if he wanted to apologise for the unexplainable mysteries of flying.

For an instant, Mrs Boulton's eyes misted after hearing Diana's friend. All at once, she realised what a fine character that Flying Dutchman possessed.

Jan had also used his hands to explain his flying manoeuvres. Looking at Diana and her mother, he continued. 'When you climb up very high on a nice clear day and you're close to forty thousand feet, the sky above you is no longer light blue but becomes much darker. I can well imagine the higher you go the darker it becomes. Well, Diana?' He hesitated a moment while facing her. 'Does that describe some of your feelings and experiences?'

Diana beamed. 'Yes, oh yes, Jan!' she confirmed. 'You've described it even better than I could. You know, within a few weeks, I'll be transferred to another plane, the Miles Master. It's frightfully fast but my brave instructor told me I'm ready for it.'

Her mother raised one hand. 'Now, Diana, take it easy. Don't push things, please. We do want you all in one piece, don't we Jan?' Her dark eyes twinkled in a friendly way when she said those words to her daughter. 'I don't want you two to stay here loyally keeping me company. I assume you have a great deal to say to one another without mother being present,' she laughed at them. 'What are your plans? You have the late afternoon and all evening ahead of you.'

'I think we shall do some shopping, Mother,' Diana said. 'You don't mind, do you?' Diana stared questioningly at her mother who shook her head. 'Then we might have dinner somewhere, maybe at Claridge's and then,' Diana stopped a moment, gazing teasingly at Jan, 'maybe I'll tempt this coura- geous Dutchman into dancing with me after dinner. Shame on you, Dutchie, you can't dance.' As she smiled at him, Jan noticed the tiny crow's feet at the corners of Diana's blue eyes for the first time, as if she had been staring into the sun's bright glare for a long time. It pleased him no end.

'Don't pay any attention to what she says, Jan,' Mrs Boulton said. 'It took me a very long time before I got Diana and Jane to dancing lessons. Well, off you go and enjoy your- selves – you've certainly earned it.'

Long after they had left the apartment, Mrs Boulton sat alone, deep in thought. She liked Diana's choice. Jan was a fine, decent boy with character, but having flown over Europe more than a hundred times, he would be really risking his life when he returned south to fly missions once again. What would become of her daughter, now so happy and carefree, if something should happen to her Flying Dutchman?

If Diana's heart should be wounded again, what would the consequences be for her, poor girl? Those awful, sombre thoughts sent a chill down her spine. And she prayed aloud, 'Dear God in Heaven, please protect those two! They're still so young.'

Jan and Diana were oblivious to everything happening around them. Arm-in-arm, they walked along, peering into shop windows, looking at each other, laughing at nothing – they were so happy to be together again. That afternoon, he bought her a warm shawl and a pair of leather gloves. She spoiled him with a new tie and a metal money clasp.

Later, they went to Claridge's, where they had dinner. Sipping coffee afterwards, Jan drew a small package from his pocket. 'A small surprise for you, Diana,' he said. 'And many thanks again for all you did for me on the houseboat.'

Her face reflecting her surprise, Diana stared at him. 'May I open it right now?'

'Go ahead,' he smiled. 'It's just a small thought.'

When Diana opened the package, she saw a small gold ring inside. She took it out carefully. Holding it up against the light from the chandeliers, she noticed an inscription: 'To Diana.'

Her eyes misted instantly with emotion. 'Oh, Jan, how kind of you. How did you know it was my birthday today? I thought you'd completely forgotten. Did you know I'm also of age today? I'm a free woman!' she chuckled happily. Then she laughed delightedly, tossing him a meaningful glance.

Jan gazed around mysteriously, as if he had to hide a secret from others who might overhear him. Playfully, he put his index finger to his lips with a 'sshh' sound. 'Your age and date of birth, my dear Diana, have been supplied to me by the Dutch Secret Services here in London. They've been following you ever since we met. Haven't you noticed?'

They burst out laughing. Once again, when she looked into Jan's eyes, Diana felt that sensation of being swept up into a world of kindness and love.

For a second, she had to fight her emotions to hold back the tears of absolute, total happiness – she barely managed to control herself. She bent over to him, kissing him softly on both cheeks. 'I'll remember this moment forever.' She looked straight into his eyes as she spoke.

But their happy reunion was rudely interrupted at that point by a voice from behind them.

'Hey, you two lovebirds, what are you doing over here in hiding?'

It was Kees. 'May I keep you company for just a second? I'm waiting for someone.'

Controlling the slight irritation the intrusion caused her, Diana turned to Kees. 'Hello, Kees. Long time no see, huh? How are things with you? Have you completely recovered? How are your injured ribs doing and how is that Dutch squadron performing? Jan never tells me anything.'

'Oh, you know, Diana, I do feel fine and healthy again, but at Woodvale we're getting lazier by the day. What kind of war are we Dutch fighter pilots waging anyway?' he asked with a sneer. 'Jan and I are doing very little flying; nothing of any real importance.' Kees shrugged his shoulders in a typical gesture of annoyance.

'You'll see,' Diana said. 'One day, there'll be the big show and suddenly all of you will be flying operationally again. And if you allow me to say so, Kees, you'll be scared stiff every time you have to cross the Channel to face the Germans again.'

Kees nodded in agreement. 'You may be right. One day, when I've downed one drink too many, I may tell you how scared I really feel at times – but let's not spoil the evening with dark thoughts. Ah, there's my friend!' Kees exclaimed, quickly getting to his feet. 'Be seeing you both. Bye for now.'

After the short intermezzo with Kees, Diana had a naughty gleam in her eyes. She watched Jan with a curious expression.

'Well, my dearest Flying Dutchman, where's your courage? Are you going to dance with me? Just for my birthday. Or do I have to drag you out of that comfortable chair and pull you onto the dance floor? I hear music from the other room. Come on, Jan. I'll lead. Don't be shy now, please,' she insisted, noticing the annoyed expression on his face. She got to her feet, offering him both her hands and pulling him up, accompanying a reluctant Jan to the dance floor where many couples were already dancing.

Diana put her arms around his shoulders and slid into his strong arms. They moved with the others to the rhythm of a slow fox-trot. The band played 'Moonlight Serenade'. They danced cheek to cheek to the melodious tune made famous by Glen Miller and his orchestra.

To be able to dance with her tall Dutchman, Diana had to move on her toes. Jan bent over her, whispering in her ear, 'You know, Diana, I think I would do much better on the dance floor if I wore Dutch wooden clogs!'

Surprised by his remark, she looked up at him, and caught the humour twinkling in his eyes. She pressed up hard against him, feeling so completely happy with him right then.

Returning to their table, they heard the dreaded sound of an air raid warning. Worried, Diana consulted him. 'Let's not waste this fine evening sitting in an air raid shelter. It may be nothing at all and we'll have lost precious time. Jane and I have a small place not too far from here. My mother rented it for both of us. Let's walk there now. Jane's on duty tonight anyway. No one will disturb us.'

They left Claridge's and walked slowly arm-in-arm through the dark deserted streets of London. Once safely at her place, Diana pulled her key out of her shoulder bag to open the front door. As she switched on the light, Jan saw a cosy, warmly furnished little apartment consisting of a sitting room, a kitchenette, bedroom and bathroom. The living room was elegantly decorated; there was an open hearth with everything prepared for it – paper, small pieces of wood, as if the elves had come visiting before them. One only needed to light a match to get the fire going.

There were a number of framed photographs on the mantlepiece above the open fire. In one of them, Jan was seated in the open cockpit of his Spitfire, looking towards the camera. 'Diana, where did you get my picture?' he asked, curious.

'That's my little secret, Dutchie,' she replied. 'Jan, would you mind lighting the fire? You'll find the matches on the table. In the meantime, I'll make coffee. You'll have to stay awake tonight and listen to all my stories about flying an airplane.'

He laughed. 'All right! First the fire and then we'll take off!'

'What does that mean? Where do we take off to?' She reached up to him, kissing him eagerly on his willing lips.

Diana left to prepare coffee in the kitchenette. After Jan lit the paper, the room started to fill with the rich aroma of coffee and, a few minutes later, with the tang of smoke and burning wood.

He lay back on the sofa, relaxing completely, but he got up as soon as Diana placed a tray on a small table in front of him. On it stood two cups filled with black coffee, plus two ballons filled with amber cognac.

'Make yourself comfortable, Jan. Just lie down. Take it easy. We have to relish these moments together – every single one,' she insisted.

Lazily, Jan smiled at her. 'You do spoil me. I'll finish this war as one of the most pampered pilots of the modern age!' He stretched his arms out towards her, reaching for her. 'Come here,' he begged with his hand. 'Let me hold you and give you a nice birthday kiss.'

Before moving into his waiting arms, Diana turned all the lights off. Now only the fire's glow illuminated the room, with the weird, restless flames in the hearth reflecting so beautifully on her silky, lustrous, blonde hair. To his surprise, Jan noticed how the flames danced in her blue eyes. He loved her – completely.

They stayed like that, holding each other and not speaking a word, for a long time, silently watching the mystic dancing of the yellow-red burning flames. They let time drift by. Softly, Jan whispered, 'I love you.'

Diana turned her face to him while her hand caressed his cheeks and her lips slightly parted to kiss him. Softly, she said, 'I'm so happy, I'm afraid it won't last. Can so much happiness go on forever, Jan?' She spoke as if she addressed the question more to herself than to him. 'Is it a concession – of God perhaps?' She stirred in his arms. 'Please hold me tightly.' She wanted to share the night with him. 'Let nothing ever come between us,' she sighed.

Jan put a finger to her lips. 'Don't say anything. Let's enjoy and value every moment of happiness.' He stared into the fire. 'We don't know what the future holds for us. In a way, we are like grains of sand in the process of time. Our happiness cannot be just an intermezzo on earth. There has to be more, Diana.' Tenderly, he stared into her eyes. 'If it's in the cards, we will live to be happy together once the war is over. If not ...' His voice trailed off as utter silence descended on the room, as if a sudden dark shadow had passed between them only to fade away again, yet leaving behind an ineradicable sign.

Right then, the all-clear signal sounded. Smiling gently at her, he said, 'Listen, even the war leaves us alone.'

Deeply in love, they spent the night together. The millions of bright stars in the dark universe over London twinkled, lighting up something of unique magnificence – love on wings.

Two young pilots racing wingtip to wingtip, streaking just above the white clouds in the sky, on a flight of tenderness and love.

Could it last?

XX

AFTER THE wonderful week with Diana in London, Jan returned to Woodvale, to the Dutch 322 Squadron. During the following weeks, he had to perform some specialised flying, a number of shooting exercises, formation flying, cannon tests and shooting at low level at the wreck of a ship close to Southport, the well-known seaside resort.

There were times when Jan decided to drink nothing alcoholic any more. When the weather turned bad and the pilots were grounded, they soon became bored, and passed the time away at the bar drinking too much. During Jan's periods of abstinence, he went to bed earlier and slept much better as a consequence. Sometimes when sitting alone in his room, he would take a piece of drawing paper and a pencil to design figures of aerobatic manoeuvres he thought he could perform with his Spit. Just like a composer scribbling notes on the bars of sheet music, Jan made drawings of what he thought he might be able to perform.

Jan had been asked on several occasions to give a demonstration of his excellent flying techniques for visitors to Woodvale.

One day, he was required to demonstrate to HRH Prince Bernhard of the Netherlands what his Spit could do in the way of aerobatics. Another day, he was asked to give a demonstration of his flying abilities to a group of workers from the

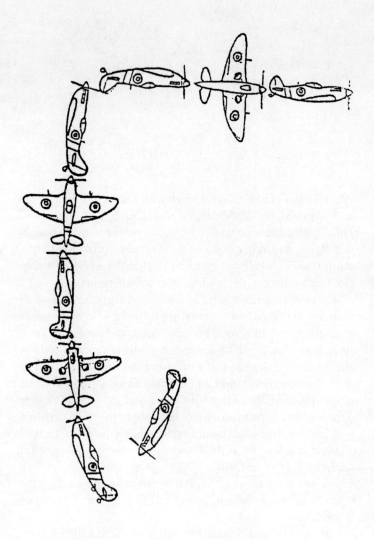

A Spitfire manoeuvre from Jan's diary
(1) A vertical right or left barrel roll ending with a horizontal flight

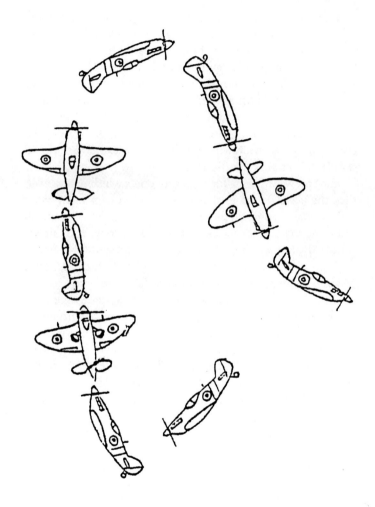

A Spitfire manoeuvre from Jan's diary
(2) A vertical barrel roll ending at the top of the climb with a one-turn spin

Fairey Aircraft Factory. Jan accepted and promised to give the visitors a good demonstration.

The group's leader asked Jan if he could show them just what a Spitfire could do under maximum stress. He took off and climbed to an altitude of nine thousand feet, from which he dived to the airfield, pulling out at the very last moment, and flashed flat over the heads of the factory workers at over 400 mph. Then, at the airfield boundary, he pulled up sharply and made a double vertical climbing barrel roll – one of the most difficult manoeuvres a Spitfire can do. After two complete turns around the plane's axis, it came to a virtual standstill – a kind of vertical stall in the air.

His Spit was hanging for an instant on its whirling propeller; then the plane started to slide downward on its tail. Jan didn't feel any real pressure on the elevators or the rudder. The aircraft just hung there in the air like a dead leaf, floating, without any control. By losing altitude, he managed to gain some pressure on the controls again. He worked the rudder with his feet, slowly regaining command of the plane now falling sideways; subsequently, he made a spin downwards, turning three times, and neatly pulled the Spit out of it just before hitting the ground.

Afterwards, Jan flew over the field at maximum speed – over 400 mph at a height of only 100 feet. Then, after passing the boundary of the field, he pulled up sharply again, made a tight turn, dived and came back over the field making slow barrel rolls at an altitude of 200 feet, the lowest height at which he had ever performed these rolls in his Spit. One wrong move and the plane would lose altitude and he could hit the ground at more than 300 mph.

He aimed the Spit at the factory workers standing very close together; at the last possible moment, he pulled up sharply, streaking over their heads. He grinned with pleasure in the small cockpit when he saw how they all ducked, fearing he might strike them with the propeller.

At last, Jan ended his flying show with a number of loops and Immelmans at only 2,000 feet. He concluded his display with his most daring stunt, flying at a height of only 30 feet, his Spitfire upside down, speeding over the field. Finally, Jan landed the plane elegantly and taxied slowly to the tarmac, parking his aircraft.

Leaving the cockpit, he jumped athletically to the ground, and received a loud ovation from all the assembled workers for the marvellous demonstration. They crowded around him and some of them insisted on shaking hands with him. They thanked him and told him enthusiastically how much they had appreciated his flying display of that morning. They also told him they now realised even better that what they built performed fantastically in the hands of such an exceptionally good pilot. But then Jan really could get the last ounce of flying out of his Spitfire.

His Dutch colleagues had to admit that, too!

As there was no tension of war at Woodvale, and as the squadron did not make enough planes available for training, there were too many pilots doing too little and as a consequence drinking too much, producing low morale throughout the entire squadron. The weather certainly did not help much to improve the dreary situation.

During the evening hours at the bar in the noisy, smoke-filled room, there was heavy drinking and the singing of Dutch songs. It was all so terribly empty, meaningless, totally void of any significance to Jan. A few days later, trying to record in his diary what had been said or discussed, he couldn't even recall a word of importance or interest having been exchanged by the men.

One day at Woodvale airfield, after he had downed a few beers before take-off, Jan overshot the runway at the end of his landing run. Fortunately, his Spit suffered no mechanical damage. Jan decided then and there to completely stop drinking any alcoholic beverages, even beer. He realised only too well that beer and flying do not mix very well. His latest decision separated him even further from the other Dutch Squadron pilots. Sipping lemonades at the bar while others got drunker by the moment, Jan became steadily more irritated with the whole setup, more than he wanted to admit. To him, it was all such a negative, empty show.

Instead, he began early morning gymnastics, doing his exercises regularly to keep himself in good physical shape. He performed more than thirty push-ups every morning.

During one of his London leaves, Jan found out one of his best friends from The Hague – Cees Bloem, with whom he had studied at Delft Technical High School – had managed to escape from Holland and had finally arrived in London.

Jan immediately dropped all his other leave plans in order to find out where his friend was staying. After numerous phone calls, he finally located Cees. They met again after two and a half years and were both anxious to exchange experiences from Holland and England. Excitedly, they discussed the latest news and information while enjoying lunch at the Kensington. Later, they walked to the Dutch Club, animatedly continuing their conversation.

Cees told Jan the latest news about his parents. Jan's mother and father were in good health, and lived in a cosy villa in the eastern part of the Netherlands, not far from the German border. The German authorities in The Hague had banned his father from his own house close to the North Sea coast and had forced him to live close to Enschede.

For the next few days, Jan and his friend Cees continued their conversations. Jan also introduced Cees to Diana, on leave in London. Diana and Cees liked each other instantly. When he finally returned to Woodvale, Jan wrote in his diary:

> This last leave has been one of the best ever in London. Seeing my friend, Cees Bloem, and talking to him again was the highlight of my short holiday. Am I glad he made it safely to England! When he spoke to me about conditions in Holland, I became even more aware of what terrible suffering the Dutch in general are experiencing.

On Tuesday 7 September, he wrote:

> Today was a special one for me. As Flight Commander,
> I led a group of twelve Spitfires. All the pilots were
> Dutch. The exercise went well. I'm very pleased I fully
> commanded eleven other Dutch pilots in formation and
> got them to follow my commands. I wonder what my
> father would have said if he'd seen me as the number
> one pilot of a group of Spitfires. Today was a good day.

On Friday 24 September, he wrote in his diary again:

> Weather bad. No flying today. Went to a cinema. While
> purchasing my ticket, I noticed three small boys, each
> around twelve, who looked at me inquisitively. One of
> them shyly approached me, asking, 'Sir, would you
> kindly accompany us inside; otherwise, we're not
> allowed to enter and we'd like to see the movie too.' I
> laughed good-naturedly at them and took them under
> my wing. We passed the doorman together. When we
> were seated in the dark cinema, I remembered so well
> how my father had also once tried to take *me* into a
> cinema in The Hague before the war. I was twelve years
> old then and the movie was reserved to spectators over
> fourteen. My father said to the doorman, 'My son is
> twelve years old and I take complete responsibility.' The
> doorman adamantly refused despite my father's
> straightforward and honest approach. However hard he
> tried, I was not allowed inside. I remembered it all so
> clearly today when I saw those three youngsters lolling
> around in front of the cinema.

During the months of October and November, the pilots of
322 Squadron made several flights to Llanbedr airfield in
Wales where they participated in shooting courses. Jan had
been there before at the end of 1941, learning to fly the Spitfire. Now he had to shoot at targets for gunnery practice.

On the 8th of December 1943, he received a letter from the Dutch Air Force Office in London, informing him he had finally been promoted to Flight Lieutenant. In Dutch military terms, it meant Captain in the Reserve Air Force. It also meant Jan, before reaching the age of twenty-three, had achieved a higher military rank than his father during his military duty at Soesterberg in Holland, in the Great War. Although he realised it was over six months late, he perceived it as representing a satisfactory acknowledgement.

In his diary, Jan wrote:

> If I should reach the end of the war, I might try to become a commercial airline pilot, maybe even with KLM. I might also try to become a technical manager of the Dutch Airline, since I've gained such comprehensive experience here in England. Or I could return to Delft and finish my engineering studies at the Technical High School. I wonder, though, if I shall be able to find the necessary patience to study that dry technical material after the war's great excitement. If I should marry Diana, I'll also need a salary.

Jan could now face his father, being a Captain, having shown tenacity, courage and perseverance, qualities his father appreciated in a man. His father was often stern in his judgment, but once he trusted a man, he became a good friend throughout life.

To Jan, the outlook seemed promising and his future bright, despite his doubts about the effective chances of becoming a technical engineer.

On 18 December, his birthday, he received a silver beer tankard from Kees and a number of his squadron colleagues. He felt pleased. They had remembered the date. Diana also gave him a call, making the day complete. Jan was then 23 years old. Finally, on 30 December 1943, the squadron was transferred to Hawkinge airfield, in the south-east of England close to Dover. When 322 Squadron took off from Woodvale, and Jan saw the field disappear beneath the wings of his Spit, he said out loud in the cockpit, 'Thanks for nothing, absolutely nothing!' He hated the place, the boredom and inactivity. He felt he had completely wasted over 200 days doing nothing of any value while the war had continued relentlessly, without halting for even one minute!

Jan, totally aware of all the goings on around him, perhaps thought of himself as some kind of white knight on a white horse, helping the weak and disapproving of the guilty; yet he was also fully aware his opinion happened to be invariably correct.

All the wasted time he had lost at the lonely Castletown airfield, in the cold north of Scotland after flying operationally as an active member of a pleasant, dynamic British squadron commanded by the marvellous Squadron Leader Duncan Smith – known as Smitty – weighed heavily on his mind.

Now, he had to add to it all the wasted months at Woodvale, the lonely, boring periods of inactivity he had been obliged, forced, to sacrifice there. He laid most of the blame on the inefficiency of the inept, lazy London Dutch officials of the Dutch Air Force brass. In his opinion, they were largely responsible for having kept him and the other pilots of 322 Squadron away from operational flying for such a long period. Jan considered it all such a complete, total waste of his valuable time.

Jan strongly believed the Dutch fighter pilots had been utterly misused: they could have flown regular missions over Europe damaging the infernal German war machine during those wasted months.

He thought it was essential to let Dutch pilots fight against the Luftwaffe and the Nazi oppressors of Europe as much as humanly possible, for three weeks at a time, with one week of rest in between.

Since he was young, impatient, and also rather obstinate at times, he was bound to clash with the inefficient Dutch bureaucracy in London. In fact, he repeatedly expressed the very low opinion he had of them in his diary.

The forward operational Hawkinge airfield proved to be no improvement at all; on the contrary, it turned out to be worse than Woodvale. It consisted of a grass field without runways. In addition, the dispersal huts had been badly neglected because most of the buildings had been destroyed or severely damaged during the 1940 Battle of Britain and had been only partially repaired.

Hawkinge was located close to Dover and on a clear day one could clearly distinguish the French coast: it was a new experience for the Dutch pilots. However, the field also happened to be within range of German long-range artillery which sporadically fired on them from France – not a very pleasant sensation at all.

During the first cold winter days of 1944, the entire airfield made a spooky, depressing, dreary impression on Jan and his Dutch colleagues. Doors squeaked loudly, the wind rattled windows mysteriously; in a way, the whole macabre atmosphere resembled a Boris Karloff movie, with the latter rambling through the empty corridors of a dilapidated, derelict castle.

The pilots were accommodated in a country manor where, for the first time since he'd been in England, Jan had a room all to himself. It was an improvement. Yes, his promotion in rank, plus a certain seniority, was advantageous to him now; at least, that's what he thought – completely unaware of what lay ahead.

Mess was half an hour's walk from the manor. A pleasant stroll on a bright day but rather annoying when rain or wet snow fell – as it did frequently during those dark, interminable winter days. All in all, Jan did not find the place an improvement over Woodvale at all, with the exception of having a room to himself and, of course, taking part in the air battles over Europe again.

Jan took advantage of the first days to work out a number of personal matters – like a new parachute and a Mae West life-jacket. He also put in a request for new flying goggles. At the end of the first day, he drank a beer at the bar, which he noticed was well-stocked. The next day, the squadron had to fly sector recces to become acquainted with the south coast area. Folkestone and Dover, with its white cliffs so easily recognised, were the two towns close to the new base.

On 4 January 1944, Jan went operational again. On that day, he twice escorted bombers flying to France. When he returned from his second flight, he phoned Diana.

'Hello, how are you?'

'Fine, and you?'

'I've just come back from France. The aerial circus has started all over again. From now on, Diana, we should coordinate our leaves as much as possible. I'm much closer to London.'

'Take good care of yourself, Jan. Please do it for me.'

After the short phone call, Jan felt much better. At Hawkinge, he was only seventy miles from London, quite an improvement compared with the long train ride from Liverpool. It would facilitate his visits to Diana.

This time around, 322 Squadron was equipped with Mk Vb Spitfires – certainly not the most modern aircraft around, but reliable. However, the Luftwaffe had outfitted their squadrons with Focke Wulf 190 A-8 fighter planes equipped with two machine guns and four rapid firing cannon. It was a top-notch plane, much faster than the Spitfires of Jan's squadron. The new Focke Wulfs were durable, and technically superb planes as far as handling qualities were concerned. A formidable antagonist, not to be underestimated.

The German aircraft designers in the Messerschmitt and Focke Wulf factories had not been idle. What they had developed was far superior to the Mk Vb Spitfire in flying characteristics. In a short period of time, the faithful Spit had become an inferior airplane in performance. Again, Jan had to face the Luftwaffe in an obsolete aircraft, just the same as during the 1940 May days in Holland.

The Mk IX Spitfires were technically a great step forward and a match for the latest German fighters, but they were only made available to British squadrons. These new planes had four-bladed variable pitch propellers and many other technical innovations that considerably improved their performance.

Jan had to make do with the flying equipment the RAF provided to the Dutch pilots. It was definitely not the best, nor the worst – just a middle-of-the-road situation he had never liked.

At home in The Hague, his father had taught Jan it was always important to offer guests the best in the home. Having risked his life to escape from Holland all the way to England, Jan obviously expected the best from his hosts when fighting a common cause together; but the RAF evidently was not of the same opinion.

Nor did the stingy Dutch government-in-exile find it necessary to purchase better fighting planes for their 'finest'. Their motto seemed to be 'Better dead than an extra pound spent'!

Jan thought it was exactly the same as it had been during the years before the war, when socialist governments refused to spend extra money to arm the Dutch military with better, more modern arms to protect the Netherlands against the German threat.

But it was all right to send their 'finest' up in the air, in 25-year-old antiquated flying coffins to fight against the sleek modern Messerschmitts provided by the Luftwaffe for their 'finest'! What gall those nauseating, cheap, despicable, hypocritical, political villains had turned out to have, feigning courage at the expense of the young pilots! And how many young dead as a consequence?

They had sat safely on their fat buttocks, in secure command posts, sending inexperienced Dutch pilots to their deaths. And now, four years later, the Dutch government-in-exile in London repeated exactly the same terrible infamy!

Angrily, Jan wrote in his diary: 'They should prosecute those responsible in London for premeditated, cold-blooded murder!'

But, thinking it over the next day and weighing all the factors involved, Jan tore the page out of his diary in disgust and threw it in his waste-paper basket torn in small pieces. He felt thoroughly fed up fighting the inept apparatchiks who sent the 'finest' to their deaths thanks only to inborn Dutch stinginess.

The planes assigned to 322 Squadron were mediocre; the airfield was lousy – definitely not the best. Fighter planes from other squadrons sometimes set down at Hawkinge. One day, a Hawker Typhoon landed: it was the most modern aircraft the RAF employed at that stage of the war. Jan walked around the parked craft and admired it.

As a fighter aircraft, the Typhoon had not lived up to expectations, but as a low-level attack plane with its four 20 mm cannon it had turned out to be a most successful, formidable anti-tank weapon. This was clearly demonstrated on 7 August 1944 in the Falaise massacre, during which many German tanks, armoured cars and trucks were wiped out by many Typhoon fighters breaking up a German counter-offensive against American army forces.

Letting his hand slide over the smooth wing surface, Jan considered it an excellent finish. The plane was a great step forward in fighter design.

Once again, Jan was regularly airborne. At times, 322 Squadron had to escort as many as seventy bombers in one mission to the Continent. Once in flight, Jan was always rather impressed by such a mass of aircraft when meeting them at rendezvous in the skies over England. They had to fly in close formation to protect each other from fighter attack.

He could well imagine how terrified Luftwaffe pilots must be when faced with carrying out an attack on such a massive, well-armed group of bombers over France or Germany.

Jan also considered the immense courage demonstrated by the 'famous few' of the Battle of Britain when they repeatedly attacked those tight formations of Luftwaffe bombers and fighters as they came over once, twice or even three times a day from France. Guts and fighting spirit happened to be qualities Jan admired and respected in a man – just as his father did.

Every time Jan flew over occupied Europe, he became more aware of the intense anti-aircraft fire over a number of targets. It seemed to become heavier and more concentrated day by day. The number of bombers being lost was still considerable if one took into account the increasingly sporadic, reduced fighter opposition of the slowly weakening Luftwaffe. But by now the anti-aircraft units on the ground were scoring heavily.

It saddened Jan to see from his small cockpit that a bomber he was escorting was going down in flames after being hit by ground flak. There was nothing, absolutely nothing, he could possibly do to help the unfortunate wounded or dying.

On several occasions, operating over north-west France, Jan met with anti-aircraft fire of impressive intensity. All those grey-black puffs of smoke from exploding shrapnel around his plane acutely reminded him of his own vulnerability. As Joyce had told him, 'You're not invulnerable, Jan.'

One day, the Dutch pilots of 322 Squadron were briefed by an intelligence officer. He informed them that the Nazis were actively working on a number of new secret weapons. The German military needed launching ramps to get these lethal threats of destruction off the ground. Blown-up photographs were shown but were not very clear or sharp. The pictures showed a kind of short upwards inclined track, that could be compared to a very short railway.

The intelligence officer explained that the ones that had been discovered and photographed all seemed to be aimed at the south of England. What these new weapons were exactly, or what precisely they looked like and how they performed, was something no one really knew at that stage.

The pilots were told to look out for them during their low-level flights over north-west France and to report immediately if they had been located. It was of the utmost importance to the Allied war effort.

The squadron was involved in many ground attacks on trains originating in Germany and travelling towards the French coast where the launching sites were thought to be installed. The Allied High Command wanted to destroy as many of the necessary supplies as possible on this route in order to deprive any secret weapons of required materials.

The first months of 1944 went by with Jan over the Continent twice a day over and over again. He was rapidly approaching the figure of 150 operational missions over Europe.

During those days, 322 Squadron finally received new aircraft – the Mk XIV Spitfire. It was equipped with a 2,050 hp engine and a five-bladed variable pitch propeller enabling the pilot to climb rapidly to great altitudes. One of the Dutch pilots took it up one day to 44,000 feet; the highest Jan managed to achieve was 42,600 feet. But Jan was given the honour of picking up the squadron's first unit at the factory.

After their move to Hawkinge, the squadron was transferred again on 10 March 1944, to Acklington – close to Newcastle in Northumberland, on the north-east coast. At this airfield, to their bitter surprise, the Dutch pilots and maintenance staff were forced to sleep in tents, a backwards step in conditions after the already mediocre accommodation offered at Hawkinge. It was quite a setback, a kind of degradation and a very unpleasant one, indeed!

The new task for 322 Squadron was to escort bombers to launching sites in north-west France.

On 23 April 1944, the squadron was transferred yet again – this time to Hartford Bridge, west of London. The lodgings consisted once again of those damn small tents. It was a severe disappointment for the already weary Dutch pilots. When it rained – a frequent occurrence during that time of year – the field became a mud bath. On one occasion, returning from a late mission over Europe, the pilots found their mattresses and private belongings floating in brownish, dirty water which had invaded their tents. In some spots, the mud was ankle deep and the blankets floated around in the slush. They even had to sleep on their wet things that night. The following morning, the cold, shivering pilots had to be awakened with whisky and warm clothes to get their strained, abused muscles working again. Jan thought it a shameful state of affairs – the way they were being treated by the Dutch brass in London was really disgusting.

Equipped with the new, modern Spitfire, the squadron was now employed to protect the southern coast of England from the inquisitive Luftwaffe reconnaissance planes that were trying to penetrate English airspace and discover what progress the Allied Forces were making in building up their super arsenal of weapons for the upcoming invasion.

Regular flights at altitudes of 33,000 feet and higher required precise, disciplined flying techniques because the Spit cockpit was not pressurised. The pilot had to be very careful in using the oxygen mask and supply, and also had to keep an eye continuously on fuel consumption – he had exactly seventy minutes of flight time at his disposal. If the mask did not fit well, or if it slipped down during the flight because of a sudden move by the pilot, he unwittingly started inhaling rarefied oxygen-poor air, instead of the pure oxygen he was supplied with. After half an hour or less of flying in those conditions, the pilot could lose consciousness. The squadron lost one of its pilots in just that way due to the silent, treacherous, invisible killer. The young pilot had just returned from leave; half an hour later, his Mk XIV was seen mysteriously crashing vertically into the English countryside at an incredible speed.

Under these hazardous conditions, so fraught with danger, Jan regularly had to fly at high altitude, intently searching the dark blue skies for Luftwaffe reconnaissance intruders. On 30 April 1944, he carried out his first high altitude patrol, and during May Jan made nineteen high altitude patrols over southern England. During June, he flew twelve high altitude patrols. Each flight lasted for more than an hour and ten minutes.

Climbing to these pre-assigned altitudes over England provided Jan with a clear picture of the immense invasion build-up. Thousands of English and American tanks were parked on the sides of narrow British country roads. Tens of thousands of jeeps, trucks and lorries were tightly parked in green fields.

These regular flights showed Jan how enormous an organisation was needed to land an army overseas. The British Expeditionary Forces had escaped from Dunkirk practically empty-handed. Now, four years later, they were going to return, fully armed this time, ready to fight and defeat the most formidable war machine ever created by the Germans on the Continent. In front of the Allies stood the intimidating Atlantic Wall – a line of fortifications along the Normandy coast facing England.

Allied bombers and fighters had to soften up that impressive defence before the final onslaught on Fortress Europe could be carried out. General Eisenhower was going to expect much from their pilots.

The courageous Battle of Britain fighter pilots had, on several occasions, fought three, four or even five times a day, but it had only lasted from the middle of July until the middle of September 1940 – a period of sixty days only, during which they had not flown at all when weather did not permit. In fact, on 19 August 1940 the weather turned bad and the Battle of Britain fighter pilots were grounded for five days, recovering their strength.

The war's fate had been decided in that short span of time. Many of the great fighter pilots were later transferred to less dangerous activities. They had performed their fine deeds in an intense, hectic period of two months and had gained a unique, well-deserved, historic victory.

However, in the air battle over Europe, Jan regularly, inevitably, month after month, had to face heavy anti-aircraft fire from the ground – plus Luftwaffe fighters who had not yet been beaten at that stage. The tense, demanding activities had begun to affect his physique; and the situation had been exacerbated because the Dutch pilots in 322 Squadron were offered such lousy accommodation – cold tents on a soggy airfield!

It was a bloody scandal!

For the expense of just a few thousand pounds, the Dutch authorities in London could easily have provided better lodgings for the overworked and exhausted pilots of 322 Squadron; but they did absolutely nothing for their 'finest'!

In his diary, Jan wrote: 'Shame on those unconscionable ones who do this to us and who are responsible for our wretched conditions.'

Not even the German and Italian POWs in England were being housed in such inhumane accommodation. They slept in heated barracks while the Netherlands' 'finest' had to sleep in damp, cold tents for months on end.

Seldom – if ever in the history of human conflict – has a government demonstrated the kind of total indifference towards the fate of their 'finest' as the Dutch government-in-exile in London!

At this point, Jan felt dead tired – he'd been engaged in many operational flights over Europe, sometimes as many as twice in a single day. Every flight lasted for more than two hours at least. And once he'd made it back to his base, he was forced to crawl into a small tent and try to go to sleep beneath a damp blanket. The British climate was very definitely not a great help either. Meanwhile, the Dutch bureaucrats in London enjoyed sleeping in their warm beds.

But Jan had at least been finally promoted to the rank of Flight Commander. He'd also received the Flying Cross – a decoration created by the Dutch government-in-exile – for his war bravery. The RAF may well have overlooked what he and the others of 322 Squadron had achieved during their stay in England fighting for a common cause.

On one of his leaves to London, Jan reluctantly showed the citation to Diana. It read:

> We, Wilhelmina, by the Grace of God, Queen of the Netherlands, Princess of Orange Nassau, etc., etc., on the recommendation of the War Minister, have approved, on the 31st of December 1943, the decoration of Jan Leendert Plesman, a fighter-pilot of the Dutch Military Forces, posted with the Fighter Command of the Royal Air Force of the United Kingdom, for his courage, energy and drive, capability and perseverance during numerous flights, many of them of an offensive character above enemy-held territories, involving him in many air battles for a continuous period of fourteen months.

After reading the citation, Diana felt proud her Flying Dutchman had at last been recognised as a brave man. She also admired the fresh extra stripes on his uniform sleeves. She knew he had earned them with consistent tenacity while fighting the enemy, but she also realised there were considerably deeper fatigue lines in Jan's face. At times, even with her, he looked and acted very, very tired. He had aged visibly in a short period of time. Trying to keep death at bay is a compelling, tiring activity. It was showing in him.

Diana insisted he should apply for a long leave; she told him firmly it was quite obvious he was doing far too much while his life was at stake all the time.

'Jan,' she begged, 'please don't exhaust yourself.' She added with concern, 'You have really done more than your share during the last two years, darling.'

But Jan remained obstinate and deliberately ignored her remark. He told her instead, 'Now's the time to get the damn war over with! I have to do my small share to damage what's

263

left of the German war machine as much as I possibly can. The quicker it's all over, the sooner everyone can go home.'

This time, however, Diana didn't agree with him at all. She angrily stamped her foot and insisted, 'Jan, you must relax more. Your nerves are much too strained. They're like violin strings pulled too taut. If you don't take it easier, a string may snap. You mustn't go on pushing yourself this hard!' As she spoke, dark anger shone in her lovely blue eyes. But she meant it, her gaze was firm and unwavering. 'There really is a limit to what any one can humanly bear,' she insisted.

Jan remained stubborn. 'Up till now, Diana, I've resisted all the strains. I do believe the war will be over soon. You'll see.' But his voice slurred; he sounded very tired and wasn't in the least convincing to her.

Diana shook her head. Her obstinate Dutchman didn't want to listen to her valid reasons. She wondered what she could do to influence him. Softly, she asked, 'What are you trying to prove, Jan? That you're a superman? You know you're stubborn. You've accumulated rights and you're entitled to a long leave which would give you back your strength. Why then do you insist on flying over Europe every single day?'

There was deep concern in Diana's voice. 'What's the sense of it?' Her voice quivered a bit and her eyes misted over for just a second of frustration. 'Won't you do it for me, Jan?' she asked, almost petulantly. 'You've still got a whole life ahead of you.'

Jan quickly took her into his arms, pulling her tight against him. Facing her, he spoke with a tinge of sadness. 'I love you more than anything else in the world but, my dearest Diana, this is a duty I must perform. The awful conditions in Europe under German occupation force me to carry on as I'm doing. Please, please try to understand that,' he begged her.

Diana firmly shook her head. 'Jan, I simply don't. I want you to make it through the war alive so that you can see your parents again and start a new life.'

Jan stared silently at Diana for a long time, then spoke, emphasising each word. 'When I was in Paris, at the very beginning of 1941, I made a promise to a certain Monsieur Mohr, who was KLM's Director for France. I promised him I would do all I could within my limited powers to liberate the people on the other side of the Channel. The poor man died in a concentration camp in Poland after helping hundreds of fugitives to escape to the south of France. I simply can't excuse myself now by saying "I'm very tired chaps, I need a short holiday." Do you understand that, Diana?'

She shook her head stubbornly, 'No, I don't. You have to think of yourself. You've got to stay alive. Jan, can't you get it into your hard Dutch head that I love you? That I want to share my life with you after the war is over?' Diana's eyes were disturbed as she glanced at him. 'Do you understand what I mean?' And she put the emphasis on 'you'.

They went on arguing, but Diana got nowhere in her efforts to dissuade her obstinate Flying Dutchman from continuously flying operationally and to convince him to ask for the long leave he was fully entitled to.

It was the first argument they'd had since they met. Jan had taken Death along as his silent flight companion on operational missions for far too long. He knew by now how things really stood. The odds were very definitely not stacked in his favour. Death already held its hand out to him, eagerly beckoning for its next victim. Perhaps he would be the one.

During this period of operational flying, Jan had tried several times to contact Geert at his airfield, but with each phone call he had been informed Geert was on a mission or had just left for London. Jan was glad Geert had finally become operational on heavy bombers. He hadn't made it on to the famous Mosquitoes, but he'd been transferred to Lancasters. Jan had also written to him, telling him how everything was going in 322 Squadron. But he had received no reply. It was strange, because Geert always wrote back immediately.

One day, Jan decided to make another phone call to his friend's base, insisting on talking to him. This time, the call was passed on to the base's Commanding Officer.

'Hello, who's speaking?' the man asked.

'Flight Commander Plesman, sir. I'm with 322 Squadron. I'm a friend of Geert Overgauw, one of the Dutch pilots stationed at your base. I've been trying to contact him for some time now without any luck. Can you perhaps tell me where I can reach him, sir?' Jan asked politely.

There was a moment of subdued silence at the other end of the line following his question. After a few seconds, Jan began to think they had been cut off, but the officer started to answer Jan's question, emphasising each word. 'I regret to inform you Geert Overgauw did not return from his last mission over Holland. The objective was Deelen airfield, close to Arnheim. Judging from the reports submitted following the unfortunate mission, I must presume he was killed in action along with all the crew members aboard. There's no hope he might have become a prisoner of war because none of the other pilots on that particular unfortunate mission reported any survivors bailing out of the stricken aircraft on its way down. I'm sorry. It happened on his thirty-seventh operational mission overseas.'

Jan managed a barely audible whisper. 'Thank you, sir.'

He placed the receiver carefully back on its cradle, as if it was responsible for the devastating news. With incredulity, he stared at it for a long time.

That was all. 'I regret to inform you ...' Jan was stunned, deeply upset, desperate. His best friend – with whom he had shared so many adventures – dead!

Tears ran down Jan's cheeks; he would never talk, nor joke, nor gripe with Geert any more. Nor would they ever again grumble together as they had done so many times before – like two angry bears – about the Dutch bureaucracy in London.

They were never going to drink a Dutch jenever again – in the Dutch Club or anywhere else in the world. It was over, the last word had been said. It was all finished. The curtain had finally come down and that was that. It was final – irreversible!

Jan was extremely upset by Geert's death. The poor fellow had had to overcome so many problems to finally become an operational pilot. During his stay in England, he had met with many disappointments, with bad luck, and now – after thirty-seven missions – his life had ended right in the Netherlands.

Later, Jan heard that, while over the central part of Holland, close to Arnheim, the Lancaster commanded by Geert had been directly hit in its bomb bay by anti-aircraft fire. Still laden with bombs destined for a target in Holland, the aircraft had exploded in mid air. Crew and plane had gone down in thousands of pieces – and, of all bitter and incredible coincidences, it had happened very close to the house where Geert's parents lived.

They had seen it happen in front of their own eyes, without knowing at the time that the heavy bomber exploding in the air and fluttering down in flames was commanded by their only son. A cruel twist of fate! Big metal pieces fell on the flat Dutch countryside, causing several explosions. The only signs left were the craters – deep holes in the ground, smoking after the impact in a sinister way.

For Geert Overgauw, it had all come around full circle. Death, which had been waiting patiently, had finally reaped its human harvest. The scythe had been swung, neatly cutting off Geert's life on earth.

Bitterly, Jan grieved over the waste of a fine and good young man, honest and modest, lost forever. A good friend he would miss badly. For nearly four years, Geert had been away from Holland, his home, his parents; and now, on his last flight, his life had ended practically on his own doorstep. As if Death had made a kind gesture!

After all they had been through together, this dreadful news was the definite end of the line. 'I regret to inform you …' That was it. That sinister sentence meant the irreversible end. Death had successfully reached out again.

The rest of the day was very sad and restless for Jan. He felt on edge, not knowing what to do or how to keep his mind from concentrating on the tragic event. He made two other phone calls to others he knew well but the only answer he got was that they too were gone. They had not returned from overseas flights, and were assumed to have been killed in action. The last phone call left Jan stunned. He hung up and gave up, afraid the next call would mean another death.

That evening, spiritless and grieving, Jan drank far too much at the bar. He kept swearing at the Nazis and the Germans in particular, for all the misery they had brought to the world. Becoming incredibly drunk, he shouted at the top of his lungs, 'Those lousy Huns! Those goddamned, rotten bastards! Now they've also got my best friend Geert!' Then he kept on mumbling drunkenly to himself, angrily staring at his half-filled glass.

Nobody dared go near him. Jan stood alone at the bar while the other pilots stood around anxiously watching him becoming drunker by the moment. At that point, he resembled a wounded grizzly bear, still standing, swaying on his feet, badly hurt yet still erect and dangerous.

The small barman had thought it safer to move out from behind the counter, afraid of the strong, drunken Dutchman in front of him making threatening noises in a language he didn't understand. Turning around, Jan wearily stared ahead of himself without seeing anything in particular. The tiny veins in his eyes had turned red; the whole room blurred in front of him. He barely managed to stay on his feet; his brain, in an alcoholic mist, was not functioning correctly any more.

Finally, Jan took one last drink and, holding his glass in his right hand, raised it shakily towards the ceiling. He stared at the glass and its contents for a long time, unsteady on his feet, wobbling from side to side. The other pilots observed him, worried he might collapse. There reigned a moment of deadly silence. Then, with one furious movement, Jan smashed the glass on the floor with a terrible force, splintering it into hundreds of tiny fragments.

Raising his closed fists up in the air, tears of utter frustration running down his cheeks, in a shocking fury, Jan stamped his feet angrily on the floor, yelling at the top of his voice, 'Godverdomme, you're the creator, but to me you seem to be the destroyer of life!'

That night, the pilots of 322 Squadron had a terrible time trying to get Jan into bed in his drunken stupor. It took five of them to hold him firmly until he stopped ranting and collapsed into a near coma.

If anyone had described the ugly scenes to Diana, she would not have believed it – her kind, well-mannered, gentle Flying Dutchman behaving like that. But it had happened – the result of Jan's deep grief and utter defeat at having to lose his friend Geert forever.

The next day, after the commotion had died down, Jan's Commanding Officer did not allow him to fly an operational mission. That evening, uneasily shifting on both feet, with a splitting headache, standing at the bar, he apologised to the others. He was drinking only lemonade.

They understood Jan so well; it could – and did – happen to any of them. His colleagues were fully aware that the one dressed in a black cape kept his scythe ready for them too, at any time, at any moment during their dangerous missions.

XXI

TOWARDS early evening on 5 June 1944, the pilots of 322 Squadron were summoned to the mess, where many other pilots based in the same area had already gathered. When they were all seated, in a hushed, tense silence, Wing Commander Oxbridge informed them the Allied Armies were going to invade Fortress Europe early the next morning by landing on the French beaches.

This sensational, unique information caused great, enthusiastic cheering among all the pilots. They rose to their feet, back-slapping each other emotionally. Finally, after four years, the biggest and most important military undertaking would become a reality. The unexpected news gave rise to wild claims that the war would be over soon.

Jan also was extremely satisfied. At last the time had come to even the score with Europe's brutal oppressor. Maybe, he reasoned, he might be reunited with his family in Holland by the end of the year. That same night, with many wild emotions whirling in his brain, he returned to base with the other Dutch pilots. As usual, his cold damp camp bed awaited him in the small tent which served as his temporary accommodation.

The next day, Operation Overlord was in full swing. An endless stream of fighters, light, medium and heavy bombers, and Dakota aircraft pulling gliders filled with airborne troops flew over their base on their way to the French coast. But strangely enough, 322 Squadron did not participate in the early operations during the first days of the giant military invasion of occupied Europe.

The eager young Dutch pilots stared angrily up at the sky, observing the masses of aircraft steadily heading eastward. They were offended, and also disappointed they'd been left out of the very first massive attacks on the Continent and the hated enemy.

On 20 June, yet again, the squadron had once more to transfer to another base—this time to West Malling, an airfield between Dover and London.

On 24 June 1944, Jan was resting in a deckchair at the new base, on standby for action. He was enjoying the warm sunshine on his pale features, drowsing and relaxing after the excitement and chaos of the transfer. It was a beautiful day.

Suddenly, out of nowhere, he became aware of a rather strange, distant sound. He'd never heard anything like it before. He compared it to a running automobile engine with a ruptured exhaust pipe.

He stood up smoothly from the chair, anxiously searching the sky, his right hand shielding his eyes from the sun's bright glare, looking in the direction from where the strange, staccato noise had originated. At last he noticed an ugly kind of flying machine, consisting of a short, cigar-shaped fuselage with stubby wings. Attached to the body but located on top of it rested a kind of long tube from which the peculiar loud popping sound resulted.

'Well, I'll be darned,' Jan said aloud to himself.

To his utter surprise, the monstrosity was not equipped with a propeller. He'd never seen such a strange flying contraption before. Studying it as it passed overhead, Jan estimated its speed to be about 400 mph, which was considerable for such an ugly craft. When it sped over the airfield, everyone rushed out of the building in concern, curious also to see the revolutionary new object pass overhead. It flew at an altitude of about 3,000 feet. All the pilots commented on the strange noise of the engine propelling the unusual flying contrivance. It seemed like a kind of robot machine on wings.

It left a black exhaust trail, easily visible from a plane cruising above it. Jan reckoned he could have easily spotted it when flying at a higher altitude. The flying contraption disappeared over the horizon, on its way to London.

An hour later, Jan heard the strange noise again and saw another one coming over on its way to the big city.

Later, listening to the BBC news, they learned the Germans had launched a new kind of warfare against London, bombarding it at random with flying bombs, the so-called V-1s – short for *Vergeltungswaffen*.

Standing at the bar that evening, the pilots animatedly discussed the new weapon and its consequences. They argued vigorously about how to prevent it from reaching its objective, London. One of the pilots asked Jan, 'What do you think should be done to shoot them down?'

He shrugged. 'Well, I'm not sure, but I believe it flies a bit faster than the Mk Vb Spitfire. Maybe the Mk IX Spits could catch up with them in level flight. I should also think the Typhoons and Tempests could keep up with it in horizontal flight. Shooting down a target on a steady fixed course without a pilot aboard to take evasive action shouldn't be too difficult. You could dive from above its course to gain more speed and then, at the right range, fire with cannon. Perhaps that would explode it harmlessly in the air. I assume one must keep a certain, safe distance to avoid being blown up along with the flying bomb,' Jan concluded, guardedly giving his opinion.

'Yes,' argued Kees. 'I do agree. There's a fair chance of downing it. We'll soon be briefed on the tactics to be applied in order to bring these flying robots down.' They all laughed nervously. 'But having no pilot on board gives us a chance to try tipping it over by manoeuvring one's wings under the flying bomb's stubby ones. If it were flipped over, its gyros might go mad and it could crash in the countryside without doing any damage,' Kees commented hopefully.

Another pilot said, 'But you could damage your wing tip doing it that way. Yet I do agree it could be a solution.'

When the prototype V-1s had been demonstrated to Hitler for the first time, the Luftwaffe had flown a captured Spitfire to prove its horizontal speed insufficient to let it catch up to a V-1 in flight. The Führer had been impressed and immediately ordered the production of the first so-called Victory weapons; but none of the German top brass had apparently been courageous enough to explain to Hitler that the Spitfire – if it dived down to gain speed – could catch up with the V-1 over a short distance and shoot it down.

Fortunately for the Allies, Hitler was completely ignorant with regard to aviation matters. He had also completely misunderstood the sensational Messerschmitt 262 jet fighter, twenty years ahead of its time, and had forced the manufacturer to change it into a light bomber, delaying its introduction for two years. If he had not interfered, daylight bombing of Germany would have probably become impossible.

In any event, diving on V-1s is exactly what British pilots were instructed to do when the V-1 offensive started; the threat of flying bombs was considerably reduced after that.

During the next couple of days, the pilots of 322 Squadron watched many of the new weapons pass over their airfield – even during the night. But their instructions for the time being were to continue to escort the bombers heading for the V-1 launching sites in France.

Because of a bad weather forecast, Jan had obtained a short leave to London. While walking with Diana in Oxford Street, Jan again heard the sinister, unique sound of a V-1, but this time over the city. He tensed immediately, grabbing Diana's arm and pushing her against a wall, protectively shielding her with his body.

In amazement, she cried out, 'For Heaven's sake, Jan, what are you doing?' But when she saw Jan's tension as his eyes searched the sky above, Diana realised something awful was going to happen.

At that very instant, the staccato sound stopped abruptly. Both saw the V-1 dive towards the ground emitting a sinister, high-pitched whistling noise which became louder by the second. The flying bomb seemed to be hurtling straight at them, approaching at an awful speed. It seemed to be pointing directly at Oxford Street. Then there was a tremendous explosion, and they saw a big cloud of black smoke mushrooming above a row of buildings not far from them.

'What was that, Jan?' Diana asked in a small voice from her protected position, looking up at him uneasily, and at the same time curiously watching the surroundings over his broad shoulder.

Grimly, he smiled at her. 'You've just experienced a close call from a flying bomb. That was a V-1, Diana. We see them regularly coming over our base heading for London. That's how I immediately recognised the strange noise it makes.'

Diana was startled. 'What a dreadful thing! It strikes anywhere as soon as its engine stops, doesn't it, Jan?' she asked, concern showing on her features.

Without saying anything, Jan nodded, as they heard in the distance the screaming sirens of ambulances and fire-engines approaching the site of impact.

'This isn't a war any longer; it's just plain manslaughter,' Diana continued. There was anger in her voice.

'I agree with you, but what can be done about raving mad Hitler in Germany? There are even rumours about a new kind of rocket, a V-2 that may be fired at London once the V-1 campaign is over. That madman in Berlin doesn't know when to admit defeat and stop the darned war.'

Jan took a deep breath. 'Those lousy German generals had the gall to send millions of their young soldiers to their death for four years, mangled by that infernal German war machine, yet none of them had the guts to kill that madman, the bastards!' Jan spoke heatedly. 'I spit on the German generals and their officers who prostituted themselves completely to Hitler! They are just as responsible for the war and the continuation of it as devil Hitler himself, along with his degenerate Nazi gang!' Jan exclaimed angrily.

'Can you imagine, Diana, not one of the tens of thousands of high ranking Wehrmacht, Luftwaffe or Navy Officers showed enough courage to kill that madman in order to save his own country from absolute destruction. No,' Jan added bitterly, 'the German General Staff and their officers are just as responsible for what Germany has done to us all as Hitler is.'

Diana had read and heard about these infernal new weapons, the V-1s, but she had never been so close to their brutal effects. She realised now what a close call she'd had – right in the centre of London. Now she knew what it was all about.

'Jan, I don't know much about those things, but I do think you're absolutely right.'

Continuing with their shopping, they later heard the menacing noise above their heads again. She looked up at the sky and saw the small air-monster clearly outlined and passing overhead. Excitedly, she pointed a finger at it, silently observing its trajectory. The purring sound of its engine could be heard clearly – then it suddenly stopped.

Diana saw the small stubby-winged plane keel over, hurtling down to earth. She instinctively jumped into Jan's arms for protection. He quietly reassured her. 'Don't worry. This one will go down far away from us.' He smiled kindly and encouragingly into her anxiety-filled eyes.

'Are you sure?' He detected a touch of concern in her lovely blue eyes, like the serenity of a deep pool being disturbed by the casting of a stone into its depths causing ripples on its tranquil surface.

He tenderly kissed her on the forehead. 'Sure, darling. Come on, we have to finish our shopping.' Just then, they heard a loud explosion in the far distance. Unfortunately, another V-1 had reached its target, London.

After Jan returned from leave, he exchanged ideas with colleagues who'd seen many V-1s come over the field during his absence. They informed him about the new techniques they had discussed.

A pilot should not get any closer than 600 to 700 feet to a V-1 in flight otherwise the pursuing plane and its pilot could be hit by debris from the exploding flying bomb. Not only that but exploding the infernal machine caused considerable pressure waves in the air that could throw a plane on its back. Already, several pilots of other squadrons who had ventured too close had been killed instantly by the infernal robot machine.

The right technique was to wait patiently while cruising at 6,000 feet, awaiting instructions from ground control detailing the direction from which the flying bomb was approaching the English coast. Then, after identifying the object, dive down towards it to shoot it down. An alternative was to move one's wing tip beneath the flying bomb's stubby wings and try to tip it over. A number of pilots from other squadrons had already brought down several that way. It was a tricky operation requiring a lot of flying skill, but it worked!

At last, 322 Squadron was also assigned the task of shooting down the V-1s coming over from France, Belgium and Holland.

On 22 June, when Jan was sitting quietly on standby, reading *The Times* at his leisure, a voice came over one of the loudspeakers, announcing, 'Prepare for action! Flying bombs on their way!'

Jan immediately threw down his newspaper and ran to his plane. He jumped into the cockpit, adjusted the seat belt quickly, and switched the engine on. It fired instantly. For a second, he let it warm up; then he headed for the centre of the field and took off. He was airborne only minutes after the warning had been given. Circling at 6,000 feet, he waited patiently to be informed by radio of the exact direction from which the flying bombs approached. Then he was instructed which one was to be his.

Jan could see it moving beneath him on its steady course towards London. He pushed the joystick sharply forward, aligning the Spitfire with the V-1's flight path ahead of him. When he was about a thousand feet behind it he opened fire with his four cannon. He could clearly see the tracer of his ammunition moving over the stubby wings of the flying bomb; adroitly adjusting his own flight path, he saw the tracer enter the V-1. But oddly enough nothing happened and Jan felt utterly disappointed.

'Verdomme' he exclaimed aloud in Dutch, in his small cockpit. He persisted, because he was still slightly gaining on the V-1, giving his engine full throttle in order to position himself for further hostile attack. After the distance between the Spit and his quarry had shortened, he fired again. This time the little monster exploded into a big, bubbling ball of orange-red flames straight ahead of him. The resulting debris hurtled through the air, slowly, even majestically, fluttering to earth.

His plane shuddered and vibrated madly from the conflagration's after-effects. He barely managed to keep the situation under control. Then he levelled off, and reduced engine power and speed to return to his base in an excellent mood. Happily, he whistled a Dutch tune in the cockpit. He had managed to shoot down his first V-1! At last he had damaged the German war machine. On his way back, he decided to have his plane completely checked by the ground staff. After landing, the mechanics meticulously serviced the Spit and less than one hour later, he received an all-clear for further flights.

Jan was elated. He had never been sure if he had really shot down a Luftwaffe plane, even though he had been convinced during several air duels that he had probably damaged a few. The one in Holland, over Rotterdam, he regarded as a good probable. But now at last he had damaged the enemy! It was a small success but he was satisfied with the result and a bit proud of it. His ego was greatly stimulated by this event. At the bar that evening, the drinks were on him.

During the next few weeks, Jan managed to shoot down a number of other flying bombs and, on one flight, on 14 July, during a 55 minute flight, he actually managed to shoot down two 'pilotless aircraft' as he wrote in his pilot's log book.

Once a V-1 had been launched from a ramp, it headed for the Channel and on towards the east or south coast of England where at first it met with concentrated anti-aircraft fire from the ground. Most of the anti-aircraft batteries protecting London had been advanced to the coast after the V-1 offensive had really begun to threaten London.

During the second stage of its flight, having survived the anti-aircraft barrages, the flying bomb was chased by Spit-fires and Typhoons. After the fighter planes had taken shots at it, the bomb still had to fly through a dense barrier of balloons equipped with long, hanging cables before it finally and infernally reached its target, London, and caused its many victims.

One afternoon, Jan was in the air again, cruising at 6,000 feet, awaiting instructions from ground control to advise him from which direction a V-1 was approaching England. He received information he could attack one which was speeding along in his vicinity. Just then, he noticed it crossing the coast and immediately confirmed the sighting of the ugly monster to ground control. He was ready to confront it, eagerly pushing the joystick forward, diving towards the assigned objective. He quickly opened the gas throttle to maximum power to shorten the distance separating him from his prey. This time, he wanted to tip it over.

The Spit gained speed quickly, shortening the range separating him from the V-1 ahead. Jan immediately posi-tioned his plane, keeping his right wing lower than the V-1's stubby one. Approaching even closer, he quickly glanced to his right. Only a few feet separated the hunter from his quarry.

The V-1 in flight, so very close to him, impressed Jan considerably. The mere sight made his flesh creep. He could even spot the rivets in the hellish machine's metal plating. At that moment, Jan was travelling at just under 400 mph parallel to one ton of explosives, a mere ten feet distant from the ugly monster. Should it detonate just then, he would be blown apart into a thousand pieces along with his faithful Spit.

Carefully, Jan lifted the right wing tip, causing it to touch the short, thick left wing of the flying bomb and hold it there for a second. Then he shifted his joystick hard to the left, and in one quick move, made his right wing rise sharply, forcing the stubby wing upwards. The V-1 suddenly turned over. The flying bomb, completely out of control, dived towards the ground.

Banking sharply, he watched the hellish explosion take place in a green field of the quiet English countryside below. A satisfied smile crossed his lips; this one would not reach its assigned target either and hadn't caused any damage to London. Jan felt happy to have contributed his little share in destroying it, saving so many human lives.

When Jan returned to base, he was told at debriefing that pilots, from that day on, were no longer allowed to use the tipping technique. The Germans had caught on to it and Jan had barely escaped being blown up with the flying bomb he'd just downed. Death had given him a reprieve but Jan had not been aware of it.

The Germans, clever improvisors, had installed pressure buttons beneath the extremity of the V-1's thick wings; once the buttons were depressed, the flying bomb exploded instantly. A pilot trying to lift a V-1's wing would surely be blown up with it. From now on, the V-1 represented a deadly danger to pilots.

The tipping had become too dangerous an operation, and 322 Squadron lost one of its own pilots when he forced the wing of a V-1 he was chasing and was blown to smithereens with it.

In the middle of July 1944, 322 Squadron was again transferred, this time to Deanland, an airfield equipped with a PSP (pierced steel plate) runway. The Dutch pilots soon learned how put the Spitfires down on this runway, but it was a rather tricky operation, especially when the surface became wet and slippery due to rain or damp.

The Mk XIVs also had to be exchanged for Mk IX Spitfires. This was a small step backwards in the quality of the planes from what they were accustomed to. Even so, the Mk IX Spitfire was one of the best the RAF had to offer the Dutch pilots.

At the new base, the pilots were again forced to sleep in small tents. Jan found it most irritating, humiliating and very tiresome. Despite his rank and seniority, when he returned dead tired from his missions each evening he had to crawl into the dreary, improvised lodgings to rest and try to catch up on sleep during the cool damp nights, not to mention the annoying mosquitoes and tiny pestering flies keeping him awake at night, depriving him of his much needed sleep.

The way in which these Dutch pilots were mistreated by the indifferent Dutch Government top brass in London stood out as an outrageous scandal. These authorities seemed to find it perfectly normal for their 'finest' to be accommodated for months on end in such god-awful conditions. It was practically an invitation for the reaper to take his pick of the physically exhausted pilots. It seemed as if the Dutch Government top brass couldn't care less about the fate of the Netherlands 'finest'.

Much better temporary lodgings could have been provided for a relatively small financial outlay with Nissen huts or wooden barracks. But the Dutch bureaucrats apparently didn't see things that way. The Dutch in general carry an inborn trait, stinginess – really a grocer's mentality – as Jan's father had told him many times.

Jan hated the incessant transfers from one airfield to another. He had barely become acquainted with the new surroundings and bearings of the airfield when he had to pack up again and be transferred somewhere else. It was certainly harmful to the already low morale of the tired pilots of 322 Squadron.

By this time, out of pure necessity, they had become experts on how to keep their camp beds, mattresses, blankets and private belongings dry when it rained; and it poured frequently in the wet English climate.

During the night of 10 August 1944, Jan shot down another V-1. It was 322 Squadron's last victim as they went about bringing down the so-called Victory weapons of the Third Reich.

The V-1 campaign against London lasted from 15 June to the first days of September 1944, when victorious Allied troops overran the launching sites in France.

A few of the mean killers continued to come over from Belgium and Holland where they were launched from well-hidden ramps in forests. One ramp was located close to The Hague as well. In all, about 8,500 were fired against London from France during the summer and autumn of 1944, and caused considerable damage. Fortunately for the hard-pressed Londoners, most of them were shot down by anti-aircraft batteries which became more precise after the first few weeks. The fighter squadrons also took their share of V-1's out of the sky.

Jan managed to shoot down eleven of the flying robots alone and one along with another pilot. His official score on the blackboard of 322 Squadron was eleven and a half, which put him in second position on the honour list. At least the ones he had shot down hadn't reached London – their primary objective. He had only slightly damaged one wing tip, easily repaired by the ground staff.

Altogether, 322 Squadron had inflicted a good deal of damage on the V-1 air offensive. The Dutch pilots shot down more than a hundred of the 'doodle-bugs', Hitler's *Vergeltungswaffen*.

During August, Jan flew frequently; between 2 and 12 August, he flew twenty low patrols and shot down three V-1s.

His operational activities were noted in his pilot's logbook, as in this extract:

11 August:
 Escort to 100+ bombers to Douai; 1 hour 50 minutes
 Escort to 10 Halifaxes; 1 hour 20 minutes
12 August:
 Target cover at Montrichard; 2 hrs 15 minutes
13 August:
 Patrol Nogent-Evreux; 2 hrs 15 minutes
 Escort 36 Marauders; 1 hour 55 minutes
14 August:
 Escort Marauders to Esternay; 2 hrs 30 minutes
 Area patrol Falaise-Argentan; 2 hrs 20 minutes
 Escort 100+ Lancasters to Brest; 2 hrs 45 minutes
15 August:
 Escort 100+ Lancasters to Bruxelles; 2 hrs 20 minutes
 Rodeo Namur Cambrai; 2 hrs 25 minutes
16 August:
 Escort Marauders; 1 hour 45 minutes

And so it went every day, flying once or twice over occupied France meeting heavy anti-aircraft fire from the ground. On 27 August he had to escort 200 Halifax and Lancaster bombers to Hamburg in Germany. It was the very first time Jan had flown over enemy Germany, a flight of 2 hours 30 minutes.

At the end of August, the squadron was called on once again to attack ground objectives in north-west France.

During the months of May, June, July and August Jan flew practically every day without any let-up, without a well-earned rest! It badly affected his physical state. Jan felt very tired as did the rest of 322 Squadron.

As Flight Commander, Jan had become the leading, number one pilot of three groups of three Spitfires each. Kees, as usual, flew as his wingman. On missions he was always right behind Jan's Spit.

That was how they attacked the ground objectives. After each low-level pass at a moving train or at trucks on country roads, they regrouped at a rather low altitude, flashing over the French countryside, to form as small a target as possible to avoid the heavy, intense flak. They changed their angle of flight for the next attack so they would suddenly show up from quite a different direction to the one the enemy were expecting.

On 30 August, Jan flew over France twice. The next day he flew another two missions. Every time he returned, he had to sleep in that damned little tent on the airfield.

That night, hearing the steady rhythm of raindrops falling on the canvas, he was vividly reminded of a very close call he had experienced on a transfer flight from Woodvale to Llanbedr in Wales. It had been on 27 November 1943 that death had almost reached out for him. That afternoon he had to deliver a Spitfire to the very same airfield in south-west Wales where he had received his final training on Spitfires at the end of 1941. He knew the Llanbedr airfield and its surroundings well.

He had taken off in bad weather; the forecast along the route had been for heavy clouds and a low overcast. After twenty minutes of flying, Jan assumed he would clear the clouds to find the sea below. But when he came out of the overcast, he found himself still over land which disturbed him thoroughly. Returning to altitude again, flying over the 10/10 dark grey clouds, he finally spotted a gap in the thick soup below him and quickly descended in tight spirals before it could close again. He knew he was flying in a southerly direction but still could not get beneath the menacing weather elements to try and establish his position. Not being able to see the ground, he was forced to climb to a higher altitude again. It was all a rather dangerous business while flying over the hilly Welsh countryside.

Where was he?

Where could he land?

How the heck could he get down safely?

The rain drops drummed and spattered incessantly against the cockpit's Plexiglas hood. Jan was all alone in the small confined space with nobody to help him out of a desperate-looking situation.

Anxiously he kept observing the altimeter needle as if it could give him any indication.

Jan, with a troubled mind, wondered where the hell he was. Every now and then, as if from the bowels of Hell, a blinding flash of intense white lightning seemed to race towards him at an incredible speed through the dark, threatening clouds in which he found himself, only to leave him again in Stygian darkness. These intense blinding flashes disturbed and impressed Jan considerably.

Would he get down in one piece, Jan asked himself.

The faithful Spitfire shuddered under the impacts, bucked and lurched wildly, tossed about by the heavy turbulence which seemed to reach out for him with sudden, unforeseen, unpredictable, angry force as if to test his perseverance. Jan needed all his flying skill and experience to overcome and control this unexpected situation. All his senses were fully alert.

His earphones produced a lot of annoyingly loud static because of the bad weather. The fierce lightning and threatening thunderclaps isolated him completely from ground control. He could not possibly reach Llanbedr control tower. In all probability he was still outside its radio range; he'd have to fight it out all alone, by himself.

Not knowing his bearings, latitude or longitude, Jan could do little more than continue to follow a procedure used when lost. The weather being what it was, however, try as he might, he still could not establish his position.

After flying for forty minutes in shockingly bad weather conditions, Jan began to feel anxious. Observing the fuel gauge, Jan realised that he only had ten gallons of fuel left. It seemed to him as if the elements of nature were lining up against him. Frantically, he tried to ask for a vector to the nearest field, but all he heard again was loud static. He was still too far away from any ground station to obtain clear reception and get a fix on his location.

Realising the situation was becoming more critical by the minute, Jan began to weigh seriously his chances of bailing out and leaving his faithful Spit.

Then, as if by a miracle, he noticed the sea and coastline beneath him through the murk. He immediately started to circle down in tight spirals, approaching the headland at a high speed and streaking over rocky formations at a very low altitude. The red warning light on the instrument panel came alive, blinking incessantly at him, indicating he had fuel enough for only a few more minutes of flight. At that stage, he seriously wondered what fate had in store for him.

Jan was in a desperate emergency situation, with a feeling of despair he found difficult to control welling up inside him. He didn't know what to do: bail out with his parachute or still try for a landing somewhere, possibly risking his life.

At that very instant, as through a God-given miracle, when he already thought everything was totally lost, an unexpected opening appeared in the clouds.

At the last moment, Jan spotted a patch of countryside in front of him that showed no obstacles. Just before the plane hit the ground, he switched the engine off and made a belly landing. He found himself in a small, wet field of grass close to Aberporth on the west coast of Wales, south of Newquay, Cardiganshire.

The Spit hit the ground hard, shooting forward, bouncing and roughly sliding over the long, wet grass. There was little he could do to influence the landing's outcome. All he could do was bump passively up and down in the bucket seat of the cockpit. The Spit finally came to an abrupt halt.

Jan was relieved – the damage to the plane seemed limited to a bent prop and a radiator filled with earth and grass. Not too bad a result after all, he thought!

It was a painful, harrowing experience – the very first prang he'd ever suffered during his flying career – yet he felt grateful to be alive.

Taking his time, Jan loosened the safety belts, slid the Plexiglas hood back and then deeply inhaled the fresh, cool Welsh air into his lungs, which made him feel slightly better. After the steady engine noise for nearly an hour, and the incessant, insistent rattle of the fierce raindrops beating on the perspex cockpit hood, he now became aware of a total, immense silence absorbing him, as if he were completely alone in a huge, ancient cathedral, completely cut off from the outer world by thick stone walls. Jan sat motionless, feeling utterly impressed, emotionally overwhelmed.

It felt as if he had entered into another time dimension. As if he floated through the endless expanse of the universe alone, soundless, as if carried by invisible wings. Was this an omen?

Slowly and carefully, Jan climbed out of the cockpit on to the wing root, where he stood for a moment, his mind going back over the sensational, threatening events of the past half hour. This time, he didn't need to jump down from the wing, he merely took a step forward to stand on the wet grass.

Forlornly, Jan punched the Spit's fuselage with his clenched right fist, exclaiming aloud, 'I'm sorry, Spittie. It was all my fault.' Then he walked away to search for a house or a cottage from where he could make a long-distance phone call to Woodvale. He had to inform operations control he had 'safely' landed in Wales but unfortunately not at his destination, Llanbedr!

Death had kindly extended a reprieve to Jan, but from that moment on, each dawn would carry a special meaning to him.

During the last minutes of the complicated, harrowing flight, Jan had not been afraid, only rather upset because he had lost his way. It was his first accident in three years of flying in England. Nothing like that had ever happened to him before.

Jan felt very bad about it and wondered what his father would have said had he been able to relate his Welsh experience to him.

Jan admitted to himself he had been rather nonchalant preparing for the flight. Flying without a map had been a mistake in the first place, although he had not been able to see anything of the ground during the major part of the ill-fated flight. The heavy static in his earphones had also prevented him from obtaining the necessary information from ground control so they might guide him to a nearby emergency airfield.

Jan also felt some anger well up inside him because he was convinced the ground staff at Woodvale had not provided him with a full gasoline tank. A Spitfire had a flight range of about one hour and twenty minutes in the conditions in which he had been flying. But he had been without fuel after fifty flight minutes! Something didn't add up!

Jan suspected a sneaky yet dangerous habit of some of the ground personnel. Every now and then they tapped a little high octane plane fuel from the full tanks for secret use in the cars of pilots and maintenance staff. However, Jan told himself, he should have made absolutely sure of the fuel level of his tank before take-off, especially since he knew he'd be facing rather bad weather. He made a firm resolution to be extremely careful in the future.

This was Jan's very first crash-landing during his flying career and he regarded it as symbolic of the miserable period he had spent with the Dutch squadron at Woodvale.

Kept awake by the steady rain drumming on the tent canvas, Jan was jerked back to reality while stretched out on his field bed at Deanland. Though already drowsy, he realised with a start it was Diana's birthday the next morning. He wondered what it held for the two of them? He planned to see her in London and spend an evening with her.

Uninterrupted, for 138 interminable nights, Jan had been forced to sleep in a damp tent. It had definitely made an impact on his physical condition. Mentally and physically, he felt exhausted – not a good frame of mind at all for a fighter pilot, who should always be on his toes and ready to face the unexpected. Especially during missions over the Continent.

And why? Because of the mean *krentenkakkerigheid*, the mean stinginess so typical and so deep-rooted in the mentality of the heartless Dutch bureaucrats working for the Dutch Government in exile in London at the time.

For four months he had flown without interruption on operational missions over occupied Europe. Jan badly needed a break, an interval, a pause, but the top brass in London acted if they were not aware of it. They should have ordered Jan to be grounded for at least sixty days but they did nothing.

XXII

AFTER JAN returned safely from a rodeo over France on the late afternoon of 31 August, he immediately phoned Diana.

'Hello, Aussie pilot. How's your flying coming along?' he asked cheerfully.

'Jan,' she exclaimed happily. 'How nice to hear your voice. How are you?' she asked, showing her interest in his well-being. 'Are you feeling very tired? Do you think you could be free tomorrow evening?' There was a moment of silence and then she continued, 'Do you remember, Dutchie, how much tomorrow means to me?' Jan heard her chuckle as she asked the question while using the nickname he didn't like very much.

'Of course,' he laughed. 'How could I ever forget? A charming young lady from Australia is celebrating her birthday in London tomorrow. If it's at all possible, she'll meet a stubborn Dutchman from Holland. How does that sound to you?' he asked jokingly.

'Absolutely positive! Then, you really do think you'll be able to make it, Jan? I shall be very happy to see you again. I've also prepared a little surprise for you, but I won't tell you about it now.' She giggled, and heard Jan's laughter on the other end of the line.

'All right then,' she said. 'Shall we say around eight tomorrow evening?'

'Confirmed! I have plenty of leave on the credit side, as you know so well. If you don't hear anything to the contrary, I'll be there. It's at Jane's flat, correct?'

'Yes. Well, that's settled. How are you doing, Jan? I'm so happy to hear your voice. Over here, I've made a lot of progress with my flying. I'll tell you about it tomorrow.'

Jan hesitated a moment before speaking. 'Diana, I must tell you, your party may most probably be the last one I can attend for quite a while. I've heard rumours the squadron may be transferred overseas in a few weeks' time.'

'Oh, no!' Diana exclaimed. 'I'll miss you terribly. Well, let's not think about it right now. See you tomorrow at eight o'clock. Okay?'

'Confirmed, dear Diana. Be seeing you my sweet, dear Aussie. Bye for now.'

'Bye, my dearest Flying Dutchman,' she murmured softly.

The next day, 1 September, was a beautiful day with a deep blue sky, but as ruthless destiny would have it the day turned out to be the blackest ever for 322 Squadron – three pilots would not return from their flights over western France.

That morning, Jan felt reasonably good. He had not slept too badly in his small tent. After the day's operational activities he was going to join Diana to pass a few happy days in her company in London.

At ten o'clock, the squadron took off for Lille in northwest France. When crossing the French coast at cruising altitude, Jan could clearly make out the greater Paris area in the far distance, spread out over quite a large part of the countryside. It really impressed him.

The sweep they made went smoothly. They shot up military traffic they had discovered on a winding country road, leaving quite a number of burning trucks behind as testimony of their attack. When Jan, leading the flight, had noticed the convoy moving eastward, he had immediately informed the other Dutch pilots they should follow him.

They swept down from the sky like hungry eagles on their prey, coming in behind the convoy at a very low height. At one point, when Jan found a big truck in front of him, he opened fire with his cannon. He clearly saw how the tracer bullets entered the heavy lorry. The enemy soldiers frantically jumped out of the vehicle, but several no longer moved after the heavy bullets had struck the target. The survivors looked like little moving dolls frantically running for cover after the surprise strafing had begun.

Once it was all over, the planes safely returned to their base, Deanland. In his pilot's log book, Jan wrote 'Rodeo; duration 1 hour 30 minutes'.

Early in the afternoon, they took off again, this time to attack a railway close to St Omer, a small town near Calais.

Seated in the cockpit of his Spitfire ready for take-off, Jan mused. 'I hope to be back around four o'clock. That'll give me plenty of time for a shower and a good cleaning up so I can prepare myself to reach London in time for my appointment with Diana.'

The squadron became airborne again. Three groups of three Spitfires each, flying towards the assigned target. Jan flew in the lead position which he liked and preferred. He could clearly distinguish the French coast below him as he crossed it close to Calais.

When the nine Spits flew over the area in tight formation, Jan's attention was caught by a freight train slowly proceeding along the tracks as if inviting an attack. It consisted of a loco-motive and four bogie vans proceeding in the direction of St Omer.

He radioed to the others to prepare for a low level attack on the train and follow him. He started to dive towards the slowly moving target. At about a thousand feet above the quarry, doing close to 400 mph, to Jan's utter amazement he saw the freight carriage roofs slide open, uncovering anti-aircraft batteries which immediately opened intense, concen-trated fire on the attacking Spitfires.

Jan had no choice but to fly through this dark wall with lightning flashes and exploding shrapnel. He flew through heavy orange-red tracer aimed steadily at him and curving towards him from the barrels of lightweight cannon and heavy machine guns set up on the train. It looked to Jan as if red-hot iron rods were being shot at his aircraft, as if he were flying into one solid mass of fiery tentacles sinisterly reaching out for him.

'The bastards!' He muttered angrily to himself.

He pushed the firing button on his joystick and saw the tracers of his ammunition speed towards the freight train and enter the carriages. Then, with a terrific ground speed, he passed very low over the still moving train. Forcefully, he pushed hard rudder with his feet and aileron-control with his right hand to enter into a flat turn, with the other eight Spit-fires streaking right behind him.

Speeding extremely low over the flat French terrain, Jan completed his steep banking manoeuvre while at the same time observing how people busy in the fields were pointing in his direction. Having completed his turn, he approached the freight train again. By the time he had his Spit aligned on the target, he knowingly faced the inferno of the intense anti-aircraft fire again. He clearly made out the German gunners behind their infernal weapons excitedly pointing in the direction of his approach. Black smoke slowly drifted over the carriages, indicating one or more were already on fire. Once again, hundreds of explosions filled the air through which he had to pass to get another shot at the slowly moving target. Bursts of fierce gunfire closed in on his flight path, getting closer by the second. It looked like a wall of fire through which he had to steer his faithful Spit. Hot metal fragments formed a curtain through which he had to proceed, just like the multi-coloured flowering explosions of fireworks.

His plane bucked and jolted as if it were flying right through an electric storm. Continuous streams of bullets sinisterly illuminated by tracer were curving up at him as if searching out for him and the others still following behind. Jan had never experienced such massive, intense ground fire coming up at him at such close range.

Flashing over the carriages again, he felt a shock at that very instant – a severe one that rocked his plane. He realised in dread he had been hit, and badly. The Spit started to vibrate violently – he could barely hold the joystick in his right hand. Jan suddenly became aware he no longer had any pressure on the elevator or the rudder. Jan was now desperately fighting for control of his Spit and for his own life.

Jan's heart pounded wildly, and to his utter despair, he felt neither of his legs responding to his commands – there was no compliance in them any more. Whatever he attempted to order mentally, there was no response, no movement.

'God!' he whispered frantically. 'Please help me now! Please, dear God!' he softly begged, already feeling a first bout of nausea seizing him.

Jan became aware of a warm, sticky feeling as if something syrupy steadily descended along his back. Desperately glancing down at his legs, he noticed an ever-widening ring of light pink arterial blood quickly spreading over his trousers and the narrow cockpit floor.

Though now semi-conscious, Jan realised he'd been badly hit in the back despite the armour plating meant to protect him.

'God … oh … God … please … let … me … meet … Diana … tonight,' he sighed faintly, already feeling weaker because of the considerable loss of blood.

Jan did not feel any pain but only the sensation of the fresh warm blood spurting out of the terrible wound in his back, running abundantly down his thighs, down his legs to his feet. The wet spots on his trousers rapidly increased in size. He still managed the necessary willpower to speak orders into the microphone in front of his mouth, instructing the other pilots in the formation: 'Re … form …'

It was the very last word the other Dutch pilots heard their Flight Commander pronounce.

Despite their frantic calls to Jan, all they got was deadly silence in return. After being badly hit, his wonderful, elegant fighting machine the Spitfire, – its tail now mangled in a mass of ruptured metal – went into a steep dive from 5,000 feet, inexorably pressing him forcefully into his bucket seat.

Whatever Jan tried to do, he could not move to try to slide the canopy back with his bare hands. Despite his desperate efforts, he did not succeed, becoming weaker by the second.

He was still conscious enough to see the ground coming up at him at terrifying speed during the last microseconds of his life. Images, clear as crystal, flashed through his mind, which still functioned, was still active. Oddly enough, a kind of grim smile took shape at the corners of his mouth, as if he had found his final destination at last.

He pictured his house in The Hague in brilliant images of vivid colours, his school, his friends, Geert, his father and mother waving at him. Then, as through a dense white haze, Diana's face became stronger, clearing the other images away. Her photographic likeness steadily took on strength, imposing itself over the others which faded and receded.

She looked so pretty, beautiful, ethereal – he loved her.

He felt very weak. The last move he made, with extreme difficulty, was a protective, reflex gesture, putting both arms in front of his face. During the last milliseconds of his life, he sadly whispered, 'Diana.'

Then a tremendous blow, and blackness.

It was all over. Jan had finally fallen. He was dead!

Two other pilots had also been shot down by the heavy anti-aircraft fire from the train's cannon. Fortunately, they had not been wounded even though their planes were damaged. They managed to reach a safe altitude which enabled them to bail out of the planes and save their lives with parachutes. Kees had been to the right of Jan, somewhat behind him, when the

Flight Commander had initiated the ill-fated attack. It had all happened so suddenly. He saw Jan's plane get hit, observing in absolute horror how the tail of his Spitfire had been torn off in flight. Kees had shouted into his microphone, 'Jump, Jan! For God's sake, jump, man!'

But nothing had happened. Kees saw Jan's Spit – now consisting only of an engine, two wings and a probably badly wounded Jan in the cockpit – streaking at an incredible speed and fully out of control. The plane hurtled vertically down towards the French soil below.

Terrified by the awful spectacle, Kees saw how Jan's plane crashed into the ground. The impact was horrendous and Kees figured Jan had died in a thousandth of a second.

It was all over for Jan. Their Flight Commander had definitely reached the end of the line.

Circling around the disaster spot, Kees could only see a crater-like deep hole in the open green countryside. It was smoking after the terrible crash.

Death had patiently waited for four long years but had finally reaped with success.

Jan had died close to the border between Belgium and France where he and his bosom friend Geert had crossed into France on their bikes while escaping from occupied Holland on their way to England to fight the hated Nazis.

For Jan Plesman the circle had come fully round!

Four years of fighting had come to an end in an open green field in the countryside of northwestern France.

The Air Ministry communiqué that evening mentioned him as missing in action. But Kees and the other pilots who had survived had not seen him leave the cockpit of his badly shot-up Spitfire as he was going down. They knew with absolute certainty that their Flight Commander, Jan – their best pilot- was no longer alive.

At last, after four years in England, the 'White Knight' had fallen. The gifted, courageous son of a dynamic, visionary father was lost forever. It was a terrible, irretrievable waste – a loss not only for his family but also for the Netherlands. That young man could have gone forward to such a promising future.

He had served his Queen and country with the same devotion and loyalty that his father had inspired in him.

XXIII

KEES HAD suffered a terrible shock in seeing three Spit-fires downed in an instant as the exchange of fire between the train and the attacking planes continued. Now he reformed the six remaining Squadron Spitfires to fly back to their base.

Forlornly, he sat in the cockpit, his vision momentarily blurred by tears, nerves completely shattered. And he felt angry. He had also flown too much for the past months, and now that Jan had been shot down, he felt the intense nervous strain of flying operations every day without any break.

After the six planes had landed, the pilots and ground staff crowded around Kees who stood dejectedly, ill at ease, leaning in exhaustion on the wing of his Spitfire.

'What happened, Kees? How could we lose three pilots all at once?' a young pilot asked nervously.

Kees shook his head. 'The train was a flak trap – filled with anti-aircraft batteries hidden beneath the freight car roofs. From the air, it seemed to be just like any normal freight train. I would have attacked it just like Jan did. I would have done exactly the same thing. In fact, we finally shot the damned train up, but that won't bring our pilots back!' Kees exclaimed bitterly.

'How many parachutes did you see, Kees?' one of the pilots asked.

'I saw two, and you?' he inquired eagerly, intently studying the other's face.

'Me too. Only two chutes opened.'

Kees said, 'I wonder what happened to the two who managed to bail out over occupied territory. I hope they've found shelter and safety with the French Underground.'

'Let's hope so!' one of the pilots commented.

Sadly, Kees told the others, 'As usual, I was flying right behind Jan's plane. When he banked away after the dive, the belly of his plane was hit. I saw the tail shear off in mid air. He was too low to do anything about it and, at that speed ...' His voice trailed away. Getting hold of himself again, he continued, bitterly, 'His Spit went totally out of control. Poor guy, there was nothing he could do about it any more. With his mastery in flying Spits, he would have saved his own life but, without a tail, it was completely hopeless.'

One of the younger pilots shook his head. 'The squadron won't be the same without Jan. Still, we have to keep on going. There'll be other targets to shoot up over Europe tomorrow.'

'Yes, I know,' Kees commented thoughtfully. He slowly walked to the debriefing session as if there were lead in his boots, now that he had to report what had happened during that disastrous flight.

When the news became known, everyone in 322 Squadron felt shocked that an experienced pilot like Jan had been shot down and killed. Nobody ever expected he might not return from a search and destroy mission because he was such a capable, excellent pilot. But now, he'd no longer be around to narrate his experiences during briefing and debriefing sessions.

Kees knew Jan had an appointment with Diana for that evening in London. How could he ever break the news to her? He couldn't possibly imagine what words to use. How could he face her and just say, 'Jan is dead.'

As soon as he got the chance, Kees phoned Jane. 'Jane, this is Kees,' he said. 'I just got back from a sweep we made this afternoon over France. Something terrible has happened! Jan was shot down. He had an appointment with Diana tonight. How are we going to give her the dreadful news?'

In a small voice, Jane asked, 'Is he wounded, Kees? Or is he a prisoner of war now?'

'No, Jane, Jan is dead.' Uttering that awful word shocked Kees more than he wanted to admit.

'Oh, no! That's terrible! He was such a fine fellow! He was the best I ever met and now this!' Jane's voice broke.

Kees waited patiently on the phone. 'Are you still there, Jane?' he asked, concerned.

'Yes.' He heard her sniffing. 'I'm still here – just give me a moment to get myself together, please.' Then she added, 'I'm going to ask for a compassionate leave at once. We'll go to Diana together. That'll be the best thing to do. Where shall we meet? Diana wanted our flat tonight. Let's meet downstairs. You know where it is, don't you?'

'See you at eight, then.' Kees hung up. His hands were shaking. He was extremely tired, flying every day without interruption. It was far too much and it showed after the terrible shock of seeing Jan's plane go down in front of his very eyes.

Now he phoned Bristol and asked for Captain Parmentier, KLM's chief pilot, to inform him of the sad news. 'Captain Parmentier, this is Kees speaking. I have bad news to report, sir. Jan was shot down over St Omer this afternoon. I flew right behind him and saw it all happen right in front of me. The tail of his plane was hit and sheared off in mid air. He went down vertically. No parachute. I'm sorry, sir. It means the definite end for him, with no hope of survival.'

'Oh, my God! That's terrible! And we're so close to the end of this damn war! A few months from now it will all be over. It's going to be a terrible shock to his father. If I may so, Jan happened to be his favourite son. A terrible shock!' Parmentier repeated softly.

'I know, Captain Parmentier. Jan always said that if his turn ever came, it would all be over in a second, in a flash. The ones who are left are those who have to bear the shock and that's worst.' Kees' voice broke for a second.

'Ja, he was not afraid of dying. We discussed it sometimes when he came to visit me. Still, now that it has happened, I feel very sad. He was such a fine boy. Thanks for phoning me, Kees. I will see to it his family is advised. Please do take care of his personal belongings. So often, valuable papers, notes and other things disappear when one of the pilots doesn't return. Goodbye.'

After the two phone calls, Kees undressed and took a long hot shower, then he drove to London in his small car to meet Jane.

He saw her already standing outside the flat, on the pavement. He immediately noticed how very nervous, sad and tense she looked. He felt exactly the same way. How could he ever face Diana with the disastrous news?

'Jane, let's take a walk first. If I have to go up in this state of mind, feeling as I do, I'm afraid I'd have a nervous breakdown. There must be someone strong enough to break the terrible news to her. It won't be easy to tell her by degrees.'

Uneasily, Jane said, 'You must tell her. I don't think I can do it.'

Kees eyed her sadly. 'I also have the present Jan bought Diana for her birthday with me. It will break her heart now. It's such a cute gift. We bought it together.'

Kees felt terribly tense, as if a great weight had been placed on his shoulders. 'You know, Jane – if Jan had only taken that long leave he was fully entitled to, nothing might have happened. He had accumulated at least sixty days of rest to his credit. I don't know why he felt so strongly about it, but he seemed transfixed with the idea that another little push would topple what remained of the German war machine and we could all go home. I really don't know what drove him so much lately.'

They kept on walking and Kees continued as if it were the only way to relax his strained nerves. 'All the squadron pilots are over-tired these days. Those damned tents in which we are forced to sleep are really the last straw when you come back from two or even three sweeps over Europe in one day. The way we're treated as pilots is scandalous. It's a bloody shame no better accommodation is provided for us. Those Dutch Ministry chaps in London all sleep nicely in their warm beds at night. We, who have to do all the dirty work, are forced to sleep on camp beds in small tents on the airfield. The Dutch brass really take advantage of our good will to the limit. You know, we've been sleeping for over a hundred and forty nights in those damned tents and there's no end to it in sight.'

Kees dark eyes reflected his deep anger. 'Those bastards in London could have done so much for us and did so little!' he added, seething.

Jane nodded, not knowing exactly what to say to her angry Dutch friend after his long monologue. 'All right, Kees. Let's keep on walking for a while. Maybe you can give Diana the present later.'

Silently, arm-in-arm, they kept walking for a few blocks without saying anything, each caught up in sad thoughts. Then Kees turned to look at Jane and took a deep breath.

'I am ready,' he said. 'I think I can do it now. Let's go back and give her the bad news.'

Jane grabbed his arm even harder. 'I also phoned my mother. She promised to be at the flat around eight too. It might be better for us to inform Diana first; then my mother can take care of her later. Oh, Kees! How terribly sad this all is!'

'That's most sensible. Your mother is such a strong-minded woman. Jan told me so. She'll certainly take care to comfort poor Diana.'

Slowly they walked to the flat and, with heavy hearts, headed up the steps. With his index finger and thumb, Kees nervously turned up the extreme tips of his thick, dark moustache, not knowing how to face the emotional scene awaiting him.

XXIV

DIANA HAD flown a great deal during the weeks prior to her birthday. The instructor had allowed her to fly the Miles Master, a plane that could be compared to the Spitfire in its flying characteristics.

She felt in excellent physical shape. She was so proud of her achievements, having made considerable progress as a pilot. Her newly gained experience would bring her ever closer to Jan.

She expected, after a few more months of training, to fly the Spitfire, the plane she most wanted to master. When she had moved on to controlling such a plane, she too could streak through the air at close to 400 mph. Her dream to be much closer to her Flying Dutchman would then be fulfilled.

Diana had arranged her life in such a way as to keep busy all the time, fully aware Jan was regularly engaged in operational flying. Yet she'd been able to obtain a leave to spend her birthday together with him. She considered herself a very lucky girl.

After his call to her, she looked forward eagerly to their meeting – especially because it was her birthday. In a way, she was curious, tickled and titillated at the thought of what kind of gift he would present her with. Not that it made the slightest importance, but still.

302

Before leaving the airfield that morning, she had phoned Jane in the early hours, asking for her help in making food purchases for the exquisite meal she planned for this all-important occasion. Jane, now working in London, had immediately agreed.

At midday, 1 September 1944, Diana took the train to London. Seated by the window in the half-empty compartment, she noticed to her surprise how sharply her face was reflected in the rain-covered glass. Studying her own image, she concentrated her thoughts on Jan and herself.

What would happen to the two of them when the war was over? Would he return to Holland, to his parents and perhaps forget her? A cold chill ran through her and she trembled for a second. No, she convinced herself, that was impossible. They were so deeply in love and he was a gentleman. Would he ask her to marry him then? And how was she going to accept that great change in her life? Would she spend the rest of her days living in Holland? She wanted so to meet his parents – his father, and especially his mother – to see how they'd come through the ordeal of the last years of horrible war. Yes, Diana decided, she would accept living in Holland should Jan ask her. And slowly, Diana's head sunk to her chest and she dozed off.

Arriving at the flat she shared with her sister Jane, Diana noticed it was four in the afternoon; she had plenty of time to prepare what she had in mind for the evening.

When she entered the kitchenette, she found all the items she'd asked for neatly packaged on the sink with a small note from Jane: 'Hope it tastes as good as it looks. Bye, and have fun, the two of you.'

Diana had made precise plans for dinner. She wanted to prepare a cheese soufflé to be accompanied by cool, sparkling, white Riesling wine, with a main course of roast beef. She felt sure her Dutchie needed the good meat after all the operational flying he'd been subjected to lately. Now that she herself was up in the air on a regular basis, she realised only too well what all those young pilots had to endure when they were over Europe practically every day, carrying out all sorts of dangerous missions.

She busied herself around the kitchenette, now and then consulting a cookbook; when everything was exactly as she wanted it, she began to set the table.

There would be no one else save the two of them and she wanted a romantic atmosphere. She placed two candelabras on the table: she planned to light the candles just before eight. Jan was always punctual. She would pamper her Flying Dutchman tonight. He was such a nice, handsome, strong man and it was good to be with him, even though he seemed so terribly tired the last time they'd met.

She looked at herself in the mirror, putting on a touch of make-up – just the little bit she needed. She also put on a new summer dress she'd bought a few weeks earlier but never worn. She wanted to show it off exclusively on this occasion. It was white with a blue floral design; she had liked it immediately when she'd spotted it displayed in a shop window.

Diana put a few flowers in a small crystal vase and placed them at the centre of the table. Then she opened one bottle of white wine and one claret to go with the meat course.

She whistled a popular tune and executed a few dance steps through the room. How she would spoil him that night! It was twenty to eight – time to put the soufflé in the heated oven. She wanted to have one quick drink with him and then she'd tell him to sit down at the table so she could make a triumphant entrance with the soufflé she had purposely prepared for him.

Diana had intentionally arranged all this to show her Dutchie Australian girls could also cook. She was certain he'd be very surprised. With a tender look in her eyes, she surveyed the table arrangement, and adjusted a thing here and there. She felt completely satisfied. And ready for him. A few minutes before eight, she stole one last glance at the oven to see how the soufflé had started to rise. She had everything under control as she desired.

Just then, the doorbell rang. Her heart beat a bit faster. It was Jan! Now she had to make a choice between the perfection of the soufflé and a friendly welcome for her Dutchman.

She quickly walked to the front door, opened it from the inside, and left it ajar. Hurrying back into the kitchen, she checked her masterpiece for the evening. It had already risen nicely in the terracotta pot. From the kitchenette, she shouted, 'Be right with you, Jan! Sit down and make yourself comfortable! I'll be with you in a second!'

Diana switched off the oven, leaving the soufflé inside. It would rise even further and stay that way without burning or shrinking in size. She'd have sufficient time to prepare the drinks. She felt superb: everything was going the way she had planned.

Returning to the sitting room, she cried out in surprise when she noticed Kees and Jane. But Jan was nowhere in sight and he was the one she was expecting.

Cheerfully, she exclaimed, 'Hello there, you two! This is wonderful. Two more guests for my birthday. To tell you the truth, I only prepared for two.' And she smiled both happily and apologetically at them. But there was something about the way her two unexpected guests behaved that struck her. Suddenly, an ice-cold feeling of foreboding seized her.

Nervously, Kees stared at Diana. She looked so lovely, so frail and now he had to tell her the shocking truth!

Slowly, his eyes misted over – he couldn't possibly control himself. The shock of Jan's death had hit him so very hard, too. The image of Diana blurred in front of his eyes.

'Diana …' he began but stopped, desperately trying to regain control of his voice. 'Jane and I didn't exactly come here for your birthday,' he somehow managed haltingly.

'Something terrible happened this afternoon.' Kees swallowed hard, staring compassionately at her.

At first Diana could not grasp what he was trying to tell her. Worried, her eyes shifted from Jane to Kees and back again. Then, at last, her eyes fixed on Kees. 'Has something happened to Jan?' she asked with a shudder. 'Please, Kees, tell me – don't hide the truth.' Her voice sounded strained. 'Do … you … mean … to … tell … me … it's … the … end?'

Diana couldn't go on, she barely managed the halting question as the blood drained from her face, turning it ash white.

'Is … he …' Her voice broke. 'Is Jan … dead?' she finally asked, tightly gripping his uniform sleeve.

Kees couldn't utter a word. He merely acknowledged her question by silently moving his head up and down. Helpless and forlorn, he stood motionless in the middle of the room, not knowing what to do or say to soften the terrible blow of the appalling and cruel tidings.

Diana gasped. She had to do something or she would faint. Despite the mind-numbing shock the news of Jan's death had caused, Diana suddenly pivoted around and rushed into the kitchenette where she lifted the soufflé out of the oven after putting on fireproof gloves. She whispered to herself, 'I've got to keep myself busy!'

Through the mist of her tears, she could hardly see the results of her efforts but it was perfect, it was beautiful. The soufflé had risen above the red terracotta pot's rim and the crust was the right brown colour just as she had intended it to be. Carefully, she lifted it up. While tears streaked down her pale cheeks, she gently put it on the table with Jane helping her. No one spoke; they stood there in silence, admiring Diana's masterpiece as if they were paying their respects.

Diana's voice, shaking with emotion, sounded so thin as she said, 'Look at it … I prepared it … for my Dutchie … and it turned out perfectly … and now …' Her voice choked. She fought hard to gain control of herself with an extreme effort. 'And now … he's not here … with me … to enjoy it … to be proud of me …' she sniffed desperately.

She turned around, hiding her face in both hands, repeatedly saying, 'No ... no ... no!' Diana wept desperately, her body wracked with silent, choking sobs. Jane went to her, putting her arms protectively around her sister's shoulders. 'I'm so sorry it had to be him.' And she cried too.

Kees stood there helplessly, unable to utter one comforting word. He just couldn't manage to offer his condolences or say anything to help Diana in her agony.

At that point, her mother entered the apartment. 'Jane and Kees – I suggest you two take a walk,' she said. 'Please leave Diana and me alone for awhile. Come back in half an hour.' Silently, they left the apartment, softly shutting the front door behind them.

Having heard her mother's voice, Diana turned around meekly, like a helpless lost child, walking to her. Delicately, Mrs Boulton took Diana's hands in hers, putting them around her own neck gently, drawing her daughter into her outstretched arms with a gesture of infinite love. She held her tightly against herself, comforting Diana with softly spoken, encouraging words, letting Diana weep out her immense grief on maternal shoulders. She herself could well have cried out against all the misery that damned war had caused her daughter.

She felt the silent shaking of Diana's body. Not a word was spoken. Then Diana pulled back from her mother's embrace and stared at her, saying, 'This is it, mother ... I haven't been ... very lucky ... in love ... have I?' She sniffed, and continued. 'I thought ... I hoped ... and prayed ... that despite the war, my love for Jan could go on and on. But ... it was not to be ...'

Her mother interrupted her. 'No, my child. You have really met with such bad luck. Jan was such a fine, decent young man – so kind, so well behaved and gentle, so sincere. The world shouldn't lose such outstanding young men like him.' She spoke with soft gentleness. 'There are so few around. The world is rapidly losing its values and traditions and a young man like Jan shouldn't really have left us.'

Sadly Diana nodded her head. ' I know. Just the same, mother, we lost him. He felt so tired lately. On the 14th of August he flew operationally for more than seven hours over occupied Europe, on the 15th for nearly five hours and the same on the 27th. On the 31st he was more than four hours over Europe with those nasty Germans shooting at him. The poor darling must have been exhausted.'

'How true, Diana,' Mrs Boulton confirmed.

'They should have forced him to take the long leave he was fully entitled to. But they didn't. They should have ordered Jan to stop flying operationally. To take up the long two months break. To me, it seems as if the Dutch authorities in London actually and shamelessly handed him to his death. They don't seem to put much value on the lives of their finest.' There was deep anger in Diana's voice.

Mrs Boulton eyed her daughter with compassion. 'You're so right,' she said softly.

'He yearned so much for the war to end this year so he could go home and meet his mother and father again in Holland. And now, mother,' Diana hesitated a moment in search of the right words, 'we're so close to the end and he isn't there to enjoy the occasion he died for.'

In deep silence, Mrs Boulton stared at her daughter. Then she spoke. 'It will be a terrible shock to his parents when they're informed about it. Jan was such a fine fellow. There are not many like him.' Having to talk about Jan in the past tense upset Diana's mother more than she cared to admit and her dark brown eyes misted.

The front doorbell rang. Jane and Kees had come back.

Mrs Boulton poured all of them a strong whisky. 'Come on,' she urged, 'drink them up. Maybe they'll make us feel a little better. You too, Diana.'

Once they were seated, Kees pulled a small packet from his pocket and hesitatingly handed it to Diana. 'I found it on Jan's pillow in his tent. We bought it together. I know he wanted you to have it for your anniversary. It's his birthday present to you.'

With a questioning glance, Diana stared at her mother who nodded back. 'You might as well open it now. It will probably hit you hard, but better now while I'm here with you.'

Diana tore off the wrapping paper and slowly opened the little box. It contained two silver wooden clogs. One bore the inscription 'Aussie', the other 'Dutchie'.

Sadly, Diana recalled the night at Claridge's when she had insisted on dancing with Jan. A mournful, wan smile played on her lips as she remembered his remark about wearing wooden clogs.

Holding the charming gift in her right hand, Diana silently looked at the other three and then rose to her feet, delicately placing the two silver wooden shoes – very, very carefully – close to each other on the mantlepiece, next to the framed photograph of Jan sitting in the open cockpit of his Spitfire, facing the camera.

For a long time, silent, as if in deep prayer, she stared at his picture. Ineffably sad, barely audibly she whispered, 'My dearest, dearest Jan ... my brave Flying Dutchman ...'

Epilogue

AFTER THE 1939–45 war was finally over, a Victory Parade took place in London. But Jan Plesman, like so many others, was not among those who marched in triumph or flew over. They had sown, but they would not reap the sweet fruit of their sacrifices. To mankind, they left behind a heritage of freedom to be enjoyed.

Posthumously, Jan was decorated by the French government with the Croix de Guerre. His father received the French Ambassador at his house when he presented the decoration in an emotionally charged atmosphere.

When St Omer was liberated in late 1944 by the Allied Forces, 322 Squadron officials tried to locate the spot where Jan's Spitfire had crashed into the ground, but in the short time available, they were unable to find a clue.

After the war, no Dutch government ever even showed any gratitude by trying to locate the place where Jan Plesman disappeared so that he might have an honourable funeral. A sickening ingratitude and disgrace after he had served his country and Queen with devotion and loyalty!

Jan's dynamic father also made an effort to have the disaster spot located. He strongly desired to give his beloved son a decent last resting place. He had mentioned in a letter to Jan, ' We will have to pay a tribute to those who died to make it all possible.'

No one so far has been able to find the wreckage of Jan Plesman's Spitfire nor his remains.

No funeral was ever held for Jan Plesman!

Like the famed Flying Dutchman, he disappeared, never to return, leaving behind a never-fading image of a fine, decent, kind, honest, capable, intelligent young man, of an excellent pilot who, on his last flight on 1 September 1944, had taken off to his final destination.

A destination at the end of his last flight where he might expect to make a last dignified landing, to be welcomed by those who had already arrived before him.

There, at last, at twenty-four, he would find rest and peace forever! Jan Plesman's gift to humanity was his life so that all of us could live in freedom.

His colleagues in 322 Squadron wrote about him: 'Today, 1 September 1944, we lost Air Reserve Captain Jan Leendert Plesman. He was our finest pilot.'

The following words were contained in a letter addressed to Flight Commander Jan Plesman when one of the Dutch pilots of 322 Squadron did not return from an operational flight over Europe:

The best fall and do not return. Those we needed most and from whom we could expect so much in the future, will not be here for the occasion.

There is a duty, but also a privilege for those who remain to carry on united, hand in hand, to understand, to work towards a Free World.

We look forward to a world of Freedom in which each and every individual can and must express himself or herself in complete liberty, without the slightest burden of oppression or tyranny.

To reach that goal, your young lives are put at stake. But if your efforts are crowned with success, millions of people all over the world will be grateful to you for your accomplishments and perseverance.

Albert Plesman

The future belonged to the younger generations. Those airmen died so humanity could live in freedom. No further oppression from the Nazis, nor the Soviets, nor any other tyrannical repressive system.

Freedom of thought, freedom of expression, freedom of speech – those were the privileges reserved for those who survived. In the air war against the Nazis, 55,000 Allied pilots and airmen of many nationalities perished – sacrificed their most precious possession, their lives, so that others might achieve the objectives they died for.

On 21 October 1948, Koene Dirk Parmentier – one of KLM Royal Dutch Airline's finest, most capable pilots died at the controls of a Lockheed 049 Constellation during a landing in bad weather conditions at Prestwick Airport in Scotland. He was only 44 at the time. He had spoken to Jan in Bristol many times, helping him get past his lowest moods.

Jan's brother, Hans Plesman, died on 23 June 1949, in the crash of a Lockheed Constellation L749, at Bari, Italy. He was captain of the aircraft, on a non-stop flight from Cairo to Amsterdam, which mysteriously came down from a 23,000 feet cruising altitude. The exact cause of the accident has never been clearly established. He was only 31 years old when it happened.

Jan's father passed away on 31 December 1953. The dynamic founder of KLM Royal Dutch Airlines died at only 64, on the very last day of the year, from internal bleeding. He left behind a profitable airline. Many people in Holland said his thesis consisted of three letters only: KLM.

As far as the writer has been able to ascertain, Diana Boulton died in a car crash.

Fifty-six years have passed since these events took place. The lasting peace and the ideals that were fought for still have not been realised. Once again, all over the world, people live in fear of ever-spreading terrorism, in a political atmosphere of appeasement; there does not seem to be any bold action to finally secure a lasting peace.

312

Those who ignore the evil that man is capable of inflicting on his fellow man only need to observe the revolting atrocities committed by the Serbians during the break-up of Yugoslavia, the oppression of the Bosnian and recently of the Chechen people, and of all those others behind the Iron Curtain.

Once again, tyranny denies individual rights and human dignity while the Western governments are, as usual, divided in their reactions.

Let's not forget that man is capable of the worst brutalities, as was so clearly demonstrated by the German people between 1934 and 1945 when Hitler came to power, and during the monstrous Stalin reign in Soviet Russia.

Looking back at it all, the author wonders, 'Is the world we live in today really the ideal one for which the young ones gave their lives? Is this what they dreamt of and were ready to die for?'

It isn't! In 1934, when Hitler and his gang of degenerates came to power in Germany and still could have been stopped, government leaders of Europe were weak, unprepared to act firmly, undecided what course to follow, uncertain of what should be done to stop that demon. The political faint-hearted weaklings were afraid to act!

Sir Winston Churchill was absolutely right: the Second World War with all its horrors could have been avoided, if men of government had acted forcefully, bravely, in unison and with foresight. But, unfortunately they didn't!

Now again, we can avoid the nightmare of expanding aggression and terrorism by standing and acting united! As was written in the letter to Jan Plesman, 'To stand united, hand in hand.'

The motto beneath the 322 Squadron crest was 'Don't talk, act!' Perhaps this should always be remembered.

Printed in the United Kingdom
by Lightning Source UK Ltd.
9651300001B/3